ALTADENA LIBRARY DISTRICT
3 9270 00100 5911

D0793525

THE STORIES OF DENTON WELCH

BOOKS BY DENTON WELCH

Brave and Cruel and Other Stories
(Hamish Hamilton, 1949)

Denton Welch. A Selection from His Published Works,
ed. Jocelyn Brooke (Chapman & Hall, 1963)

Dumb Instrument,
ed. Jean-Louis Chevalier (Enitharmon Press, 1976)

I Left My Grandfather's House
(Lion & Unicorn Press, 1958; Allison & Busby, 1984)

In Youth Is Pleasure
(Routledge, 1945; E.P. Dutton, 1985)

The Journals of Denton Welch,
ed. Michael De-la-Noy (E.P. Dutton, 1984).
Unabridged version, edited by Jocelyn Brooke,
was published by Hamish Hamilton (U.K.) in 1976.

A Last Sheaf
(John Lehmann, 1951)

Maiden Voyage
(Routledge, 1943; E.P. Dutton, 1984)

The Stories of Denton Welch,
ed. Robert Phillips (E.P. Dutton, 1986)

A Voice Through a Cloud
(John Lehmann, 1950; E.P. Dutton, 1984)

THE STORIES OF DENTON WELCH

Edited by
Robert Phillips

E. P. DUTTON | NEW YORK

Published in the United States by E. P. Dutton,
a division of New American Library,
2 Park Avenue, New York, N.Y. 10016

Library of Congress Cataloging-in-Publication Data

Welch, Denton.
The stories of Denton Welch.
I. Phillips, Robert S. II. Title.
PR6045.E517S7 1985 823'.912 85-25382
ISBN: 0-525-24364-X

Published simultaneously in Canada by
Fitzhenry & Whiteside Limited, Toronto

COBE

DESIGNED BY MARK O'CONNOR

10 9 8 7 6 5 4 3 2 1

First Edition

Contents

Preface

Denton Welch, the writer, did not surface until Denton Welch, the painter, was made an invalid in a vehicular accident which eventually caused his death.

Prior to being knocked off his bicycle by a "woman driver" (as he said) on June 7, 1935, the twenty-year-old Welch was a student at Goldsmith School of Art at New Cross, painting and planning a career as a painter. The accident changed all that. His spine was severely fractured—irreparably so—and he suffered many other internal injuries, including kidney damage. Eventually tuberculosis of the spine developed. By his own count, he lost seventy pounds (though he always exaggerated).

Much of the thirteen years that remained of his life was spent in bed, though he did manage to ride a bicycle and to drive his baby

Austin. He also continued to draw and paint. (One example adorns the jacket of this book.) But most of his creative energy went into writing. His sick-bed became his studio. Like Clare and Keats, illness gave him more rather than less time to produce. "That obscene accident," as he came to call it, saved Welch from the fate he most feared, that of becoming "a precious young man in a gallery." In his *Journals* he explains: "Being ill made me think of being great and famous. They are always linked together in my mind. I must not be so ill that I cannot be famous."

Famous he was, at least in his native England. During the last years of his short life (1915-1948) and during the years of publication of his posthumous books, he enjoyed considerable popularity and critical acclaim. His books were blurbed by Dame Edith Sitwell (". . . that very rare being, a born writer") and admired by Vita Sackville-West, Cyril Connolly, E.M. Forster, John Betjeman, Herbert Read, John Lehmann, and others. They sold well, and had considerable impact. It has been said that perhaps the only other contemporary work that had a comparable effect upon servicemen and the young was Connolly's *The Unquiet Grave.*

Welch published three books in his lifetime—two novels, *Maiden Voyage* (1943) and *In Youth Is Pleasure* (1945); and a short-story collection, *Brave and Cruel* (1948). He sent advance copies of the latter to friends a few days before his death. His best books were published posthumously—*A Voice Through a Cloud* (1950), the unfinished novel on which he worked to the day he died, sometimes only a few minutes at a time before headaches and failing vision plagued him; and the *Journals* (1952), which first appeared in a bowdlerized and truncated version and was recently reissued more or less as written. Welch kept the *Journals* between 1942 and 1948.

Unlike some novelists, for whom the writing of short stories is merely a diversion and the results of secondary importance, Welch regarded his stories as a significant portion of his *oeuvre.* In executing them he consumed a significant portion of his energies. In fact, *A Voice Through a Cloud* might have been completed had he not abandoned it at one point to write the stories that eventually became *Brave and Cruel.* Enough stories were written to fill a second collection, *A Last Sheaf* (1951), which also contains poems and painting reproductions.

Welch's stories were never published in book form in America, while his novels and *Journals* were. It may be true that publishers intended to get around to publishing Welch's stories after the novels, then found the climate inhospitable. Some American critics did not cotton to his precocity, his obsessions with narcissism, minutiae, suffering, homoeroticism, hedonism, and nostalgia. As Welch himself noted, some Americans called him "a snip and a snob, effeminate and obnoxious, saying that I sit better with Miss Sitwell than I do with them."

(Not that the British were universally receptive to his work: When "The Barn" was published in *New Writing and Daylight*, the *Spectator* reviewer remarked, "Mr. Welch has produced another tremulous and sexy story in the manner of his *Maiden Voyage*, all about a fat woman in stays, and the contrasted beauty of a tramp who comes to sleep in the barn." Readers of this volume will discern that *that* is not what the story is about.)

By being difficult to categorize, Welch's work has given certain critics an uneasy time on both sides of the Atlantic. His first novel was promoted as a travel book, his second as autobiography. His best piece of reportage was included with short stories in his second collection. An anonymous reviewer in the *Times* (London) *Literary Supplement* noted of Welch, "Like some wines, this manifestation of the English spirit, with its undertones of snobbery, ultra-sensitivity, and sexual ambivalence, tends to travel badly." Pervading all his work is a strange mixture of sophistication and naiveté.

Whatever reasons one may advance for the stories' unavailability in this country, quality is not one. They bear the same characteristics of his longer works—his ear for dialogue, his eye for detail, his taste for sweets—as well as his instinct for revelation of character and intolerance of inferiors. His *Journals* confirm the suspicion that much of what he wrote was autobiographical, and one can only marvel at his near-total recall.

Here, nearly four decades after composition, are the stories of Denton Welch for American readers, twenty-six in all. I have included all the stories from *Brave and Cruel* and *A Last Sheaf*, with the exceptions of the 72-page "A Novel Fragment" (which is exactly what its title purports) and "Sickert at St. Peter's" (which is reportage; an account of a visit with painter Walter Sickert, it would properly have become part of the enlarged *Journals*, together with accounts of visits with Dame Edith Sitwell and Lord Berners). In addition, I have included seven uncollected stories. Their texts are supplied by the Harry Ransom Humanities Research Center, The University of Texas at Austin. These have never appeared in book form. They were selected from a larger number of manuscripts, most of which seem unfinished. (One beauty, "John Trevor," is lacking two key pages and is therefore unpublishable. Perhaps in time those missing pages will surface.)

Readers unfamiliar with Welch will find this volume an accessible place to start. Those who already admire his work will find all his strengths (and weaknesses) and preoccupations. The stories are simple, spontaneous, sure, fresh, and naive. They are relatively free from influences and highly original. He writes of the joys of physical existence ("The Barn"), the fragility of human relationships ("The Judas Tree"; "The Diamond Badge"), early awareness of pain and illness ("The Trout Stream"; "At Sea"), and sexual frustration ("The Fire in the Wood"). The majority are about childhood and adolescence, the need for love and respect, social hypocrisy, admiration for the ruthless, and his absolute horror of bad taste. Welch explores these themes with all his senses. When the eight-year-old protagonist of "The Coffin on the Hill" licks the brass trim of a porthole, he does so in order to sensually realize the ship he is on. This is a figure for Welch himself. Has any other story-writer included more sights, tastes, smells, and feelings?

The same eight-year-old has a doll which Welch describes as neither male nor female, "but a sexless being, like an angel." So too are many of Welch's protagonists androgynous figures, representing the duality within himself. In a number of stories, Welch almost certainly adopted the Proustian Albertine strategy and changed the sex of a protagonist from male to female. These include "The Fire in the Wood," "The Hateful Word," "Anna Dillon," "Weekend," and "Alex Fairburn." Censorship was more strict and sexual freedom less prevalent than it is today.

While Welch made these sex changes in material that often was autobiographical, the reader should be cautioned against assuming every story is based upon personal history. "In the Vast House," for instance, seems autobiographical but a reading of his biography reveals that it is not.

Every story he wrote, real or imagined, is distinguished by sharp and distinctive imagery. Note this description, a scene from a bus window ("The Earth's Crust"):

> Along the pavements thronged the people, like bottles walking; their heads as inexpressive as round stoppers. What if some god or giant should bend down and take several of the stoppers out? I thought. Inside there would be black churning depths like bile, or bitter medicine.

Or this description of an invalid ("The Diamond Badge"):

> I could just discern the little dumpy figure of Andrew on the bed. Somehow his richly striped dressing-gown, turned now to black and pale grey, made me think of a squat cold-cream jar, or a fat tube of toothpaste with the used part neatly rolled up. . . .

This is admirable writing, especially when one realizes it is a ruthless self-portrait. (It is curious that a writer of such fine poetic prose should have been such a bad poet. Welch left dozens of undistinguished, Housmanesque poems, some published in *A Last Sheaf* and a posthumous book of verse, *Dumb Instrument*. Others mercifully are still on deposit at The University of Texas.)

At this moment, Welch's work is finding an American audience. All three novels have been reprinted here, and the augmented *Journals*. With publication of *The Stories of Denton Welch*, the *oeuvre* is ripe for assessment. One attempt at assessment has already appeared in *The Nation*, an essay by Brad Gooch that I applaud because it emphasizes Welch's pleasing discontinuity and his teasing touches, the obvious fun.

I hope we are not too quick to categorize, to pin down, this elusive writer. Part of his artistry is his artlessness. No product of writers' workshops, he wrote purely from a natural and uninhibited sensibility.

The stories in this volume are not arranged chronologically. Rather, I have attempted to effect a counterpoint of themes and protagonists. I have Americanized spellings. Occasionally I altered Welch's punctuation—when it was most confusing or incorrect. He loved to sprinkle dashes and semicolons upon the page like so much paprika on moussaka, a practice his British editors did nothing to discourage. I have restored a few censored phrases when this recreates a more powerful text. Some of his underground slang fell victim to Mrs. Grundy's blue pencil in the forties.

Gratitude is due to the late Lester G. Wells, who first introduced me to Welch's work; William Whitehead, editor-in-chief at E. P. Dutton, who first conceived this book; Margarette Sharpe and Jesse L. Crowell, Jr., of the Harry Ransom Humanities Research Center, The University of Texas at Austin; and Mark F. Weimer, of the George Arents Research Library at Syracuse University.

—ROBERT PHILLIPS
July 1985

Some of these stories first appeared in *Contact, Cornhill, English Story, Horizon, Life and Letters, New Writing and Daylight, Orpheus II, Penguin New Writing, Vogue*, and *World Review*.

THE STORIES OF DENTON WELCH

When I Was Thirteen

When I was thirteen, I went to Switzerland for the Christmas holidays in the charge of an elder brother, who was at that time still up at Oxford.

In the hotel we found another undergraduate whom my brother knew. His name was Archer. They were not at the same college, but they had met and evidently had not agreed with each other. At first my brother would say nothing about Archer; then one day, in answer to a question of mine, he said: "He's not very much liked, although he's a very good swimmer." As he spoke, my brother held his lips in a very firm, almost pursed, line which was most damaging to Archer.

After this I began to look at Archer with more interest. He had broad shoulders but was not tall. He had a look of strength and solidity which I admired and envied. He had rather a nice pug face with insignificant nose and broad cheeks. Sometimes, when he was animated, a tassel of fair, almost colorless, hair would fall across his forehead, half covering one eye. He had a thick beautiful neck, rather meaty barbarian hands, and a skin as smooth and evenly colored as a pink fondant.

His whole body appeared to be suffused with this gentle pink color. He never wore proper skiing clothes of waterproof material like the rest of us. Usually he came out in nothing but a pair of grey flannels and a white cotton shirt with all the buttons left undone. When the sun grew very hot, he would even discard this thin shirt, and ski up and down the slopes behind the hotel in nothing but his trousers. I had often seen him fall down in this half-naked state and get buried in snow. The next moment he would jerk himself to his feet again, laughing and swearing.

After my brother's curt nod to him on our first evening at the hotel, we had hardly exchanged any remarks. We sometimes passed on the way to the basement to get our skis in the morning, and often we found ourselves sitting near one another on the glassed-in terrace; but some Oxford snobbery I knew nothing of, or some more profound reason, always made my brother throw off waves of hostility. Archer never showed any signs of wishing to approach. He was content to look at me sometimes with a mild inoffensive curiosity, but he seemed to ignore my brother completely. This pleased me more than I would have admitted at that time. I was so used to being passed over myself by all my brother's friends that it was pleasant when someone who knew him seemed to take a sort of interest, however slight and amused, in me.

My brother was often away from the hotel for days and nights together, going for expeditions with guides and other friends. He would never take me because he said I was too young and had not enough stamina. He said that I would fall down a crevasse or get my nose frostbitten, or hang up the party by lagging behind.

In consequence I was often alone at the hotel; but I did not mind this; I enjoyed it. I was slightly afraid of my brother and found life very much easier and less exacting when he was not there. I think other people in the hotel thought that I looked lonely. Strangers would often come up and talk to me and smile, and once a nice absurd Belgian woman, dressed from head to foot in a babyish suit of fluffy orange knitted wool, held out a bright five-franc piece to me and told me to go and buy chocolate caramels with it. I think she must have taken me for a much younger child.

On one of these afternoons when I had come in from the Nursery Slopes and was sitting alone over my tea on the sun terrace, I noticed that Archer was sitting in the corner huddled over a book, munching greedily and absentmindedly.

I, too, was reading a book, while I ate delicious rum-babas and little tarts filled with worm-castles of chestnut purée topped with caps of whipped cream. I have called the meal tea, but what I was drinking was not tea but chocolate. When I poured out, I held the pot high in the air, so that my cup, when filled, should be covered in a rich froth of bubbles.

The book I was reading was Tolstoy's *Resurrection.* Although I did not quite understand some parts of it, it gave me intense pleasure to read it while I ate the rich cakes and drank the frothy chocolate. I thought it a noble and terrible story, but I was worried and mystified by the words "illegitimate child" which had occurred several times lately. What sort of child could this be? Clearly a child that brought trouble and difficulty. Could it have some terrible disease, or was it a special sort of imbecile? I looked up from my book, still wondering about this phrase "illegitimate child," and saw that Archer had turned in his creaking wicker chair and was gazing blankly in my direction. The orchestra was playing "The Birth of the Blues" in a rather remarkable Swiss arrangement, and it was clear that Archer had been distracted from his book by the music, only to be lulled into a daydream, as he gazed into space.

Suddenly his eyes lost their blank look and focused on my face. "Your brother off up to the Jungfrau Joch again, or somewhere?" he called out.

I nodded my head, saying nothing, becoming slightly confused.

Archer grinned. He seemed to find me amusing.

"What are you reading?" he asked.

"This," I said, taking my book over to him. I did not want to call out either the word "Resurrection" or "Tolstoy." But Archer did not make fun of me for reading a "classic," as most of my brother's friends would have done. He only said: "I should think it's rather good. Mine's frightful; it's called *The Story of my Life,* by Queen Marie of Roumania." He held the book up and I saw an extraordinary photograph of a lady who looked like a snake-charmer in full regalia. The headdress seemed to be made of white satin, embroidered with beads, stretched over cardboard. There were tassels and trailing things hanging down everywhere.

I laughed at the amusing picture and Archer went on: "I always read books like this when I can get them. Last week I had Lady Oxford's autobiography, and before that I found a perfectly wonderful book called *Flaming Sex*. It was by a French woman who married an English knight and then went back to France to shoot a French doctor. She didn't kill him, of course, but she was sent to prison, where she had a very interesting time with the nuns who looked after her in the hospital. I also lately found an old book by a Crown Princess of Saxony who ended up picnicking on a haystack with a simple Italian gentleman in a straw hat. I love these 'real life' stories, don't you?"

I again nodded my head, not altogether daring to venture on a spoken answer. I wondered whether to go back to my own table or whether to pluck up courage and ask Archer what an "illegitimate child" was. He solved the problem by saying "Sit down" rather abruptly.

I subsided next to him with "Tolstoy" on my knee. I waited for a moment and then plunged.

"What exactly does 'illegitimate child' mean?" I asked rather breathlessly.

"Outside the law—when two people have a child although they're not married."

"Oh." I went bright pink. I thought Archer must be wrong. I still believed that it was quite impossible to have a child unless one was married. The very fact of being married produced the child. I had a vague idea that some particularly reckless people attempted, without being married, to have children in places called "night-clubs," but they were always unsuccessful, and this made them drink, and plunge into the most hectic gaiety.

I did not tell Archer that I thought he had made a mistake, for I did not want to hurt his feelings. I went on sitting at his table and, although he turned his eyes back to his book and went on reading, I knew that he was friendly.

After some time he looked up again and said: "Would you like to come out with me tomorrow? We could take our lunch, go up the mountain and then ski down in the afternoon."

I was delighted at the suggestion, but also a little alarmed at my own shortcomings. I thought it my duty to explain that I was not a very good skier, only a moderate one, and that I could only do stem turns. I hated the thought of being a drag on Archer.

"I expect you're much better than I am. I'm always falling down or crashing into something," he answered.

It was all arranged. We were to meet early, soon after six, as Archer wanted to go to the highest station on the mountain railway and then climb on skis to a nearby peak which had a small rest-house of logs.

I went to bed very excited, thankful that my brother was away on a long expedition. I lay under my enormous feather-bed eiderdown, felt the freezing mountain air on my face, and saw the stars sparkling through the open window.

I got up very early in the morning and put on my most sober ski socks and woollen shirt, for I felt that Archer disliked any suspicion of bright colors or dressing-up. I made my appearance as workmanlike as possible, and then went down to breakfast.

I ate several crackly rolls, which I spread thickly with dewy slivers of butter and gobbets of rich black cherry jam; then I drank my last cup of coffee and went to wax my skis. As I passed through the hall I picked up my picnic lunch in its neat grease-proof paper packet.

The nails in my boots slid and then caught on the snow, trodden hard down to the basement door. I found my skis in their rack, took them down and then heated the iron and the wax. I loved spreading the hot black wax smoothly on the white wood. Soon they were both done beautifully.

I will go like a bird, I thought.

I looked up and saw Archer standing in the doorway.

"I hope you haven't put too much on, else you'll be sitting on your arse all day," he said gaily.

How fresh and pink he looked! I was excited.

He started to wax his own skis. When they were finished, we went outside and strapped them on. Archer carried a rucksack and he told me to put my lunch and my spare sweater into it.

We started off down the gentle slopes to the station. The sun was shining prickingly. The lovely snow had rainbow colors in it. I was so happy I swung my sticks with their steel points and basket ends. I even tried to show off, and jumped a little terrace which I knew well. Nevertheless it nearly brought me down. I just regained my balance in time. I would have hated at that moment to have fallen down in front of Archer.

When we got to the station we found a compartment to ourselves. It was still early. Gently we were pulled up the mountain, past the water station stop and the other three halts.

We got out at the very top where the railway ended. A huge unused snowplow stood by the side of the track, with its vicious shark's nose pointed at me. We ran to the van to get out our skis. Archer found mine as well as his own and slung both pairs across his shoulders. He looked like a very tough Jesus carrying two crosses, I thought.

We stood by the old snowplow and clipped on our skis; then we began to climb laboriously up the ridge to the wooden rest-house. We hardly talked at all, for we needed all our breath, and also I was still shy of Archer. Sometimes he helped me, telling me where to place my skis, and, if I slipped backwards, hauling on the rope which he had half-playfully tied round my waist.

In spite of growing tired, I enjoyed the grim plodding. It gave me a sense of work and purpose. When Archer looked round to smile at me, his pink face was slippery with sweat. His white shirt above the small rucksack was plastered to his shoulder blades. On my own face I could feel the drops of sweat just being held back by my eyebrows. I would wipe my hand across my upper lip and break all the tiny beads that had formed there.

Every now and then Archer would stop. We would put our skis sideways on the track and rest, leaning forward on our sticks. The sun struck down on our necks with a steady seeping heat and the light striking up from the snow was as bright as the fiery dazzle of a mirror. From the ridge we could see down into two valleys; and standing all round us were the other peaks, black rock and white snow, tangling and mixing until the mountains looked like vast teeth which had begun to decay.

I was so tired when we reached the long gentle incline to the rest-house that I was afraid of falling down. The rope was still round my waist, and so the slightest lagging would have been perceptible to Archer. I think he must have slackened his pace for my benefit, for I somehow managed to reach the iron seats in front of the hut. I sank down, still with my skis on. I half-shut my eyes.

From walking so long with my feet turned out, my ankles felt almost broken.

The next thing I knew was that Archer had disappeared into the rest-house. He came out carrying a steaming cup.

"You must drink this," he said, holding out black coffee which I hated. He unwrapped four lumps of sugar and dropped them in the cup.

"I don't like it black," I said.

"Never mind," he answered sharply, "drink it."

Rather surprised, I began to drink the syrupy coffee. "The sugar and the strong coffee will be good for you," said Archer. He went back into the rest-house and brought out a glass of what looked like hot water with a piece of lemon floating in it. The mountain of sugar at the bottom was melting into thin Arabian Nights wreaths and spirals, smoke-rings of syrup.

"What else has it got in it?" I asked, with an attempt at worldliness.

"Rum!" said Archer.

We sat there on the terrace and unwrapped our picnic lunches. We both had two rolls, one with tongue in it, and one with ham, a hard-boiled egg, sweet biscuits, and a bar of delicious bitter chocolate. Tangerine oranges were our dessert.

We began to take huge bites out of our rolls. We could not talk for some time. The food brought out a thousand times more clearly the beauty of the mountain peaks and sun. My tiredness made me thrillingly conscious of delight and satisfaction. I wanted to sit there with Archer for a long time.

At the end of the meal Archer gave me a piece of his own bar of chocolate, and then began to skin pigs of tangerine very skillfully and hand them to me on his outstretched palm, as one offers a lump of sugar to a horse. I thought for one moment of bending down my head and licking the pigs up in imitation of a horse; then I saw how mad it would look.

We threw the brilliant tangerine peel into the snow, which immediately seemed to dim and darken its color.

Archer felt in his hip pocket and brought out black, cheap Swiss cigarettes, wrapped in leaf. They were out of a slot machine. He put one between my lips and lighted it. I felt extremely conscious of the thing jutting out from my lips. I wondered if I would betray my ignorance by not breathing the smoke in and out correctly. I turned my head a little away from Archer and experimented. It seemed easy if one did not breathe too deeply. It was wonderful to be really smoking with Archer. He treated me just like a man.

"Come on, let's get cracking," he said, "or, if anything happens, we'll be out all night."

I scrambled to my feet at once and snapped the clips of the skis round my boot heels. Archer was in high spirits from the rum. He ran on his skis along the flat ridge in front of the rest-house and then fell down.

"Serves me right," he said. He shook the snow off and we started properly. In five minutes we had swooped down the ridge we had climbed so painfully all morning. The snow was perfect; new and dry with no crust. We followed a new way which Archer had discovered. The ground was uneven with dips and curves. Often we were out of sight of each other. When we came to the icy path through a wood, my courage failed me.

"Stem like hell and don't get out of control," Archer yelled back at me. I pointed my skis together, praying that they would not cross. I leant on my sticks, digging their metal points into the compressed snow. Twice I fell, though not badly.

"Well done, well done!" shouted Archer, as I shot past him and out of the wood into a thick snowdrift. He hauled me out of the snow and stood me on my feet, beating me all over to get off the snow, then we began the descent of a field called the "Bumps." Little hillocks, if maneuvered successfully, gave one that thrilling sinking and rising feeling experienced on a scenic railway at a fun fair.

Archer went before me, dipping and rising, shouting and yelling in his exuberance. I followed more sedately. We both fell several times, but in that not unpleasant, bouncing way which brings you to your feet again almost at once.

Archer was roaring now and trying to yodel in an absurd, rich contralto.

I had never enjoyed myself quite so much before. I thought him the most wonderful companion, not a bit intimidating, in spite of being rather a hero.

When at last we swooped down to the village street, it was nearly evening. Early orange lights were shining in the shop windows. We planked our skis down on the hard, iced road, trying not to slip.

I looked in at the *patisserie, confiserie* window, where all the electric bulbs had fluffy pink shades like powder-puffs. Archer saw my look.

"Let's go in," he said. He ordered me hot chocolate with whipped cream, and *croissant* rolls. Afterwards we both went up to the little counter and chose cakes. I had one shaped like a little log. It was made of soft chocolate, and had green moss trimmings made in pistachio nut. When Archer went to pay the bill he bought me some chocolate caramels, in a little bird's-eye maple box, and a bar labelled *"Chocolat Polychrome."* Each finger was a different-colored cream: mauve, pink, green, yellow, orange, brown, white, even blue.

We went out into the village street and began to climb up the path to the hotel. About halfway up Archer stopped outside a little wooden chalet and said: "This is where I hang out."

"But you're staying at the hotel," I said incredulously.

"Oh yes, I have all my meals there, but I sleep here. It's a sort of little annex when there aren't any rooms left in the hotel. It's only got two rooms; I've paid just a bit more and got it all to myself. Someone comes every morning and makes the bed and stokes the boiler and the stove. Come in and see it."

I followed Archer up the outside wooden staircase and stood with him on the little landing outside the two rooms. The place seemed wonderfully warm and dry. The walls were unpainted wood; there were double windows. There was a gentle creaking in all the joints of the wood when one moved. Archer pushed open one of the doors and ushered me in. I saw in one corner a huge white porcelain stove, the sort I had only before seen in pictures. Some of Archer's skiing gloves and socks were drying round it on a ledge. Against another wall were two beds, like wooden troughs built into the wall. The balloon-like quilts bulged up above the wood.

"I hardly use the other room," said Archer. "I just throw my muck into it and leave my trunks there." He opened the connecting door and I saw a smaller room with dirty clothes strewn on the floor; white shirts, hard evening collars, some very short pants, and many pairs of thick grey socks. The room smelled mildly of Archer's old sweat. I didn't mind at all.

Archer shut the door and said: "I'm going to run the bath."

"Have you a bathroom too—all your own?" I exclaimed enviously. "Every time anyone has a bath at the hotel, he has to pay two francs fifty to the fraulein before she unlocks the door. I've only had two proper baths since I've been here. I don't think it matters though. It seems almost impossible to get really dirty in Switzerland, and you can always wash all over in your bedroom basin."

"Why don't you have a bath here after me? The water's lovely and hot, although there's not much of it. If you went back first and got your evening clothes, you could change straight into them."

I looked at Archer a little uncertainly. I longed to soak in hot water after my wonderful but grueling day.

"Could I really bathe here?" I asked.

"If you don't mind using my water. I'll promise not to pee in it. I'm not really filthy, you know."

Archer laughed and chuckled, because he saw me turning red at his coarseness. He lit another of his peasant cigarettes and began to unlace his boots. He got me to pull them off. I knelt down, bowed my head and pulled. When the ski boot suddenly flew off, my nose dipped forward and I smelled Archer's foot in its woolly, hairy, humid casing of sock.

"Would you just rub my foot and leg?" Archer said urgently, a look of pain suddenly shooting across his face. "I've got cramp. It often comes on at the end of the day."

He shot his leg out rigidly and told me where to rub and massage. I felt each of his curled toes separately and the hard tendons in his leg. His calf was like a firm sponge ball. His thigh, swelling out, amazed me. I likened it in my mind to the trumpet of some musical instrument. I went on rubbing methodically. I was able to feel his pain melting away.

When the tense look had quite left his face, he said, "Thanks," and stood up. He unbuttoned his trousers, let them fall to the ground, and pulled his shirt up. Speaking to me with his head imprisoned in it, he said: "You go and get your clothes and I'll begin bathing."

I left him and hurried up to the hotel, carrying my skis on my shoulder. I ran up to my room and pulled my evening clothes out of the wardrobe. The dinner jacket and trousers had belonged to my brother six years before, when he was my age. I was secretly ashamed of this fact, and had taken my brother's name from the inside of the breast pocket and had written my own in elaborate lettering.

I took my comb, face flannel and soap, and getting out my toboggan slid back to Archer's chalet in a few minutes. I let myself in and heard Archer splashing. The little hall was full of steam and I saw Archer's shoulders and arms like a pink smudge through the open bathroom door.

"Come and scrub my back," he yelled; "it gives me a lovely feeling." He thrust a large stiff nailbrush into my hands and told me to scrub as hard as I could.

I ran it up and down his back until I'd made harsh red tramlines. Delicious tremors seemed to be passing through Archer.

"Ah! go on!" said Archer in a dream, like a purring cat. "When I'm rich I'll have a special back-scratcher slave." I went on industriously scrubbing his back till I was afraid that I would rub the skin off. I liked to give him pleasure.

At last he stood up all dripping and said: "Now it's your turn."

I undressed and got into Archer's opaque, soapy water. I lay back and wallowed. Archer poured some very smelly salts on to my stomach. One crystal stuck in my navel and tickled and grated against me.

"This whiff ought to cover up all remaining traces of me!" Archer laughed.

"What's the smell supposed to be?" I asked, brushing the crystals off my stomach into the water, and playing with the one that lodged so snugly in my navel.

"Russian pine," said Archer, shutting his eyes ecstatically and making inbreathing dreamy noises. He rubbed himself roughly with the towel and made his hair stand up on end.

I wanted to soak in the bath for hours, but it was already getting late, and so I had to hurry.

Archer saw what difficulty I had in tying my tie. He came up to me and said: "Let me do it." I turned round relieved, but slightly ashamed of being incompetent.

I kept very still, and he tied it tightly and rapidly with his ham-like hands. He gave the bows a little expert jerk and pat. His eyes had a very concentrated, almost crossed look and I felt him breathing down on my face. All down the front our bodies touched featherily; little points of warmth came together. The hard-boiled shirts were like slightly warmed dinner plates.

When I had brushed my hair, we left the chalet and began to walk up the path to the hotel. The beaten snow was so slippery, now that we were shod only in patent-leather slippers, that we kept sliding backwards. I threw out my arms, laughing, and shouting to Archer to rescue me; then, when he grabbed me and started to haul me to him, he too would begin to slip. It was a still, Prussian-blue night with rather weak stars. Our laughter seemed to ring across the valley, to hit the mountains and then to travel on and on and on.

We reached the hotel a little the worse for wear. The soles of my patent-leather shoes had become soaked, and there was snow on my trousers. Through bending forward, the studs in Archer's shirt had burst undone, and the slab of hair hung over one of his eyes. We went into the cloak-room to readjust ourselves before entering the dining-room.

"Come and sit at my table," Archer said; then he added: "No, we'll sit at yours; there are two places there already."

We sat down and began to eat Roman *gnocchi.* (The proprietor of the hotel was Italian-Swiss.) I did not like mine very much and was glad when I could go on to *oeufs au beurre noir.* Now that my brother was away I could pick and choose in this way, leaving out the meat course, if I chose to, without causing any comment.

Archer drank Pilsner and suggested that I should too. Not wanting to disagree with him, I nodded my head, although I hated the pale, yellow, bitter water.

After the meal Archer ordered me *crème de menthe* with my coffee; I had seen a nearby lady drinking this pretty liquid and asked him about it. To be ordered a liqueur in all seriousness was a thrilling moment for me. I sipped the fumy peppermint, which left such an artificial heat in my throat and chest, and thought that apart from my mother who was dead, I had never liked anyone so much as I liked Archer. He didn't try to interfere with me at all. He just took me as I was and yet seemed to like me.

Archer was now smoking a proper cigar, not the leaf-rolled cigarettes we had had at lunchtime. He offered me one too, but I had the sense to realize that he did not mean me to take one and smoke it there before the eyes of all the hotel. I knew also that it would have made me sick, for my father had given me a cigar when

I was eleven, in an attempt to put me off smoking forever.

I always associated cigars with middle-aged men, and I watched Archer interestedly, thinking how funny the stiff fat thing looked sticking out of his young mouth.

We were sitting on the uncurtained sun-terrace, looking out on to the snow in the night; the moon was just beginning to rise. It made the snow glitter suddenly, like fish-scales. Behind us people were dancing in the salon and adjoining rooms. The music came to us in angry snatches, some notes distorted, others quite obliterated. Archer did not seem to want to dance. He seemed content to sit with me in silence.

Near me on a what-not stand stood a high-heeled slipper made of china. I took it down and slipped my hand into it. How hideously ugly the china pom-poms were down the front! The painted centipede climbing up the red heel wore a knowing, human expression. I moved my fingers in the china shoe, pretending they were toes.

"I love monstrosities too," said Archer, as I put the shoe back inside the fern in its crinkly paper-covered pot.

Later we wandered to the buffet bar and stood there drinking many glasses of the *limonade* which was made with white wine. I took the tinkly pieces of ice into my mouth and sucked them, trying to cool myself a little. Blood seemed to rise in my face; my head buzzed.

Suddenly I felt full of *limonade* and lager. I left Archer to go to the cloak-room, but he followed and stood beside me in the next china niche, while the water flushed and gushed importantly in the polished copper tubes, and an interesting, curious smell came from the wire basket which held some strange disinfectant crystals. Archer stood so quietly and guardingly beside me there that I had to say: "Do I look queer?"

"No, you don't look queer; you look nice," he said simply.

A rush of surprise and pleasure made me hotter still. We clanked over the tiles and left the cloak-room.

In the hall, I remembered that I had left all my skiing clothes at the chalet.

"I shall need them in the morning," I said to Archer.

"Let's go down there now, then I can make cocoa on my spirit-lamp, and you can bring the clothes back with you."

We set out in the moonlight; Archer soon took my arm, for he saw that I was drunk, and the path was more slippery than ever. Archer sang "Silent Night" in German, and I began to cry. I could not stop myself. It was such a delight to cry in the moonlight with Archer singing my favorite song; and my brother far away up the mountain.

Suddenly we both sat down on our behinds with a thump. There was a jarring pain at the bottom of my spine but I began to laugh wildly; so did Archer. We lay there laughing, the snow melting under us and soaking through the seats of our trousers and the shoulders of our jackets.

Archer pulled me to my feet and dusted me down with hard slaps. My teeth grated together each time he slapped me. He saw that I was becoming more and more drunk in the freezing air. He propelled me along to the chalet, more or less frog-marching me in an expert fashion. I was quite content to leave myself in his hands.

When he got me upstairs, he put me into one of the bunks and told me to rest. The feathers ballooned out round me. I sank down deliciously. I felt as if I were floating down some magic staircase for-ever.

Archer got his little meta-stove out and made coffee—not cocoa as he had said. He brought me over a strong cup and held it to my lips. I drank it unthinkingly and not tasting it, doing it only because he told me to.

When he took the cup away, my head fell back on the pillow, and I felt myself sinking and floating away again. I was on skis this time, but they were liquid skis, made of melted glass, and the snow was glass too, but a sort of glass that was springy, like gelatine, and flowing like water.

I felt a change in the light, and knew that Archer was bending over me. Very quietly he took off my shoes, undid my tie, loosened the collar and unbuttoned my braces in front. I remember thinking, before I finally fell asleep, how clever he was to know about undoing the braces; they had begun to feel so tight pulling down on my shoulders and dragging the trousers up between my legs. Archer covered me with several blankets and another quilt.

When I woke in the morning, Archer was already up. He had made me some tea and had put it on the stove to keep warm. He brought it over to me and I sat up. I felt ill, rather sick. I remembered what a glorious day yesterday had been, and thought how extraordinary it was that I had not slept in my own bed at the hotel, but in Archer's room, in my clothes.

I looked at him shamefacedly. "What happened last night? I felt peculiar," I said.

"The lager and the lemonade, and the *crème de menthe* made you a bit tight, I'm afraid," Archer said, laughing. "Do you feel better now? We'll go up to the hotel and have breakfast soon."

I got up and washed and changed into my skiing clothes. I still felt rather sick. I made my evening clothes into a neat bundle and tied them on to my toboggan. I had the sweets Archer had given me in my pocket.

We went up to the hotel, dragging the toboggan behind us.

And there on the doorstep we met my brother with one of the guides. They had had to return early, because someone in the party had broken a ski.

He was in a temper. He looked at us and then said to me: "What have you been doing?"

I was at a loss to know what to answer. The very sight of him had so troubled me that this added difficulty of explaining my actions was too much for me.

I looked at him miserably and mouthed something about going in to have breakfast.

My brother turned to Archer fiercely, but said nothing.

Archer explained: "Your brother's just been down to my place. We went skiing together yesterday and he left some clothes at the chalet."

"It's very early," was all my brother said; then he swept me on into the hotel before him, without another word to the guide or to Archer.

He went with me up to my room and saw that the bed had not been slept in.

I said clumsily: "The maid must have been in and done my room early." I could not bear to explain to him about my wonderful day, or why I had slept at the chalet.

My brother was so furious that he took no more notice of my weak explanations and lies.

When I suddenly said in desperation, "I feel sick," he seized me, took me to the basin, forced his fingers down my throat and struck me on the back till a yellow cascade of vomit gushed out of my mouth. My eyes were filled with stinging water; I was trembling. I ran the water in the basin madly, to wash away this sign of shame.

Gradually I grew a little more composed. I felt better, after being sick, and my brother had stopped swearing at me. I filled the basin with freezing water and dipped my face into it. The icy feel seemed to bite round my eye-sockets and make the flesh round my nose firm again. I waited, holding my breath for as long as possible.

Suddenly my head was pushed down and held. I felt my brother's hard fingers digging into my neck. He was hitting me now with a slipper, beating my buttocks and my back with slashing strokes, hitting a different place each time, as he had been taught when a prefect at school, so that the flesh should not be numbed from a previous blow.

I felt that I was going to choke. I could not breathe under the water, and realized that I would die. I was seized with such a panic that I wrenched myself free and darted round the room, with him after me. Water dripped on the bed, the carpet, the chest of drawers. Splashes of it spat against the mirror in the wardrobe door. My brother aimed vicious blows at me until he had driven me into a corner. There he beat against my uplifted arms, yelling in a hoarse, mad, religious voice: "Bastard, Devil, Harlot, Bugger!"

As I cowered under his blows, I remember thinking that my brother had suddenly become a lunatic and was talking gibberish in his madness, for, of the words he was using, I had not heard any before, except "Devil."

The Hateful Word

Flora Pinkston noticed the German prisoner as soon as she came out of the ironmonger's. He stood near the bus stop, wearing a too-romantic rust-brown cloak which fell to his knees in graceful points. His long hair fitted his head so sleekly that it looked like a thick gold skullcap. Its regularity repelled her a little; she wished the wind would ruffle it. She was not surprised when she saw him glance furtively in a shop window, then draw out a little blue comb and run through the shining strands.

"Poor boy," she thought a little contemptuously; "he is a prisoner with nothing to cherish but his golden hair."

He was a little man, several inches shorter than herself, and probably half her age. She tried not to mind the thought of her fortieth birthday looming nearer and nearer—hadn't she been through all that time and time again? Whereas he—he could be only twenty-two or twenty-three at the very most. "Probably even less," she thought, taking in the simplicity of his expression, the innocent smoothness of his face. She wondered whether she liked the pointed delicacy of his nose. He held his mouth with that precision often seen in Germans. Did it make him look rather missish? A little, as if he repeated "Prunes and prisms" several times every night before going to bed.

Where the cloak fell open in front she saw that he wore the shortest of battle-dress blouses above dark, full trousers. The tight little blouse reminded her of an Eton jacket—a monkey jacket. Men called them "bumfreezers," she mused, remembering her husband with a smile.

Had she done all her shopping? The picture cord, the hooks, the creosote and Harpic? She had them all; but was there anything she needed at the chemist's? And should she go to see what sort of fish there was, or was Trevor sick of all kinds, and all methods of cooking it?

Heavens! Although her thoughts had wandered back to her, her eyes had still been fixed on the little prisoner, and now he was smiling shamefacedly, as if he could no longer ignore her gaze. What ought she to do? Could she just smile her apologies for staring, then get into the car and drive off? Or would he be dreadfully disappointed? He looked as if he were steeling himself for an encounter, as if he expected to be addressed by her at any moment. How lonely he must be feeling standing on the pavement of this bustling little English market town. No one but herself had even stopped to stare at him. His russet cloak and burnished hair aroused no spark of interest.

Impulsively Flora took a step towards him; she moved with long, easy strides, as if lazily conscious of an elegant, well-dressed body.

"You going my way?" she asked in her casual, brassy voice. "Can I give you a lift? Masses of room."

She waved a hand, indicating the empty car. It was characteristic of her not to modify the superciliousness of her tone, to use a phrase like "masses of room" which he would probably not understand.

The little prisoner was all smiles and anxiety.

"Please," he said, bobbing his head both in acknowledgment and answer. Somewhere in the "please" a question also lurked; he was not quite sure of the part expected of him.

"Come on, then," Flora said, overriding his hesitation, sweeping him towards the car. He sat in the seat beside her, his arms hugging his chest. He would make himself as small as possible. He would touch nothing, lean on nothing, be as little trouble as a brown-paper parcel.

Flora wished he would relax; she hated the thought of so much tautness near her. She could feel her own muscles tightening.

"Have a cigarette?" she said, pointing to the pigeonhole in front of him. "Matches and everything there."

This led to the further awkwardness of having to refuse when he immediately held out the packet to her first. She could see him taking one, putting it in his mouth, cupping his shaking hands round the flame of the match. They were clean hands, which still looked dirty because of the ingrained blackness of hard work.

What on earth were they to talk about? She knew no German at all. Surely he would ask to be put down soon.

"You like the English countryside?" she asked, waving a proprietary hand at the fields and orchards they were passing.

The little prisoner gulped, took hold of himself and said: "Oh, I like—I like *very* much."

There was silence again. At last in desperation Flora said:

"Just let me know when you want to be dropped?"

"Please?" the German said in gentle bewilderment.

It was only then that Flora realized that he had no journey to make, that he had got into the car simply because she had invited him.

"Lord! I've landed myself!" she thought. "I shall have to ask him in for a drink, smile and be kind, then get rid of him quickly."

She turned down a lane, then into an even narrower drive through a nut orchard. Soon the attractive little house came into view. Flora never ceased to enjoy its smooth cream weatherboarding, its tiny Gothic sash windows and the delicate iron porch with gracefully curving roof.

"Come in and have a drink," she said, not looking at him but busying herself with her parcels. He darted forward to help, grabbing packages from her feverishly. Once more she wished that he would calm himself.

In the long, low drawing-room he stood about, desperately ill at ease till she almost forced him into one of her snug French chairs. Even then he was afraid to lean back lest his hair should touch the pale apricot watered-silk.

"A bit late for tea," Flora thought. "Besides, it's Margaret Rose's afternoon out—much easier just to give him beer as I thought at first. Perhaps Trevor will be in soon; things may be easier then."

She went to the rather plain Georgian doll's house and took out a bottle of beer and some tomato juice. She laughed at herself for keeping the drinks in such a place. It seemed a rather coarse and vulgar thing to do; the little house was worthy of better treatment. One day she would have it repaired carefully and try to find some old furniture for it. In the meantime it served as a bottle cupboard very well.

"My name is Flora Pinkston," she said, pouring out the beer and passing it to him without asking if he wanted it. "What is yours?"

"I am Harry—Harry Diedz." The little prisoner tried to make the name sound as English as possible, but the unfamiliar "Harry" came out as if spelled with two "e" 's at the end.

"Silly to Anglicize his Christian name," Flora thought.

"What part of Germany do you come from?" she asked.

"Thuringia."

"Are your people still there?"

"Oh yes; I have letters every week."

"What did you do before you were in the army?"

"I was glassworker, like my father."

"Did you like that?"

"Oh yes, I like."

The little prisoner gazed into the distance, as if reliving all the pains and pleasures of being a glassworker.

"Do you like music?" Flora asked.

"Very much." He gave a little hissing intake of breath.

"Which composer do you like most?"

"Mozart."

"Who else?"

"Wagner, but not so much."

"Do you box?" Why should she suddenly ask him this? Had the stockiness of his little body put the idle question into her head?

"Sometimes a little—I try," he laughed, putting up his hands in mock defense. "There is very good man at the camp; he teach me. But I like football."

Flora heard the turning of the front-door handle. Good. Trevor was back. Conversation would be less like a dreary cross-examination. He would know what to say to the little prisoner.

But when her husband came into the room, he looked anything but conversational. He was tired from his day in London; he still clutched his neat black briefcase as if unable, even at home, to free himself from his clients' problems.

He looked at the German prisoner, then glanced away. This was another of Flora's vagaries. He could hardly control his annoyance.

"Oh, Trevor, this is Harry Diedz," Flora was saying. "He likes Mozart better than Wagner and football better than boxing, and before the wretched war swallowed him up he used to blow the most beautiful glass objects in Thuringia."

Was there any need for this silly "party" brightness of Flora's? And since, presumably, she had invited the prisoner herself, why should she go out of her way to make him look foolish? Poor little devil. He was so horribly embarrassed, standing there, scraping his boots together and half holding out his hand.

Trevor nodded perfunctorily, then sank into a chair.

"What can I get you, dear?" Flora asked with a curious unexpected meekness. "A whiskey and soda?"

She went to the doll's house again and brought out a decanter and siphon. She had not offered Trevor's whiskey to the German, but she showed no compunction in producing it now.

Trevor drank deeply, lugubriously. He was too dejected to talk; he longed to be left alone so that he could stretch out his legs and relax.

"Why not show your friend the garden, before it's dark?" he suggested, turning to Flora with a set look in his eyes.

Flora saw the look and understood. She led Harry out into the garden much in the same way that she would take a little dog for an airing before bed. They walked between the currant bushes, past the vegetables and out on to a little lawn under an old weeping willow. Trevor liked doing the garden himself, only sometimes having an old man to dig or clip the hedges. Now, because he had been so busy in London, the garden looked a little bedraggled. The grass was rather too long and a few weeds had sprung up in the borders.

"Do you like gardening?" Flora asked, to break the silence.

"Yes, very nice," said Harry, with such feeling that an idea suddenly came to Flora. Why shouldn't he help Trevor sometimes in the evenings? Surely Trevor would be pleased to have someone to mow the grass, or to do some of the other less interesting jobs. She turned to Harry at once.

"My husband is so busy in London that he can't spare much time for the garden at the moment. If you're free in the evenings would you like to come in and help?"

Her abruptness made it difficult for Harry to understand at first, but when he realized that he was being asked to do something very much to his taste, for which he would probably be paid, he said: "Yes, please, very much."

The prospect of coming to this charming house and garden delighted him. It solved the problem of his evenings; it would do away with that brooding emptiness that clapped down on him after the day's work, so that he stood on the street corner, or lay in his bunk in the iron hut, despondent.

"Thank you very much," he said again with deep gratitude. "I come tomorrow night?"

Flora thought quickly. She was a little taken aback by his prompt acceptance. Had she been impulsive and silly? What would Trevor think? Would he be pleased? Aloud she said: "Yes, that will be fine." She paused a moment, dismissing him. "Can you find your own way back to the camp?"

"I think," he answered in spite of not knowing where he was.

She took him through the nut orchard, leaving him at the gate.

"You go this way," she said, pointing up the lane; "it can only be a mile or two, three at the outside."

"I find all right, Missis."

He gave his stiff little bow and turned abruptly, so that his cloak swirled out like a dancer's skirt. She left him without another glance and walked back to her husband. He was still sunk deep in the chair with his knees higher than his head. Flora thought that one could tell they were attractive knees, even through the trousers; and how large after the prisoner's compact doll-like quality.

"What a little quainty," she said, wrinkling her nose in amusement. "I took him to the gate and he said good-bye and he called me Missis."

"Why you should want to ask a German back beats me," said Trevor truculently. "It seems pretty sentimental. If they'd won the war, you'd be laughing on the other side of your face."

"Darling, don't be Blimpish, it doesn't suit you; and what does that expression about laughing on the other side of one's face mean? It always sounds faintly rude to me. It may be quite illogical, but it reminds me of the ridiculous phrase we used to shout at school: 'Base equals Face.' "

Trevor gave a wan grin.

"Well, what was the point in asking this one back suddenly?" he asked. "They've been here long enough and you've taken not the slightest notice of them."

"Darling, you know how I stare if something catches my eye. I came out of Griffith's and saw the flowing cloak and gruesomely brushed golden hair—oh, so picturesque. He saw me staring and smiled back. I felt I had to do something, so I offered him a lift; then when he'd got into the car I found he wasn't going anywhere."

"Just a straight pick-up," said Trevor laughingly. He was recovering his natural easy warmth.

Flora thought it a good moment to mention the gardening scheme.

"Will you be pleased, I wonder? I've asked him to come in the evenings to help with the grass and other boring jobs. He leaped at the idea and is turning up tomorrow."

"God! I expect he'll dig up the bulbs, break the mowing machine, and water the things that shouldn't be watered. But I don't mind; I've given up bothering. You have your blond plaything."

"Dearest, don't be crude. I did it for you. You know how tired you've been lately. The garden is really too much for you, now that you're so frightfully busy in London."

"Well, thank God you didn't offer him my whiskey," said Trevor, pouring out another drink. "That would have been the last straw."

The little prisoner appeared punctually the next evening. He had barely had time to gulp a cup of tea and gobble a bun after his hard day's work in the fields; but he was satisfied. Was he not coming to this nice house where the handsome lady, though a little terrifying, was really kind underneath? Had she not given him beer and a ride in her car? No other English person had ever asked him home. He scrambled into a clean shirt, then brushed his golden hair with special carefulness.

Trevor was not yet home, so Flora took Harry to the toolshed and showed him the mower.

"Be careful with the blades," she said; "my husband is rather particular."

"I know, I careful. Stones very bad."

Harry made a little gesture as if picking up a stone and throwing it off the lawn.

By the time Trevor returned, Harry had finished the little patches of lawn and the grass paths and had begun to clip the edges and weed the borders. He had undertaken these tasks without any word from Flora. His crisp sleeves were rolled up, showing sunburned arms. The full, dark trousers were pulled in snugly round his waist by a thick leather belt. He looked like a little model of a gardener.

Trevor, hurrying past, noted what he was doing with grudging approval and dropped some word of greeting. The little prisoner stood up and bowed punctiliously.

"How well they trained them in that army," Trevor thought. "Too damn well—a bit slavish all that bowing and obedience."

The next evening Trevor arrived back earlier and went to join Harry in the vegetable garden. Flora, helping Margaret Rose with the evening meal, looked out of the kitchen window and saw the two men working—Trevor tall, powerful, leisurely; Harry neat, and quick, like a clockwork toy.

"And they'll never think it necessary to utter a single word," she mused. "Wonderful, that acceptance of silence, even of gruffness. If Trevor's in rather a mood, Harry won't mind; he'll just go on working peacefully." Like many women, she had an exaggerated notion of the comradeship existing between men.

But it did seem as if some sort of understanding was quickly growing up between the two. Flora would sometimes catch Harry looking up at her husband with a sort of schoolboy admiration, and

Trevor would often say comtemptuous patronizing things which, nevertheless, showed quite clearly the warmer feelings they were supposed to mask.

"Poor little runt!" he would exclaim, giving the ugly word its full value. "What a life he's had. Do you know he's hardly twenty yet?"

The words sent a pang through Flora. When she went up to her bedroom she looked in the glass for a long time. She saw the ripeness of her face. Perhaps she was handsomer than she had ever been; but she did not want to be handsome. She wanted to be fresh, even a little raw. She hated herself for this preoccupation with the outward semblance of extreme youth. "It is pathetic," she told herself fiercely, "and so wrongheaded. Young people are often at their very worst. They have bad skins, neglected hair, abominable clothes, and they don't know how to manage anything. Their mouths, their eyes, their legs and arms are all over the place."

In this way she tried to fortify herself against the years to come. She ran the lipstick over her mouth, rubbing the color in carefully; she did not want *her* face to look like a chamber pot daubed with strawberry jam. Where had she read that frightful description? Was it in a novel of Joyce Cary's? She smiled at herself in the mirror and went downstairs to finish arranging the table. She liked to make it as attractive as possible for Trevor in the evening. After being immersed in the squalor and intricacy of the law all day, he needed something to make him feel civilized again. She never asked the little prisoner to stay; his gaucherie would have turned their quiet meal into an ordeal, a penance. She usually just took him out a tankard of beer, or gave it to him when he came shyly to the back door to say goodnight. She remembered again his scarlet embarrassment and pleasure when, after the first week, she offered him the money he had earned. She gave it to him very gracefully, thanking him for his wholehearted work. It was difficult for her to keep the heartless quality out of her voice, but she did look straight at him with attractive sincerity. In spite of the awkwardness of the money transaction, she suddenly found that paying him gave her a curious, sharp pleasure.

She was melted by his blushing humility and gratitude, yet at the same instant a delicious, rather shameful sense of power tingled through her.

"Paying Margaret Rose has *never* affected me in this way," she thought, trying to laugh herself out of an emotion that seemed somehow discreditable.

One rainy afternoon, about three weeks after her meeting with Harry, Flora was looking out of her drawing-room window, watching the birds on the lawn and the drops hissing into the carp pool. The whole garden was in the trimmest order now. To look at it soothed Flora; she had been sorting clothes and rearranging the furniture in her bedroom for most of the day, and she felt tired. Suddenly she saw a figure in a camouflaged oilskin coming down the drive. For a moment the piebald cape, with its patches of chocolate, green and khaki, perplexed her; then she realized that it was worn by Harry.

"But what is he doing here so early?" she wondered; "it's only four o'clock."

She went to open the door for him. He stood smiling up at her, his square little teeth looking very white and rather savage in the wet, glowing face.

"Farmer says: 'Go home early—too wet', so I come to do greenhouse," he explained. "I clean glass inside, make walls white." He ran an imaginary whitewash brush up and down an imaginary wall.

Later, when she had called him in for tea and they sat over the empty cups, smoking cigarettes, she remembered that the Louis Quinze commode, which was her dressing-table, had not yet been moved into its new position because it was so heavy. The weight would be nothing to Harry.

"I wonder," she said, "if you would help me move a piece of furniture."

"Oh yes," he said, standing up at once to wait for orders.

"It's in my bedroom."

Flora led the way up the little box stairs. She said: "Be careful not to knock your head," before she remembered how much shorter he was than most men.

They each took hold of a magnificent rococo ormolu handle and lifted out the first curved drawer. When the carcass was empty, they moved it easily across the room, fitting it between the windows. Flora sat down on the bed to admire the new effect and Harry went to pick up a drawer; but as he bent down his attention was caught by Flora's bright scarves and bags and by a small collection of old fans, scent bottles, beadwork purses and Early Victorian nosegay holders. He crouched over the drawer, not moving. Flora, looking down on his back so close to her, felt prompted to say: "You are happy to come here, Harry? You like working in the garden?"

He looked up at her with his most brilliant smile. A raindrop still glistened in the little cup at the base of his throat. The unmistakable soldier smell rose from his warm damp battle-dress.

"I like here like my home. Before I was very sad—nowhere to go; now I think every day, tonight I go to Mr. Pinkston."

"You like my husband?" Flora asked, barely conscious of her wish for him to say something appreciative of herself.

"Mr. Pinkston *very* good man, very clever, very strong . . ." Harry left his sentence in the air, finding it impossible to put his admiration into English words. He blushed a little and looked down again at the drawer to hide his awkwardness.

"This very pretty things," he murmured, touching a sequined fan delicately. The bristles on the back of his neck suddenly glinted gold against the darker, sunburned skin. Flora felt an irresistible urge to treat him as a little boy. She leaned forward blindly, to put her arms round him.

She felt Harry's body suddenly stiffen. He was utterly still, a frozen man. She put her mouth to the nape of his neck. The flesh was cool and she had expected it to be warmer than her lips. Harry gulped; she felt the Adam's apple rise and fall, like a squirrel leaping to escape, but tied by the leg. She was crying now. The hot tears falling on his neck appalled Harry. He turned, straining his head towards her. There was a desperate look of pity and unhappiness in his eyes. Flora saw it and was shocked into some sort of self-possession. Her hands fell to her sides. Mechanically she looked in the long cheval glass and saw how ugly the crying had made her. The tears had no power to smudge her make-up, but they had inflamed her eyes and lids; she had reddened sockets of a rheumy old witch. "They don't look real," she mused; "I've been got up for some production of *Macbeth*." She ran her hand over her hair, fluffing a curl, smoothing a wave. The feel of her strong, vibrant hair comforted her a little. She even tried to clear her thoughts. What had he done to her? She had thought of him as a vain, pathetic, ridiculous little person. How had he cracked her hard bright shell, so that she quivered with no protection any more? Would she ever recover from the sudden devastating glimpse of herself which he had given her?

He had scrambled to his feet and was standing awkwardly before her.

"I must go now, Mrs. Pinkston; tonight I help to play music for sing-song at the camp."

His lips worked; he was trying to add something to his sentence. The words came out in a rush of almost pidgin English.

"I am thanking you so much, Mrs. Pinkston, and your very good husband, for friending me; I so lonely before. Soon I go back to Germany; I tell them there you are like, like—" He strained after the one word to express his gratitude. "You are like mother to me—my English mother."

He was out of the room and down the stairs, leaving the hateful word tingling in her ears.

The Coffin on the Hill

Perhaps I was eight when my parents took me at Easter time up the river in a houseboat. I shall explain here that in China a houseboat is not a terraced barge, all plate-glass windows, white balustrading, frothy pink geraniums and ferns. It is a compact little motor launch fitted with saloon, tiny cabins, bathroom, and galley. In it one can explore the canals and waterways.

Part of the fascination of that journey must be put down to the fact that I don't know where we went. I only know that it was up the river Yangtze from Shanghai.

For days beforehand my mother superintended packing of food, clothes, rugs, bed-linen, and drinks for my father.

Boy, Cook and Coolie were coming with us. When I went to visit them in the kitchen, they gathered round me and teased me, telling me not to fall in, or the drowned people would pull me down and keep me under. Although I took it as a joke, I shuddered too, seeing arms like water-weeds or octopus tentacles stretched up to grasp my kicking legs, dragging me down, not demonishly, but with a horrible, greedy sort of love, as though they wanted to keep me and gloat on me forever. I thought of the dead faces; the eyes, the nose, the mouth eaten away by fishes. But they were still able to weep from the holes where their eyes had been, and cries locked in bubbles escaped from the shapeless mouths.

When I told my father about these drowned men, he said that the Chinese in old times described in this way the dangerous current, which was supposed to drag people down if they struggled.

I think he saw how much I had been dwelling on the subject, for he laughed at me and made me feel excessive and unreasonable.

At last everything was ready and we drove down in the afternoon to the Bund. The great mass of shipping on the river before Shanghai alarmed me. I felt that a small houseboat could never thread its way between all the steamers, junks and sampans; but as soon as we were on board, I was so enchanted that I forgot everything but the little world of the boat. I wanted to explore the whole of it at once, and so, to begin with, I did nothing but run up and down the deck in a mad, excited way. When I was a little calmer, I dived down the miniature companionway and found myself in the saloon; but my mother was there, unpacking the silver, and I was afraid she might ask me to arrange the pepper and salt and mustard pots neatly in one of the little mahogany cupboards, so I darted past her and came to the first cabin.

I tipped down the shining metal basin, pressed the hot- and cold-water buttons—quite new to me and so far more delightful than clumsy taps—then I tucked myself up in the bottom bunk and pretended to be asleep in mid-ocean; but the restraint was too much. I had to jump up, put the toy ladder into position, and climb into the top bunk where I watched the light from the water jigging and flashing on the ceiling.

By now we had begun to chug gently up the river. The city was left behind and I could see green banks through the porthole. I heard Boy talking in the galley; being still too restless to settle, I thought I would go and see what he was doing.

I found him preparing tea, while Cook and Coolie squatted on their haunches and played a game with little round discs. Boy was singing to himself in his high cracked voice. It was something intricate and tricksy as yodelling, and I longed to be able to copy him when he produced his piercing little trills and grace notes. They were sad and keen and sweet, like some fruit vinegar.

When he had finished the egg sandwiches, I helped him take the tea to the bows, where my father and mother were sitting, with rugs over their knees, for it was still cold.

My father watched and smoked and drank many cups of tea, while my mother and I ate the sandwiches, Cook's crusted sponge cake and the American cookies. As we sat there, perched up in our wicker chairs, like three figureheads, I felt that we were part of some marvellous, rich procession, and an important part too—grotesque and strange perhaps, but significant. The touch of nightmare was there because the little boat, so perfectly compact and self-sufficing, was all at variance with the flat land, the little frog-green ponds and the clusters of curling grey roofs half-hidden in the bamboo groves.

Sometimes mangy dogs came out of the villages to bark, and once we passed a squeaking wheelbarrow, loaded with people sitting back to back, and looking in their quilted clothes like so many rolls of bedding. How they chattered amongst themselves, and how extravagantly the wheelbarrow-man groaned and grunted and chanted! He was half-naked, and the wind was biting; yet the sweat poured off him. Some of the people pointed at us and were clearly being witty at our expense, finding us very ridiculous and amusing.

Before it was really dark, my mother suggested that I should go to bed, hinting that I would then be able to get up very early in the morning. I hated the thought of sleep, but I knew I had to go, so I said good night to my father without kissing him and went down alone. My mother would come later to see me in my bunk.

The pale eyes of the portholes gleamed on each side of the saloon and there was a faint glimmer over the surface of the lockers. The sound of the engine came to me and the lapping of the water. The air seemed weighed down and given some deep dreaming meaning by the scent from lovely bulbs, which I think must have been China New Year flowers; or were they hyacinths?

I touched them, and I touched the delightful green pom-poms

on the minute curtains. Leaning forward and putting out my tongue I licked the brass rim of one of the portholes, in order to realize the ship with all my senses. Then I curled up in a corner of the fitted seat and felt like a mole, or some other perfectly happy blind animal, burrowing deeper and deeper, coming at last to its true home.

My mother found me there and chased me into the bathroom and stood over me until I had cleaned my teeth and done everything else in her own approved way; then she saw me into a top bunk in one of the cabins and put beside me the curious doll which I insisted on keeping; though some grown-ups told me that I was too old to play with it—to say nothing of being quite the wrong sex.

Leaning over the side of the bunk and clutching the doll, I began to tease my mother, pretending that she was getting me to bed early, so that she could drink cocktails with my father—for whenever my mother drank a toast or took a sip from my father's glass, just to please him, I would officiously remind her of her principles.

After we had kissed and hugged and she had left me, I began to talk to the doll, whose name was Lymph Est. I have had to invent that spelling, because the name has never been written before, and I cannot, of course, explain what the words mean. They just came to me one day, and I repeated them over and over again, until they turned into an incantation.

The doll was neither masculine nor feminine, but a sexless being, like an angel. It was broad and squat, and it wore a kind of convict's outfit—meager trousers, jacket and cap of bottle-green corduroy. Its white silk face was painted with black eyes, the shape of greatly enlarged fleas, and it had a scarlet mouth, like the slot of some rococo pillar-box. Two red dots did for nostrils. It possessed no hair or ears.

I used to talk to it, not because I believed it was alive, but because I needed an audience for my hopes and plans—an image that would not answer.

"Do you like this ship?" I now asked Lymph Est. And then I began to tell over all its delights and beauties, until the cataloguing of them sent me to sleep.

I woke to find long grasses poking through the porthole. We were moored close to the bank and I could smell the earth. Leaving Lymph Est on the pillow, I ran up on deck in my dressing-gown. Everything was hidden in a soft mist, but the sun was gradually melting a way through. I longed to go on shore to explore the unknown land, but Cook was already making the breakfast, while Boy laid the table and Coolie pretended to dust with a bunch of cock's feathers on a long bamboo; just as if we were in a palace antechamber, twenty feet high, instead of in a miniature saloon, where even I could touch the ceiling by standing on the lockers.

I remember smell of coffee and smell of oatmeal porridge on that morning, and then my mother making scrambled eggs with butter and cream in the chafing-dish. I watched the eggs curdle and thicken, saw my father's portion put on a piece of anchovy toast, but mine on a plain piece. As I ate, the mouthfuls seemed to stick halfway, still leaving the void of excitement underneath.

Soon after breakfast the last shreds of mist evaporated, and then we saw in the distance, on the left bank, a group of buildings shining in the sun. Boy said they might be part of a monastery, and this made my mother want to visit them at once; so the engine was started and we moved on. My mother kept looking through my father's field glasses and telling us what she could see.

"There are ruinous pavilions round a courtyard," she said; "and a sort of paved way leading down to the river."

She passed the glasses to me, but I was not good at adjusting the lenses and only produced a milling, curving blur. But in a little time we were before the monastery and I could see it all for myself.

Stone carvings of lions and horses guarded the paved way, and through a thick brown mat of ancient grass pierced this year's acid blades, hiding the bases of the statues and the steps up to the broken pavilions. Directly in front of us bulged a granite incense burner, rather like a witches' cauldron. The lip was broken, and I did not think it very beautiful or interesting, but for some reason my mother fell in love with it. As soon as the little gangplank had been put out she ran on shore and started to stroke the harsh surface with her hand.

For a few moments we were unnoticed, then the monks came down to us in a little group. I stood still and watched, never before having seen shaven heads or thick dusty black robes or clacking wooden rosaries. The monks were very young, with faces as smooth as mushrooms, and they were smiling shyly and secretly and had their hands hidden in their sleeves. When they were within a few feet, I caught a curious smell both animal and aromatic, and it filled me with uneasiness.

My mother smiled at them and bowed, and my father nodded more awkwardly, but neither could speak Chinese, so Boy was called hurriedly to act as interpreter.

Boy told us that the monks were pleased to see us, but we must not expect any entertainment, for they were very poor and their monastery was falling into decay. Boy waved his hand rather contemptuously in the direction of the collapsing buildings. Altogether he seemed to treat the monks with very little respect.

It was now quite clear that we were being asked for money, and my father began to fiddle with coins in his pocket, wondering, I suppose, how best to make a present to the monks. At last he thrust two or three silver dollars into the hand of the spokesman, muttering as he did so: "And they'll only gamble it away or spend it on opium, I expect."

To give jokingly and ungraciously was with him a convention that meant nothing at all, but I was afraid that the monks would understand his words and resent them.

Of course they did not. They were all smiles and charm and urbanity. They asked Boy if there was anything that the lady would like, and when he translated this, my mother's eyes went straight to the incense burner.

They gave it to her at once, smiling at her for wanting the broken thing, telling her that all this side of the monastery had been abandoned, only one wing at the back being kept in repair.

Although my parents had often condemned rich Americans for carrying off Spanish cloisters and black-and-white Cheshire manor houses to their own country, they neither of them seemed to hesitate over the incense burner. Perhaps it was not important enough to trouble them; in any case it was soon being carried to our boat by several of the strongest monks. My father walked in front to show where it should go on the deck.

When it had been lashed to the rail at the top of the companionway, my father gave the monks cigarettes, which they smoked ceremoniously as they watched us glide into midstream. We waved to them and they waved back. Their faces had all gone sad and thoughtful, and I felt that they were prisoners chained to their ruin, but longing to go exploring with us. I had the idea that a monk's life was nothing but a waste of idleness, and I decided that they would all go mad in the end.

Soon they were out of sight and I could wave to them no more; then I turned to the incense burner and started to examine it with my mother. Under the mud in the bowl we found the burnt marks of the joss-sticks. These made me think of sacrifices in the Bible, and I imagined white lambs and newborn babies being slaughtered and then roasted in the bowl by a High Priest with a knife as long and curving as a scythe. The more he slaughtered, the more holy he felt. I could almost smell the meat sizzling. What had begun as an alarming fancy, ended up by merely making me hungry.

Without saying anything to my mother, I went to get the green tomato chutney and two forks. Pickles were for me the symbol of the free, grown-up life, and I pretended that I liked them better than sweets.

My mother smiled when she saw what I brought for a mid-morning tid-bit, but she took up a translucent green fragment on her fork, and sat with it poised before her. She was looking at the low hills far away, and I wondered what she was thinking about, she was so still and smiling. I watched her, while the tang of the chutney roughened my tongue and dried up my mouth. . . .

Once we passed a pagoda with fairy-like grass growing on its many roofs; and then there was a beautiful little white marble bridge over a canal. I remember too somewhere logs floating in the water. I was sure that they were dangerous to our small boat, having heard stories of icebergs and steamers; but although I waited for the tearing, crunching sound, nothing happened and we sailed on smoothly.

When we stopped again, it was at the foot of a hill which stretched back from the river in a long arm. My mother suggested having our picnic at the top of the ridge gazing out over the land; so my father took up the picnic case and I a little basket, and we started to climb up through broken terraces and tangled bushes.

It was not long before I saw that the whole hill was a huge graveyard. Walls that had looked like curved garden terraces were really horseshoe graves, and there were simpler ones, where the coffins had not been buried, but little windowless, doorless brick houses had been built round them.

It did not seem strange to us to take our picnic to the top of this dead city and eat it there, surrounded by ten thousand hidden skeletons. In China there are graves everywhere.

My mother chose a bank where the grass was blown flat by the wind. Below us the land stretched away endlessly; and I could just pick out our little boat on the curling white river. My father said the position was too exposed, but he acquiesced with mock resignation, and made a business of taking off his coat to shield the spirit lamp.

The leather picnic case was old. Plated flasks and sandwich cases fitted round a square kettle, which appealed to me strongly because of the delicate cap and chain on the spout. Apostle teaspoons and knives with yellowed ivory handles were arranged in a fan shape on the stained green satin lining of the lid.

My mother began to open the cases and take out chicken bones, Russian salad, chocolate cake, and oranges, while my father poured himself out a drink from the wrong flask and grimaced when the babyish white trickle appeared. He made coffee for my mother by throwing spoonfuls into the boiling kettle. She said that the drink was not a success, but I was delighted when she allowed me to color my milk with it.

I gnawed my drumstick and ate little pieces of piquant stuffing. There was roasted brown skin to crunch, messy salad to be played with, and then the cake, black and rich as leaf mold. The pieces of orange at the end seemed to tingle all through my mouth, cleaning away all other tastes that had ever been.

When my father was lying on his back with a cigarette between his lips, and my mother was motionless, lost in the view, I got up and ran away from them without a word. I went to explore the graves, hoping to find some ancient coin or ornament hidden under a stone, or just lying on the ground, undiscovered, but for all to see.

I jumped down from terrace to terrace, clambered under bushes, lifted stones, but found only beetles and insects. I was wondering what to do next, when I saw at the end of the ridge one of the simpler brick graves which seemed to be broken open. I hurried towards it, feeling a little afraid, but hoping for great things.

The whole of one corner had collapsed. I could see the coffin quite plainly and when, trembling with excitement, I bent even closer, the coarse weaving of a piece of cloth jumped out at me from a crack in the rotting wood.

These things were so exactly as I had expected them to be that I saw through the coffin and the shroud to the skull, the loose teeth, the clots of hair, and the white bone. No need to pry any further. My dreadful pictures had come true. The imprisoned, concealed smell of the monks had been bad, but there was a worse, more evil smell here—a smell that was forcing me to know what happened in the end. Rotting wood and cloth and human bone were changed now. They were dead.

I knew that I must never say a word, that I must just walk away as if nothing had happened, but when I turned to the place where I had left my father and mother, they were no longer there. I saw only the picnic things spread out on the grass.

I started to run; and every now and then I called out to my mother in a very even plain voice that perfectly expressed my fright. There was a hollow sound in the curved arm of the hill, but no human answer.

I came upon my mother just when I had begun to feel that I might never see her again. I turned the corner of a peeling stucco wall, and there she was, framed in one of those charming completely round Chinese doorways. She smiled at me slumberously and serenely. It was clear that she had wandered away to meditate in that forgotten tomb garden.

I ran up to her and stood, breathing hard, but not touching her or saying anything. She seemed the very opposite of all that the coffin held, but this only made my confusion worse, for I knew that she would come to it at last; and that knowledge was unbearable.

I would have liked to say, "Up there you can see a rotten coffin with some rotten cloth poking through a crack, and under the cloth . . . there's a rotten man," but I knew that it was forbidden, that if I did so she would frown and gaze into me to discover what had been left at the back of my eyes. Then she would turn away and say with careful casualness, "Darling, you oughtn't to have looked," and I would be made to feel peering and a little indecent.

So I said nothing, but took her hand and walked back with her to the picnic place, where my father, back from the bushes, was now packing up the case and scattering crumbs for the birds.

We said very little as we climbed down again to the boat. The clouds were gathering and pressing lower, and soon after we had settled ourselves in the saloon I heard rain pattering down on the deck. The surface of the river began to hiss and boil, and such a delicious feeling of snugness was created that tremors ran through me and I pressed Lymph Est hard against the cushions of the seat under the portholes where I was lying. My father took up the book that he had been reading to me at home, and my mother started to work on her neglected piece of petit-point. She had not touched it for months, but now she sorted the wools with quiet pleasure and began to put stitches into the conventional acanthus leaf. Her hand rose and fell like a sparrow snatching crumbs from the canvas.

I listened with one part of my mind to my father. He was reading something about the ancient rivalry between Genoa and Venice. The heroine's name was Maria. I remember, because my father *would* pronounce it in the English way, although my mother insisted that the "i" should be "e" as in Italian.

The other part of me talked to Lymph Est. I got a sort of mournful, gruesome pleasure out of saying over and over again: "Tomorrow we go back."

We were amongst the ships again in the thick of the river traffic, with hooters droning and the shouts of bargemen ringing out, making me believe that something terrible was about to happen.

Boy, Cook, Coolie, my father and mother, were all packing and tidying, preparing to leave.

I lay in my top bunk with Lymph Est held above my head. I was trying to pretend that the journey had only just begun, but I knew it was over and that we were back in the hateful confusion of the city.

I suddenly remembered the drowned people, and I saw again the piece of shroud poking through the coffin on the hillside. An extraordinary impulse seized me, making me hold Lymph Est out of the porthole above the water.

For a moment I hesitated afraid, yet longing for the pain and the sight I would never forget; then, as if absentmindedly, I relaxed the grip of my fingers and shut my eyes.

When I opened them again, I saw Lymph Est's squat limbs, silk face, whorish black eyes, and scarlet mouth all framed in the mud-green water. No dead men dragged it down. The kapok stuffing kept it floating perfectly. Lymph Est was unmolested and serene and doomed.

And as I watched it sailing away, I was pierced by my own wantonness, and I started to call out for help.

Coolie ran along the deck with a boat hook and tried to fish Lymph out for me, but it was beyond his reach. I watched it disappear between the coal barges; and as I looked for the last time on that extraordinary face, my feelings were so interwoven and twisted that I felt mad.

Boy, Cook, Coolie all comforted me so gently. What was I to do? Was I to take everything to myself, hypocritically, pretending that it had been an accident? Even if I dared to explain, what could I say?

Had I sacrificed Lymph Est just to cause a sensation, to fix people's interest on myself? The knowledge of what I had done was not clearly revealed to me; but now I know that I gave Lymph Est to the river because of the corpses at the bottom, and because of the thing wrapped in cloth on the hill.

The Fire in the Wood

On the edge of a pine wood in Hampshire there is a little concrete box which dates from the time when such architecture was still fashionable and rare. It looks a little forlorn and posturing now, but inside it is comfortable enough. My story begins on a grey afternoon in April, when a young woman let herself out of this house and started to walk up the path through the trees. She was going to meet an old friend of her mother's. Mrs. Tuke drove over once a month at least to see Mary and take her back to tea, but she would never come quite all the way. If she stopped at the top of the hill and waited for Mary to climb up to her, she told herself that she had been wise and not wasted her petrol.

As Mary walked over the uneven rain-washed path, she felt pleasantly tired and at ease. She had been working all morning on one of her needlework pictures. Into this one she had stitched real shells, coins, fossils, beads, buttons, sequins, fur, feathers, beetles' wings, skeleton leaves and human hair. She was always looking out for new things to use. Once she had worked in a gruesome eagle's claw off an old brooch; another time she had found some sheep's teeth in a field and taken them home for dragon's fangs. Mary often chose to do fierce beasts. This morning she had made flashing eyes for her lion out of two old steel beads—their facets caught the light and glinted hungrily—then she had worked its tongue in the glossiest, flossiest crimson silk, so that it looked almost dripping with saliva. She had finished by doing a little to the rocks and groves in the background.

The thought of romantic landscape brought Mary back from her picture to the Scotch pines and rhododendrons all round her. She knew the history of this wood and always took pleasure in the artificiality that lay just under its present tangled wildness. The local great lady of early Victorian times had designed it to surround her new stone mansion, which was to have risen from the levelled site at the top of the hill. But something had happened and the house was never even begun. So the pink serpentine paths, the artfully planted trees and shrubs encircled nothing. Every year the pines had grown taller, the rhododendrons more dense, the paths less visible. Bracken crept over the ground, and the seeds of other trees planted themselves.

In some places the rhododendrons had bulged across the paths, blocking them entirely; in others they had sprung up, then joined black, sticky witches' arms and fingers, twisting and gripping together until long tunnels were formed where all the light was green and cobwebs hung down to madden human faces. Some lone bushes had climbed twenty feet into the air, as if determined to pour down their leaves in a hard and glittering cascade.

But if the rhododendrons were gross, almost threatening in their growth, the pines that rose out of them were splendid; they were great pythons, their serpent scales all mauve, brown-pink and silky in the sun. There was no sun now, but Mary always imagined the trees glinting and iridescent, at their most beautiful. She paused for a moment, leaning her face against one of the trunks and gazing up to where the grey-blue pine needles frisked and frolicked like mad pom-poms or bottle-brushes. She felt a little drugged and swimming, as if she could never stop gazing on, on, beyond the needles into the limitless grey of the sky; then she was seized with the strange conviction that the tree might suddenly collapse into itself, like a giant telescope, sucking her into the ground with it. . . .

It was the smell of smoke that broke the spell. At first it came to her faintly and she thought nothing of it, it had only been enough to bring her eyes down to the earth again. She walked on quickly, anxious not to keep Mrs. Tuke waiting.

Just before she reached the point where two paths crossed, she smelled the smoke again; this time it was stronger, it stung her nostrils a little, but she was still unperturbed. She thought of forest fires and put the thought away from her comfortably; she was lazy and dreamy from work and from staring into the sky. She would soon have to turn to the right down one of the green tunnels which led to the road. On her other side a thick bank of rhododendrons hid everything behind it.

Mary stood still when she came to the crossway; she had heard a snap and crackle of flames, and, above her, whales and cornucopias of white smoke were bellying out of the branches. With a sudden excitement she ignored her green tunnel and ran through the opening on the left.

She was in a little clearing; straight before her blazed a great fire, and behind it stood a man with a fork. He was young. His rough smoky hair crowded down to his eyes. He wore an old striped collarless shirt, unbuttoned and tucked in, so that a V of brown chest reached almost to his worn cord breeches. These were held up by a thick, cracked leather belt, polished with long use. The heavy brass clasp kept flashing in the light from the flames. Mary could just see that it had some device on it. Everything about the man held her, she seemed unable to take her eyes from him. His whole body was so covered with little smears of mud and charcoal, little bits of moss, twig and leaf, that she found it easy to imagine him rising out of the ground itself.

"Well," he said at last, staring back at her through the shimmering air above the flames, "good afternoon."

His voice was startingly northern. He was mocking her, mimicking a genteel politeness to shame her for staring. Under the dry tangle of hair his dark eyes glowed hot and truculent. He threw on more rhododendron branches and pine needles. The dark oily leaves, despairing and surrendering utterly, sucked up the fire in one demoniac rush. The needles spat like squibs. His image was broken by the sudden leaping of the flames. The dancing, quaking features looked even more lowering than before; the mouth was so pouting that Mary almost expected to see the wet inner side of his lip.

"Hullo!" she gulped, flashing out a vivid smile and leaning forward, as if in her anxious friendliness she would do all she could to make it easy for him to criticize or gibe.

The man leaned on his fork, hunching his shoulders so that they looked too powerful and heavy for his legs in the tight-fitting breeches. Mary thought of Sinbad carrying the Old Man of the Sea. The slender legs were Sinbad's, the shaggy head and glowering eyes belonged to the Old Man crouching on his back.

"You're burning the branches?" she ventured, aware of her own inanity, yet feeling that she must speak.

"Aye, I'm finishing up for the day, burning the rubbish."

The vowels all changed, the singing, flowing tone were like a lullaby to Mary—she had never been to the North. But what had happened to the man? She had expected him to sneer at her obviousness. He was still withdrawn and careful, but there was no more attack in his voice. Perhaps her lack of assurance had softened him, even made him a little contemptuous of her.

"All the straight ones are coming down," he volunteered, turning to look at the three felled pines which threaded in and out of the crushed bushes.

For the first time Mary was able to take in what lay beyond the man. The long pines lopped of all their branches made her think of primitive bronze needles, lost by some long-dead giant woman. Although to walk in the wood was one of her everyday delights, she found that she could only regret the trees dispassionately, as if their destruction was inevitable, a law of God—not her affair. She wondered why she felt no resentment against the woodman, and made herself exclaim with shocked surprise: "Do you mean all the straight trees through all the wood?"

"Aye," said the man, "that's right."

He was looking at her with a faintly puzzled amusement. She might have been a pigmy at a fair, or a grotesque little dog. Mary was about to harden herself against this affronting look, when she saw his eyes dodge away from her uncertainly, almost fearfully. He began to skewer branches on his fork, until gradually his face grew calm again. Now he was patient and far away, like a man quietly enduring the extraction of a thorn, or the dressing of a wound.

Suddenly a motor-horn blared out. It continued to blare; for Mrs. Tuke was deaf and harsh sounds gave her no pain. She could never believe that gentle ones would be heard.

"Oh! I must go," said Mary, starting guiltily, like a child caught playing truant.

The man looked up at her.

"Happen somebody's impatient-like."

He gave an amused unconcerned little grin and turned back to his work.

In her perturbation Mary began to run.

Soon she was leaning through the car window and kissing Mrs. Tuke's soft amazing cheek, all crazed with tiny lines, like the crackle on porcelain. The brown reproachful monkey eyes looked up at her.

"My dear, I thought you had forgotten."

"I do hope I haven't kept you too long," Mary panted; "but I've just been talking to the man who's cutting down the trees; he says all the straight ones are to come down."

Her voice was excited.

Mrs. Tuke's eyebrows went up.

"Oh, but how dreadful!" she said. "Aren't you terribly upset? You love the wood so much. It's no good; it doesn't do to love anything; if one does, the thing is sure to be destroyed."

There was deep monkey melancholy in her voice, bitter, hopeless and lazy.

Mary got into the car beside Mrs. Tuke. She turned to smile at the companion Miss Martin, who all this time had been sitting in the middle of the back seat, holding herself aloof, so that she could welcome Mary, uninterrupted and in her own way, after Mrs. Tuke had finished.

She was much more carefully dressed than Mrs. Tuke. Instead of a knitted beret, rather like an egg-cosy, she wore a correct and tasteful hat. She came from Bradford, and under the refinement in her voice Mary was pleased to catch faint echoes of the woodman's vowel sounds. She wanted Miss Martin to go on talking so that she could think of the woodman saying: "Happen somebody's impatient-like," or, "Aye, that's right." She even liked to remember his gibing "Good afternoon."

And all the time she saw him standing there, gazing at her through the flames, his eyes smoky, sullen, questioning.

It was almost dark before Mary felt that she had stayed long enough with Mrs. Tuke. She had tried several times to suggest leaving, but always Mrs. Tuke's sad eyes had looked out at her and stopped the words. The eyes must have changed so much less than the withered face; they were bright, quick-moving, sometimes melting into sudden sweetness, sometimes diminishing into far away unfeeling bird's points. Now, when Mary made the darkness an excuse, the eyes showed bitterness for a moment, then resigned themselves.

"Yes, perhaps we ought to start," said Mrs. Tuke; "you have that dark walk through the wood before you."

This was what Mary had been longing for all through tea. She had thought of it through every subject. She wondered if her abstraction had been noticed. Miss Martin, she felt sure, noticed everything.

As soon as she had kissed Mrs. Tuke once again and left her on the edge of the wood, Mary went straight to the place where the fire had been. She knew that she would find no man there, but she wanted to run her foot through the velvety ash, look into the apricot heart, so lovely, still stirring, falling, crumbling, like a dying salamander.

The wood was so still that she could follow the sound of Mrs. Tuke's engine until it faded from a cat's purr into nothingness. She looked round at the torn rhododendrons and fallen pines. In the darkness white scars, where the branches had been lopped, glimmered all up the sides of the trunks. It was as if each tree had many blind eyes with marble lids.

Mary noticed how cleanly, how close to the ground the pines had been sawn. She went up to one of the low smooth bases and touched it with her finger. With a shock she felt stickiness. It was oozing its turpentine, its blood.

In that moment the scene became an execution in a dream for her. Here was the great white neck with the severed head beside it; and there were the dying embers where the instruments of torture had been heated. The bushes had been torn and trampled by the eager mob. But now they were all gone, and she had come at night to sew the poor head on to the shoulders again, to wash the mud and spittle from the lips and close the eyes. . . .

Mary jumped to her feet, frightened by her own fantasy. All over the wood silence and darkness coiled under the leaves, gathered there to skulk and swell. Soon the whole countryside would be overwhelmed. Mary turned to go home, and a heavy bird flapped screaming out of a bush above her. She bowed her head, walking very delicately and quickly in the middle of the path. She would disturb no other more terrifying thing, if she could help it.

II

Mrs. Legatt with the tea tray woke her in the morning. Mary looked up through narrowed eyes and saw that, as usual, Mrs. Legatt's gaze was fixed far beyond her; it was as if she were forever calculating difficult sums in her head, and so had no time for faces or scenery. She had looked after Mary for the last three or four years, indeed ever since Mary had come of age and had a house of her own. Her two aunts had not liked the thought of Mary living by herself. They told Mrs. Legatt to keep a careful watch over her health and her spirits, explaining that Mary had been a very delicate child, and, in their opinion, rather a morbid one, inclined to shut herself away from companions of her own age.

Mrs. Legatt had smiled and appeared to listen to the aunts, but it is doubtful if, from the first day of their meeting, she had ever looked closely at Mary, or studied anything about her. She cooked well, was not over house-proud, but adequate; in the times between her work she floated in her own private dream.

When Mrs. Legatt had left the sleeping-porch, Mary sat up and sipped her tea. The large doors were folded back so that the whole of one side of the porch was open to the wood. The air was cold, making the chatter of the birds seem even more piercing than it was; beyond the chatter Mary could hear other noises. Children were laughing, shouting to each other excitedly; then there was a mysterious swish and crack, and a dull tremble in the earth. She knew that the woodman was already at work.

She wanted to jump out of bed at once and run to watch him, but she made herself write in her diary until breakfast, then she bathed, dressed, collected her drawing things together, and went down the outside staircase, which jutted from the house like a clumsy flying buttress or a swimming-bath chute.

Very soon she was under the trees, climbing up to the place where the fire had been. The children's voices came to her as if bounding and rebounding off the trunks. The whole wood seemed to be shaking with excitement. Once she heard the bright ring of metal on metal, and this made her hurry more than all the other noises.

When Mary came to the clearing of yesterday, she was amazed to see how it had changed. It was now a wide space where hard light poured down on saplings which looked too weak to bear it. Great trunks lay on the ground; everywhere were crushed and mangled rhododendrons. Children ran about, delighting in this ruin. Some had boxes on wheels in which they piled the fat white satisfying chips and smaller branches; others just laughed, tumbled, screamed, or chased each other. Beyond them Mary saw the woodman, stripped of his shirt, kneeling on the ground beside an older, less powerfully built man. They were sawing through a pine so close to the ground that the blade almost skimmed the peat and pine needles. They took and gave the saw with a lovely and laborious rhythm. Mary guessed that they were father and son.

Every now and then the older man wiped his hand across his mouth and sat back on his haunches. While he rested for the few moments, there seemed a bitter patience in his kneeling, in the bowing of his head. Was he telling himself that he was a fool to do work that was now too hard? Was he grumbling against the world? The son's patience seemed perfect and unquestioning.

Before she should be noticed, Mary crouched down by a torn bush and started to draw. She contrived some sort of indication of the thighs and tucked-up legs, but when she tried to catch a position of the young man's rippling shoulders and swinging arms, she felt helpless, frustrated by her lack of skill and quickness. She found herself marvelling at the brownness of his skin so early in the year, at the curve and flow of all his muscles. Once again her eyes became fixed on the worn brass clasp winking and glinting like some great eye or jewel in his stomach.

But now the children were drawing nearer and nearer, moving

up behind the protection of their handcarts and baskets. Mary scowled at them and bent lower over her drawing, but they were not to be discouraged. Soon they were all round her, peering over her shoulders, pressing against her arms. They smelled of their clothes and food and of themselves. Wood smoke and pine needle smell had caught in their hair. Their heavy serious breathing was only broken by little sniffs, coughs and gurglings inside. The first one to speak pointed with turpentine-blackened finger at the drawing and exclaimed: "Coo! isn't it good?" His voice sounded artificial, self-conscious.

Mary gave up trying to draw and sat back, waiting for the tree to fall. In those waiting moments the children behind her were plain and bare, shorn of all their pretenses.

At the point when the sawing became most difficult and the men most concentrated, one of the smallest children broke away from the group and started to do a sort of sleepwalking dance right under the tree. The child was dressed all in soft dirty blue—blue combination suit, blue cap tied down over its ears with a blue woollen scarf. Its tiny wax face was divided by a stream of blackened snot. It talked to itself and sang and waved its arms. Dancing there under the tall pine, it looked unnaturally minute. It might have been a goblin or dwarf.

As soon as the young woodman saw it, he called out angrily: "Who's bloody looking after that kid? It'll get killed."

He snatched it up in his arms and turned to the children and Mary. Nobody claimed it, so Mary felt bound to go forward and take it from him. Its arms and legs hung down like a stiff doll's. Mary put it on the ground and held one of its hands. The man's look was too full; he was recognizing her, linking her with the child and condemning her neglect.

"Is it a little boy or a little girl?" he asked; "it's dressed so funny."

"I don't know, it's not mine," said Mary hurriedly; "I just thought I'd keep it out of your way."

"What's its name?" the man asked the children.

After a pause one of the older boys called out: "It hasn't got a name. It lives with Mrs. Wooler; and it's a little boy." He spoke contemptuously, as if all the world should know these facts about a child who, in any case, was not worth a thought.

"Well, why don't you keep it by you?" the man demanded.

"None of us looks after it; it follered us up here," the boy explained sulkily.

Mary led the child back, feeling burdened with it in some dim way, because it had no name. She wondered if it was an orphan put out to foster parents. She thought of all the years of neglect before it.

The man had knelt down and begun to saw again. In a few minutes there was a delicate quiver at the base of the tree. The men jumped back swiftly. For an instant the pine seemed to hold its breath with the little crowd; then it swivelled and swung down, like a huge guardsman fainting on parade. The pine needles whipped through the air, making the rushing, swishing noise. Branches cracked against other trees. When the trunk smashed on to the ground a dumb thump ran under the earth, rising up to hurt the soles of the feet. The children jumped up and down and screamed. After the tension of waiting, all their actions were extravagant. Some let out long dramatic sighs, others made whistling noises of amazement. The quick ones darted forward to seize the best chips. There was a scramble round the men, who were already hacking off the branches with their axes.

Mary still held the nameless child's hand; but now she let go musingly. The child at once began its dance again, mouthing its own words and song notes. Was it too young to talk intelligibly? Or was it an idiot child? It blew small bubbles on its lips, utterly happy in its isolation from the other children and the world.

Mary watched until it disappeared between the saplings. The child had both attracted and repelled her, so that she was confused, more than ordinarily uncertain of herself. To forget the child and its fate, she turned quickly to see what the men were doing. They were measuring the tree. The son called out and the father wrote in a dirty red notebook, then marked the base.

The children were all quarrelling and scrambling for the chips, so Mary decided to do some quick drawings while she was free of them. She got something down, but part of her regretted the lines, wished that the paper was still blank. The lines were not interesting enough to make up for the loss of pure whiteness. She had spoiled what was there, not made something new.

While she brooded in this way, her eyes were down on the paper so that at first she was unaware of the melting away of the children. When she looked up, only a few stragglers were left. All the rest had gone back to their dinners. The men had made a little pyramid of their axes and the saw, and were pulling black dented tins and old beer bottles from the bracken. The father walked off and settled himself against a trunk, but the son stretched up and took a swig from his bottle of cold tea. His back was arched; he slapped his chest and stomach with satisfaction and said: "Ah!"

Then he looked at Mary tucked up against her bush. She was pretending to be busy with her last drawing, afraid that he would ask her what she was doing, mock her with his mimic politeness; but he said: "When I'm having my dinner, I'll keep still and you can do my photo lying down."

"But won't you mind keeping still?" Mary asked, taken aback.

"I won't mind if you don't," he said. "You're doing the work."

He lay down where he was and started to eat his bacon sandwich and his bread and cheese. He had propped himself on one elbow, with the bottle and the food spread out before him, making an interesting arrangement. Mary began at once to draw. She wanted to please him, to repay him for his trouble, but she was afraid that her sketch would be formless and dead. In her anxiety, her hand began to shake a little.

Suddenly the father called out: "Is she doing yer, Jim?" as if the whole affair were a great joke. He startled Mary; his amusement made her uneasy, but perhaps she was grateful for it too. She had expected glum heaviness; now both the men seemed tolerant. What had happened to the young one's smoking eyes and sullen mouth of yesterday? To her they had been such an important part of him that she felt this calm sleepy man posing for her was a different person. She could not yet fit the sides of his nature together; and so her mind was fixed on him. She felt a vague alarm, being uncertain of his next mood.

When the dinner hour was over, Mary made herself hold out the drawing to the two men. The father said: "Aye, that's good! She's got yer, Jim," but the young one just smiled and nodded. As soon as the father moved away to fetch the axes, Mary found herself speaking hurriedly and urgently.

"I'd like to do a painting, but I couldn't do it here, with all the children."

There was a pause. Mary was afraid of the emptiness between them. Then she heard him saying smoothly: "I could come along after work for a bit, if you like. Do you want me with my axe?"

He smiled, as if posing with his axe were rather ridiculous, but woman's whims should be indulged.

Mary darted a look at him, then bobbed her head, like a small bird eating.

"I live very near," she said. "I'll come up to show you the way. What time?"

"Five," he said, grinning.

She gave another little nod, then gathered up her things and hurried back to her own lunch. She wanted to get away from the man so that she could think of him more clearly. She wanted to picture his rough stiff hair, his changing eyes and tawny skin. She wanted to see him sitting for her still as stone, the burnished axe-head gleaming like white fire.

III

Mary told Mrs. Legatt that the woodman was coming to sit, and asked her to prepare a good tea. Mrs. Legatt looked at her as directly as she ever looked at anyone.

"It's not often you want to do portraits from the flesh," she said in her rather strange, chanting tones; "you like to make things up, or do those fancy needlework horrors; I can't say I'd want one in a house of mine, if I had one."

"You'd rather I tried to paint a straightforward portrait then?" Mary asked, wanting to talk about the woodman.

"Well, that depends on what he's like; it's no good trying to make a silk purse out of a sow's ear, you know."

Conversation with Mrs. Legatt was always like this; after a plain statement, a warning, a proverb, she would slip away or lapse into silence. With her there was no continuation, no further step.

Mary turned her mind to her paints, her easel and her board. She would have everything ready, so that no time should be lost when the man came.

Just before five she went into the wood to bring him back. She found him alone at the far end of the waste; he was wiping down the axes and the saw with an oily rag.

"It's quieter now," he said, smiling half at her, half to himself; "all the kids gone to their tea, and my dad's just taken the motorcycle combination. It's a good thing I came on my push-bike this morning—sometimes I do, so we can go home separate—I must have known you'd be doing my picture."

Here he gave his old mocking grin, but with a subtle difference; it was tamed, and Mary felt no uneasiness. She watched him finish his job, then thrust the saw, the iron wedges and one of the axes into a clump of dead and sprouting bracken. He pulled the fronds this way and that to mask his hiding-place.

"Do you always do that?" asked Mary, recapturing a little of her childhood excitement over anything buried or hidden.

"Aye, it saves taking 'em back," he said; "nobody'll tamper with 'em there."

Mary thought that she would always like listening to his voice; the north-country stress and intonation would suddenly strike her again, just when she imagined that she had grown used to it.

She saw him go towards a bush and pull out a roughly painted grass-green bicycle. Instead of the usual slim seat, it had a thick broad clumsy saddle. The effect, for some reason, was embarrassing to Mary. Did she think of the bicycle as a spare athlete burdened and humiliated by a grotesquely swollen behind? Jim noticed her quick glance away and said: "It looks a bit funny, but it's much more cum-fort-able for long journeys like. Those little ones fair cut you in half. I got it off my dad's old motorbike."

He started to walk beside her, the axe on his shoulder, a greasy army satchel swinging from his arm. With his other hand he grasped the handlebars in the middle, forcing the bicycle over the difficult ground. His size and his burdens made Mary feel rather trivial; she might have been a whippet pettishly following a too serious-minded master. Anxiety gathered to sweep over her; Jim was now her guest. She tried to think of something to say.

She felt easier when they were standing together in the little polished hall, so rigid and still after the swaying tangle of the wood. Jim looked about him with gentle inquisitiveness; he seemed to be thinking, "So she lives in this quite different sort of house!" Perhaps he was a little bewildered, but his trustfulness eased Mary.

She took him up the shining artificial stone stairs, glancing back once in time to see him hesitate, then withdraw his hand from the polished copper rail, as if he had decided that it was too glistening to touch. At the top of the stairs they passed the open bathroom door. Jim at once asked if he could wash, and Mary went to the linen-cupboard to find him a clean towel; but he protested that he was much too dirty to use it, so she left him with her own used one. She went into her workroom and drew the little table up to the stove for tea.

When Jim came out of the bathroom, his mat of hair was sleek and wet, although tufts here and there were already breaking away from the smooth surface. His nose looked bigger and his eyes had lost some of their tarry gleam. For a moment Mary felt dashed, deprived of something; then, without effort, her idea of him broadened to accept this more commonplace indoor appearance.

Mrs. Legatt, bringing in the tea tray, gave Jim a casual sidelong glance, as if he were quite the most usual thing to find in Mary's room—and yet perhaps not quite the most usual. Mrs. Legatt's filmy glances always left this doubt in the mind. Was she really only dreaming, brooding on her wrongs, counting her blessings? Or was she storing the sights and sounds around her for another day? She put down the tray without a word and Mary began at once to pour out the tea and pass toast to her guest.

It was not an easy meal. Jim leaned forward in his chair and ate slowly; Mary pressed things on him and strained to find words. She was glad when she had him on a stool near the great blank panes of the window. He had rested the axe across his knees in a way that she liked. His hair was growing drier and rougher every minute. She squeezed out her colors and began.

There was silence in the workroom for some time. Mary painted intently, noticing nothing until the thick creamy mess on her board became unmanageable.

"I've put too much paint on," she said, looking up and smiling ruefully. Then she saw that Jim was as still as a frozen man. In his broad throat a vein pulsed thickly. One flap of his open shirt trembled, as if a little wind blew only on that part of him. His grip on the axe had tightened until all his knuckles were white, like bare bones.

"Shall we rest now?" said Mary softly, afraid of the effect of her words on him.

His eyes flickered, then came back from far away, a look of awkwardness, even of pain flashing across them; he was aware of self again.

"I've never known anyone sit quite so still," said Mary.

Jim smiled, losing some of the tenseness that had turned him into a caricature of himself.

"Aw, it's easy work sitting still." He leaned forward a little. "May I have a look?"

The question was shy and gentle. Mary swung the picture round, hating to show it, but feeling that he had a right to look.

"My!" he said with quiet unconsidered admiration; "but I'm afraid it's a bit too handsome."

"It's only a beginning; I've hardly got anything down yet," said Mary hurriedly.

Jim laughed. "You mean you'll make it more rough, get it more like me later?"

The blood flushed up into Mary's cheeks; she bent low over her palette and began to scrape vigorously with the knife.

Jim looked out of the window. The light was failing rapidly; already the barn and squat tower on the far hill had been changed into some mysterious Gothic-revival church shrouded in blue mists.

"I must go," he said; "I've got a twenty-mile bike ride in front o' me."

Mary looked blankly at him, hating to think of this journey added to all the strain of his long day.

"I don't always bike it," he reassured her; "I told you; sometimes I come in my dad's sidecar, but other times we want to be independent-like."

"You shouldn't have sat to me for so long," said Mary; "I had no idea you had far to go. I thought you lived quite near."

"It's not far; I can do it easy," Jim said scornfully; but Mary knew that, in spite of all his strength and vigor, he wished that the ride were not before him.

She got up at once and offered him the biscuits, then she poured out two cups of cold tea; they stood by the stove, eating and gulping hurriedly. There was silence, but less awkwardness between them. Still munching a biscuit, she led the way down the flying-buttress stairs to the road.

Jim swung his leg over his bicycle, then settled himself in the ribald seat, with the toe of one foot on the ground. He turned to her: "I'll come again tomorrow then?" The words were half a question, half a statement.

Mary nodded impatiently, longing for him to start while there was still some light. She watched him crouch over the handlebars, turn into the road, and disappear. Cocked up in the saddle, with head and shoulders down, he had looked formidable and inhuman, reminding her of a piston rod or an ancient battering ram.

She started to walk back to the workroom, taking slow steps, thinking of the woodman speeding through the dusk, all his stiff hair blown flat. She climbed up the stairs, opened the glass door; and the first thing she saw was his axe, where he had left it, by his stool. In the half-light its diamond flash had melted to a moonstone glimmering. She knelt down, then lifted it and felt along the blade with one finger. She experienced the delicate, dangerous bite of the metal. It was almost as if her finger could not leave the magnet of the edge until it had been slit and she had tasted the sour blood. She put her cheek to the cold steel cheek; she pressed her nose flat against it, while tingling silver wires seemed to dart up to her brain. She remained for some moments in this strange kowtow. Then she shouldered the axe, took up her torch, and went back into the darkening wood.

After a little searching, she found Jim's hiding-place. The torch suddenly glinted on the ugly shark's grin of the saw. Mary laid Jim's axe to sleep with the other tools in the bracken, pulling the fronds across again as she had seen him do.

IV

Jim came the next afternoon, and the next, and the next, until Mrs. Legatt grew used to making tea into a larger, more satisfying meal. She would look at Mary's picture and say: "Yes, I think it's progressing very well; if only you don't lose that 'natural' look."

About Jim himself she said very little. Once she remarked on his quietness and politeness; another time she exclaimed: "That's a terrible long journey after a hard day's work. What a pity he doesn't live nearer!"

It may have been on the fifth or the sixth afternoon that Jim came in later than usual and Mary saw at once from his sober look that he was really tired. Although there were still great blank spaces in their understanding, they knew some part of each other by now. Mary let him in and took him upstairs, almost without saying a word. She turned on the taps in the basin, pushing the thick dirty towel that he liked towards him. He bent to wash; then she saw that his hair was full of tiny twigs, papery fragments of burnt leaf, and little curling beards of lichen. Before she had thought clearly, she had picked up her comb and run it through his stubborn thatch. A shower of little pieces fluttered down to the blackened water in the basin. Jim looked up, his face glowing and slippery and dripping. He laughed, spluttering a little water over her.

"Quite a natural-history museum," he said with a return to his lofty, sarcastic manner. Afraid that she had offended him, Mary offered him the comb, as if giving up a badge of office; but he had turned back to the basin and was scrubbing his face with the towel. Later he took the comb and whipped the wet clots and tails from his forehead, grooving them into the still dry hair.

They went into the workroom and sat down by the stove. Jim had brought fat creamy chips in a sack; now he fed some to the flames, and the heat glowed on their faces.

Mrs. Legatt came in carrying muffins, heavy and soggy, with something good about them. They spread them thickly with jam and sipped the steaming tea from great breakfast cups which Mrs. Legatt always used now, out of respect for Jim's sex.

When the tea was cooler and Jim drank deep, half his face seemed swallowed up in the white moon of the cup. Over the rim his eyes glowed, shifted, melted, surrendering to the comforting heat.

They lay back against the cushions. Jim filled his pipe, and began to roll a cigarette out of the same damp dark tobacco. He licked the paper delicately, then twirled it quickly down and offered the weeping cylinder to Mary.

"Hope you don't mind my spit," he said, laughingly, apologetically; "better tuck those ends in, if you can."

But Mary had taken up her scissors and was snipping off the odd strands of tobacco. She wondered why she was so delighted with Jim's crumpled cigarette.

Soon smoke was wreathing out of their mouths, flowing up to make a soft octopus above their heads. It hovered there, stretching out tentacles, merging, twining, melting, vainly trying to reach into the corners of the room.

Looking down at the length of Jim's body on the sofa, Mary thought that he looked like Gulliver. His knees were higher than his head; he was pinned down by his tiredness, just as Gulliver had been trussed and strapped across with the Lilliputians' spider-thread ropes. She saw him with the eyes of a Lilliputian. He was some giant of enormous size and weight. And his skin was not skin; it was too tough, too permanent. It was the finest book calf, tanned to last for centuries.

Why was Jim always reminding her of the pictures in her nursery books? Sinbad, Gulliver, even Rip Van Winkle, when his hair was full of the woods, his hands black as peat, and his wellingtons caked with mud and grass and moss. Was it because of his clear outlines, his separation from her? Did these give him the legendary quality? He was a woodman, and woodmen were linked with charcoal burners, with bears, wild boar, Robin Hood and venison pasties.

"How brown you are!" she murmured, to explain the fixity of her gaze.

"Aw, that's because I take my shirt off," Jim said. "My dad doesn't hold with it; he says I look like a savage and one day I'll get sunstroke and that'll teach me. He says I ought to wear woollen vest, shirt and waistcoat same as him; but I like to feel free. What's the sense o' getting more hot an' mucky than you need?"

Jim knocked out his pipe and stood up; his sense of duty not allowing him to idle any longer. He took up the pose, waiting for Mary to go to her easel and begin.

As usual Jim sat with Spartan steadfastness. Mary tried to think only of her painting, but it was impossible for her to ignore his signs of strain for long. The vein in his throat throbbed more heavily than ever; the shirt flap trembled all the time.

"Let's stop now and go back to the stove," she said at last; "I've done quite a lot; besides, it's getting too dark."

Jim put his axe down, then slowly rose to his feet, stretching arms up like a man forcing with all his might against a collapsing ceiling. Behind him the light was being sucked down under the hill, sucked all away; and gunmetal clouds were surging into boneless mountain peaks. Against this wild background Mary watched his black shape. He was lowering his arms, stretching them out level with his shoulders. Now he had become a monstrous bat, escaped from some land of terrors and ghosts.

As he walked towards her over the polished floor, his wellingtons squelched, letting out little sighing puffs of air.

"Take those things off and warm your feet; they must be quite cold and clammy after all this time."

Mary was too anxious, too urgent, clutching at anything to ease his tiredness.

"But I've got to go at once. My! it's late. Just look how black it's getting!"

Before Mary could say anything the heavy curtain between workroom and landing was drawn back and Mrs. Legatt came in for the tea tray.

"We have the camp-bed, you know," she said gravely, as if stressing a profound truth which Mary in her frivolity had lost sight of.

For a moment Mary was nonplussed. She did not care for Mrs. Legatt's sudden passages from complete indifference to meddling. They were rare; for that reason all the more disconcerting. Was she prompted by caprice? Did she speak just for the sake of creating a little situation? But before any awkwardness could grow, Mary said: "Yes, why bother to go home? You'll only have to pedal all the way back here tomorrow morning; and you're tired. If you stay, you'll feel fresh. All we have to do is to put the camp-bed up."

Jim looked at Mary, at Mrs. Legatt, out of the window, down at his feet. Mary wished she could know his thoughts. Perhaps he felt trapped; or was he shamefaced because he thought that some remark had been misunderstood and twisted into a hint?

"Thanks very much," he said at last, "but I wonder what the wife'll think."

He spoke with the jovial guilt of the stage husband, turning "the wife" into nothing but a music-hall joke.

"You will stay then?" asked Mary, still uncertain. Jim bowed his head and Mrs. Legatt slid out of the room with the tray. They both breathed more easily. Suddenly Jim sat down on the sofa and started to pull off his wellingtons.

"Oh, good," said Mary at this sign.

While Jim tugged at one boot, she crouched down and began to coax the other off.

"You've no call to do that," Jim said, uncomfortably; "you'll get all mucky."

"I can easily wash," said Mary, bending lower. Her long short hair fell forward sweeping the boot. She tossed it back, at the same time jerking off the boot. She had it in her hands, close to her face; she could smell the rubber and the mud. She rocked on her tucked up legs, her mouth a little open as though crooning a lullaby.

"Eh, you look that funny with my old boot," said Jim; "did it come off sudden an' take you unawares?"

Mary looked at him; her eyes were laughing. She put down the boot, then tucked herself up in the other corner of the sofa.

Soon the smell of cooking vegetables came floating up the stairs, seeping round the thick edges of the padded curtain. Mary felt glad, knowing that Mrs. Legatt had not waited to be told, was at this moment doing her best to provide something that would not fall too far short of her idea of a hearty meal.

As they sat there together on the sofa, Mary suddenly found that Jim was talking. When she asked a question, he did more than give his usual "yes" or "no"; he even began to tell her of things without prompting, things she could know nothing of, because they happened long ago.

"When I was a lad in Yorkshire, me and my pal used to go rabbiting with my dog. Once we were in the grounds of the big house and someone jumped out at us from a thicket; and, do you know, it was the lord himself!"

Jim paused, still awed by his memory of the scene.

"He was swearing and cursing, carrying on at us something crazy. All on a sudden he caught hold of my pal Dick and gave him one with his walking stick. Dick was yelling, but the lord had him by the collar and went on basting him. I couldn't do nothing, so I ran away."

Jim looked full at Mary, smiling to hide the little bit of shame that still remained.

"After that, Dick wouldn't go with me nor talk to me; but what could I do? Not likely I could take on the old lord, and me only ten—besides some people said he was a bit daft-like, though not so as you could always notice."

Mary leaned forward to throw more chips and coal into the stove. The shimmering orange cave was transformed into a little volcano in eruption; the coal fumed, shooting out tiny jets of gas, the wood snapped and bubbled, and white clouds rose. Jim, looking at the wood, was reminded of his trade.

"It took me two years to learn from my dad," he said; "and

then I messed up a lot of axes. It's a proper job to do it well; it may look easy."

"It looks anything but easy," Mary said. "I've never seen any other trunks sawn off flat with the ground as you and your father do them."

"Ah, that's how you can tell a good woodman."

Jim enjoyed her little tribute. He paused to fill and light his pipe again; when the match flared, Mary saw his eyes shining contentedly. Except for the stove's glow, they were quite in darkness now; the wild boneless peaks had been blotted out, leaving the window nothing but an oblong of heavy, sooty blue.

"Tell me some more," said Mary.

There was silence while Jim thought.

"Once we lived in a caravan and it hadn't any windows. It was all black, when you shut the door. There was bunks round the wall and quite a big old kitchen stove. When my mum cooked, all the smoke hung about, till you couldn't hardly breathe. We used to go from place to place, wherever we had a job; me and dad would cut the trees, and mum would come afterwards clearing the ground, burning the leaves and branches, like you saw me doing the first day we met. But now we've got a house, and mum doesn't come out so much; she likes to look after the home. Sometimes she fancies a change though, then she gives a hand at the end of a job."

Jim was looking at Mary. She could see the shape of his head turned towards her, the fire glowing on one flat cheek. He was all hollows and planes, a boulder drilled and scoured by centuries of weather.

He put out his hand a very little way towards her, then drew it back: "But you, you—I've never known anyone like you before; you treat me more like a brother than anything else—and me only a rough chap you saw in the wood last week."

Mary stirred uneasily in her corner. How glad she was that Jim could not see her face! His voice had changed—he was urgent and faltering, a little ashamed of putting his feeling into words. She tried to think of the right easy laughing thing to say; then it seemed so false, so trashy to hedge herself about with lightness, that she said nothing at all, only stared through the darkness at him. She could just see the soft glint of one eye and the sliding up and down of the Adam's apple in his throat. "It's like a bobbing float on the river," she thought. Why was Jim gulping? And why was his head held back stiffly just at that angle which is seen in sleepwalkers and blind people? He put out his hand again, increasing the impression. This time he let it hover above her shoulder, never touching her, but making her feel that at any moment the tingling flesh under his grasp might be drawn up to the waiting fingertips.

"I think I shall have to stroke you," he said at last, as if there were no help for it, no other way out. The voice was changed again; it was a child's voice now, soft and dreamy, with that ruthless concentration that acknowledges no other interest in the world.

Very gently he lowered his hand to the sleeve of her jersey. Mary could feel his hard palm grating over the wool; sometimes a strand caught in a piece of rough skin and was snapped. Her teeth were set on edge, but she could not move; she sat becalmed, waiting for the next stroke.

Jim began to run his fingers over her hair, starting at the top of her head, descending each wave and curl until he reached the nape of the neck. There he seemed to love the projecting bone with the pads of his fingers; he smoothed it and touched it gingerly. It was as if he were playing with a very pretty cat which yet held some hint of malice in its twitching tail.

But malice was far away from Mary. She was melted by the flowing motion of Jim's hand; she was a candle guttering into a subterranean pool; above her arched the sweating cave roof, livid, veined, amazing. A little door in her throat seemed to open then shut capriciously and terrifyingly.

"I want everything about him," she thought; "his breath, his skin, his teeth, his bones, his hair." So she jumped up and broke away. Jim, who had caught at her hand, had to follow to the head of the flying-buttress staircase.

"We'd better get your bed in before it's too late," she said, every word a disc of thirsty plaster in her mouth. She licked and bit her dry lips, regardless of the color on them. Hunger was everything, was the world, but just behind it lurked Fear, although Fear was only a grey shape, a dirty fingernail, a stream of blackened snot pouring down an orphan's waxen face.

They were between the rose trees now; against the night sky the thorny stems looked like great hairy spiders' legs hopelessly tangled.

The car in the garage was a sleeping tortoise, the folded camp-bed in the corner a giant's Swiss roll of poor quality.

"Stop making everything something else!" implored Mary; "stop saying, stop doing, stop thinking!"

She had brought no torch; they fumbled in the dark, running their hands along ledges silky with dust, feeling the sickly cream of oil beneath their feet.

"Ay, d'you know, I've got no shoes on?" laughed Jim. At last he had the bed firmly under his arm. As he passed, he banged the projecting car mirror and swore, almost with the same breath apologizing to Mary.

They were in the open again, walking apart, like two campers who have come to the end of a long empty day and have only a long empty night to look forward to.

"We are utter strangers," Mary thought; "if we were not, I would not be looking at him, would not be wanting the sight and the smell and the sound of him. He would be my friend; there would be no fear—and so I should be free again to think my own thoughts. How is it that something as tiny as fear—for fear is a bee's tongue, a fly's dropping—can overshadow the world? Why do I hug my fear to myself, afraid to let fear go?"

At the foot of the stairs Mary turned to Jim, offering help with the bed. He stood still, looking up at her on the second step, saying nothing. Suddenly he dropped the bed and gripped her in his arms. He had her against the wall of the house. On the other side of the concrete, in almost exactly the same position, Mrs. Legatt was busily cooking the supper. Mary clung to this thought, picturing every detail of the electric stove, the pots, the pans, the wooden spoons, the thickly winking bubbles in the soup. Perhaps as Mrs. Legatt bent low to stir, one of her hairs might fall into the soup. This *had* been known to happen, although Mrs. Legatt would never admit it, the very mention of a hair made her furious. . . .

"Hair, hair, why am I thinking of hair? I can feel his hair on my face, hard prickly stubble hair on my cheek, mouse-soft brush of lashes near my eyes. If I could put up my hand, I could even feel the hair along his arms, at his throat, and on his head—all different; but I cannot move, my arms are pinioned and I feel his belt clasp biting into me, his bony knee against my thigh. His face is all soft with warm dew; his polished face is melting in his own soft steaming breath. It is like fine stretched rubber, like Scottish bap-cakes damp from the oven; and I have heard those cakes called 'baby's bottoms' too; the girls at school would always call them this. If I turned my head, what would I see? I would look down the devouring blackness of his throat into his very guts. In the crimson darkness I would see everything working, striving, forcing; it would be like the engine-room of a mighty ship. I would be surrounded with wild blind energy; I would be a tiny beetle amongst the towering machines."

Mary did turn her face, and her teeth struck against his; for a moment she felt the flame-like flicker of his tongue. She made a useless little jerk away, then the imprisoned hands dropped to her sides again. Jim seemed to grip her with perfect inhumanity. She might have been a ladder he had to scale. His rough raw breathing mounted all the time.

Suddenly a little shudder seemed to pass through Jim, clutching him at the end in a moment of utter stillness. Mary felt the stillness spreading out all round them; then all at once Jim drooped, seemed almost to lie against her for support. She had the whole weight of him, not taut and springing any more, but like a sleeping man hanging about her neck. Quite dazed by his change, but feeling that she must lead now, Mary took his arms from her shoulders and made towards the staircase, shaking back her hair, rippling out her arms, slapping her skirt roughly, to rid herself of the dazed, bruised feeling. Jim still lay against the wall. He gave one sigh, full of sleep and resignation at waking and beginning all over again; then he too slapped his clothes, hitched up his breeches and rolled his shoulders under the cotton shirt. Obediently he followed her, remembering first to pick up the camp-bed from the sprouting bulbs where it had fallen.

In the lighted workroom they did not look at each other; Mrs. Legatt had already brought the supper and left it by the stove. Their little earthenware pots of soup steamed patiently; tempting onion breath rose up from the wide brown mouth of the casserole.

"Do you like stew?" asked Mary with awkward jauntiness.

"Oh, aye," said Jim, and there was silence again.

Only afterwards, when they began to put up the camp-bed and Mary thought that Jim was about to pinch his fingers, did constraint disappear. She called out a sharp warning and immediately felt easier. Jim smiled down at his hands saying, "It'd take a lot to hurt them; they're used to all kinds of treatment." He glanced quickly at Mary's very different ones. Later, on the sofa once again, he held out his palm, broad and flat, cut with little black rivers and streams, humped with shallow pink-brown hills. He frowned over the puzzling map. Mary put out her own palm. "Have you ever had your fortune told?"

Jim shook his head, but brought her hand close to his, as if he would tell them together. He glanced from one to the other several times, sometimes following a line with his finger, or touching a cushion delicately; then he turned both hands over and felt the skin on Mary's and on his own. He examined carefully the white half-moons of her unbroken, unblackened nails.

"What a difference!" he whistled, putting her hand into his, so that it gleamed like a thin silver-grey fish on a wooden platter. "Look how dainty!"

Mary, embarrassed by the adjective, made to withdraw her hand. Jim closed his over it. "Two or three of those could get lost easy in this leg o' mutton.

"I often wonder," he added musingly.

"You often wonder what?" asked Mary.

"Well—well, what it's like to be a woman."

Slow difficult red pushed its way to the brown surface of his cheeks. "I've never told nobody but you, because it sounds so daft-like; but when I'm lying in bed on my back, maybe can't go to sleep at night, I keep thinking— What's it like to be a woman? What's it like to have a great man messing you about? What's it like to have a baby?"

"Ah, that is something I can't tell you; you see, I haven't tried yet."

"Course not," said Jim, shocked into propriety by her light simplicity.

Mary wished that he had not remembered to "respect" her, for she had never felt so close to him, so eager to meet every thought and help it to live and flow. Would the barricades go up again now? Why was the question, that might have been so silly and ordinary, valuable to her? She supposed it was because it was so unexpected, so "out of character" as some people would insist. But Jim was talking again.

"If you could do it, change over like, just for a bit, I'd like to try, have a baby and everything."

Mary laughed. "You'd certainly have to change completely;

there doesn't seem to be anything feminine about you as you are. With some people it's much easier to imagine a transformation—they seem to fluctuate."

Jim looked at her as if he had not quite heard or understood her words. His eyes turned up, so that white showed under them; they looked heavy and thick and slow. Only then did Mary remember his tiredness. He must have been almost falling to sleep as he asked her what it felt like to be a woman. Perhaps that was why he came near her, touched her with his unafraid simplicity.

She jumped up quickly to leave him with the camp-bed. Jim smiled gratefully and almost before she was out of the room, he was pulling the striped shirt over his head.

Mary thought of him stripping off the socks and breeches, switching out the light, jumping into bed naked. For a long time she lay awake in her porch, staring up into the sky, watching low scudding clouds cast filmy membranes between her and the upper darkness.

She heard Mrs. Legatt come up the stairs, pause on the landing as if she were listening, drinking in all she could of the situation on the other side of the curtain. She passed on to the bathroom and Mary heard her scrubbing her plate, rinsing it under the tap. Soon there was the sucking windy sound of her pneumatic hair brush. Each rhythmic stroke was punctuated by a whistling little intake of air. The air rushed in, the air rushed out, the bristles on the rubber base rose, the bristles sank; in, out, in, out, in, out—until Mary felt that she was at last being charmed into sleep.

When she awoke later, she was puzzled then alarmed by a strange bull-frog droning. In her drowsy state she tried to explain it to herself as the sound of Mrs. Legatt brushing her hair; but part of her knew that this could not be true—that she could not still be brushing, nor, even if she were, could she possibly make so much noise. Then with a sudden stab she remembered Jim, knew that he was snoring. The thought of him had assailed her too violently. She felt hopeless, a little sick, drained of all love of life. Her sense of desolation made her think of a raw white dusty ruin in a desert strewn with bones. She looked out of the ruin, through the crumbling loopholes; her jaw was bound with coarse linen grave bands. She felt stifled with cloth and dust and deadness.

Surprisingly Mrs. Legatt was up at six to get the breakfast; for Jim had said that he must be in the wood early. Mary heard her moving about and, without bothering to dress properly, put on trousers and a fisherman's jersey over her pajamas.

She stood outside the workroom curtain and asked if she could come in. Jim was sitting on the edge of the bed, pulling on his socks. The laces of his breeches were still undone, but he stuffed his legs into the wellingtons just as they were. When he looked up, his face was brownish-pale and clouded. Mary saw that the bed was scattered with pieces of leaf and twig and moss that must have clung to his skin underneath the clothes. She was reminded of yesterday, when she combed his hair. The memory was sour, and to shake it away she went over to the stove and started to push the rake in and out vigorously. She put on more coal, shut the door and waited, crouching on the floor until the little gleam began to swell and flame.

They hurried through their porridge. Mary burned her mouth and quickly poured cold milk into her spoon. Jim swallowed his rasher of bacon between great gulps of scalding coffee. It was not the breakfast that Mary had planned. It was eaten in haste with no thought or pleasure, and their hearts and bodies were numbed. In spite of her thick jersey a little shudder ran through Mary.

"Eh, someone walking over your grave? These mornings are chilly-like."

Jim looked down; his sleeves were already rolled up and goose-flesh covered his arms.

There was no time for cigarettes or Jim's pipe. They hurried out into the wood carrying the axe between them like a baby-chair. Mary knew that it would have been more sensible to let go of the head, so that Jim could swing it on to his shoulder; but for some reason she still grasped it. She had to trot beside him in the way that had made her feel trivial. She felt guilt too, for in spite of all their hurry they were late. Already they smelled wood smoke and heard the ring of a hammer on a metal wedge.

"Looks like my mum's come too," said Jim; "dad'd never go burning the rubbish yet awhile."

Mary wanted to turn and run; she wondered what stopped her. Why had she even come out into the wood with Jim so early? Was she afraid to lose sight of him? And how would she meet the inquisitive, burrowing eyes of his father and mother?

They reached the cleared ground, passing the motorcycle under a clump of rhododendrons. Beyond the clump a plump woman was bending to gather up an armful of small branches for her fire. As soon as she looked up and saw them, she came forward eagerly, still hugging the branches to her bosom, so that her smiling bun face glowed through the waving leaves. She was wearing her husband's dungarees, or so Mary thought, for the square masculine garment seemed to be filled out and cushioned with jerseys and a scarf. On her head was a wool-work beret absurdly like the one Mrs. Tuke so often wore; for an instant Mary was transported to that first afternoon, only a week ago, when she had come upon Jim—then she was back again, staring at his mother behind the leaves, looking for sharp suspicious eyes, but finding only a sweet smile of welcome and interest.

The woman turned to speak to Jim.

"I came with dad to help tidy up and see if anything had happened to you; but dad said not to worry, you'd be all right with the lady who was doing your picture."

Here she gave Mary another shy smile.

"There's no call to worry about me, Mother; I'm old enough and ugly enough to look after myself."

Jim turned from her churlishly and looked down at his boots.

"Well, dad will be getting proper mad at me," he added at last, with a rather desperate jauntiness. Suddenly lifting his eyes to Mary's face, he jerked out: "Good-bye for now," and stalked off through the ragged bushes.

Mary watched him go, gazing all the time at the sweaty patch between his shoulder blades; it was like the shadow of a cloud hovering over a striped field. She heard the father call out archly: "Where you been, lad?" She was reminded at once of the mother by her side.

"I hope you didn't worry about Jim," she said, anxious to make up for Jim's gruffness, anxious to be liked herself; "he came in tired, then I painted till it was almost dark, so Mrs. Legatt, who keeps house for me, thought he ought to put up on the camp-bed."

Did that sound too careful? Was Mrs. Legatt dragged in clumsily, unnecessarily?

"It's that good of you to look after our Jim," the woman was saying; "it's too much, all that pedalling after a hard day's work."

She paused. "Father was telling me about the picture. Have you got it handy? I *would* like to see it—that is, if it's quite convenient."

"Oh, yes," said Mary, bringing her eyes back from the distance again; "I live just on the edge of the wood. Won't you come and see it now?"

"Thank you *very* much."

Jim's mother dropped her bundle of branches and began to bank the fire. Mary, watching her, was suddenly touched and melted by the bulging figure; the mother was so eager, so friendly; and she knew almost all there was to know of Jim. Her voice was different from his; she had lost more of her Northern accent, so that her native forms of speech were made to sound more purring.

When she had finished patting and poking the fire, she wiped her hands up and down the dungarees.

"You do get in a shocking state doing this work," she said, smiling anxiously at Mary; "that's why I wear these things," she held the pockets out, rather as a clown does; "they're dad's, of course, by rights."

They began to walk back to the house in silence. The mother was bashful and Mary kept seeing Jim's back retreating between the trees. When they had almost reached the gate, Mary began to make excuses for her portrait, protecting it beforehand against the woman's eyes.

"I'm afraid it's not very good," she said. "I haven't painted many people; but you might just be able to recognize your son."

The mother was not listening; she was gazing at the little square house through the thin trees.

"Oh, my, is this your house? Isn't it nice! I've only seen a road house done like that before."

"Well, I'm not very fond of it outside," said Mary, shepherding her into the hall as quickly as she could.

The mother looked about her in silent admiration.

"My! it's lovely," she murmured at last. She looked down at the polished floor and was painfully reminded of herself.

"I hope I'm not bringing in a lot of mess from the wood." She lifted her feet with the shy awkwardness of a child, then stood very still, afraid of showering leaves or twigs.

In her eagerness to make the mother feel at ease, Mary began to open cupboard doors, turn back rugs, draw curtains, to show off their color and design. She brought out everything that might give the mother pleasure. Taking her into the kitchen, she introduced her to Mrs. Legatt, who was wiping over the enamel of the stove.

Mrs. Legatt gave Jim's mother one of her strange faraway looks and continued to wipe. The mother bobbed her head and said: "My!" once again. She had fallen in love with the fitted kitchen cupboard and glanced back at it as Mary led her to the foot of the stairs.

In the workroom Mary moved the picture forward, hiding her head behind it so that she might miss the mother's first expression.

"It's him all right," she heard her say with a sort of dreamy love that seemed at that moment more for the picture than the man. Mary looked round the picture and saw that the mother's eyes were glowing; her smile held up her cheeks in firm little cushions.

"I want to do a lot more yet, if Jim will come again," Mary said, heartened by the mother's pleasure.

"But they've got to start a new job tomorrow!" the woman exclaimed; "dad got word of it last night. It's a big job in Wiltshire and he doesn't want to miss it; that's why I've come to help clear up."

She looked at Mary with real concern.

"How'll you get your picture finished now?"

"But there are lots of pines still standing," Mary said, trying to cover her dismay.

"Not good straight ones; there're only four or five of them, I should say. If dad and Jim work hard, they'll get them done all right."

"You don't think they'll want to come back after this new job?"

"No, dad likes to finish things up clean and have done with them."

Mary stopped herself from further silly questioning or hoping. She ought to have known that they were going; perhaps she really had known. Otherwise why had she come into the wood so early? Why had her eyes followed Jim's back as though she were never to see him again?

"Well, I'll have to try to finish it without him," she said with mechanical brightness; "it doesn't matter, even if I do spoil it."

"You won't spoil it!" pleaded the mother. "I like it so much I'd want to buy it now, if I had enough money and knew what you'd be asking."

Her hand went to her pocket.

"Oh! no, you must have it," said Mary, eager only to check her movement; "that is," she added more thoughtfully, "if Jim doesn't want it himself. I suppose he ought to be asked first."

"They haven't got a proper home yet; they're living with us."

"Jim is married then?" said Mary, feeling rather bewildered.

"Oh, yes, didn't he tell you that?"

"Perhaps he did just mention it; I wasn't sure if he was serious."

"He's a funny lad; sometimes he'll tell you anything, other times he's like an oyster. Yes, he's married all right; but I'm afraid she's not the right woman for him. I think he knows it too now, but he won't hardly talk to me for knowing it first, so I can't tell properly any more what's going on in his mind."

"Why isn't she the right woman?" Mary asked.

"Because she's no good," snapped the mother, her round sweet-natured face stiffening into ugliness. "But what am I thinking of?" she added in her old gentle voice; "I must get back to that fire of mine at once."

She looked at Mary wistfully.

"I'll come with you and help," Mary volunteered.

"Oh, would you? But you mustn't mess your clothes up helping. You just sit by the fire and talk to me. I *would* like that."

The mother's eyes went to the picture for one last look. She gathered courage to mention it again.

"And—and you'll really let me have Jim's picture?"

"Yes, if you like it."

"Oh, it's lovely, lovely."

The woman made a little movement as if to take the picture with her.

"I've just got to do a little more, then when it's dry, I'll send it to you," Mary said.

"Thank you ever so. I expect Jim told you where we live, but I've got it all written down here on an envelope from my sister in Sheffield, so shall I leave you that for safety?"

The woman pulled a dirty crumpled envelope from her pocket and passed it to Mary.

Mary took it smilingly but with unseeing eyes, not wanting to know either Jim's surname or his address. Still keeping her eyes from it, she put it in a drawer.

They went out into the wood again.

Soon after Mary was settled on a log near the fire, the woman returned to the subject of Jim's wife.

"She had another fellow before, you know; but he went overseas. That's why she married Jim. I think maybe the baby isn't Jim's at all; she had it very soon. Jim's so softhearted he'd never let on though."

"Is it a boy or a girl?" asked Mary, trying to draw the woman from the mother to the child.

"Well, it's a boy, but you know it's not right."

"How 'not right'?"

Mary waited, dreading the answer; she could see that the mother wanted to sink down and enjoy the depths of human trouble with her.

"Not right in its head. It can't even sit up properly yet; it just lies back and dribbles. And now the doctor says it won't get any better and'll never learn to talk; so she's trying to get a London place to take it. She doesn't seem to care; and I think it's all her fault. She wouldn't feed it you know, though the doctor said she should, and she had lots of milk. She had one of those pumps. She only thinks about herself, having a good time. She's no good."

Mary, sitting on her log, not allowed to help because of her clothes, had nothing to take her mind from the hideous picture of a breast pump, a whorish wife and an idiot baby. The mother's sanity and worth counted for nothing now; they were destroyed by her hate.

The mother had stopped working and come close to her; she was bending low, looking into her eyes with painful earnestness.

"I have a little girl that isn't quite right too, you know. Did Jim tell you?"

Mary shook her head, unwilling to speak. The hurt reluctant look deepened in the mother's eyes.

"But it wasn't my fault. She has the epilepsy. Nobody can blame me."

The mother's voice rose on the last words; she stared into the wood angrily, as though defying the trees and crumpled bushes to contradict her.

"Once a month we go to visit her. We can't have her at home because she might cut herself bad, or fall in the fire when nobody's near. Oh, it's terrible, her poor face and arms! All little cuts and scars. You see, when the fit's on her, she just falls down anywhere;

she doesn't know anything till it's over. It's a terrible thing, *terrible.*"

Mary's picture changed to a young girl falling. There she lay on the rough bricks, mad parrot screeches bursting through the spittle bubbles on her lips, her whole body shaken with violent tremors. For some reason Mary was suddenly reminded of that other scene of horror she had imagined, so long ago, last week, when she saw the glimmering white base of a pine tree and turned it into a giant's neck left to bleed in silence after the clamor of his execution.

But the mother was still looking at her intently; there was more to come. Mary made a primitive little gesture of refusal, but it passed unnoticed.

"D'you think they're good to them in those hospitals? Do they treat them all right?"

The voice was urgent, entreating, uncertain; the mother was willing to be blind if she could but be blind enough.

"I don't know about them," Mary said palely, drained of all feeling, tired to weakness, only anxious now for some chance to get away.

"Sometimes when we go to see her she's very good, sometimes not so good. She makes a great noise; I wonder if they get angry—maybe slap her perhaps."

"I don't know," Mary repeated desperately. She watched the bulging padded woman heap on more branches. Sizzling, whipping flames and greedy flashes were now darting through the pile. They were like lizards made of lightning. They swallowed up the black skeleton fingers and the horny polished rhododendron scales until grey robes of smoke poured from the heart. It was as if some ragged emperor imprisoned in there had shaken out the endless mole velvet of his train.

The woman did not seem to be truly aware of the flames. She fed them with no expression on her face. The hate was gone, the shame and anxiety, even the wish to keep Mary with her. The eyes were two raisins in a smooth steamed pudding.

"I am dressed in blankness too," Mary thought, seeing herself on the log, her hair hanging down, her mouth set, her hands in her lap. "If I could escape now!"

She jumped to her feet, then stood, uncertain of her resolution to run away so rudely.

"Oh, you don't have to go!" the woman exclaimed. "It's a treat for me to have someone like you to talk to. I get a bit lonely with only the men all day. I'd like to show you the letter from my sister in Sheffield. Poor thing! she's had a terrible time; her husband fell off a ladder and she's been up days and nights waiting for the worst; but—"

"I must go," Mary broke in; "I've left everything at home. I haven't even dressed properly."

The matter-of-fact excuse came out grotesquely, all the words too sharp and thin. She began to walk rapidly away, confirmed in her first purpose by the appeal in the mother's eyes. She would not stay, she would not give comfort, she would not be kind and gentle; she was filled with her own trouble. She would take it into the heart of the wood where she could pour it out alone.

The mother was calling after her; she flapped her hand shamefacedly, half said "good-bye" and quickened her pace. She thought of the mother now as a plump Bologna sausage fitted disgustingly into a tightly quilted bag; her little woollen hat was the protruding navel at one end. "Children call them belly-buttons," she mused; "that's what it is, a belly-button on a sausage."

In her agitation she was walking nearer and nearer to Jim and his father; she looked up and saw Jim's naked back twinkling between the pink-brown trunks only a few yards away. It rose and fell as he hacked with his glittering axe. The father was bending solemnly examining the teeth of the double saw. The children scurried in all directions, fighting for Jim's flying chips.

She wanted to slip past them all without a word, but one of the children called out, and the father looked up.

"Hullo! you in a hurry?" he teased.

She never answered. She saw Jim pause and look over his shoulder; he wore the smoldering sullen look she had seen first. It was as if she had never known him. He was the stranger in the wood again. She began to run.

Late that afternoon she was still in the wood, lying now where she had tripped over a root; it had seemed so much more comfortable not to get up and force on through the bushes. She had rolled into a little hollow with pine needles, and the sun stroked her back; she had the pine scent close to her nose. Beyond this far ridge, where few people came, the trains shunted and whistled in the little country slum that had grown up round the station. They were great crooning beasts, hissing and soothing her to sleep. . . .

A child crawled through a tunnel made by dogs and appeared in the little opening. In its journey on hands and knees it had found a dead thrush with sodden feathers. It clambered to its feet and held the bird up, showing no horror at the sight and smell of death. Slowly it began to twist and arabesque round Mary, sometimes pointing at her with the bird, sometimes sweeping it up above its head and running absurdly, breaking its own solemn rhythm. Under its breath it was muttering and singing all the time.

The blue combination suit was dirtier than ever now. There were thick cakes of mud on the knees. The child's hands were caked too, and a sort of crust had collected at the sides of its mouth where the bubbles broke.

When at last it grew tired of its dance and lulling incantation, it stood still and looked about it for a moment; then very gently it laid the dead thrush in the soft nest of Mary's outspread hair.

She found it there, when she awoke.

The Barn

I turned and skidded obediently on the little patch of lawn at the side of the house. My brother was teaching me this accomplishment and he was an exacting master. I looked over my shoulder at the last brown wound on the grass. It was meager, not bold and fierce like the gashes my brother made.

"Don't be such a funk, Denton!" he yelled from his position under the crab-apple tree. "You can't skid properly unless you turn and jam your brakes on as hard as you can."

He snatched the bicycle from me, threw his leg over it, pedalled furiously for a few moments, so that I felt he must certainly end in the hedge, then turned violently, making a superb chocolate fan on the emerald grass.

I was lost in admiration. He was so ruthless and competent.

"Now do it again!" he ordered, severely.

I mounted on the gravel path, tore on to the little lawn as wildly as I dared, overshot the appointed skidding-place by a few feet, and tried desperately to turn where all the scattered crab apples lay. Of course my wheel caught on one of the bright, hard little fruits, and I suddenly lay sprawling beside the madly revolving pedals of my bicycle.

I was hurt and dazed, but I dared not show it; so I laughed and smiled anxiously, and then, in desperation, picked up one of the little red balls and bit into its crisp white acid heart. I felt the juice skinning my teeth, roughening my tongue, making it feel like a cat's tongue.

I made no attempt to get up, but lay there indolently, thinking of the cleanness of the apple, smiling slackly. I knew that this behavior would disgust my brother, but I had to wait until I had recovered a little self-respect. I could not jump up straight away, still shaken, looking flustered and foolish.

Paul turned from me contemptuously and was about to walk into the house when my father appeared at the French window with a note in his hand. He held it out to Paul saying:

"Take this to Mrs. Singleton for me, will you?"

My brother jerked his head away sullenly. He hated encountering other people.

"Can't Denton take it, Daddy?" he asked.

"Why should he when I've asked you?" was the reply.

"Because he doesn't mind. He likes old ladies!"

And with this last shouted jeer, my brother darted down the path and was away into the fields, no one knew where.

"I expect he'll have a guilty conscience about that later," said my father comfortably, then turning to me: "Will you take it, Denton, since he's so silly?"

I felt proud. This was something I could do easily. I was not nervous of people, unless they were other children or rude old men. I hated the very thought of an old man. It spelled dirt and bad temper to me. With women it was different. I felt that, whatever they were like, some part of them was human and could be reached.

I took the note, and leaving the bicycle still lying on the grass,

I walked out of the garden, between the tiny box hedges, into the lane.

Mrs. Singleton was our landlady. When my parents had rented her house for the summer, she had moved out with her Colonel, her dogs and her grown-up daughters to the army hut which had been re-erected on the edge of their land, at the far end of the lane.

I walked down the lane keeping close to the brook and looking down into its depths. Hosts of tiny minnows flapped their fins to hold their position against the current. I loved the brook. The house was called after the brook, but Brook House somehow did not sound romantic; it sounded dull.

As I got nearer to the army hut I composed my face and took the letter from my pocket. I had a deep snobbish pity for Mrs. Singleton, because we had turned her out of her dignified house, where her family had lived for a hundred years, into this squalid little army hut.

The front door was open, and some soiled gym shoes lay beside it. I gave a quiet, well-bred, rather furtive knock, and the door swung with an unpleasant creak.

"Who's there?" shouted Mrs. Singleton, peremptorily. Her voice came from the room on the right of the hall. It sounded so hard and questioning that I became uneasy.

"It's me," I said childishly.

I can only imagine that, from this, Mrs. Singleton imagined me to be one of her daughters, for the next moment she appeared before me in all the glory of soiled and elaborate corsets, which reached from her bosom to her pale grey thighs. She wore no stockings, and the suspenders dangled uselessly against her heavy blue-veined legs. Her hair was like a nest made by some very slovenly rook.

With an exasperated, outraged exclamation, she turned about—displaying her huge, grey blancmange buttocks—and fled into her bedroom.

From there she carried on a ladylike and furious conversation either with me or with herself. I could not tell which, for I was too frightened to listen or to distinguish the words.

She emerged at last in the ruin of a feathered *peignoir.*

With a queenly and austere gesture, she held out her hand,

making me feel that it was *I* who had appeared before *her* in a semi-naked and disgusting condition. She took the note in silence and shut the door. I too felt that it was no time for small talk.

Rather shaken by the horror, I walked slowly back to Brook House, wondering what to do with myself. My brother, I knew, had disappeared for the rest of the day. As I walked drops of rain began to fall. They hissed into the brook and spat against my face.

I entered by the stable-yard gate, and walked over the cobbles. The puddles were growing between the big curved stones. Outside the disused barn I stopped, and pulled at the huge, crazy door. It opened creakingly. I went in and shut it after me.

I was in darkness which smelled of dust and mice and hay. Chinks and cracks in the walls shot beams of light into the blackness.

I climbed on some boxes, then caught hold of a beam and swung there, like a monkey. I gnashed my teeth and contorted my face. I gibbered and hung on with one hand as I scratched under my arm with the other.

I grew hot, swinging in the darkness, and my arms began to feel the strain. I broke my last imaginary peanut between my teeth and spat as disgustingly and coarsely as I could on the invisible floor; then I sank down on the boxes and thought that I was miserable and lonely indeed.

And as I lay there I decided to be a slave who had to sweat and labor in the barn all day. But slaves had to be naked. I put my hand inside my flannel shirt and felt the flesh on my chest. Slowly I leaned forward and began to pull the shirt over my head. It was straining work, for I was sitting on the tails. When my body was free of the shirt and my arms were imprisoned in it above my head, I looked down at the vague whiteness of my skin. I thought of the men I had seen, with tufts of strong hair on their chests and under their arms. It was ugly and beautiful at once, I thought.

I caught hold of the beam again and swung about fiercely, hurting my arms, straining the muscles as I pulled myself up. I swore not to stop pulling until I had rested my chin on the top of the beam. At last, with a shudder of pain and pleasure, I brought it to rest there on the rough, beetle-eaten oak. The harsh wood grazed the soft skin on my throat.

Then slowly and gently I felt my trousers slipping. They slid caressingly over my hips and fell with a soft plop to my ankles, where they caught in bunched-up folds. I still hung there, supported by my chin and my tingling arms. Soft draughts of air blew deliciously against my complete nakedness.

"Now I am a criminal whose feet have been tied together, and whose body has been stripped by the hangman," I told myself. "I shall be swinging here till late at night, when my friends will come to cut me down."

I hung there not moving, living passionately my idea of a criminal on a gibbet; while the rain beat against the great barn door, and drops fell from the roof.

Gradually, as my strength gave out, I sank nearer to the ground, until my arms were stretched out agonizingly. There were still some feet to fall to reach the ground. I decided to drop, although I knew that my feet were trapped in the trousers. I fell in a crumpled mass, and lay on the barn floor with the short pieces of hay pricking me. I felt the smooth, satiny mounds of bird-droppings against my flesh. Slowly and wearily I put on my shirt, pulled up my trousers, ran my fingers through my hair, and went in to tea.

Towards evening, as I sat in my little room, polishing my favorite possessions, an ugly Japanese ivory, a Chinese agate chicken, and a painted tear-bottle (how many times had I tried, without success, to catch my own tears in it!). I heard the cook go into the library and begin talking to my father. This was unusual, and I stopped polishing and waited to hear any of her words.

As she opened the door, about to leave the room, this remark floated up the staircase-well:

"He wants to know if he can put up in the barn for tonight, sir."

I heard my father say: "I'll come and see him." Then he followed Cook into the back of the house.

I waited excitedly. Who wanted to put up in the barn for the night? I looked on it as my barn, where I did secret things. When my father came back I ran down to him.

"What's happened, Daddy?" I asked.

"Nothing. A tramp only asked Cook if he could sleep in the barn because it's raining so hard, and I said of course he could." My father made a gruesome horrific face and added: "I hope he won't murder us all in our beds tonight!"

I was fascinated and frightened.

"May I go and see him?" I asked urgently.

"Certainly not. He doesn't want to be stared at. Cook has given him something to eat, and then he wants to go to sleep in the hay. He's very tired."

I shut the door and went upstairs again, tingling with excitement. I decided to visit the tramp in the middle of the night, when everyone else was asleep.

I got ready a bundle of blankets to take out to him, and a bottle of sweets I had been given.

Impatiently I waited for supper to be over and "good nights" to be said. I lay in bed with all my clothes on, and my mother came and kissed me and put out the light.

"If only she knew!" I thought. "If only she knew—!"

She went downstairs again, and I heard her talking to my father. At last I could wait no longer for them to go to bed. I snatched up the bundle of bed-clothes and the bottle of sweets, and ran down the back stairs out into the dripping stable-yard. Then I ran back again to get my torch.

I crouched over the blankets to keep them dry. The huge door swung open easily and I turned my torch on and shone it in all the corners and into the thickness of the hay.

At first I could see nothing, then I saw him lying full-length in a deep nest of hay which billowed in soft, high walls all round him. He was asleep, and as I stood still I heard the heavy rhythm of his breathing.

I tiptoed up to him, and, too curious to be considerate, shone the torch full on his face. For a moment the face remained still and grey and smooth as marble, except for the crisp stubble on his chin. There was no expression. He looked beautiful. Then, as he suddenly woke, his face broke into a cobweb of connecting lines. His eyes and his mouth fell open in fear, and he shouted out hoarsely: "What's that? Who's that?"

I was frightened at the change I had brought about.

"I've only come from the house," I whispered urgently, "to bring you some blankets and some sweets."

"Let's have a look at you, mate," he said. "Shine the torch on your face." I obeyed, delighting in the word "mate."

"How old are you?" he asked.

"You'd better guess," I said, playing for time, wondering how many years I could add to my age without appearing too absurd.

"Oh, I see—" His voice trailed off and I was afraid he was going to fall asleep again; I snatched at the first thing and asked:

"And how old are you?"

"What do you want to know for?"

Then he relented and added: "I'm twenty-four, if that's any good to you."

It was clear that I amused him. This upset me.

"Do you like sleeping in this barn?" I questioned him almost severely.

"It's not a bad old place. Better than being under a hedge on a night like this."

"I'd like to do what you do," I said earnestly, looking at him. "I'd like to walk miles every day, and sleep in a different place every night, and get my own food."

"Oh, no you wouldn't, mate; you'd be much too soft. You'd be half dead after a day of it," he jeered.

I handed him the sweets, feeling deeply hurt; although it was comforting that he still called me "mate" after seeing my face. I looked up at the beam above our heads and said abruptly:

"I do exercises in this barn on most afternoons."

"Getting your muscles up?" he jeered again.

Since he would not take me seriously, I fell silent. I pointed the torch so that the beam lay on the length of his figure in the hay. He had the sort of body that I wanted to have when I grew up. It was not tall, but solid and compact, and rounded. Through a rent in his trousers I could see his hard thigh. I thought how different his flesh was from Mrs. Singleton's. And at the thought of her, hot blood rushed up into my cheeks.

"I'm going to sleep in the hay too!" I said.

"What for? Ain't you got a bed?" he asked coldly.

"I want to try it," I said.

"You'll cop it if your ma finds out," he warned me humiliatingly.

I looked at his body again. I could smell it now in the warm hay. I had a hard, quite callous feeling that the blankets were too clean to be put over him.

"Are you warm enough?" I asked. He did not answer. The

next moment I heard his deep rich intakes of breath. Wrapping myself in the blankets, to stop the hay from pricking, I lowered myself gently beside him. Deep, deep, into the hay I sank, until we were in one nest. He did not wake again, but stirred a little in his sleep, turning towards me. I drew as close as I dared to him and lay, my head close to his chest, so that I could feel the rhythm of its rising and falling.

All night we lay together there. Towards dawn I woke up to find that he now lay face downwards and that he had thrown an arm over me. I waited, not being able to sleep any more, hoping that he too would wake up.

When he did, he looked straight into my eyes from a few inches away and smiled. He was not teasing me any more; he had accepted me.

Slowly he raised himself in the hay and jerked his clothes this way and that, readjusting them. This was his morning toilet. He ran his hand over his face, rubbing his eyes roughly, and crackling the stubble on his chin.

"Well, I must be getting along," he said.

"I'm coming too," I announced.

"Don't be bloody daft," was his answer. I took no notice, but began to roll up the blankets. I wondered whether to take them with me, but decided that they would be too heavy. I hoped that he would unpack some of the food Cook had given him, but he didn't; he just went on hitching his knapsack up and ignoring me.

We went out into the weak sunlight in the slippery cobbled yard. He took no notice of me, but trudged on out of the yard into the lane, past the twinkling brook through the village, and out on to the heath-like stretch beyond. There he sat down and I sat too. In perfect silence he offered me a piece of cake and cheese. We munched together and he drank cold tea from his tin.

At last he stood up, and looking at me harshly, compellingly, he said:

"Now go back, you silly little bugger."

Narcissus Bay

One summer, when I was staying with my mother at Wei-hai-wei in China, I remember seeing four men and one woman coming down through the woods from the mountain. Two of the men had their hands tied behind their backs; their chests were naked, and they had thick ropes round their necks. The other two held these ropes, which they made to curl and ripple as they drove their prisoners on. The woman walked behind. Her dusty black hair was torn down over her face and shoulders. Blood oozed from cuts on her scalp; a patch of oiled paper had been stuck over one gash, and her lips were swollen and bruised. White cotton puffed out of the sharp tears all over her quilted clothes. She was crying and shaking her head exaggeratedly. In her hands she carried a thick stick broken in two. Where the bark had peeled off, I saw blood on the white, silky wood.

I stood dumbfounded, watching them pass out of the lemon-colored light under the leaves into the biting sunshine. The woman as she passed me held out the broken stick in pantomime. She ran her cries together, making them into a sort of whining song. The two men holding the ropes jerked the necks of their victims, swore at them, spat on their yellow-brown backs. Then the little procession moved on down the rocky path to the town.

I watched until they disappeared round a bend. My fascinated eyes came back to the cool leafy place where I was, and I could hardly believe what I had seen. I pictured it all to myself again, and the story was unfolded. I saw the men beating the woman outside a thatched hut, close to a smoldering fire. She had exasperated them in some way and they both set on her. But her screams at last roused the village policemen, who came running to help her. They threw ropes round the necks of her attackers, and tied their hands behind their backs.

Now they were all going down to the courthouse in the town, where the woman would show the bloodstained stick and tell her story. She was nursing her tears—just as I had done myself—because she wanted the judge to be sorry for her.

This all came very vividly to me. Perhaps the woman's expressive dumb-show had made it easy for me to reconstruct the whole story.

I thought again of the blood seen through her matted hair. It was the most barbarous sight I had yet seen and I held it to me with all the violence of new possession. I could not have rid my mind of it if I had tried.

Gradually the picture so overwhelmed me that I began to hate the glade where I had first seen the sight. I darted away, down towards the beach, and did not stop running till I felt the sand under my feet.

On the beach I found two girls I knew, playing outside their bamboo-matting bathing-hut. They were both older than I was; they had reddish down on their thick arms and legs, and their lips were full and well shaped. They treated their Belgian governess with the utmost harshness.

Now, as I approached, they called out and said that they had decided to eat nothing for the whole day. They would touch no meat, no sweet, no wheat, no beet; no fruit, no root; no nut, no gut —. They rhymed until they had nothing but nonsense words left; then, to fill a gap, I said, "Where is your mademoiselle?"

"Elle est grosse et grasse," chanted the elder girl, taking no notice of my question, pleased only to have an opportunity of abusing her governess. She repeated her sentence several times in a very loud voice and curved her hands in and out in imitation of the repulsive lines of mademoiselle's body.

I knew then that their governess was quite near, though hidden. I guessed that they had driven her into retreat behind some rock, where she was knitting. They would go on insulting her until they were tired of the game.

I wondered whether to tell the girls about my extraordinary experience or not. I really wanted to keep it to myself, but I had not the control. I wanted, too, to describe the horror to them and the unreal, magic atmosphere.

I began to tell them about the ropes, the wounds, the blood, and the broken stick. They listened contemptuously, sometimes throwing out their arms and legs, or twitching their nostrils in disbelief. But I knew that I had stirred them.

"What a liar!" the younger one said when I had finished. She said it mildly, as if she'd known me to be one for a long time.

"Which way did they go?" the other asked with heavy sarcasm; but her eyes were watching sharply.

"Towards the town," I said. And immediately they were away, over the sand and the rough tufted grass. They were running down the white road and mademoiselle had risen up from behind her rock and was screaming to them to come back.

"Mary! Rosalie!" she cried, but they never turned their heads. Hopelessly she started to run after them. The town was forbidden and she did not know what she was going to say to their mother.

I watched her fatness jellying for a little; then I turned away and searched for fan shells along the beach. Once or twice I had found softest pink ones and ones of coral scarlet, but now I found nothing. I wondered whether to go home or to go on to the end of the bay and have tea with Adam Grant and his mother.

I decided to visit Adam. I was still restless. My thoughts were seething and my body tingled. I would arrive a little early and perhaps a little dirty, but I hoped Mrs. Grant would not mind.

I walked slowly over the wet sand, close to the waves; but I soon reached the stone steps and the rock pools. I idled on the steps, leaning on the iron rail and staring into the depths of the pools from above. At last I climbed up to the terrace and found Adam lying there in a wicker chair. He looked up and told me importantly that he wasn't very well, he wasn't allowed to bathe, and his mother had pinned a flannel band round his stomach because she thought he had a chill there.

This struck me as ridiculous and rather disgusting in hot weather, and I said, "But what good will that do?"

"Of course it's the thing to put on for a chill in your stomach," Adam replied pompously; then he pretended to go on reading his book.

I stared at him. He was rather a fat boy with hair like coconut matting. I laughed to think of the flannel band round his stomach. Still he kept his eyes on his book; but I smiled, knowing that I could make him drop his show of indifference.

"Today I saw two men with ropes round their necks, and a woman who'd been beaten all over," I said flatly, without any color, to give my words their greatest effect.

Adam's head jerked up.

"Where? When did you see it?"

He seemed about to run out to look for the sight as the girls had done.

"Oh, it was a long time ago, up on the edge of the wood," I said languidly.

Adam poured out questions and I answered them with maddening slowness and vagueness. The story filled him with excitement, but at the end he remembered to say, "How awful for two men to beat a woman like that!"

He was still showing horror at the brutality, when his mother called out in a boisterous singsong voice, "Tea's ready!" and we both got up to go into the cool shaded dining-room.

There we found Mrs. Grant and another, younger boy, who, with his nurse, was also staying in the house. We sat down at the long narrow table and Mrs. Grant began to pour out. While Adam passed the bread and butter, I watched her. She was a soldier's wife, and I had the idea that she was very superstitious. Perhaps I exaggerated, but I imagined that her religion was made up of patent medicines, charms and unmeaning rites—such as the pinning of the flannel round Adam's stomach. I felt sorry for her—she was so very benighted and unaware of real things.

The other boy was silent. He was nervous and puzzled because he believed nearly everything that was said to him.

I looked at the tea and saw that it was good: peanut butter, brown bread, chocolate biscuits, and sponge cake. At first I was pleased; then I began to feel out of sympathy with everyone, and I longed to get away and be alone.

We played in the garden after tea, hiding behind the huge hollyhocks, springing out at one another.

Adam told the younger boy to eat one of the dead flower heads, then to drink some slimy green water in an earthenware crock. He shouted at him, "If you sit on the lavatory seat too long a swordfish will come up and bite you."

I saw Derek's face jump. He really believed it, and the thought was going to frighten him forever.

Adam followed up his success with other horror stories.

"If you swim into a jellyfish and it stings your face, it'll blind you; and if even a baby octopus gets hold of you it can suck the life out of you. A shark too can bite a leg off as easy as anything. Once they brought a man in with no arms or legs left."

Derek put his arm across his mouth and bit the flesh. His eyes were terrified. He wanted someone to deny the stories, but I was too lazy and uninterested to do so, and his nurse was far away, gossiping to Mrs. Grant on the verandah.

Adam made a lunge at him with a pole and when he flinched said, "What's the matter? I was only pretending that I was harpooning a whale."

To get away from us Derek ran into one of the bathrooms and locked the door. Adam climbed up to the window and made terrible faces through the glass; then he said, "You won't sit on the seat, will you, because of that swordfish."

At this Derek burst into tears and wailed so noisily that his nurse came and reprimanded us all, not sparing Derek. I could see his eyes still puzzled, terrified, longing to find protection somewhere. I turned away, ashamed for myself and ashamed for him.

His nurse began to undress him for bed. I heard the bathwater splashing.

Adam followed me out on to the rocks below the terrace. I disliked his stomach band, his fleshiness, his superstitious mother, and wished he would leave me. I wanted to be alone to watch the orange sun sink down into the sea.

To get away from him I moved from rock to rock until I was on a level with the pools. Still Adam followed me. I remembered that he was not supposed to bathe, and lying down on the edge of a pool I dipped my arm in and said, "How lovely the water feels this evening!"

"But you know I'm not allowed to bathe," he said accusingly.

"Aren't you?"—and I rolled into the delicious water with my shirt and shorts and sandals on. I beat about with my hands and shouted out my delight.

Adam went stiff with envy and resentment, but I took no notice of his venomous remarks until I had played and splashed enough; then I climbed out and said, "Lend me a lantern, I'm going home."

It was not really dark enough for a lantern, but I wanted to carry a lighted one along the beach.

Adam grudgingly found me his and I lit the candle; then, after asking him to say good-bye to his mother for me, I set out along the ribbed sand.

The oiled cotton of the lantern was painted with large scarlet and black characters. I danced and jumped about, making the light bob up and down and throw shadows like ghosts. Showers of drops fell from my soaking clothes. Far out in the bay the phosphorus was beginning to fringe the wavelets.

The scene of the early afternoon came back to me with sudden violence. I saw again the woman and the four men winding down through the trees; and for some reason my thoughts jumped to the shrine which I knew was on the mountain above them. My mother and I had once climbed up to it and eaten our picnic on the thymy grass in front. With my fingers I had picked out the little rock plants, like the flat round bottoms of artichokes.

The walls of the shrine were covered with peeling vermilion plaster and under the black curling roof were gods with little plates of food set before them, and joss-sticks, and gold and silver paper money scattered everywhere.

The clouds came down so low that they turned into veils of rainbow mist when the sun shone through them.

I thought of the utterly still, deserted place and I thought of the baked mud gods, all painted bright and gilded, gazing down, unmoving, caught in a trance, just watching everything, holding up their fingers, flashing their eyes and teeth forever.

The Judas Tree

As I was walking home from the art school one day, a rather plump, middle-aged man in shaggy tweeds passed me and then looked over his shoulder. He had a smooth round face with red veins on his cheeks, pepper-colored hair, and a carelessly trimmed moustache. He carried a little bunch of spring flowers—hyacinth, narcissus, daffodils—and in his other hand was a knotted walking stick.

The first time he looked round, his face wore no expression, and it reminded me of a beefy moon or a dart board; but when, a few yards further on, he turned again, the skin round his eyes was crinkled into a kind and sleepy smile. He slowed down, then held out the bunch to me and said, "Like to smell?"

I was surprised, but I bent down at once and put my nose to the cold flowers. Their rich breath filled my head. A little tingle of excitement ran through me. I waited to see what would happen next.

When I raised my head I saw that the man was looking down on me with a sort of hungry benignity impossible to resist. It was as if he were saying, "Oh, you are young and silly and unprotected, and I am old and wise and unused. If only we two could combine!"

I felt that I had to treat him with great consideration, and this feeling threw up a slight barrier of pretense. I was a little uncomfortable.

"They are lovely," I said, referring to the flowers. I nearly asked if he'd grown them himself, but the more I hesitated, the more inquisitive and pert the question sounded. I was tongue-tied and silent.

We were walking together over Blackheath now, near the church, and the pit where they light bonfires on Guy Fawkes's night. I expected the man to say good-bye soon and branch off in some other direction, but he stayed at my side and every now and then looked down at me. He was tall.

"Where do you go to school?" he said at last, smiling again in his disarming way.

I was nettled, but also obscurely complimented. I think I felt, "Well, I must look simple! Nobody knows what's going on in this head."

"I am an art student," I said trying not to sound stiff.

"Oh, that's interesting!" and his face lit up, as though an idea had come to him.

"Do you know what a Judas tree is?" He stared straight into my eyes, then added, very surprisingly, "I've been a schoolmaster for thirty years, and I can always tell when a boy is lying."

"I was going to say that I didn't know." I felt repulsed at once by this flashing glimpse of another side of his character. I recognized the schoolmaster's unnecessary parade, the overemphasis.

"Well," he said sweetly, returning to his earlier manner, "it is a wonderful tree that bears great rose-colored flowers; and the amazing thing is that the flowers appear before the leaves! Judas, you know, after he had betrayed our Lord, repented and took back the thirty pieces of silver to the chief priests. But when he had told them that he had betrayed innocent blood, they gave a terrible answer; they said, 'What is that to us? See thou to that.' So he threw down the silver in the temple and went to hang himself. He found a bare tree, climbed up into the branches, tied the rope; then jumped. The next morning the whole tree was lighted and hung with marvellous Judas-colored flowers. And the Judas tree, from that day to this, always bears its flowers before its leaves."

When he had finished this story, the man's face was rapt. He seemed transported. To take him away from the dangerous subject of the Bible, I said, rather stolidly, "Why do you call the flowers Judas-colored?"

"Don't you know that Judas had red hair?" he rapped out. "I've collected every picture I can lay hands on, and nearly all the painters from the early Italians downwards have given Judas red hair. Sometimes it's curly, sometimes it's straight, but it's almost always red." Then he gave me the names of one or two famous painters who had *not* given Judas red hair. He blamed them for inaccuracy, saying that their Judases failed and had not nearly enough evil in them, because of the mistake.

"Don't you think I've proved now that Judas had red hair? Could so many painters be wrong? There must be something in it." He looked at me sharply and anxiously, as though he wanted to make me agree.

I nodded and said, "I expect you're right," then thought this weak, so added what I really felt.

"It is all such a long time ago that nobody can really tell. Perhaps all the painters followed a tradition which was started by a man who hated red hair and so gave it to the villain in his picture."

The man was infuriated. "Of course Judas had red hair!" he thundered. I was able to picture him in front of a class at school, abusing the boys violently.

We walked on in silence. Still the man didn't leave me. I was about to turn to the right pretending that I lived in that direction, when the man, with all his fierceness gone, said: "I'm wondering if you could do something for me, since you are obviously a clever lad." I moved about uncomfortably in my clothes, wondering what was coming.

"Could you paint me a picture of Judas hanging dead from the Judas tree, with the beautiful rose-red flowers all round him? You could do the flowers very large, and I want Judas really dead. His tongue must be hanging out, black and swollen. It would make a wonderful picture, and I've been trying to get it painted for years."

He looked at me with intense, excited eyes. He had begun his speech cajolingly, with the remark about the clever lad, but he ended on the same vibrant note as before. It was clear that he lived for Judas and the Judas tree.

"Won't you have a shot at it?" he pleaded when I did not answer at once. "I could give you a great deal of help over the details. I've got some enlarged photographs of the flowers, and I know exactly how a hanged man looks. His head lolls on one shoulder just like this—." Here he stopped abruptly and, drooping his head to one side, showed the whites of his eyes and the whole length of his tongue in a hideous imitation of death.

"I could sit like this for you, if you liked," he said, still holding the pose. I wished he would stop distorting his face, so I told him how convincing he looked and moved on. He hurried after me.

"I thought at one time of having real red hair, cut from a human being, or, if that's not possible, from a red setter, for my Judas, but my sister, who lives with me, tells me that an oil-painting in which real materials are also used is in very bad taste. Do you agree?"

He seemed wistful, wanting me not to condemn his idea as fantastic.

"I think to have the whole picture in paint would be safer," I said carefully; "but I'm afraid I could never do it for you. It would be much too difficult. I wouldn't know how to begin on such a subject."

We had almost crossed the heath. I should have gone along Chesterfield Walk to reach my rooms on Croom's Hill, but the man said: "You *must* come home with me and see my reproductions of Judas; and if my sister's in she will give us tea."

Again there was the tingle of excitement in me, the feeling that some sort of adventure might be unfolding. I had been growing a little restive, but this invitation reawakened my interest. I wanted to see his surroundings.

"Oh—thank you," I said, "I'd like just to look at your pictures, but I *mustn't* be late back." I hoped in this way to make any sudden retreat seem necessary, not rude.

Somewhere behind the Green Man we turned down a long

street of mid-Victorian yellow brick houses with dog-tooth moldings over the doors and windows.

"We live a bit further down, on the left," the man said, then, realizing that he did not know my name, he demanded it in his schoolmaster's manner.

I told him and he seemed to weigh it in his mind, as if trying to assess its worth.

"Mine's Clinton," he returned solemnly.

"Oh, we have a girl at the art school called Clinton," I said. "She comes to the fabric-painting class, and she's going to teach art."

He frowned and looked uncertain for a moment, then he said stiffly: "She is no relation—no relation at all. I can trace my family back to the thirteenth century."

The last sentence, so naked, so irrelevant and disagreeable, chilled me. I said nothing.

"If they've got any books on heraldry at your art school you'll be able to look up quite a lot about my family," he said smolderingly, *willing* me to be awed.

I still said nothing and he began to boast about his family so outrageously that I wanted to laugh. Could he be serious? I had known nothing like it since early school-days, when children vied with one another over motorcars, the size of houses and the number of servants kept.

I was relieved when he put his key into the front door and dropped the subject of his family as abruptly as he had introduced it. We were in a dark hall now. He led me to the door of the back room, then threw it open. I saw a grand piano, a large old portfolio stand, and books in low cases, lining the walls rather meagerly. Opposite the one French window was a dilapidated brown sofa.

"Sit down, sit down," the man said expansively. I was his guest now, no longer a chance acquaintance. He wheeled the portfolio up to me, then brought out picture after picture in which Judas appeared. Some of them were charming old prints torn from books, others were shiny "Last Suppers" and richly glowing "Betrayal" scenes made for Catholic children. There were dreary photographs of great masterpieces and "details" showing every crack in the plaster or the panel. I looked again and again at evil, twisted, avaricious features, at hyacinth-curling hair, at goatee beards and at ones flowing like the little waterfalls in Japanese gardens. There was simulated love—the lips kissing while the eyes were glittering, almost radiant, with treachery. Then the torture of remorse, the last agony of realization.

But there was no picture of Judas hanged, paid out, fulfilled. For a moment I felt the lack, almost understood Mr. Clinton's preoccupation with the subject.

He was sitting very close to me now, breathing on my neck as he leaned over me to point with his stubby finger. I could smell juicy pipe tobacco, the animal smell of tweeds, and something between alcohol and the smell in chemist's shops. Was it the last traces of whiskey, of eau-de-cologne, patent antiseptic, or medicated snuff? I tried to analyze it in this elaborate way to cover my growing uneasiness. Would Mr. Clinton never move away to some other part of the room? Had he enticed me here for some criminal purpose? Was he perhaps going to try to string me up, so that he should at last have a living, kicking picture of Guilt and Retribution?

My thoughts grew so wild that in my nervousness I began to gather the reproductions together officiously and thrust them back into the portfolio. I felt that his eyes were burning into the back of my head. He said nothing. I wanted to get up and run.

"Did you like your school?" The flatness of the question came as a shock. Because I had expected strangeness, or even violence, I was bewildered. How did this man's mind work? Why at the climax did he always jump to some other subject, as if the first one no longer meant anything to him?

"Perhaps I liked it in bits," I answered vaguely, "but I couldn't have enjoyed it much, because I ran away."

"You needn't imagine that I think the better of you for that," he said.

Blood rushed up into my face. Could he think that I was proud of running away from school? The pointless snub seemed unforgivable, until I remembered that he was a schoolmaster.

He began to tell me all about himself. He had been a housemaster at a school whose name I had not heard before. Nobody had ever run away from *his* house. He understood boys, and boys understood him. It was, I was made to realize, a great loss to the school when the ridiculous rules had compelled him to retire. He was not idle, though. There was all this research on Judas to be done, and he was musical. Had I not noticed the Broadwood grand piano? Did I play?

"Only a very little," I answered cautiously.

"And can you sing?"

"I was in the choir at school until my voice broke, but now I don't sing properly," I said.

He looked at me expertly. "Perhaps you had a good treble; but what have you got now, I should like to know? Maybe something—maybe nothing. Just come over to the piano and we'll see."

I followed him in a hot state of embarrassment. Was I really to be made to sing "ah, ah, ah, ah, ah, AH, AH, AH" in that shaming way? I began to sweat a little. But a part of me was pleased. I wanted to be able to sing well, and once my voice had broken no one had bothered with it. Was my adventure to end in free singing lessons? I hoped so. Clinton looked so competent on the piano stool. I believed in him.

I began quaveringly, afraid of too much sound and of the surprising, unnatural tone of my voice.

"Louder!" he shouted.

I grew a little bolder, ascended and descended the scale, and sang particular notes which he thumped insistently, until they sounded like tom-toms in the jungle.

His hands dropped from the keyboard and there was an impressive silence for a moment; then he looked not at me, but out of the window, and said, "I can make something of your voice. Of course, you'll have to work. You'd better come here at least twice a week."

"Thank you so much," I said, really grateful, "but can you spare the time? Wouldn't it be a nuisance?"

"Nuisance! Why nuisance? It's part of my job. I've trained hundreds of lads' voices. I hate letting them go to waste."

At this point a woman's tired, rather petulant voice called from upstairs.

"Excuse me," the man said, leaving the piano stool at once; "that is my sister. I shall go up and ask her about tea."

It was long after teatime and I wondered what the sister would say. I heard them talking at the top of the stairs in low voices. The only clear words were the sister's irritable "Who is it?"

I was immediately ruffled, upset, put in a false position, and I decided to leave as soon as the man returned.

I heard him running down the stairs. He burst into the room in a young way and said, between puffs, "My sister's got one of her troublesome heads, and so I've persuaded her to stay in her room, but we can go into the kitchen and forage for ourselves." He seemed delighted about his sister's headache. He came up to me at the piano, put his hand on my shoulder and said, "Can you boil eggs, you scoundrel, eh? I bet you coddle 'em or make them like old leather boots, but come and try, while I make toast." He gave me several playful punches.

I was not expecting so much heartiness and good-fellowship. His changes in personality were too much for me. I had been hurt by his sister's words. And what was the cause of this sudden gaiety? Had he a sinister reason for wishing his sister out of the way in her room? All my misgivings reawoke and I longed to get away from him. It was easy to persuade myself that he was evil.

"But I really must get back," I said, "or they'll wonder what has happened to me." Even if I had stayed out all night no one would have worried; but I allowed Clinton to think that careful parents were waiting for me at home.

"Can't you just stay to tea?" he asked, quite crestfallen.

"I'm afraid not; it's getting so late." I moved firmly towards the door and he followed me, shambling.

"You *will* try to do my picture of Judas, won't you?" he said.

He was different again—sad, deflated, almost clinging. "And you must come here for your singing lessons."

"Oh, thank you, I will," I said.

We were through the dark hall and I was walking down the steps and saying good-bye over my shoulder in my haste. I smiled at him and tried to look pleased, but it was easy to see that I was escaping.

He stood under the porch disconsolately, then gave a little jerk with his hand and went in and slammed the door.

I sucked in deep breaths of air and ran up to the heath, free at last.

I saw nothing of Mr. Clinton for about a month after this first meeting. I did nothing about his Judas picture and avoided going anywhere near his house. I regretted the singing lessons, but would not have braved his strangeness, his unaccountable changes of mood, and the something alarming in him, even for them.

When I saw him for the second time I was with three other students. I suddenly recognized his back. He was a few feet in front of us on the pavement. He carried no posy, but he had his walking stick.

By turning my head away and talking earnestly I hoped to brush by unnoticed; but as I passed him I heard him call out, "Oh, so it's you, is it?"

"Hullo!" I said, stopping and trying to put surprise and pleasure into my voice.

"What are you doing, going home?" he asked suspiciously.

"No; we're having tea together somewhere first," I said, my eyes following the other students, who were now some yards in front.

"Have you done anything about that picture?" There was accusation in his voice.

"I haven't had a moment," I said guiltily. "I couldn't do that sort of thing at the school, you know. I'd have to do it at home."

He turned sharply and saw me looking at the backs of the other students.

"Well—hadn't you better go after your friends?" he said, somehow threateningly. "Hadn't you better leave *me* and catch *them* up?"

And in this last sentence Mr. Clinton seemed to put all the waste and emptiness of his life. It was so sad that I was melted and horrified. He who had once had fifty boys to bully and befriend now had no one at all. People all smiled nervously and backed away, as I had done. How old and mad and undesirable he must be feeling!

"Why don't you cut along?" he sneered. "Why don't you join them for a jolly tea party? You're no use here." He darted a venomous look at me and went on jeering at my dumb, nonplussed state. I would have stayed with him, but he was driving me away with every word.

"Yes, I must go," I said miserably, turning my shocked, startled face to him.

But as I turned he looked away and appeared to be interested in a black boy's head and a pipe in a tobacconist's window.

"Good-bye," I said uncertainly. He never turned.

Inexplicably wounded and humbled, I ran on to join my friends.

At Sea

Robert sat on the deck holding a book in front of his eyes and wearing a very preoccupied and intellectual expression. He was pretending to read. He mouthed words silently, smiled as if amused, then looked grave and serious. Every now and then he glanced about him, to see if anyone was noticing him. The stewardess came up with a cup of hot soup. She bent over him and said: "What! you reading to yourself! Clever lad. Here's your soup and your mother wants you when you've finished it."

Robert smiled at the stewardess and took the soup proudly. He felt rather ashamed of deceiving her over the reading, but decided that the deception was worth it, if it gave him this comfortable, proud feeling.

He began to drink the hot peppered soup and to crumble the hard water biscuits. He could never understand why biscuits of this extreme dullness were made. "Even grown-ups can't really like them," he thought, although he knew how perverse and disgusting their taste in food could be sometimes.

When he had finished the soup and made sucking noises against the lip of the cup in imitation of some voracious animal, he went down to the cabin. He was always annoyed when Americans called cabins "staterooms." It reminded him of palaces, of death, of politics, of candles round a coffin in a cathedral. It was showing-off and pretense. Rooms on boats were cabins.

His and his mother's cabin on "A" deck had really been designed for a drawing-room to a suite, but it had been partitioned off for this particular trip across the Atlantic and two beds had been put in. The walls were covered with dull panels of grey and rose tapestry. There were canework and gilt chairs and nothing much else, except a rather smelly little washstand which had been hurriedly installed. The mixture of commercial luxury and improvisation was surprising. Robert was both impressed and depressed by this particular cabin, different from any he had shared with his mother before. She, as an American with her older sons at school in England, was always travelling backwards and forwards; and wherever she went she took Robert.

There she lay on the bed, still in her nightdress. She did not feel very well and had decided not to get up till lunchtime. She was reading *Science and Health, with Key to the Scriptures* by Mary Baker Eddy, but when she saw Robert she raised her head and smiled. Robert thought for the thousandth time, "My mother is young and pretty, most people's mothers look old and ugly." Always he felt this when he looked at her; especially if, as now, she were a little bedraggled and unwell. When in the morning she asked him to kiss her before she was absolutely awake, when her eyes were still heavy and she felt almost damp from the warmth of the bed, he would have the curious proud feeling mixed with distaste. And sometimes he would not kiss her until she was quite awake and smiling, with her curly, fried-bread-crumb-colored hair fluffed out and pretty.

"Darling," she said now, "which dress shall I wear? You choose and put it out with nice stockings and shoes."

Robert thought swiftly and methodically. He knew his

mother's clothes well; not her underclothes—he did not understand them and did not want to, they seemed too fragmentary and bitty—but her day dresses, her coats and skirts and especially her evening clothes, interested him deeply. He would often tell her that something did not suit her. He had even used violence on things of his mother's that he did not like. Once he had pulled off and mauled a mustard-yellow hat with a velvet bow which he could not bear.

This being the period of the late nineteen-twenties, the dress which Robert chose for his mother to wear at lunch was extremely short. It was of light soft beige wool and had a very broad shiny black belt that looked as if it was made of creased American cloth. He put out cobweb-thin flesh-colored stockings and a pair of snub-nosed snakeskin shoes with very high heels.

His mother looked at what he had laid out.

"Darling, do you think snakeskin goes with that wool?" she asked tentatively.

"Yes, why not? It's just right," he answered with matter-of-fact emphasis.

"Oh well—if you think it looks nice. Tell me, what have you been doing on deck all morning?"

There was a slight pause, then Robert said rather desperately, "I—I've been reading." His voice grew bolder, more brutal towards the end, as if he were daring his mother to gainsay him.

"Reading!" she echoed incredulously. "You reading! Why, Miss Hawethorne told me that she could only get you to spell the simplest words out; and whenever I've tried to get you interested, you've always become sulky or implored me to read to you myself. Darling, you mustn't pretend you can read when you can't; and you *must* learn to read so that you needn't pretend. It's terrible; you're really quite old now. Perhaps it's my fault for taking you about so much, but you really must try to get hold of it, then you'll love sitting all alone and reading the most wonderful things; Shakespeare and the Bible and *Science and Health*, and *Alice in Wonderland* and Michael Arlen."

"I *can* read," said Robert obstinately, his cheeks burning with shame. "The stewardess thought I could anyhow," he added. It was a poor little spark of defiance and bravado.

"You are not to pretend and you're not to lie. You can't read and you know it and you're ashamed of it. Don't let Mortal Mind get hold of you and keep you back; know that as God's child nothing can stop you from learning."

"I *can* read!" Robert almost screamed at his mother. He was on the verge of tears. She leaned forward in the bed and smacked his face hard.

"You are not to lie. No gentleman lies," she said with icy contempt. This change from the religious to the social field was startling and disconcerting. The hardness in her voice frightened Robert. It was so much more difficult to follow her now that she was not talking about realities. God was real. Wickedness was real (in spite of what his mother and Mrs. Eddy said) but gentlemen didn't seem real at all. He knew that gentlemen lied; the very fact that they called themselves "gentlemen" was a lie.

He looked down on his mother on the bed. He had not cried when she smacked his face, although her hand had stung, and he had been shocked and startled. If he had cried, she would have been more victorious. He wondered what to do to regain his integrity and pride. He thought of smacking his mother's face in return, but he didn't quite dare do so, for the heat was leaving him. He thought of discomforting her by pulling back the bedclothes or by some hurting remark, but suddenly another idea came to him and he quietly went over to the clothes he had laid out and began to put them away again.

"Robert, don't put them away; I'm just going to get up and bathe," his mother called, but he took no notice. When he had shut the huge wardrobe trunk again, he left the cabin, without another word.

He wandered about the deck, then went into the writing-room and began an imaginary letter on the elaborately hideous ship's notepaper. The letter was to begin in English, but there were to be long passages in French and Italian, and there was even to be a snippet of Russian. He had it all planned. He began legibly enough, "Dear Friend, Here I am at sea," but as his small stock of real words gave out, he began to invent ones, and when he came to the sections which were to be in foreign languages, he twirled and twisted and jabbed with the pen until he had made an extraordinary pattern on the paper.

"That ought to do," he said to himself at last, having covered several pages. He looked at the elaborate scribble carefully, as if he were reading an important document through and checking it;

then he took an envelope and licked it portentously. He sealed it down and wrote a most imposing address. The flourishes and capital letters were grand enough for a royal proclamation.

He took this letter out with him on deck again; and when he thought no one was looking, he posted it in one of the enormous open-mouthed ventilators. He threw it up in the air. He saw it hover, then disappear down the black throat. He wondered where it would go. He associated the bowels of the ship with the bowels of the earth, and thought of ugly black demons seizing on his scholarly letter and reading it with interest and delight.

The gong for lunch sounded. Robert went to wash his hands. He smeared down his hair with his wet hands, as this always proved to his mother that he had washed. He wondered again why it was considered so despicable not to wash before meals.

He went into the dining saloon and saw his mother already at their table. She had on the dress he had chosen, the stockings and the shoes. She was smiling and talking to a friend over her shoulder. She looked well and happy. There would be no more talk of gentlemen and lies.

"Darling," she said, "you *were* naughty to put all my clothes away again, but now don't sulk anymore. Come and have minced chicken and rice. You know you love minced chicken and rice."

Robert did not smile, but was immediately submissive to his mother, at least in spirit if not in words.

"Can't I have curry and all those things to put on top?" he asked with very little hope.

"Darling, the chicken and rice will be so much nicer. They don't really know how to make curry well on this ship."

Robert allowed his mother to order the whole meal with no more resistance. He looked about him and saw the woman at a nearby table whose looks he so admired. She was utterly different from his mother; cold-colored, not warm; tall, not small and childish; graceful and studied and rigid, not gay and spontaneous and completely unself-conscious. She held her back so straight when she bent forward. The effect was overpoweringly impressive to Robert. It was like a marble goddess leaning down from a cloud. When she put her elbow on the table and turned and twisted her wrist, the poised utterly careful mannerism bewitched Robert. He found himself imitating her, both consciously and unconsciously. He tried leaning towards his mother in the same rigid way. He held up his napkin with the drooping, fallen-bird posture of the left hand. He wiped his mouth as if it were made of precious porcelain.

He did not love this woman at all. Something about her was even repellent to him; but his admiration for her knew no bounds. The ceremoniousness of her disciplined Diana-like body fascinated him. She was with a handsome young Jewish man, who morning and evening showed a great deal of cuff and the most beautiful emerald and diamond links. She spoke to him slowly, graciously, coldly smiling now and then with her archaic Greek-sculpture smile.

"Darling, stop staring and eat your chicken," his mother said, recalling him.

After lunch they went out into the vestibule and sat down in deep chairs and had coffee. Robert poured out and passed a cup silently to his mother; then he saw his mother's new friend Mr. Barron approaching. He turned his back a little more and pretended to be occupied with the coffeepots. He opened the lids and looked inside, even pretending that the skin off the boiled milk had stuck in the spout. Mr. Barron, so delicate and spectacled and poor and gentlemanly looking, clapped him on the back heartily and said, "Aha, looking after your mother well? I like to see a chap looking after his mother."

Mr. Barron smiled as broadly as he could, but, owing to the refinement of his features, he only managed to look like a skeleton.

Robert's mother smiled back at him gaily and said: "Come and sit down and have coffee with us. Robert will pour you some out and get another cup for himself."

Robert looked at Mr. Barron and said: "I wasn't looking after my mother, I was only pouring out because I like playing."

There was a slight pause. Robert's seemed such an unnecessary childish contradiction, yet it held in it a deep antagonism. Mr. Barron was embarrassed and so grew even more unnaturally hearty.

"Come, come," he said boisterously, "this'll never do. We all know that you'd do *anything* for your mother. And quite right too. I don't think any fellow could wish for a more charming one." Here he made an awkward, deeply sincere bow towards Robert's mother, and immediately grew red at this foreign gallantry.

Robert watched the pantomime with cynical, taunting eyes;

then he said something preposterous to shock and terrify Mr. Barron into retreat forever.

"I wouldn't let them put a red-hot poker into my behind, as they did to King Edward the Second; so you see I wouldn't do *anything* in the world for her."

"Darling!" his mother said in shocked and laughing surprise, "whoever told you of such a thing?"

"Miss Hawethorne," said Robert flatly. "I asked her what they did to him in the dungeon and she told me. She doesn't think people should beat about the bush, and she says I'm old enough to know the truth."

"Yes, Robert, but if you're old enough to know the truth, you're old enough to know when to mention things and when not to mention things. It's not right to say things like that just to be surprising. Talk about them seriously, not in a silly way."

Mr. Barron was now so nonplussed by Robert's dislike that he was pressing cigarettes on Robert's mother when he knew that she did not smoke because she was a Christian Scientist. He looked at her with deep admiration and respect.

"I've asked a few people to tea in my cabin, won't you come too and dance to the gramophone afterwards?" he asked at last, still gazing at her rather too reverently. Robert was not conscious of feeling jealous of Mr. Barron, he only wished that his mother would not waste time in his company. There was so much for them to do together. His mother was teaching him how to do her petit-point, and now he had nearly done all the left ear of the squirrel in her beautiful embroidery. He was getting so good that they could silently work at each end of the canvas. Only sometimes did he have to ask her to match wool or thread the needle when the wool came unravelled. It was a joyful time, doing the embroidery with his mother.

His mother was half-accepting, half-refusing the invitation.

"We were going to do some more work together and I was going to paint you one of those weeny little pictures you liked, and you said I had to learn to read properly," Robert burst out in a torrent.

"Yes, darling, but we've got plenty of time to do all that. It's very nice of Mr. Barron to ask me and I'd like to go."

"What am *I* going to do then!" Robert screamed, betrayed. "*I* can't sit eating too many little cakes. *I* can't go dancing! And afterwards you'll drink cocktails. They'll make you drink cocktails, and you know what Mrs. Eddy says. She says Scientists don't need such false stimulants; she even thinks tea and coffee are wrong."

Robert looked at his mother in a brokenhearted way.

"Mummy," he burst out in a sudden strangled melodramatic voice; "don't go dancing in his stuffy cabin and drinking cocktails. It's Error trying to get hold of you."

Mr. Barron's extreme discomfort made him lift himself on his hands and waggle from side to side uneasily.

"I think I—er—" he began.

Robert's mother was furious with her child for being so uncontrolled and primitive.

"Robert, stop talking nonsense and go away, if you can't be civilized. Leave Mr. Barron and myself alone; you've bored us quite long enough with your pretentiousness and your tantrums."

She turned towards Mr. Barron with the most engaging of smiles and seemed to snuggle down to a long cozy talk.

Robert got up. He was torn with horrible pangs of shame and frustration.

As he passed Mr. Barron he made the vulgar whorish gesture of lifting his foot and displaying the whole sole in contempt, at the same time looking over his shoulder with a sneer on his face. He had seen two schoolgirls doing this in America and it had impressed him. The showy insolence of the unsuitable gesture comforted him for a moment.

He saw Mr. Barron's skeleton, hearty, terrified smile grow from ear to ear.

"Please overlook his impossible behavior," he heard his mother say. "He must be left alone at the moment, but when he recovers I shall see that he apologizes to you. Where on earth did he learn that disgusting trick!" Then she laughed, quite genuinely amused through her anger. And this was the worst thing of all, her refusal to take his protest seriously.

He went up to the "winter garden" which was always more or less deserted until teatime. Here the large palms stood about between panels of elaborate Edwardian lattice-work. Trellis roses were painted dimly and delicately on the lattice. There were large gloomy mirrors.

In one corner he saw smoke rising from behind a cane-work

chair. He went up and found the woman he and his mother privately called Princess Bonbon. She was reading and smoking a fat Egyptian cigarette. She was indeed some Bourbon princess, but was of English birth. She seemed to have no husband, at least not on the boat. When Robert's mother first told him who she was, he was thrilled. He knew all about Marie Antoinette from Miss Hawethorne and was always longing to ask the Princess Bonbon how her husband's ancestors linked up with this fascinating queen, but he never dared. He knew it was wrong to appear even to notice that she was a princess. But he felt that she must be different. You couldn't be ordinary with Marie Antoinette tacked on somewhere behind.

He looked at the Princess Bonbon carefully once again. Again he saw a smear on her teeth of the cerise lipstick which she always wore. He had never seen her without this rather frightening ornamentation. It was as if the teeth had become delicately bloodshot. She was an awkward, lanky, very English woman, whose clothes were too brightly colored and artistic to be smart. Her face was plain and flat, as if the bone structure had fallen in slightly. The bright cerise lipstick made her pale skin look grey-white and uneven in pigmentation, almost blotched. In spite of magenta chiffon scarf, diamond clip, peacock and mustard jerkin and bag, she looked colorless and effaced, tired, angry, wasted.

"Hullo, Robert," she said; "come and talk to me. I'm all alone here."

He went directly up to her and stood very straight with his head bowed respectfully. At that moment his manners were perfect. He was ready to treat any woman, but his mother, with the most extreme chivalry. He waited for the Princess to ask him to sit down. She patted the stool where she had put up her feet and he sat down beside her not very attractive shoes. She had chocolates in her lap and she held out a big pistachio nut one and he, although he did not care for this sort, opened his mouth dutifully and let her thrust it a little too far in. He munched, making as little noise as possible. He became awkward and uneasy, not knowing what to talk about after the tumultuous scene with his mother and Mr. Barron.

"Would you like to come and see Joey?" asked the Princess suddenly. Joey was her liver and white spaniel which was kept in a special kennel at the farthest end of the boat deck. She was always talking of Joey, bemoaning the fact that he would have to be left in quarantine for six months as soon as they reached Southampton.

"Yes, let's," said Robert, pleased and relieved at the suggestion. He stood up and held the Princess's chocolates and book, while she put a little more lipstick on her mouth. She saw in the mirror the pink stain on her teeth, and rubbed them in a workmanlike fashion with her thin handkerchief. Robert thought how foreign it looked, with its profusion of embroidered flowers, its large coronet and rococo initials. "It's French or Italian," he thought. His mother's handkerchiefs were plain, smooth, delicate, lovely.

The Princess Bonbon led the way and Robert followed a few paces behind, like her page or squire.

They climbed up to the boat deck where the biting wind struck them. The Atlantic, unbelievably monotonous and real, came as a shock too. It was an endless carpet, bulging and yielding, because of the draught along the floorboards beneath it.

Joey rushed at them, madly straining on his chain. The Princess, having brought nothing for him, gave him chocolate after chocolate out of her box. Joey swallowed them as if they'd been flies.

"It's no good," said Robert. "He's too greedy even to taste them!"

"Oh, the darling, darling, darling," said the Princess, dropping on her knees and clutching the scrambling Joey to her. He licked her face, mauled her chiffon scarf, bit the checked bag. Then he tore away to the extent of his chain, as if suggesting a ten-mile walk.

They marched him up and down the deck for about twenty minutes. They talked very little between themselves but a great deal to Joey.

"Oh pet, petkin, petskin," cried the Princess, "I can't bear to think I'll be parted from you for six months in a few days' time."

At last they grew so cold without overcoats that they had to leave him. He whined dismally, danced on his chain, implored. The Princess's heart was wrung. She turned quickly away and said, "Mr. Barron's asked me to his cabin for tea and drinks and dancing; come with me, Robert, and give me moral support."

"That's where my mother's gone," he said, suddenly remembering the whole ugly scene in the vestibule.

"Do you like that Mr. Barron, Princess?" he asked, on impulse. He had never called her "Princess" before. Now he seemed to warm to her and long for her to say something spiteful about Mr. Barron.

"I think he's a very nice man, don't you? So clever and quiet, and yet quite gay at the same time."

"Why does he smile like that?"

"Like what, Robert?"

"Sort of like a dead man."

"I think he's rather nervous, like so many sensitive people."

"He offers my mother cigarettes and cocktails and he knows she thinks they're wrong."

"He only wants her to have a good time. I think he admires your mother very much, and quite naturally. She is very attractive."

"Do you think so?" Robert was delighted; the annoyance of Mr. Barron was quite forgotten.

They reached the door of Mr. Barron's cabin and heard noises of amusement and gaiety. The gramophone was playing "My Cutie's due at two-to-two on a big choo-choo."

Robert pushed the door open for the Princess and stood back as he had seen grown-up men do. The room was very smoky. People were sitting on the bed and others had overflowed into Mr. Barron's private bathroom. He himself was mixing drinks while Robert's mother was sitting childishly hunched up on a chair, pouring out tea as if she'd been hostess. She held out cups for anyone to take. She was like a charming eighteenth-century street hawker. The cups were her wares; her mouth, a little open, seemed to be singing their goodness.

There was a slight stir when the Princess came in with Robert. They brought a completely different, unconvivial atmosphere with them. Mr. Barron hurried up, still holding the shaker, and in his nervousness offering it to the Princess to drink out of. She smiled her flat, plain smile. Nothing seemed to matter. She could not be happy. People began to chaff Robert and offer him sips from their various drinks; until one managing soul thrust her tea into his hand and forbade him to sip another cocktail or to eat another alcohol-soaked cherry. Robert refused even to look at his mother; but he knew that she had left the tea and had accepted an Old-fashioned cocktail. Then he knew that she was dancing with Mr.

Barron and that others were dancing too. All the couples could do was to circle on the small patch of bare carpet, but their activity set up a rhythm and vibration through the whole, fairly spacious cabin.

Robert lay down on the bed and shut his eyes. He felt a little sick from the cherries and the sips and the Princess's pistachio chocolates. Someone tried to make him eat bread and butter but he would not.

Fat tears squeezed out of his eyes. He tried to hold them in by shutting his eyes still tighter but they always managed to wriggle out. He dashed them on to the eiderdown where they made little dark splashes.

The Princess Bonbon came and leaned over him and saw that he was crying.

She said, "What is wrong, Robert, dear?" then feeling ineffectual she went over to his mother and touched her shoulder as she danced with Mr. Barron.

"I think Robert's rather overtired or feeling ill; shall I take him back to your cabin?" she asked.

Robert's mother immediately left Mr. Barron's arms and went up to the bed.

"What is wrong?" she asked rather coldly, bending down.

"Go away, pig," he screamed, then turned over on his face and buried it in the eiderdown.

He felt his mother's hands on his shoulders and her warm breath on his neck. He wriggled his shoulders violently and kicked back his legs. He knew that he was about to make the most terrible scene. He had the sudden fear that his nervous excitement would make him lose control of his bladder. The shame, if this happened, would be terrible, but he also thought with detachment that it would be funny to wee-wee on Mr. Barron's soft bed.

"Don't be troublesome, Robert," his mother said briskly. "It is so bad to make scenes in public. People never do it. They think it very ugly and in very bad taste."

This mention of good taste, correct behavior, and public opinion struck Robert as extraordinarily frivolous and wicked.

"I don't care what anyone thinks," he shouted into the thickness of the eiderdown; then he sprang up and ran into the center of the cabin. The two or three dancing couples stared at him. He felt with horror the sudden warmth on the inside of his leg. His mouth fell open. He screamed some abuse at his mother, then with tears pouring down his face he ran from the cabin, slamming the door behind him.

He made straight for his own cabin; there he snatched up his towel and flannel and rushed to the bathroom. He locked himself in and gave himself up to a fit of weeping; then suddenly his heart went quite hard and he felt ashamed of himself. He got on to a stool and crouching over, dipped his head deep into a basin full of cold water. Afterwards he washed his clothes methodically and efficiently and pressed them against the hot-water towel-rail until they steamed and gradually grew dry. He dressed himself again and left, quite emptied, chastened, apart; a hundred miles from the world, the ship, his mother, everything.

He got ready for bed early and waited until the stewardess brought his hot milk and biscuits. She had also managed to filch a striped ice cream for him from the dinner menu. She always brought him some delicacy, apart from the plain milk and biscuits. Robert thanked her and then, after she had made her few nice gossipy remarks and left, he went over to one of the portholes and threw the ice cream as far out to sea as possible. Striped ice cream of this sort made him feel sick, but he would never have told the stewardess this.

After he had cleaned his teeth as his mother had taught him (up and down, not across) he lay down on the bed, and shut his eyes, still leaving the light on. He felt that he wanted to cry again, but the hardness in him poured contempt upon his other self and instead he began swearing at his mother with the worst oaths he could invent. The only real swear words he knew were "damn" and "bloody," and so he twisted and elaborated these with fanciful beginnings, endings, middles.

Suddenly the door opened and he knew that his mother was about to enter. He shut his eyes even tighter and began to breathe deeply. He tried to make snoring noises. She came over to him and touched him. He took no notice. He knew she was bending low over him. He showed no sign and tried to imagine himself turned to granite. His mother shaded the light away from him and started to change for dinner. He heard the tinkling of rings and other things on the glass-topped table, and the soft plop of garments being shed. He made his eyes into narrow slits and watched her impatiently doing up her dress at the side. He saw her leaning forward to the mirror and making up her face in a slap dash way; a dart of lipstick, a slash of black pencil, the cream rouge in two little balls on her cheeks smudged in and in until they almost disappeared. He was anxious to see the whole effect of her before she went in to dinner. He could tell how unhappy and out of patience she was. She would go in to dinner, ready to shock and surprise, to appear startling. She had put on her bizarre black dress with tulips made of dyed feathers dangling from one shoulder almost to her hips. The dress showed her knees in front and swept down in a curve behind like a half-moon.

She got up and snapped the light off with a vicious flip.

Robert gradually floated further and further into sleep. . . .

When he next woke the light was on again and he saw his mother in the middle of the cabin; she looked lost, unhappy and unwell. He knew that it was late. He knew that she had been dancing and that she was very tired. He wondered if she had drunk cocktails or champagne or any other intoxicating drink.

She came over to him gently, and he smelled the tobacco smoke which had soaked into her clothes from the choking air of the ballroom. It came out in waves, mixed with her scent.

When she saw that he still pretended to be asleep, she turned away to undress, then, as if too ill and exhausted to go on, she fell down on her bed and began to say fanatically but softly: "There is no life, truth, intelligence, or substance in matter. All is Infinite Mind and its infinite manifestation."

Robert knew how ill she must be feeling. She lay still holding on to the eiderdown, waiting in a trance to feel better.

He opened his eyes and looked at her; he could not go over to her or touch her, but he longed to help her. He formed his face and mouth carefully into the right shape and then began to sing very gently.

"What is thy birthright, man,
Child of the perfect One;
What is thy Father's plan
For His beloved son?"

He waited a moment to gather breath and to remember the second verse correctly.

"Thou art Truth's honest child,
Of pure and sinless heart;
Thou treadest undefiled—"

He had forgotten what came next. He was overcome with the beauty and sadness of his own singing. He was going to cry because his mother was ill on the bed. He wasn't going to help her. He was going to cry.

He jumped angrily out of bed and crouched by her on the floor. He held her hand and arm fiercely. They neither of them said anything, but his mother was breathing deeply, trying to master her illness and pain.

"Sing, darling," she said after a pause. "It's lovely when you sing for me."

He still held her arm tightly and untenderly as if it were the spar of a ship and he a man in the water. He knew so many hymns, but only the first verses of them. He wanted to sing something so consummate and wonderful that his mother would turn over and smile and be happy forever; but he knew that she was dying and that she could not save herself. He only knew this sometimes in a flash. At other times he would be completely hypnotized by her gaiety and liveliness into believing that she was not ill at all and that she would live forever.

Now he decided to sing,

"Eternal Mind the Potter is
And thought the eternal clay;
The hand that fashions is divine,
His works pass not away."

His mother was growing less tense, she sighed, turned towards him and smiled.

"Don't cry, darling," she said humorously, for the tears were now streaming down his face, "don't cry, I feel so much better." But he could not stop, they poured down and he made no sound, only stared at his mother, his eyes boring deep down into her. He could not sing anymore, he could do nothing, only watch his mother and let the tears stream down bitterly.

The Trout Stream

How well I remember that first visit to Mr. Mellon! My mother and I had been asked to spend the weekend at his great villa near Tunbridge Wells. He was an old friend of my father's, and since my father was abroad at this time, I think he imagined that we were lonely, sitting in our Kensington hotel, looking out at the fossilized trees in the gardens of the Natural History Museum.

We set out on a dark rather foggy afternoon in early autumn. The light under the dirty glass dome of the station was thick and yellow. The train was just about to start and we had to run down the platform to reach a coach. As I skipped along by my mother, I suspected nothing. I was excited by the hurry, rather pleased that we had to scramble in this way; but when the door of the first coach had been wrenched open and my mother's suitcase tossed on to the rack, I saw that there was something strange about her. She stood, swaying a little, a sort of smile on her face, her bag still open, although the porter had been tipped. I thought that she was about to move her hands and head in rhythm, perhaps even to hum a song. Then the middle-aged man opposite had jumped to his feet, had taken hold of her, was touching *my* mother! Between the little white tufts of hair above each ear, his chunky lips were working up and down in agitation. He was saying: "Oh, is there anything I can do, madam? Lean on me. Shall I get a doctor?"

He seemed impossibly fussy and protective. He was turning my mother into one of those fainting, delicate women I had heard about in stories, when really she was the strongest, most capable mother anyone could want. Why! running was nothing to her; she could dance and swim and ride and play all sorts of games. No one in the carriage would know this now, because of the man. They would all think her a weak woman who had to be held up, fanned with newspapers and given smelling-salts.

I looked up in amazement and said: "What is happening, Mummy?" Then I pulled at her to make her sit down, for she was still standing, with her head almost against the man's shoulder. Slowly the train began to move out of the station. My glance darted up to the vast glass roof, so far away and threatening; it returned to my mother fearfully. But she was recovering. Her smile lost its sleepwalking quality before my eyes. She looked up at the man and thanked him charmingly for his attention, explaining that she had only felt faint for a moment; then she sat down beside me and took my arm.

We said nothing at first, each, I suppose, feeling relieved and yet shy. I was impatient with her, too, for giving the wrong impression to the people in the carriage; I had always been proud of her youthfulness and vigor. I was not to know that this was one of the first signs of the illness that was to separate us soon.

When we were near the end of our journey, my mother told me not to say anything to Mr. Mellon or his housekeeper about her faintness, since she wanted no sort of to-do now that she was well again. So it was in a rather strained and careful mood that I left the train and went towards the long black car that was waiting for us. Already we were coming within the influence of Mr.

Mellon and I must let no word slip. The car itself with its high old-fashioned body and glittering carriage lamps, already lighted, was a disappointment. I had expected a man of Mr. Mellon's wealth to have a Rolls-Royce, and here was something that I could not even give a name to. Still it was good to have darkness outside, but to be in the warm padded box with my mother, to be smelling the slightly aromatic dried-up air and playing with the scent bottles, matchboxes and engagement tablets of old cracked ivory—the cracks were black, like my nails when I was sent to scrub them.

On the outskirts of the town we left the wide avenue and turned in between large clumsy gates. The car lamps glistened on the fresh paint, showing the branches of monkey-puzzles and rhododendrons beyond. There was a little lodge of grey and red rubbed brick. Everything was hard and ugly and beautifully kept. It reminded me of public parks or cemeteries; and this effect, together with the shock of my mother's passing illness, and her wish that nothing should be mentioned, all helped to oppress me, so that I dreaded coming to the end of the long curling drive, where Mr. Mellon and his housekeeper would be waiting for us.

I suppose it was this wish to shut the world away from me that has made me forget almost all the details of our arrival. Just the sight of three huge plate-glass windows, curtained and lighted from within, remains. We were approaching them quickly; then there was the crunch as the wheels braked on the gravel under the granite porch.

It is the next morning that is still so clear. It must have been the hour before lunch. I know that my mother took me into the room where Mr. Mellon always sat, the one with the three long windows.

It overlooked the gravel, the starfish flower beds and the whole stretch of lawn in front of the house. The sun was pouring in, draining the fire of color, making the invisible flames seem rather overpowering. I had been told that Mr. Mellon was an invalid, so his wheelchair did not surprise me. Only the plaid rug across his knees made me wonder fearfully what the legs could be like underneath. Were they all withered away? Were they like drumsticks when the chicken has been eaten? The face beamed at me. I thought it looked like a very large, scrubbed, kind potato. There were only little mounds and valleys, all colorless and smooth with no wrinkles. Mr. Mellon held out his hand and I went up to his chair. He held me against his side. He seemed extraordinarily fond of children, I thought; too fond to be quite comfortable, for I was conscious of his big body so close, the hardness of the wheelchair and the heat of the fire. Then the door opened and Mrs. Slade the housekeeper came in.

Mrs. Slade was the smiling, confident hostess, and yet somehow it was clear that she was no unpaid wife, friend, or relation; perhaps her very competence set her apart. My mother had explained to me that she was half-Javanese, but I could not quite accept her appearance and kept gazing at her whenever I thought that it would not be rude. I did not like her very soft, creamy skin, or the almost freckled duskiness round her long eyes, but their strangeness held me. I thought the grey seemed out of place in her black hair, for her body was flat and supple, like a young person's, and she was very small.

She began to ask my mother how she had slept, whether she had been brought exactly what she liked for breakfast; then she went over to the fire and wheeled Mr. Mellon back a little, as if she knew, better than he did himself, what was comfortable for him.

"It's nearly time for drinks," she said brightly, and turning to me so that I too should be included in her attention she added, "My daughter Phyllis will be down in a moment; she is just washing her hands. It is so nice for her to have someone of her own age to play with."

I was a little alarmed by Mrs. Slade's efficiency, afraid of that smiling hardness. She seemed not to be aware of my nature or my mother's. Her mind was always occupied with the arrangements of the day; and the comforts and pleasures she planned for us were made to sound like duties. She was like the harsh little lodge, the monkey-puzzles and the sharp-edged drive.

The drinks were brought in by one of the tall Indian servants in his red turban and long white coat. As soon as he had left, Mrs. Slade turned to my mother and said: "The Indians are new since you were here last, aren't they?"

"Yes, where did you get them?" asked my mother.

They were indeed remarkable; all tall and silent in their red and white uniform. Ever since we had arrived I had been wanting to know why they were in this English villa. I knew that Mr.

Mellon had made his fortune in the East, but it had been the Far East, not India.

Mrs. Slade was explaining.

"We had so much trouble with English servants that at last we thought we would try these Indians; they work as a team. A friend of Mr. Mellon's told us of them."

"They seem very good," my mother said.

"Yes, I think they do their work well on the whole, and the cook makes excellent curries. You will see; we are to have one today."

This was delightful news to me, since curry was almost my favorite dish.

All this time Mr. Mellon had been beaming at me, at my mother and at Mrs. Slade, sometimes saying a word, but usually leaving the conversation to Mrs. Slade. Now he took from his pocket a little gold box and I was suddenly excited to see the lid blaze with large initials in diamonds. The initials were too big for the box, making it seem crusted and clumsy. I was still more excited when he opened the box and took snuff. Noticing my fascination he held out the box to me. I went up to him again and took it, but did not dare to smell the snuff, imagining that I would sneeze or choke at once. I just held the box and drank in its great value and the beauty of the diamonds.

"I thought only old people, people in history, took snuff," I said uncertainly, thinking of wigs and swords and other things my mother had told me of.

"I take it because I mustn't smoke, you see," Mr. Mellon said, then added: "You like my box?"

For one intoxicating moment I thought he was going to give it to me. What would it feel like to possess a diamond-studded snuff-box? But he was only amused by my reverent interest. I felt he was almost laughing at me.

"I've another one here," he said. "I wonder if you'll like it better."

He fished in his other pocket and brought out a box with a little urn of flowers on it. The urn, the flowers and ribbons were in every color of precious stone. I tried to name them: ruby, sapphire, emerald, pearl—I knew no more.

"Oh, yes!" I said with a sigh of wonder and amazement.

Could I be really holding such boxes? What would happen to them when Mr. Mellon died? They seemed more desirable to me than anything else I had known.

Suddenly Mr. Mellon took the boxes back from me, slipped them carelessly in his pockets and said with complete irrelevance: "One day when my legs are better, you and I will go out in the woods behind the house and climb up to where the white elephant lives. I'd like to show him to you."

I was nonplussed. I knew that Mr. Mellon was paralyzed and could never walk again. I knew that there were no white elephants—certainly not in England. Was this a game of make-believe? I was painfully embarrassed.

Mr. Mellon saw it and laughed. I turned to my mother for help and guidance.

"Ah! here is Phyllis at last," broke in Mrs. Slade. "How long you've been!"

I guessed that Phyllis had been keeping away on purpose, for she was a dark heavy girl with nothing at all to say. Her eyebrows met in the middle and already she had black hairs on her arms. She stood against the wall, utterly impassive and confident. I could not help thinking her very ugly, and it was a shock to my self-satisfaction when Mr. Mellon showed even more delight in her arrival than he had shown in mine. He asked her to bring him one of the little cocktail tit-bits, then when she stood by him, he put his arm round her shoulders and said: "Phyllis is a good old sort, isn't she! I've been talking about our white elephant, saying we must visit him when I'm up and about again."

Phyllis's response to this was a sort of grunt that seemed both sullen and lazily good-natured. It was as if she knew his nonsense of old, but was ready to put up with more of it, since he was good to her.

At lunch I was surprised to see so many Indians; there seemed to be one for each of us, and they came and went with such silent smoothness. Sometimes there was the lowest murmur behind a screen, sometimes Mrs. Slade made a sign with her hand; and her eyes followed them constantly. I felt the strain of her watchfulness and saw that she ate in quick abstracted snatches, hardly looking at her plate.

But the curry was what really occupied my attention. There was rice bright gold with saffron, chicken in its glistening brown sauce; then came innumerable little dishes of condiments. I suppose we had chutneys, Bombay duck, chopped coconut, egg, parsley, peanuts and many other stranger things I still cannot name. I know that I piled them up until I had a little mound, then dug into it joyfully with my spoon.

As soon as I had satisfied my greediness a little, I began to look about the room; at the walls covered with a heavily embossed gilt paper in imitation of Spanish leather, at the sticky landscapes and still-lifes in plaster frames almost a foot deep. Out of the windows I could only see lawns, laurel hedges and the corner of a white conservatory all cast-iron spikes, silvered poppy-heads and Gothic tracery. A sense of the deadness of things began to oppress me. I thought that all Mr. Mellon's possessions looked as if no one had ever wanted to use them or enjoy them. I wondered why he had them and kept them in such perfect condition.

Mr. Mellon's long head now seemed to me to be like a peeled satiny log. Phyllis next to him was like some coarse little fair negress, unaware of anything but food. Her mother's much more delicate Eurasian face with its smile and its strain filled me with uneasiness. I looked at my mother with relief, kept my eyes on what always pleased me. Here was the only object that did not seem strange or ugly or inauspicious to me.

Mrs. Slade must have planned that our first lunch should have an Eastern flavor throughout, for we finished with tinned mangoes. The long spoon-shaped slices swimming in syrup disappointed me, because the preserving had made them taste more like peaches than anything else, but I had a second helping, since Mrs. Slade seemed to expect it.

Afterwards Phyllis took me into the paddock to show me her pony. A groom brought it out, but then left us alone together. I was feeling at a disadvantage, because Phyllis had changed into riding-breeches and looked even tougher and more self-sufficient than before. I thought too that I would probably be expected to ride as I was, in shorts, which would mean two raw patches on the insides of my legs. And what if I should fall off, or show any sort of fear? Phyllis would just look away, hardly even bothering to be scornful. The visit to the paddock was an ordeal.

Phyllis stood for some time with her arm on her pony's saddle, doing nothing. The running together of her thick eyebrows gave an effect of frowning, but I think she was really looking at me with no expression at all. At last she said: "Are you fond of riding?" She might have been asking if I liked cleaning my teeth or performing some other irksome duty.

"Yes, last year I rode every week," I explained, "but now we are living in London."

At this Phyllis gave my bare knees a glance and remarked: "But you haven't got any breeches"; then she swung herself on to the pony and trotted briskly to the other end of the field. I watched her go, wondering how soon I could leave without seeming rude. I wanted to explore the grounds by myself.

As she returned, I tried to show some interest, but Phyllis passed without a word. Her face was set; she might have been all alone. I felt that my welcoming smile must look silly indeed.

Several times she rode round the field, solemnly, without taking any notice of me; I was only saved from the growing awkwardness of my position by the sudden appearance of Mr. Mellon and Mrs. Slade. My eyes had wandered towards the house rather longingly; and then I had seen what looked to me like the strangest of little horseless carriages. It was approaching down one of the winding yellow paths, threading in and out of the trees very rapidly and smoothly.

Soon I could see that it held Mr. Mellon with Mrs. Slade sitting at his feet. Mr. Mellon waved his hand, as if beckoning, so I ran to the gate of the paddock and let myself out.

They had stopped in the protection of a bank of shrubs with mottled leaves, and against this bright yellow and green background their faces looked very pale. I saw that the little carriage was an elaborate motor or electric bathchair. Mr. Mellon's head was framed in the folds of the calash hood, while Mrs. Slade squatted cross-legged on the tiny space left on the platform in front of his feet. Seen thus, sitting before him like a little Buddha, she was stranger than ever to me; but I also thought her smile seemed happier and more spontaneous, as if she really enjoyed fitting herself so ingeniously into the bathchair and racing down the garden paths with Mr. Mellon. She suggested that I might like to try riding in her position and rose from the platform like a dancer, hardly using her hands, and with her legs still crossed. Mr. Mellon said: "Yes, you just see if you can fit in as neatly as Mrs. Slade, and then we'll go for a fine ride."

I crouched on the platform uncomfortably, afraid to lean back for fear of hurting Mr. Mellon's legs, or of feeling them against me. I imagined terrible skeleton legs that could not bear even the lightest touch. Mr. Mellon turned the chair round and we began to glide almost silently towards the house. We passed Phyllis, still riding round the paddock. Mr. Mellon waved; she gave us a glance, seemed to take in the fact that I was sitting at his feet, and returned one wooden gesture.

"I expect you and Phyllis get on like a house on fire," Mr. Mellon said: "she's as good as any boy at riding and playing games. You should see her throw a cricket ball!"

Again I wondered that Mr. Mellon could show such fondness for Phyllis; she seemed so very unenticing to me.

We were now passing the house and reaching the wooded ground behind. As soon as the path began to rise a little Mr. Mellon said: "I know I told you about the white elephant that lives at the top, but we'd better not go to see him today. It's not very good for the chair to pull two uphill, and I expect Mrs. Slade's wondering where we've got to."

I was only too pleased to drop the subject of the white elephant and agreed that we ought to go back at once; but when we were near the front door, Mr. Mellon suggested leaving me, so that he could go back to Mrs. Slade and bring her up to the house in the chair.

As I wandered into the hall, I thought dimly that Mr. Mellon also enjoyed riding in the chair with Mrs. Slade. It might be one of their chief pleasures. I knew he admired her for being so small and supple that she could fit on to the footboard where no one was supposed to sit. I wondered if they ever went out of the grounds in the chair, taking a picnic perhaps and a book; and if they did go out, did people stare to find her sitting there at his feet like an Eastern idol?

How quiet the house was! I guessed that my mother had gone upstairs to write letters or to read on her bed. I began to want to know about the other rooms leading off the hall. I had only seen Mr. Mellon's room and the dining-room. Very gently I opened one of the heavy mahogany doors and found myself in what must have been the drawing-room. The first thing that caught my interest was a cabinet filled with Japanese and Chinese ivories; some too large to have been made out of only one tusk. There was a smiling woodman with a basket of sticks on his back; a woman in fantastic ceremonial dress; then I saw it—a man crouching down, holding out one hand beseechingly. He must have been a beggar; he was naked except for a few rags and so wasted that there seemed to be no more than a film between me and his tiny skeleton. It was a moment before I realized that the little creatures running over him were rats and that they were gnawing his flesh. The carver had shown the tears in the skin, the rats' minute beady eyes, the teeth of the agonized man. Looking deeper into the open mouth, I saw even a tongue curling back convulsively.

What a horrible thing this delicate ivory was to me! How could anyone carve such hideousness so lovingly? How could another human being be found to possess it? And yet the little figure fascinated me; I had to turn it over in my hands until every detail had been taken in; then I shut it back into the cabinet and left the room tingling.

Tea was being laid out on small tables in Mr. Mellon's room; I went in and found my mother already there. I wanted to tell her about the little starving man, to take her into the drawing-room and show it to her quickly before the others returned; but something held me back. It was as if the sight were indecent and I did not dare to share it with her.

Soon we were all eating scones and guava jelly, sandwiches of several different sorts, and little cakes brightly decorated with silver balls, crystallized violets, rose petals, and little spikes of angelica. Mr. Mellon said to me: "You'll want to be with Phyllis again after tea; grown-ups aren't nearly so much fun, are they?"

I wriggled, trying to think of something to say that would not slight Phyllis, yet would show that I preferred the company of the grown-ups.

When tea was over, I managed somehow to get out of the room alone. Perhaps I put on the grave air that children assume when they want to be "excused." Once free, I waited in my room until I felt that Phyllis had settled to some amusement without me; then I stole downstairs again and let myself into another of the unknown rooms.

This one was a sort of study, or perhaps, because of its size, it might have been called the library, although books were not the most important part of its furnishing. A huge roll-top desk stood in the middle of the room and round this were spread all types of wild animal skins: lions, tigers, leopards, polar bears, brown bears. All their heads were mounted, with fierce glass eyes staring, and pink plaster tongues, rough as sandpaper, hungry for the taste of blood. These roaring mouths seemed just to have loomed up through the floor, so that I could imagine the flat skins gradually filling and taking shape after them, until I would be surrounded by living wild beasts.

"But how can Mr. Mellon wheel his chair in here with so many heads on the floor?" I thought; then I began to notice how unused every object in the room looked. The books were all shut away behind glass in the rather small bookcases. There were no magazines lying about. The ashtrays glistened. Even the blotting paper on the desk was almost without ink stains.

I sat down on the polar bear and had begun to ponder again on the peculiar deadness of Mr. Mellon's possessions, when the door opened softly and my mother looked in.

"Darling, don't prowl so," she said, coming across to me, still rather quietly; "they might not understand how fond you are of things. They might think you were being too inquisitive."

"I expect they think I'm playing with Phyllis," I answered.

"Well, anyhow, let's say good night and go upstairs now; it is nearly your bath-time."

"But Mummy, have you ever seen so many animals with stuffed heads in one room before?" I asked, to keep her for a few more minutes from taking me to bed.

Should I try to hold her interest by telling her about the little rat-eaten ivory beggar? But once more I put the idea from me.

When I was bathed and in pajamas and dressing-gown by the imitation logs that glowed so rosily on the hearth in my room, I said: "Mummy, who will have Mr. Mellon's snuffboxes when he dies?"

My mother frowned a little.

"We don't want to think about people dying."

"But I want to know," I persisted.

My mother seemed to be wondering whether to tell me something or not.

"Has Phyllis explained that Mr. Mellon is going to adopt her?" she asked, lifting her eyebrows.

"No, Phyllis hardly says anything at all." Then the full meaning of my mother's words came to me and I added excitedly, "Will *she* have the snuffboxes and everything then?"

"I expect so, darling, but it won't be for a long time, so don't talk about it or think about it anymore."

But once in bed, with the lights out, I thought of nothing else. It seemed to me the greatest waste that Phyllis should have anything more than the necessities of life; then my imagination was caught by the wonderful change in her fortunes; for, without having heard a word on the subject, I pictured Mrs. Slade and Phyllis in very difficult circumstances before they had come to Mr. Mellon.

I must have been asleep for some hours when I was woken by soft bumping sounds and the murmur of voices. The noises frightened me and even after I had recognized one of the voices as Mrs. Slade's, I felt anxious. What could be happening? There was another gentle bump. Mrs. Slade said: "There we are! Up at last!" and I heard a sort of comfortable grunt from Mr. Mellon.

I realized that she was wheeling him to bed. Could she have pulled him up the stairs alone? The stairs were shallow, but Mr. Mellon would be very heavy and awkward in his wheelchair. It did not seem possible for so small a woman. Perhaps the Indians had helped, and now she was only maneuvering some odd steps on the landing. They passed my door, still talking in undertones. Mrs. Slade's singsong voice was murmuring comforting things, as if she were talking to a child; Mr. Mellon just grunted, or replied in monosyllables.

Their intimacy surprised me, for even while riding in the bathchair together there had been some formality; and, before that, I had thought them quite cut off, in spite of Mr. Mellon's jolliness and Mrs. Slade's metallic smiles. Now they were like two old friends who no longer had to be very polite. It is true that Mrs. Slade still sounded dutiful for I remember thinking, "She hasn't finished yet!" but it was the dutifulness rather of an old nurse than of a professional hostess.

Long after all sound of them had ceased, I felt haunted. My mother's sudden giddiness in the train had fixed my mind on pain and illness, so that I had been made specially conscious of Mr. Mellon's useless legs; then I had crept into the drawing-room and seen that terrible starving man gnawed by rats. The fearful feelings awakened in me, together with what I thought of as the great ugliness and deadness of Mr. Mellon's surroundings, made me long for tomorrow when we would go back to London. Everybody had been kind, even Phyllis had meant no harm, and yet I wanted to draw away from all of them.

Only the jewelled boxes and the wonderful curry were truly happy memories.

II

I did not see Mr. Mellon again for about six years. During this time he had moved to a house of his own building, a few miles from his old villa. My mother was no longer alive, and I paid this second visit with my father on a hot summer's day.

The approach to the house had lately been planted with all kinds of ornamental shrubs and trees, ranging from green through yellow to pink and greyish blue. I found myself contrasting their gay feathery leaves with the dark glistening toughness of the monkey-puzzles and rhododendrons at the villa. The drive was so thickly planted that I could see nothing of the rest of the garden, nor did the house come into view until we were almost upon it.

It was long and low, only one story high, built of a light pinkish-fawn brick, with metal casements; apart from its squatness, the sort of house that any prosperous business man might build. When the door was opened by an English servant, I grew even more disappointed. What had happened to the Indians? Was nothing strange left? I began even to regret the ugliness which had disquieted me as a child. I would have found it stimulating now.

My eyes brightened when we were taken into the room where Mr. Mellon sat, for it was octagonal and the floor was an inlay of rubber in baby blue and pink and yellow; it reminded me of nothing so much as the top of some gigantic cake prettily decorated with soft icing.

As I walked forward to shake hands with Mr. Mellon, I felt its slight resilience.

Three sides of the octagon were of glass, and Mr. Mellon's chair stood so that he had the whole of the garden before him. While he was welcoming my father boisterously I stood looking out of the window in some wonder. It was a complete surprise to find the house built almost on the edge of a small ravine. The garden fell away at once in narrow terraces, held back by large flat rocks. More pointed rocks thrust out of the ground, and a path with stone steps wound in and out of these until it reached smooth lawns and a stream at the bottom. A small rustic bridge led to the other heavily wooded bank, where the ground sloped away more gently.

"Not bad, eh?" said Mr. Mellon, suddenly taking notice of my interest; "you'd never think we had anything like this here, would you? I must say the landscape gardener has made a good job of it—really a very clever chap."

My father went to the window to admire the scene, so that both our backs were turned when Mrs. Slade came in with Phyllis. I was the first to hear their footsteps. Mrs. Slade, like Mr. Mellon, seemed hardly to have changed at all, but Phyllis had grown into "a breasted woman," as I put it to myself. Her arms and legs were beefier than ever, and she was much taller than myself. But the full bosom gave me the greatest shock. I thought of her as the mother of fat twins. And was that *lipstick* on her mouth? Were girls who were not yet sixteen ever allowed to wear lipstick? Apart from this sudden redness, her face was much as I had remembered it. True the eyebrows had become even thicker, leaving no sign that the long fat caterpillar had ever been two smaller ones affectionately rubbing noses. The expression too had strengthened; the sullenness was now almost formidable; but I was quick to see again that it was misleading, that it arose from her eyebrows and from her quite unmalicious indifference to other people.

As soon as Mrs. Slade had greeted us with many smiles and bright remarks, and Phyllis had nodded her head and held out her thick hand, Mr. Mellon suggested that we should be shown the house and garden.

"Oh, yes," said Mrs. Slade to my father, "you've never been to this house before, have you? We like it so much now that it is finished at last. It is much more convenient than the old one; there are no stairs you see; Mr. Mellon can wheel himself wherever he likes without having to call anyone. All the floors are rubber to make things as quiet and comfortable as possible; I wouldn't have anything else now; they are so bright and so easy for the maids to keep clean."

Still chattering, Mrs. Slade led us into the garden first, to give us an appetite for tea, as she explained. She knew very little about the flowers and rock plants, but she kept drawing our attention to things by saying: "Aren't those pretty?" or "Mr. Mellon's very fond of that," or again, "I think this is rather rare, but there's nothing much to show for it, is there?"

My father was walking with Mrs. Slade and I with Phyllis, but since Phyllis said so little, I found myself listening chiefly to the other conversation. I heard Mrs. Slade tell my father about the number of men it had taken to move some of the rocks into position.

"But weren't they already here?" my father asked in surprise.

"Oh no, nothing was here—only the banks and the stream."

Mrs. Slade's voice was very high and fluting; she seemed to be amused by my father's simplicity on the subject of gardens.

"Of course," she went on, "this is not a very good garden for Mr. Mellon, most parts are so steep; but he took a great fancy to the site and *would* have the house here."

"Do you like school?" Phyllis suddenly asked, bringing me back to her with a jerk.

"Yes," I said hurriedly and quite untruthfully; "do you like yours?"

"It's all right; some of the mistresses are a bit dim. I needn't stay after next term though, if I don't want to. Mello says I can go to a finishing school abroad—I can choose where."

"So she calls him Mello," I thought; "and they're going to let her go to one of those schools where the girls just do what they like!" This further proof that Phyllis was being treated almost as a grown-up filled me with envy. How I longed to have some attention paid to my own private wishes!

We had now reached the bottom of the cliff garden; Mrs. Slade led us across the strip of lawn to the rustic bridge. I leaned on the gnarled balustrade and looked down into the water. It seemed quite shallow.

"Oh, do you know what Mr. Mellon has had done?" she asked, as if here were a topic, of especial interest to men, that had been almost overlooked; "he has had the stream stocked with trout. There are gratings underneath the water at the boundaries of Mr. Mellon's land so they can't swim away. We are hoping they will settle down and have lots of families."

I now caught a glimpse of a dark shape fanning the water with its silky tail. It held its position under the far bank; then darted away in a flash, leaving me to search for others. I thought of their bodies, soft as moleskin and with a sort of filmy shimmer over them, perhaps a little like the bloom on untouched plums. I knew very little of trout and probably confused them with my memories of lovely prune-colored carp.

But I was not allowed to gaze into the water for long; Mrs. Slade told me to cross over and look up at the terraced garden and the house.

"It is rather a good view," she said; "someone told Mr. Mellon it was like the hanging gardens of Babylon, but I don't know how he knew." She gave her little tinkling laugh.

Far away I could see Mr. Mellon in his great bow window; he looked like a captain on the bridge, I thought—a captain who had sat down and given up worrying about his ship.

After a moment he saw me too and waved. He was smiling broadly, as if I had done something to amuse him. I waved back; he took out his handkerchief and pretended to be a boy scout signalling. I wondered how long I ought to keep my eyes on him.

"We'd better not go any further now," Mrs. Slade was saying to me; "there is much more to show you, but it's rather a stiff climb back and you'll be wanting tea; perhaps your father will be able to bring you over again quite soon."

Crossing the stream rather reluctantly, I started to walk beside Phyllis again. In spite of my envy, I felt warmer towards her since our slight talk; we had never exchanged so many words before. I tried to begin another subject.

"Can you bathe in the stream?" I asked.

"Not now the trout are in it."

Her tone made me feel I ought never to have asked such a question.

"Mello says they mustn't be disturbed."

"Does Mr. Mellon ever fish for them?"

"Oh, no, he never goes down there."

"Who does fish then?"

"Nobody's allowed to until the fish have had babies; they've got to settle down."

"Well, who *will* be allowed to fish?" I persisted, rather hopelessly.

"Oh, I don't know, people who come, friends of Mello's, I suppose. He might let you, if you come next year."

Phyllis paused after this last kind remark; I realized suddenly that she was about to tell me a secret.

"As a matter of fact I *do* sometimes bathe, if you'd really like to know," she said, grandly; "there's a place where the trees lean over the water; I take off all my clothes and go in there—with nothing on," she added, to make sure that I understood her fully.

She was looking at me, trying, I think, to find out the effect of her words. Did she want me to be confused and red? Or was she hoping for a lively interest in her nakedness? Perhaps she only wanted me to admire her devil-may-care attitude towards Mr. Mellon, the carefully nursed trout, and the curiosity of the gardeners.

It was difficult to return the gaze of those sulky eyes. The thick red lips were set as though carved out of wood and painted. The whole face had the relentless quality of some Polynesian image, of African ju-ju. I felt that the only protection was for me to make my face as mask-like as her own. I tried to do this, and when she saw that I had nothing to say, she began speaking again herself.

"Of course, it's not much fun, you can't really swim, it's too shallow; I just splash about."

"Aren't you afraid of being seen?" I asked, as colorlessly and casually as possible.

"Oh, the trees make it quite private, but I wouldn't care much if one of the gardeners did come along. He wouldn't tell. Even if he did, Mello would only be a bit angry at first about his fish. I could get round him; he lets me do what I like."

This was spoken as we climbed the last few steps to the house. I was afraid that Mr. Mellon might hear through the open window, but Phyllis did not even trouble to lower her voice.

My father and Mrs. Slade had sunk down on one of the stone seats of the terrace, and when Mr. Mellon saw how hot my father was from the climb, he called out: "You'll want something instead of tea, I can guess!"

My father laughed and shook his head; but I think he was very pleased to see whiskey and soda appear with the tea tray.

As soon as everything had been brought and we were left to ourselves once more, I turned to Mrs. Slade and asked what had happened to the Indians.

A bright stare came into her eyes, she held her neck so stiffly that barely perceptible tremors ran up to her head.

"Oh, we had to get rid of them," she said, with careful smiling unconcern; "they were good at first, but we found that the cook was awfully extravagant—then we had trouble with one of the others."

There was a sudden gleam of fierceness in the soft brown eyes, as if some memory had stung her; the next moment it was drowned in smiles which asked me to believe that the Indians had been nothing but an amusing trivial episode. I wondered why the thought of the Indians should have excited Mrs. Slade; I guessed that she had been worsted in some scene with one of them, and that her Eurasian blood still felt the outrage. I had never seen her angry before; there had been a sort of quenched anxiety and a preoccupation with the details of the day, but her attitude to other people had seemed unchanging. In public at least she treated her daughter and Mr. Mellon with the same brittle sociability that she accorded to little-known guests. I remembered how as a child I had been disquieted both by her Eastern appearance and her mechanical smiles, and now a little of the uneasiness returned. I saw her as a woman who hid so much that when a spark of feeling did escape, it flashed with all the rage of the fire within. This rather sensational picture of her made me want to turn away from the long oily eyes, and the creamy cheeks that were too soft. I wanted the reassurance of my father's sleepy good-nature; even Mr. Mellon's embarrassing heartiness and Phyllis's silences were refreshing.

We sat long over tea—my father and Mr. Mellon had begun to talk about the past; and so little time was left for our inspection of the house. I felt disappointed as we hurried down a wide gallery, glancing into room after room almost without pausing.

I remember chiefly the variously patterned rubber floors, the monotonous primrose and chromium of every fitting in the kitchen, and the fantastic decoration of the bedroom which Mrs. Slade laughingly said should be mine, when I came to stay, since I was fond of "artistic" things.

The modern four-post bed had a pagoda roof with little wooden bells under the curling eaves; it was painted in dull blue, pale meat-red and yellow ochre, and all the moldings were picked out in gold. On the dusty mauve walls large dragons coiled towards each other ferociously; their claws and teeth and scales were also gilded. The chairs had elaborate lattice-work backs. Everything was so new, so mat, so European in spite of all Chinese hankerings, that I was reminded at once of some painted backcloth for *Aladdin* which I must have seen as a child; the furniture and walls had the same powdery distemper bloom, and the designs the same coarseness as the bold scene-painting.

Here, as in every other room, I looked for the little ivory carving of the starving man that had so horrified me on my first visit to Mr. Mellon; but it was nowhere to be seen; I doubt if it could have been found, even if I had not been so hurried; for everything was changed in this new house. Nearly all the floors, walls, and hangings were in the pale shades associated with babies, powder-puffs and sugared almonds, just as the shrubs in the drive had the light feathery leaves that I had never seen at the villa. There everything had been rigid and glistening and tough, here all was downy, almost scented—even the fantastic things were in pastel colors. But in spite of all changes, something of the villa's atmosphere remained. As we walked back to the octagon room to say good-bye to Mr. Mellon, I tried without success to define what spirit it was that still lingered under the soft prettiness.

Mr. Mellon was gazing out of his huge window and taking snuff; I saw him for a moment through the crack of the door before he was aware of us. His face was quite blank and empty, more than ever like a peeled trunk of wood. The welcoming smile that suddenly puckered all the features gave me a stab of discomfort, so that I wished I had not caught him as he was alone.

"Seen most things?" he called out with rowdy boyishness.

There was a flash of light as he put his jewelled box away.

"Pity you hadn't more time. All the more reason why you must come again."

He put his hand up to my shoulder to say good-bye; then, perhaps because he could no longer treat me as a child and hug me, he stretched out his other arm and caught Phyllis, who was moving towards the terrace. She allowed herself to be drawn to him with her usual seeming ill-grace; he encircled her waist, swung her gently on her feet and gave her stomach a loving pat or two.

"We'll want to see him again very soon, won't we, Phyl?" he said.

Phyllis grunted.

I was becoming more and more uncomfortable when the

opening of the door created just the slight diversion necessary for a not too unnatural escape. As soon as the heavy hand was taken from my shoulder, I turned, to see a new face hovering in the doorway.

"Yes, what is it, Bob?" asked Mrs. Slade, brightly.

"Oh, excuse me, madam, I came to see if Mr. Mellon was ready for his massage; it's his time."

"In a minute, Bob, in a minute," Mr. Mellon called from the other end of the room.

"Yes, sir," Bob said, and shut the door.

There had just been time for me to take note of Bob's curling fair hair, pink-brown coloring, and pursy cheeks. These last gave to his face the cast of an earlier century. His eyes seemed to stare a little, as though the lids were not quite full enough to cover them. He was near enough to my own age to make me conscious of his body under the white coat and dark trousers. It was as if I were asking myself: "Will I look anything like that in four or five years' time? Will I have thick legs, thick arms, deep chest? Will I look so well-fed and strong?"

He appeared to be a favorite of Mrs. Slade's, for she turned to me and said: "You've not seen Bob before, have you? He's a very nice boy; he first came only as a valet; then we had him trained as a masseur, and now, although he's only nineteen, he does everything for Mr. Mellon. It is an excellent arrangement."

Mrs. Slade might have been talking to herself, or to an intimate woman companion, instead of to a young boy; I realized that my appreciation of Bob would not satisfy. She wanted real enthusiasm.

Mr. Mellon held Phyllis till the last moment, then, as we were leaving the room, he released her with a playful spank, saying: "Off you go, Phylly, to wave good-bye."

But Phyllis did not run forward to escort us to the car; she ambled along, some way behind her mother.

My last picture was of her leaning against the open door, while, in the hall behind, Bob hurried back to the octagon room to begin his master's massage as soon as possible. Mrs. Slade was showering us with busy smiles and hand-wavings. The car started, we turned and were quickly lost in the feathery trees.

Once more Mr. Mellon, Mrs. Slade and Phyllis disappeared from my life; I did not even hear of them, or if I heard, I quickly forgot the slight mention of some unimportant detail. But when I was nineteen, a new friend at the art school asked me to his parents' home for Easter, and I accepted impulsively.

So one grey evening I found myself in a little Sussex village, standing on an unknown doorstep, feeling very reluctant about ringing the bell.

I need not have been anxious about my visit, for the house was comfortable and my friend's mother seemed really pleased to see me.

She had just returned from Egypt; it was clear that her husband and son had not listened to her experiences with nearly enough interest; she was delighted to be able to pour all her stories into a new ear, to have a listener who paid attention and seemed to want to know more.

When asking me to stay, my friend had said rather brutally: "My mother's an awful fool, you know." Perhaps she did show more capriciousness and willfulness than is quite acceptable; but in spite of these slight signs of childish whining or petty tyranny, we were soon on very good terms, even going off together to explore churches and a ruined abbey, while the others stayed at home.

When we came back from these expeditions, my friend would look at me as if he were wondering how I could have borne his mother's company for a whole morning, or afternoon. I imagined that the father also flashed glances at me sometimes; he seemed to be looking for signs of weariness or irritation, and because he could not find them, he was grateful, more polite than ever, yet somehow less friendly. It was as if he were relieved to see my easiness with his wife, but felt cut off from real communication with me just because of it. I had the vague notion, perhaps quite fanciful, that both father and son would have preferred it if I had appeared to enjoy myself less.

On the fourth or fifth day of my visit, John's mother announced at breakfast that there was to be a tea party in the afternoon. Extravagant groans came from John and his father, and once more they made me feel that I too ought to be pulling some sort of disapproving face instead of wearing the ridiculous smile of the perfect guest, pleased at any suggestion, however inane.

Both John and his father had threatened to go out; but as the time for the guests to arrive drew near, I noticed that they were looking trim and fresh, as though their faces had been dipped in cold water, their hair brushed vigorously and their ties straightened.

Tea for so many people had been laid on the long dining-room table, and I was placed next to my hostess.

"Come and sit near me and help me with the teacups," she had called in her soft screech; "John is no use, he only thinks about his own stomach."

At first I had little time to listen to conversation because I was walking round the table with cups of tea and plates of buttered toast and scones; but when I came back to my place, the fluting, warbling tones of the woman on the other side of John's mother caught my attention. There was the faintest suggestion of the electric guitar about her voice.

"But, my dear," she was saying, "you should have been there; it was fantastic, but quite fantastic! In all our eighteen months of house-hunting we've never come across anything like it. All the floors were rubber; I had the awful feeling that I was trapped in a gigantic lavatory; it was terrifying. One room was fitted up as a sort of teahouse in Chinatown, another was sexagonal, I think, if there is such a word, and it doesn't sound too rude; anyhow, all these six or more walls seemed to close in on one, and there was an enormous window which just screamed out for one of those horrible dentist's chairs."

At first her words floated in a void, but as the description grew, they seemed to link up with something in my own experience; I began to listen intently.

She was talking of the garden now.

"Darling, even the plants were weird, and there were *the* most enormous rocks—rather marvellous really, if they hadn't seemed so completely out of place. The money that must have been poured into that garden!"

Surely there could be no more doubt? It was Mr. Mellon's house and garden that were being so cruelly described. I realized for the first time that, since we were so close to the border, Mr. Mellon's place in Kent could only be five or six miles away at the most. Feeling angry with this unknown woman for laughing at tastes that I myself had always thought strange, I decided to go over to see Mr. Mellon as soon as possible; then it came back to me with a shock that she had been talking of a house that was to let or for sale, an empty house, whose key, decorated with a large label, must hang on one of the local house-agent's hooks.

Where had Mr. Mellon gone? Was he at this moment building another house somewhere else? I suddenly wanted to know all that had happened since I last saw him.

While the woman was describing the house and garden, John's mother had not spoken, but her eyes had danced. Now the words came pouring out.

"But Dulcie, didn't you know? Didn't anyone tell you about that house?"

"Oh no, *do* tell me, I haven't heard a word. Is it haunted by some horribly unclean spirit? Or has *the* most atrocious murder been committed there? I can believe anything, *anything*."

"No, it wasn't a murder, but the place is quite possibly haunted by now," said John's mother with satisfaction, her eyes dancing more than ever. A faint flush had come into her cheeks.

She was in no hurry to reach the climax of her story; she seemed to wish to savor both her own excitement and the suspense of her audience.

"Perhaps you wouldn't have heard of it," she mused; "perhaps it *is* rather a local tragedy."

"Darling, stop maundering! I'm mad to know what happened."

"Well, you remember the rock garden?"

"Yes."

"And the path leading down to the stream?"

"Yes, yes, pet, don't be so ponderous, I remember it all perfectly."

"Well, one day the housekeeper ran down the path, jumped into the stream and drowned herself."

The words seemed to tumble over each other, as if John's mother had suddenly grown tired of trying to unfold her story skillfully. For a moment I could not grasp their full meaning, then the exclamation: "It's Mrs. Slade, she means Mrs. Slade!" kept ringing in my head like some battle cry or line from a famous poem.

"But why did she drown herself?" the woman was asking, "we must know *everything*."

John's mother beamed gratefully.

"Of course I didn't know them myself, but I've heard little bits from people who did; they've all said that it was the queerest household. The man was an invalid. He seems to have been very good indeed to this housekeeper, who was half-Japanese or something of that sort; he had even adopted her daughter."

The woman called Dulcie raised her bald-looking eyebrows.

"Yes, I thought that rather an interesting point, too," said John's mother, "but anyhow, when this daughter suddenly eloped with the chauffeur, the mother was so upset that she just flung herself into the stream; and I'm told it's only quite shallow. One of the gardeners found her later."

Something had mounted from my stomach to my heart, to my head. Perhaps I had turned very red. I looked at my hostess's bright chirpy smile and understood why her son thought her so silly. Now that she had told her story she was like a bird waiting for crumbs. Her head was cocked a little to one side; she seemed to be contemplating her own winsomeness, to be modestly disclaiming any credit for the suicide which had interested us so much.

Through the surge and tingle in my head, I found myself asking her if she was sure that the daughter had run away with a chauffeur.

"Someone like that," she said, a little piqued to have her story questioned; "actually, now you ask me, I believe I did hear later that he was more the personal servant of the old man, the sort of valet-nurse."

"Was he called Bob?" I asked, unable to stop myself.

"How should I know?"

John's mother was staring at me curiously. She was about to ask if I knew the family. I picked up a plate of little cakes and started to pass them round the table. When the question came, I pretended not to hear but I answered it under my breath, to myself, "Yes, I knew them, but not very well. She wasn't half-Japanese, she was half-Javanese—I expect it was Bob who ran away with Phyllis; I only saw him once for a moment, but I can imagine it so easily with him. It must have been Bob."

People were already beginning to leave the table, to wander

into the other room or talk in groups near the windows. I decided to put down my cakes on a side table and escape into the hall.

I was out, and nobody had called my name or appeared to notice me. I could hear the chatter and smell the cigarette smoke creeping under the door. It was still quite light outside; I opened the front door and let myself into the garden.

I walked behind hedges until I came to the old stables; there I found John's bicycle and began to pump the tires. I tried the lamp and saw that the battery was fairly new. That was good. I would need it.

By great good fortune I found my way without a mistake to the village nearest Mr. Mellon's house; after that my progress was more difficult. But at last someone directed me down the right lane; I came upon his drive, and had almost passed it before something told me to look again. Yes, that was the drive; the trees and bushes were bigger, but I could recognize them.

It was dusk now; objects were beginning to lose their color and sink into each other, like lead soldiers melting on the nursery fire. I saw an orange square of light somewhere through the trees and wondered if a caretaker lived there. I was suddenly afraid of being discovered in Mr. Mellon's grounds. What explanation of my prowling could I give? I remembered my mother saying: "Darling, don't prowl so."

Pushing my bicycle into the shrubs, I walked swiftly down the drive till I came to the point where it turned and one saw the long squat house. I stood still, shocked by the blankness of the windows; they were oblong eyes over which a terrible fungus of nothingness was growing. And the porch was a great black mouth, the jaws of the whale that swallowed Jonah, the gates of Hell in an ancient wall-painting. I could not walk into the yawning cadaverous blackness under that plain brick arch; I could not even look through those neat metal casements, now that they had been turned into horrible eyes filmed with cataract. I stood back from the house, staring through its walls, picturing Phyllis and Bob as they prepared for flight. Phyllis would be packing everything of value into a small soft suitcase, while Bob waited rather desperately by the door. She would put in all the jewels and trinkets Mr. Mellon had ever given her. She would be methodical, heavy, placid; but Bob would be pulling at his collar and jerking down his sleeves. His large eyes would roll from her to the door and back again. She would take no notice of his longing to be off, until the last object had been fitted in.

Because I knew nothing of them as they were today, because I did not even know for certain that it was Bob who had gone with Phyllis, my picture seemed squalid and meaningless and dead. It was the counterfeit of a counterfeit. The bare fact that Phyllis had run away with a lover was in itself papery and unreal. I had been given no reason, only told that it was so; therefore my mind kept teasing and plucking at ideas.

At last I made myself turn from them and from the house; I would strain no more after reasons, just let thoughts float through my head, while I wandered in the garden.

It was a relief to plunge into the bushes. Somehow they were not fearful, as they might well have been at nightfall; they seemed to offer warmth, a protection against the balefulness of the house. I pushed and threaded my way blindly, till I came out on a ridge of the ravine, some way from the house. To the left I could see the great window of the octagon room gleaming palely against the sky. There was no proper path here, only a sort of gardener's track along the ridge. I walked to the end, then began climbing down from terrace to terrace, avoiding the plants by standing on the rocks. The garden was still being tended; I could see patches of softly crumbled, weedless earth. Birds were scudding across the sky, calling forlornly, as though the coming of night were some sort of catastrophe for them. When I reached the foot of the ravine, I was hot and tired; sweat had begun to sting in the scratches I had received from the shrubs and trees. I sat down on a rock enjoying the cold moistness that was already coming from it. The stream flowed near me, industriously, secretly, like some man who, thinking he is alone, sings and mutters and swears at his work.

I sat listening for some moments, then stood up and walked towards the bridge. From the other bank I looked up the tortuous path. All at once I thought of Mrs. Slade as she must have been when she ran down to drown herself. I saw her crying, crying, stumbling over the artfully uneven stone steps, chattering madly all the time. Nothing could stop her; if she fell, she was on her feet again in a moment, stockings torn, knees bleeding. She was like a wingless bat, wrapped round in a little whirlwind. Her greying hair flared out in a tangle wilder than Beethoven's; and her eyes had grown into pools of boiling tar. They were still growing; suddenly I was caught up in them, so that I plunged into the stream with her and heard them sizzle as we struck the water. . . .

I was standing now on the very brink of the stream looking straight down into the black water. The night wind ruffled the surface into little fish scales. One of the birds kept up its perplexed lost flying and calling. Darkness was gathering in the branches of the trees behind me, thickening under the rocks, turning them into grotesques and derelicts standing in puddles of ink. One was a man with an elephant's trunk which he clutched to himself desperately. Another had huge monkey ears; all the rest of him had sunk into a belly like a giant's teapot. The biggest was an ancient pugilist who had given up hope and died at last by the side of the road. He was a vast lump of sagging muscles and despair.

High up above them the dark bow of Mr. Mellon's window jutted out. I thought of him sitting there, taking snuff, staring blankly, waiting for Bob or Phyllis or Mrs. Slade to come. I saw him as a great sick bird, a turkey wrapped in flannel. How long was it before he realized that he had been deserted by all three of them? Did he watch the gardeners bringing the body up the twisting path? Where was he now? Had he found other people to look after him?

Then I remembered how fond he was of the stream, how he had stocked it with trout and told Phyllis not to bathe there.

And all the way up the cliff, back to my bicycle in the drive, I kept wondering if the fish had been very disturbed when Mrs. Slade plunged in and drowned herself.

Leaves from a Young Person's Notebook

I am thinking of that time when I spent three or four months in a nursing home on the East Coast. My room was on the third floor, with a bow window in the roof. It looked straight out to sea. When the bitter February wind blew, this jutting window shook and swayed a little. My bed was pulled right up to the glass, so I was surrounded on nearly three sides by sky and water. Down below me were some shiny-leaved bushes and part of the yellow pebbled drive; beyond stretched the blue-black tarmac of the esplanade along the cliff's edge. The isolated cast-iron lamp-posts and seats on this esplanade were piercingly sad. In my curious state of health, it was very easy for me to see them as lonely, tortured creatures rooted and anchored just out of shouting distance of one another. The loneliness of that never-ending expanse of leathery sea was horribly accentuated by those florid shapes in brittle cast iron.

Although it terrified me, I gloated on the emptiness, the negation of everything living. The suck and mumble of the waves on the beach, licking and slithering and eating, filled me with a wry, fearful pleasure. I would make words up to their everlastingly industrious, hopeless music. My words were not worthy of the music, but I would repeat them over and over again until I had lulled myself into a kind of trance. I would say, "Across the sullen rocks and slime I feel the wasting of all time," or "Meanwhile let's pass the whiskey round, with sucking, talking, human sound; unlike that rushing of the sea, which beats outside eternally." I would say these things a hundred or a thousand times, until the world and my surroundings had dissolved and I was alone in a mist, borne up on some grey woolly substance like brains, or the marrow from an ox bone.

Every morning at the same time, just after Sister Howe had brought up my breakfast, a small girl would go past with her mother, or nurse, and another child. This girl always looked up to my window, and when she saw me, propped up with several pillows, right in the corner of the window, she would turn to the woman and the other child and say something which usually made the other smile or laugh. I took it that she was being funny at my expense, for her white grinning face with its narrowed eyes seemed to wear a rather malicious expression.

After her witticism to the others, the little girl would fling another glance up at me, to make certain I was looking, then, rushing to the railings at the cliff's edge, she would bang her gloved hand along them, or self-consciously bounce her rubber ball in a way that seemed to express very clearly her pose of careless insolence and hard gaiety. It was as if she were saying, "Here am I, dancing about and bouncing my ball so beautifully and deftly, and you and all the other dull things on the earth don't mean anything at all. All that means anything is me, being clever with my ball and laughing."

And while she performed, she would sing a special yodeling song for me. She would gargle in her throat, then shoot up to the highest treble where, by rocking between two notes, she created a grotesque and extraordinary liquid tremolo. After this she would sink right down again and gurgle in her boots, making the noises of a large animal, an elephant or a hippopotamus in pain.

During her song she would look back at me over her shoulder and widen her mouth or roll her eyes; and before she was too far along the esplanade for me to be able to see, she would usually finish her act with the most frightening of gargoyle grimaces and a strange flutter of the hands which was not meant as a wave to me but rather as a final display of elegance.

The woman seemed to take very little notice of this girl. She generally hurried along holding the other child's hand and allowing this one to scamper about and behave as preposterously as she liked.

I was glad that she did not try to repress the small girl, for her performance was very strange and amusing and stimulating. I watched all her movements with great attention and tried not to show any emotion on my face; but sometimes I could not help smiling or looking self-conscious, and if the little girl was able to notice this through the glass, she would shout with laughter and bounce up and down in one place, like a pneumatic road-drill. To have made some visible impression on me seemed to give her the greatest delight, and she at once wanted to express the friendly derision in which she held me, because I had taken notice of her.

I always watched until this devil of a little girl had quite disappeared; then, no matter how cold it was, if the day was sunny, I would collect book, paper, pen and notebook and wait for Sister to take me up on to the roof. There she would settle me in the sunniest corner with a screen tied to the back of the deck chair to keep off some of the wind. She would spread an eiderdown over me, bring me a tray with tea and biscuits on it, then leave me till lunchtime.

At first I would just lie with my eyes shut, the sun on my face, and my body shivering under the eiderdown; then gradually as my skin grew accustomed to the iron touch of the wind from the sea I would throw back the eiderdown and lie only in my striped pajamas. I would next abandon the jacket of these and occasionally even the trousers; so that sometimes in mid-February and March I lay on a roof in Thanet naked.

It was a pleasure for me to watch my body burning to a tawny color and the hairs on it bleaching till they all shone with a brassy glint. It compensated me slightly for it at least gave me the appearance of good health.

Sometimes it grew so hot in my sheltered corner that I sweated. I would watch all the diamond beads forming in the shallow cross between my chest muscles; then when a sudden gust of wind caught them, I would see them dashed flat against my body, smeared and scattered. The ice of the wind suddenly striking my sweaty body made curious thrills of pleasure-pain, fear and exaltation pass through me. I thought of throwing myself from the roof and allowing the wind to carry me along, until I caught in the branches of a tree, where I would hang crucified, with my arms outstretched, until my pajamas rotted to tatters and rags, and my bones were cleaned of all flesh by the birds. I thought of them pecking out my eyes and enjoying tremendously these delicious morsels of glutinous hazel jelly. I wondered if a large bird would succeed in tearing out my tongue whole, or whether an army of tiny birds would just peck delicately at the tip and gradually work downwards until they reached the roots.

When I grew tired of lying idle, I turned from these fantasies and went on with the drawing I was doing at the moment. One of these pen drawings was nothing but faces outside a stage door. I had written "Stage Door" on the glass panel, so that no one could mistake it. There was a pimp's face, very young and jaunty and common-looking, a bearded hermaphrodite face, rather lugubrious and distinguished, a smart woman's face with hair piled up and curling Greek lips, and one of those faces which are often associated with the early Russian Ballet; the sort that has dark straight hair parted in the middle, purple brown circles under the eyes and a pouting prude's mouth sinking down at the corners into dissatisfaction and disillusion.

I don't know why I drew any of these faces; they were none of them types that I cared for or knew anything about. They just seemed to evolve themselves as I scratched the pen over the paper. Their faces were shown quite flat, like cardboard cutouts, and each one had some particular property or distinguishing mark attached to it. The artistic lady had megaphones attached to, and streaming from, the pupils of her blind eyes, the pimp had a little black thing like a lizard wriggling out of his mouth, and the smart woman had my name cruelly tattooed on her bosom and worked time and time again into the embroidery of her dress.

Once Sister had caught sight of this drawing as she bent over me with a tray, and she'd said, "Good heavens, my dear boy, what a queer drawing! Do you think you ought to frighten yourself like that—or anyone else either?"

And although she said this lightly and breezily as a good nurse should, I became so nervous that without knowing quite what I did, I snatched up a chocolate from the box my aunt had sent me, and thrust it roughly into her astonished mouth. My hand was shaking and the chocolate banged on her teeth and lips, but I achieved what I had blindly intended. It silenced her.

I brooded on this scene after she left me and I decided always to carry a box of chocolates with me, so that I could shove them hastily into the mouths of all who were about to hurt and terify me by their remarks. If the chocolates were large enough they would successfully act as temporary gags, and in extreme cases, if they were thrust with violence, they might even lodge in the throat and choke.

After lying still all day, I was allowed to dress and go down to tea in the sun-room, where I would meet any of the other patients who happened to be up.

One day I found a person of my own age there. In spite of the lard-colored hair, through which could be seen his scalp, my heart gave a leap of pleasure, for I had spoken only to older people for a whole month.

I stared at him quite openly while I ate my scone, and waited for him to say something to me across the room, but although I caught him furtively eyeing me several times, nothing happened. I became so exasperated by his obstinacy, and my own, that I was about to jump up and kick the panels of the door as I left the room, when Sister saved the situation by coming in just at that moment and suggesting that I might like to talk to Mr. Johnston before going back to bed. She led me up to him and I sat down in the basket-chair at his side. We were quickly telling each other our troubles. First he told me his, which were, I thought, on the whole unreal and hypochondriacal; then I poured mine out in a torrent. I was very conscious of the lack of restraint in all I said, but I hoped that for once this would not matter. Perhaps this could be done, I felt, in the sun-room of a nursing home to another patient who was also wishing to unburden himself.

But I was wrong. Johnston only wanted to tell me how unhappy he'd been at Cambridge, how far he liked to walk each day, and what sort of salad he had for breakfast—of all meals. He didn't want to hear about my difficulties.

And when I realized this, I made up silly stories to frighten and disgust him. I told him of pathetic drunken parties which had never been. I described how friends had taken off their trousers and danced in the street at midnight in their shirttails, pretending they were highlanders at a Caledonian ball. I told him that I had stirred a hundred aspirin tablets into a saucepan of Heinz tomato soup in an attempt to kill myself.

Here I made my eyes go rather wild and staring, then fixed them on Johnston. I saw that he was beginning to be uneasy. I was pleased that at last he was showing some feeling.

Suddenly he jumped up, saying that he was going to his room to fetch a book. I was left alone. I wondered what to do. I opened the narrow French window into the garden and stepped on to the gravel path. Nobody was about. I thought I would go for a walk. If I could manage it, I would get to the town. I started out along the deserted esplanade, with the sea washing and whining below me at the foot of the cliffs.

Twice I had to sit down on the freezing public seats, but at last I reached a narrow pathway which cut through to the center of the town.

I stood on a corner where there were two inns close together. I could hear voices, some fitful halfhearted piano music, dogs yapping and barking.

Suddenly I began to chant out loud, "Soft slow dogs that sit upon the parlor floor, watching the feet that wander here and there. Deep hard voice, crusted with smells of all humanity. Eyes searching, forever searching for that long past lover, whose breath shall never warm you more."

It didn't seem to mean much; it was slushy; but the words pleased me, as rigmaroles do.

I thought that the right and proper thing for someone else to do would be to go into one of the pubs and drink some gin for his great unhappiness. Everything seemed to point in that direction; and I wondered why the idea seemed so very unattractive to me. It appeared as a fault in me that I did not wish to drink anything at this particular black moment.

Then, even as I thought so coldly and sensibly, an upsurging mad desire swept over me to displease, to pain myself, to draw unfriendly eyes to my troubled state. I went up to the nearest inn and pushed open one of the doors. There were only a few men in this bar and I was aware of their eyes as I crossed the room rather unsteadily. The more I tried to walk evenly, the more I lurched; and they, who were not to know my state of health, imagined, I suppose, that I had already had a fair amount to drink, for they looked at me with that sort of tolerance which is so insulting.

I ordered some gin and lime juice and drank it almost at once to cover my confusion; then I had another and another and felt more able to look at the other men and perhaps even talk to them. But they still seemed to treat me with a wary curiosity, which made me imagine that there was something startling and distraught about my appearance. As the drink began to work on me I acted up to this belief more and more. I drummed on the bar with my fingers and rolled my eyes. I muttered and hummed under my breath, jerking my head this way and that suddenly, for no apparent reason. But I did not feel drunk. My sadness was growing instead of melting away. And this incapacity to throw off my sadness terrified me.

After my sixth gin I jumped up convulsively. Something seemed to be rising up inside me to stifle me. I ran across the room and threw myself against the door. Someone called out after me, "Steady on; take it easy." And that enraged me, because it was just what I could not do.

I stumbled across the inn-yard and stood in the lavatory with my head and my forearms pressed against the wall. I retched. How chastened and glorious I felt for a moment afterwards! I raised my eyes and saw written on the wall quite high up and in rough, clear capitals, GOD = GOOD = STRENGTH = POWER = LOVE. Close to it was a picture of a naked lady with a great deal of fuzzy hair scribbled on her. I put up my hand and traced with my little finger the clumsy capital letters; then, still keeping my finger on POWER, I stretched across and planted my thumb on the pencilled hair in the middle of the lady. My fingers were all splayed out and I could feel the pleasant stretch of the tendons and muscles. I heard the drip and the gush of the water down the stone wall, and because of my curious arched position over that gush of water, I began to imagine that I was a rustic bridge over a cascade in someone's ornamental water garden. And the idea was so funny, and the joining together of God's Power and the fuzzy lady's hair by my outstretched fingers was so incongruous that I felt I had to laugh. I made great booming noises which were not my real laughter. They came from my belly; I could feel it going in and out under my belt. I liked the feeling when it came back and hit the tight belt.

When I had recovered, I felt in my pocket for my pencil. I wanted to give the lady prettier, more decorative, less realisitic teats. I also wanted to regularize and classicize her features. There seemed to be altogether too much soft blowsiness about her.

I set to work and had soon turned the fuzzy lady into a peculiar sort of Russian icon madonna. She had a long thin nose, almond eyes and the most wonderful embroidered filigree pattern round each nipple. She really looked like a sacred image, I thought. The nakedness made her even more holy. I felt that I ought to offer up at least one prayer to her. So I knelt down in that dirty place and prayed.

When I got up I wanted to touch something with the tip of my tongue. I wanted to touch the creamy distemper on the wall above the cascade, then I wanted to touch the polished brass water pipe.

I went out with the chalky dry taste of the distemper mixed in my mouth with the acid tang of the brass.

I began to walk back towards the nursing home. I was feeling happier now, as if nothing mattered, and as if I had hardly any importance, even for myself. This feeling was freeing and lightening. All sense of strain had left me. I was nothing, floating in a larger mass of nothing.

But the waves beating on the cliffs and the iron lampposts in their glaring but weak pools of light brought back all my true misery, and I gave up even trying to walk properly. I stumbled along, lurching from side to side and sometimes lying on the pavement for a moment to recover myself.

Once a man helped me up and dusted me down and I shouted, "Don't dare to smack me! It's none of your business." I said it so angrily that he left me alone at once, after apologizing for being kind.

At last I got to the nursing home and let myself in again by the French window. It was late and no one was in the sun-room; I hoped to be able to creep up the stairs without being discovered; but Matron came out of her room just as I was at the top of the first flight. She looked up at me with a worried helpless look and said, "Oh, you shouldn't go out like this, without telling anyone! It's not right. How can you expect to get well if you won't make any effort? It's not fair to treat us like this, and it's ruining your chances."

Because she spoke vehemently and sincerely, I hated her at once. I scowled as harshly as I could, then went on up the stairs, gripping the banisters tightly.

In my room I stood against the wall, under the light. I leaned against the wall, doing nothing, allowing the drumming in my head to rise, listening through it to the shut-out smudged noise of the sea.

Sister Howe came in without knocking. She had been sent by Matron. There was a sharp feeling of disapproval and efficiency about her. She said, "You're a bad lad to go out like that! You must get into bed at once; it's long after your time. If you don't take proper care, you'll make yourself so much worse; and that's not what you're here for, now, is it?" And because I still looked quite blank, she gave me a helpful bustling smile and took hold of my shoulder as if to help me out of my jacket.

I let her lead me to a chair, and then I let her ease the jacket off my shoulders. All this time I just looked at her smooth marshmallow face and wondered what it was for, what it meant.

And suddenly I couldn't understand what anything was for. The room seemed a riddle, the moaning of the sea, myself, my nose, my hair, my teeth, and the gin taste on my breath.

I was so frightened by this un-understanding that I leaped up and ran to the thick velveteen curtains. I tried to climb up them like a cat. I hid myself in the folds and clung to the cloth above my head. I was crying now, letting the tears splash down my face and shoot out on to the midnight-green velvet, where they sparkled for a second, like quicksilver, before soaking into the darkness and disappearing forever.

And then Sister Howe was holding me tight, pressing me hard against her football bosom. It was like a football because of her stiff, firm uniform and her starched apron top, and because her breasts were compressed and squashed flat by my chest. I could feel the bones behind her breasts. I liked the hardness of her bones which seemed to bite down into my own bones to support me in a scaffolding.

I was quite content to let her hug me like a grizzly bear, and I let her say, "Poor boy, you're all unstrung; you're just all to bits."

And as she squeezed the breath out of me and soothed me, I began sentences which always stopped in the middle with a jerk, because there was no ending. I listened to the swamped smudging rush of the sea, and I thought that people should do dirty acts and wallow in their shame and sorrow and sink down in abasement, so that all the dirt in them could rise up to the top like scum. I thought that all shameful things lost their indecency when the earth began to quake, the fire to rage, the bombs to fall. It was the same now, when I was a baby kangaroo in Sister Howe's pouch. Nothing was disgusting, not even the tears; although I could not help likening their flow to the hot meaty rush of a nosebleed.

But when all this had been washed clean out of me by the tears, and I felt thrown up and abandoned on some desert-island shore, alive but exhausted, I wondered why Sister Howe was holding me and why I should allow it.

And I quietly went away from her and lay down flat on the bed and crossed my arms and shut my eyes and said nothing.

The tears were salt, I idly thought—and so was the wonderful, booming, wriggling skin of the sea.

The Earth's Crust

When I first went to an art school, it was decided that I should live with my eldest brother in Adam Street, off Portman Square. His two rooms were at the top of the little Georgian house and my bedroom was on the ground floor. Between us we had a woman with a tightly held mouth and contemptuous eyes, and a curate viscount who ran up the stairs and usually carried a music case stuffed with papers. In the basement lived the owner of the house and her children. She had a harsh dry cough which tickled the back of my throat whenever I heard it.

In houses where people live behind closed doors, unknown to one another, some emanation broods in the passages and especially on the stairs. Perhaps it is just vague, diffused suspicion. This house had it in particular. The embittered woman, going to the bathroom with her sponge, moved almost furtively, as if afraid of eyes staring down from the top landing; and the curate, as he bustled past me with his papers, seemed to be escaping from someone or something. Even the landlady appeared to be affected by the atmosphere. She climbed up from her basement with a look of deep anxiety and secretiveness on her face. One had the impression that she had something to hide which gave her a great deal of trouble. Yet it was all illusion, for she was a conscientious woman who kept good rooms and gave excellent breakfasts.

These were brought to our rooms on trays. I would have mine before I bathed or dressed. I usually began with iced grapefruit already sugared, then went on to scrambled eggs, toast, coffee and marmalade. And all the time I would be reading a book with the lamp on, because my old room had only one window and was dark. Although it was dark, it could have been a charming room, for it still possessed its high wainscot and old L-shaped hinges on the door; but the landlady's stained oak Cromwellian furniture and cretonne curtains had almost completely overlaid its original character.

At the last moment I would run out of the house to catch my bus, without even going upstairs to see my brother. The art school that had been chosen for me was in the southeastern suburbs. It had been chosen by my aunt, because she had once bought a print from the man who taught wood engraving there. The journey out to it was long. The bus crossed the river, passed under thundering Vauxhall railway bridge and came to Kennington, where the blackened acanthus railings of the Regency church were covered with yellow and red placards, asking for money. I would be sitting on top of the bus, right in front in order to see everything. On the other side of the road was a park with screaming children standing in the paddling pond and splashing one another. The girls had their dresses bunched up above their thighs or tucked into their bloomers. Little boys, clad only in braces and trousers, ran amok, shooting off water pistols. Girls screamed more piercingly than birds, lolled out their tongues and rolled their eyes like epileptics. There was madness in the air.

When the children had been left behind, my eyes turned to the small factory, which advertised for women to work sewing machines.

I pictured the sweatshops; the scores of pedalling feet, the darting needles, snapping thread. I saw the girls' bent heads, their hair cascading down. I smelled the sweat, the strain, the powder, the knitting, and the buns in paper bags.

Then there were the butchers' shops with pink lamps on all day to make the meat look rosy and good. I saw pigs' faces with bunches of parsley in the scalded mouths.

Along the pavements thronged the people, like bottles walking; their heads as inexpressive as round stoppers. What if some god or giant should bend down and take several of the stoppers out? I thought. Inside there would be black churning depths like bile, or bitter medicine.

So many of the people still carried sleep in their faces. Grey skin, blear eyes, rough hair seemed to show that they had been forced from their beds and were only waiting for the day's work to be done, when they would throw themselves down again.

The lunatic asylum at Peckham, so remote in its old building behind high walls, cut off from trams and buses and crowds and posters, was dreaming of another age and time. I peopled it with lunatics who knew that they were great historic figures. Queen Victoria was there with a tray of silver paper medals, which she graciously bestowed on the nurses and doctors who pleased her. Napoleon brooded; and Joan of Arc smiled in ecstasy as the flames licked up.

I always hoped to see a face appear at one of the top windows—just the glimpse of a face looking up at the clouds; but there was no sign of life.

I next tried to penetrate the walls of a great warehouse. There was furniture that had been stored there for fifty years, I told myself. Mice ran between the legs of the tables and nibbled at the doors of the huge sideboards, misled by a ghostly smell of cheese and biscuits. Moths silently munched through green baize and damask wool. The tickless clocks kept watch. The chairs held out their arms. The rolled Turkey carpets were like giant cocoons, waiting to burst open. Everything had life, but it was muffled, furtive, secret.

The "Marquis of Granby" was my stop. I would get off the bus, cross the road and enter a large building which had dusty evergreen bushes round the door. The main part was devoted to the training of school teachers, so I would run down a long, dark passage till I reached the stairs which led to the art school. I would climb up as quietly as possible, for I was usually late, get my drawing-board and pencil, and glide silently into the antique room. Students already astride their "donkeys" would glance up at me, then down again. They seemed both curious and uninterested. I was too new to have any friends. I thought that they would talk *about* me, but not *to* me. Sometimes there were only two or three girls in the room, and then they would talk about men, as if I were just another plaster cast. I was left to get down on my paper something that looked a little like the Hermes of Praxiteles.

The master, when he appeared, would perhaps say: "This is just fun—you are amusing yourself." He would say it mildly, even tolerantly, but my cheeks would tingle, and I would crouch over my drawing, as if to conceal and protect it. I had not yet learned to enjoy an art school. I would long for the end of the morning.

At lunchtime most of the students ran down to the refectory on the ground floor and had a large lunch with the schoolteachers-to-be, but I had found a shop which sold crisp rolls and butter and slices of good liver sausage. Further down the street a baker kept strange fig biscuits that I liked. With this food I used to walk down a side street of early Victorian houses—one with plaster eagles on each side of the door—until I came to a later, stone church that blocked the end. Plane trees and small patches of grass surrounded it. I had discovered that if I sat on the steps of the great west door, which was never opened, I could be in the sun and yet hidden from the road. In front of me was a trim garden and a house. I would crunch my roll and biscuits as I gazed at the beds of tortoise-shell wallflowers or at the railway line beyond, and for a few moments would feel happy and content; even the curiously rude Victorian contractor's gargoyle nearest to me would add to my pleasure. But then the isolated feeling and the useless feeling and the imprisoned feeling would sweep back over me and I would know that I was alone on a stone step with no idea of how my life was to be lived.

One day, while I was sitting there, a youngish man in a dog-collar came hurrying round the north buttress, which partly hid me. He opened the garden gate, and when he turned to latch it again he saw me. I was afraid that he was going to turn me out and reprimand me for irreverence, but instead he smiled as if quite used to seeing me there and as if he approved. He said that he had often noticed me from the vicarage windows and he was glad that I enjoyed the peace and quiet and the sun; then, just when he seemed about to lean on the gate and talk, his manner changed. He had evidently remembered that he had no time to spare. With one more smile he turned and walked quickly towards the house.

I was left with an empty feeling, as though something nice had been taken away from me capriciously. He had so obviously wished me well; I began to wonder if some shyness or stiffness in me had driven him away. I was filled with regret. He might have been a friend instead of a stranger. I could hear the clanging trains in the New Cross high street, and the dust and filth seemed to be trying to invade my retreat. I got up to go back to the school.

I walked a different way, along a footpath between fences, to delay my return for as long as possible. The class that afternoon was "book illustration," and the master who taught was so nervous that he either praised extravagantly or spat out some demolishing remark and then glided away, seemingly dismayed by his own excessiveness.

I sat on a high stool, trying to design a frontispiece for *The Way of All Flesh,* which I had chosen as my book; but it seemed hopeless. No ideas took form, and the extraordinary perversity of my materials conquered me. No one was there to help me technically or to give me the confidence which would have made my thoughts run clear. I toyed with my brushes and paints and longed for the end of the afternoon.

At last it came and I was free to get away from the school. I left the other students laughing and shouting and washing their brushes in the lavatory basins. I seemed to have no connection with them. They belonged to another world. I ran down the tunnel-like passages and let myself out into the open air.

I was filled with a sort of exultation. What should I do? Should I wander in the drab streets around me? Past the eel shop, where the writhing black things were slowly dying on zinc trays; there was a bicycle shop which blared music against the noise of the trams, and beyond that was a junk shop where I had noticed some little prints in old oval frames. They were sepia-colored by Bartolozzi, the sort I had read about. I went to bargain with the man, who turned out to be likeable and understanding, but he would not sell me the smallest one for five shillings—he wanted eight. We talked a little and I turned the pictures over and saw that one had the charming old framemaker's label still on it. I wanted that one particularly, but it was even more expensive. The man was busy. There was no place for me. I said good-bye and walked away, unsatisfied.

I walked in the direction of "home." I would catch a bus later, when I was tired. I stared at the people's faces, looking for something that I had known a long time ago or had perhaps dreamed about. But the faces told me nothing; they were set and oblivious, like slices of pallid cheese wrapped in grey muslin. So many people, yet nobody for me.

I jumped on to a bus and let the scene merge and blur and melt. The motion soothed me into a waking sleep. I sailed high above noise and dirt and danger.

At Park Lane I got off and walked into the park. There were lovers there lying in the grass, and I thought how flimsy they looked, like trash washed up on a beach, or corpses in an old war photograph. But what were their thoughts? I wondered. Were their minds filled with extraordinary things which only came to flower when they lay down? Had they forgotten all about the world outside, or did the eyes of other people give an added excitement? Would some of them be lovers for years after this day's beginning?

My questions multiplied and grew more fantastic. I think something ancient in me really condemned them as whores and lechers, but I ignored this deeper feeling and invented for them strange situations and romances.

I could not stay in the park all the evening, and I hated to go back to Adam Street alone, so I decided to have tea and ice cream at Fuller's. But when I sat down at the small round table and had the chocolate fudge sundae in front of me, my malaise increased rather than diminished. People at the other tables leaned towards one another and talked in low contented voices. Outside the traffic roared and grated. I hurried through what I had meant to enjoy, then turned into the street again.

I began to walk very slowly towards Portman Square, letting the crowd push me this way and that. Outside the house I found my brother and a friend just about to set off for the evening. They asked me perfunctorily to join them, but I looked at the friend's rolled umbrella, at my brother's smartness, and I felt tousled and callow. Their age, their sleekness and assurance made them inhuman. I said hurriedly that I had to visit an old friend of my mother's. They talked and joked with me for a moment, then walked off down the road, the friend swinging his umbrella a little.

Having said that I was going to see my middle-aged friend, I decided that I would. But when I had climbed up the stone steps to her old-fashioned flat, there was no one at home. The bell buzzed through the empty rooms. I bent down and looked through the letter-box. The hall was fawn color and dead. It seemed possible that ghosts were haunting the flat while she was away. I listened for sinister movements and voices, then turned away almost in despair. To find the door locked at that moment was a catastrophe.

I trudged back across the bridge, feeling sick and empty. It was almost dark now and the lights were lit. Near the Marble Arch I noticed a group of people not moving but standing still on the pavement outside a fun-fair. As I passed them I heard blues music, the ping of balls and wire springs, tinkle of money, and over everything the snarling voices of two people in the doorway. A young woman in black with fair, parched-looking hair confronted a man, whose tie had blown over his shoulder. A belt with a nickel buckle was pulled tightly in round his stomach. He was lifting his lip, sneering at the girl's stream of abuse, hunching his broad shoulders as he pushed his hands deep into his pockets. Then, as she paused for breath, he began. He poured contempt on her clothes, her body, her age, her voice, her class, her sex. He seemed to be trampling on everything they'd ever known or done together. I stood quite still on the edge of the crowd, too horrified and fascinated to break away. I could picture them just the night before, close to each other in the dark, or kissing like the people in the grass. Now they were murderous, searching for the worst poison and the sharpest pain.

The woman began to move away. She seemed to be broken and conquered by the man's brutal words; but all at once she darted back and slashed him in the face with her handbag. It was as if he had at last said the unbearable thing.

There was blood. The metal clasp had caught his cheek, and as he put his hand up to it, the woman burst into a storm of tears. He made as if to rush at her and smash her face in, but people in the crowd caught his arms behind him. Seeing him powerless, the woman with a strange movement jerked her head up and her tongue flashed out like a serpent's. For one moment she was quite spiritualized and transformed with hate; then she slipped through the crowd and I saw her running, half crouching, along the pavement. She was sobbing again violently. Hate was over, and only misery left.

The man turned and tried to fight the men who were holding him. The little crowd swayed. I broke away and started to run, too.

In my dismay it seemed to me as if the earth's crust had cracked and I had looked through and seen reality at last.

Memories of a Vanished Period

I saw, when I entered the room, that all the quaint accessories had been brought out, as if from glass-cases or refrigerators.

Champagne spat and frothed in glasses; a tiered, armor-plated wedding cake stood foursquare on its disc of silver paper; at the bottoms of entrée dishes, on seas of doubtful lace, floated little pastry boats filled with caviar; the summit of each pyramid of sandwiches was crowned with a gallant little flag. The flags bore these legends: "Paté," "Smoked Salmon," "Kipper."

Fat Levantine-looking ladies laughed and made jokes from behind their heavy barricades of maquillage. A sort of deep angry "Summer Bloom" seemed all the rage. Being curious, I could not help discovering the line where this Red Indian cosmetic stopped. Behind the ears, down the throat, came the natural whiteness, almost as a shock. Those stones, which are called zircons, flashed on plump fingers and heaved and fell on bosoms.

In spite of their size and heaviness, there was a curious tinselly, unreal quality about the women. I could not understand it, until I realized suddenly that they, like children or actors, were "dressed up." Their finery was sad and limp, perhaps a little dirty. I thought of the phrase "A Brave Show," it seemed so very suitable.

The men not in uniform were even drabber, more than ever bent on appearing commonplace. Only the bride's father had put on his "tails." He was a round little man with a benign white tonsure of hair, and one somehow knew how far his sweet smile must have carried him in the hard headed business world.

Everyone seemed to be making remarks about the chandelier.

"My dear, why didn't it shatter into a thousand pieces?"

"D'you mean to say the bombs merely made it swing to and fro?"

"Think of having one of those glass stalactites in your eye!"

"Aren't you terrified of it crashing down on your heads?"

"You ought to dismember it."

This last remark was made by a grey old man with a trembling under-lip. His wife corrected him in a shrill, dry shriek. "You mean dismantle, Herbert, not dismember. It isn't human."

But there the chandelier remained. Being in a rich man's house, it was, of course, a cheap reproduction—yet it had its own *rechauffé* prettiness and the same squalid gallantry as the women's clothes.

I moved into the circle round the bride's younger sister. The skin was still very young and pretty round her eyes—smooth and taut, not loose or crisscrossed like chicken's skin—and her hair might almost have been dressed with lard, it was so sleek.

"Only the back windows were blown in; wasn't it lucky?" she said.

There seemed nothing to add to this statement. I stood for a moment, trying to think of conversation, then I floated on till I came to the bride. She wore the sort of dress that has been made very quickly from a fashion paper pattern. The pins, the crinkly paper, the blue chalk, still seemed to cling to it. Its color was green, and the orchids pinned across it were also green but of a more "sickly" shade; for they were pale, a little bruised, breathless-seeming, with silver paper hiding their death-wound.

The phrase: "The bound, tortured feet of Chinese women" jumped into my head.

The bride had her back half turned to me. She seemed to be gazing through all her guests, through everything, into the distant future, or the past. Out over the park her eyes were roving, and because of her self-forgetfulness she was poised, dignified and quite human.

I did not notice her mother's approach until she was near; then I witnessed a curious little scene which I shall always remember.

With a harsh, black, permanently-waved sort of frown, the mother reached out her hand and gave her daughter's thigh a brutal pinch. "Can't you attend to your guests?" she hissed with venom.

Shocked as if I myself had been pinched, I expected the bride to start, almost to scream—at least to swear. But she did none of these things; she only walked away quietly, her trance replaced by no vivacity.

"To be pinched on your wedding day! To be pinched on your wedding day!" I kept saying to myself. I could think of nothing else.

To shake the picture from my head I turned away and looked at the bridegroom with his two friends. That extraordinary camaraderie, which only comes fully to blossom between ordinary men when one is getting married, lit up their faces. They were holding one another's shoulders, patting one another's backs, wishing good wishes, saying good-byes, joking and chaffing as they knew they should from the pages of *Esquire*. It was painful to watch, because you felt that they really had no love for one another at all.

Suddenly, before even the first guest had thought of departing, the hired waitresses began, quite openly, to pack up the remaining food and drink. They did it almost with ostentation, flapping napkins sharply with their birdlike hands, snatching up the plates of *foie-gras* sandwiches and shovelling them into paper cartons. The one solitary waiter in charge of them, being too decrepit to be snapped up by the army, the air force, or the navy, was also too decrepit to stop their uncomely, female haste. He just looked on, weakly scandalized.

I went in search of Angus, who had brought me to this wedding, and found him, tightly hedged round with friends, in a corner of the large room. I was pleased that he had deserted me, for I had been free to look at everything from outside, like a thief, but I pretended to be annoyed and bored, and said that I thought it was time for us to go. We said good-bye prettily all round and went to find our "things."

Outside, in the street, we stood for a moment watching the people pouring out of the front door into the sunlight. Here they looked even worse and more unhappy than upstairs in the drawing-room. "Cruel, cruel Sun," I muttered; then I turned to Angus to stop myself revolving all these words and phrases.

We walked to the bus, talking gaily about the other guests. Being quite unknown to me, I was able to build up the most elaborate fancies about them. Angus sometimes corrected these by the revelation of even more remarkable facts.

I had decided to take Angus to tea with Grace and Randal. I thought they might like one another as they did such different jobs (Randal was a painter and Angus used to work in a whiskey distillery); and tea we had to have, after champagne and so many curious tid-bits.

We climbed up the stairs to the fourth floor and rang the bell of the tiny flatlet.

Soon we were all sitting on the bed, drinking from big steaming breakfast-cups and looking at Grace's new scrapbook. It dated from about 1800 to 1830. First came "Gentlemen's Seats," stiff, caught in a trance, a dream of antlered deer, shaped walls, half-hidden domes of tiny temples, gazebos, ice-houses, strawberry-beds. Next came "Politicians," the older ones heavily wigged, the younger ones wearing their hair romantically brushed forward into curls and tendrils. "Beauties" followed. As is usual in such collections, only the higher walks of life were represented; there was no "Molly Flynn, the Prettiest Milkmaid in all Huntingdonshire" or anything of that sort.

We looked at each picture minutely, carefully, making many remarks. I forgot that Angus could only be expected to have the smallest interest. Being so well-controlled, he did not fidget; but at last he jumped up, saying, "I'm afraid I have to meet someone at six," then, turning to me, "Are you coming?"

Only afterwards, in the thickly carpeted, curious-smelling passage, did I realize how impatient Angus had been. "What strange hair your friend has," was all he said. "It's just like an albino golliwog's."

The person Angus was meeting at six had a bad reputation. It appeared that he asked his friends to expensive places, ordered many drinks and dishes which they did not want, then revealed the fact—wasn't it amusing—he had no money on him at all.

We jumped off the bus at the "Ritz" and went down below to an underground bar. I felt relieved as the minutes slipped by and no friend came. Angus and I drank gin and ate Smith's Potato Chips—removed from their grease-proof paper packets, of course.

The place began to fill up. A mature American film star rustled into the room, followed by a curious air force "escort." When the man sat down he twined his legs together like a little pixie on the edge of a cement birdbath.

Something very Gothic, with rings and Central European accent, was pouring out its soul to a sleek, diffident, nervous-breakdown type of soldier.

A young grandee leaned against the bar looking sober and beautiful. His double Guards' buttons punctuated him all down the front like pairs of lovers on seats in the park. I was surprised when Angus said: "That's the Duke of R."

For some reason I had expected a combination of names like Etherington Todd or Alex Miller.

Angus was beginning to talk now.

"Last week some of us were in here," he said, "and there was the most frightful smell of cat. At last we could bear it no longer, so I asked the waiter if he knew what it could be. He leaned over me and said very quietly, 'Excuse me, sir, but it is the Lady Robins who is sitting at the next table. We spill drinks over her, we try to trip her up, but nothing will drive her away. I think it is the Valerian, sir.' "

Angus and I had some more drinks and then someone resplendent in kilt and furry sporran came in. I recognized him as an actor in a country repertory company. He belonged to a rather tawdry, bedraggled Scotch family, and, before the war, had possessed an American admirer in Paris who was always kept strictly neuter in conversation. We had once exchanged two words in the pub opposite his theater.

Now I went over to him gaily, too gaily, and of course he did not know me. I felt insulted and depressed.

"It's the kilt that's done it," I grumbled to Angus. "Everything before the kilt has been obliterated from his mind."

"And a good thing too," Angus answered tartly. "That child needed a spring-cleaning very badly."

We did not speak for some moments, and I was able to notice a melting and a buzzing growing in my head. I looked at the modest strawberry-leaves, the ripe glamor-girl, the pinchbeck Highlander, the pixie-legged air force "ace" and all the other dreary people.

"Let's go," I said urgently.

Without waiting for him to answer, I jumped up and made for the doorway; then I ran rather jerkily up the stairs and waited for him in the street.

It was harsh and cold in the open. The evening had only just begun and could not be cut short so suddenly.

We plodded to the Café Royal and began to eat *hors d' oeuvre.* A peculiar feeling came over me as I contemplated the fantastic hanging confection of jagged glass which covers the electric-light bulbs. I became almost hypnotized. I identified myself with the mouse that ran up Selfridge's clock and "did not expect such a bizarre effect, so came tumbling down with the shock." I knew that I had not remembered the end correctly, and this worried me. Through dreaming of the mouse and the clock I began to lose a clear-cut consciousness of my immediate surroundings. The next thing I realized was that Angus was shepherding me to Dean Street.

In Piccadilly a soldier swore at us terribly. He followed behind, pelting us with blasphemies and filth. We giggled weakly, wondering why we had been singled out for this attention. He was so alone, so drunk, so hopeless and unhappy. Hate was seething inside and had to flow out. He poured it on to us and he had all my sympathy.

The pubs in Dean Street were full to overflowing. We fought our way in, pushing through the crowd of soldiers, whores, airmen, negroes and French sailors with red pom-poms on top. All round, I could feel their chests, their thighs, their legs (with the knees a little bent) pressing on me. Close to my ear people whispered to each other earnestly, ecclesiastically. The thimblefuls of golden whiskey spilled on dark cloth when elbows were jogged. Someone said playfully: "I'm feeling hysterical." There was warmth and dirt and love and disgust and poetry and sweat.

We stayed till closing time, then smoothly, swayingly, dancing a little sometimes, we laughed our way back to Piccadilly.

It was all so crazy, so delicious, so sad; so terribly, nobly sad; like an avalanche crashing down.

"She shall have music
Wherever she goes,"

I sang tragically.

Years, years afterwards, I thought, I shall remember this night when I was young; when we got drunk and all London was drunk with us; when lonely soldiers shouted blasphemies through the streets.

On all sides people were streaming out of doors, making jagged sections of light, like slices of cake, each time they lifted the blackout curtains. I wished that the seething and the bubbling could go on forever.

"Angus, my train!" I suddenly shouted. We both rocked with laughter at the idea of a train, then Angus became severe.

"Get a taxi at once!" he ordered. At last we found one, and as I stood at the door, saying good-bye, the sirens blew.

Drink had made my mind free to receive all impressions, and at this sound a sense of doom struck deep down.

"I shall be killed," I said with conviction and relish. "I know I shall be killed. I have been kept in London especially to be killed."

"Shut up!" Angus shouted brutally, not allowing me to wallow in the importance of death.

"Drive quickly to Victoria," he said to the man.

"Good-bye, good-bye forever, Angus!" I shrieked out of the window.

He raised his hand in a noble, archaic gesture; and I could see no more.

While the taxi sped along I began to think that nothing would happen; and I was sorry that all calamities were to be avoided. I had the sense of being cheated, which is anticlimax.

Then the guns began to go off. Livid flashes jigged about and fell over the whole city, like scarecrow fingers.

"Don't be afraid, don't be afraid," the taxi-man said, sliding back the partition window. "You're with the only V.C. taxi-driver in London. He'll see you through anything."

We dodged a street lamp, slithered round a corner on the pavement, and soon came to rest in the great well of Victoria Station.

It was dead; no lights, no noise, no trains. The hollow was filled with doom. I could not bear its silence.

"Don't stay here!" I shouted. "It's no good. Drive me to Notting Hill Gate, please."

I had decided to take refuge with Grace and Randal, since I could not get back to the country.

"Don't be afraid, don't be afraid," the taxi-man chanted automatically. I had realized by now that he also was drunk. "You're with the only V.C. taxi-driver in London. He'll see you through anything."

I sat close to the window, and as the guns flashed I talked and said mad things, asking extraordinary questions.

"Where did you get the V.C.? I don't believe a word of it. Are you married? Are you faithful? I can't bear long noses, can you?"

My merriment was mounting almost to delirium, trying to make an armor against the bombs about to fall.

"Don't, don't have an accident," I implored him as we swirled and scudded along. "Awful to die in an accident when an air raid's going on."

I paid him at the door of the block of flats and he said again: "You were safe with the only V.C. taxi-driver, weren't you?"

Affectionately we shook hands and waved; then I entered the building. The passages were littered with people who had come from their private holes to sit on the floor against the inner walls, away from all glass. Some were reading or playing cards while others talked comfortably in little groups. There was an atmosphere almost of gaiety. Propped up with many cushions were fantastic old ladies, their hair arranged in the "King Charles' Spaniel" or "Matriarchal Sheep" manner. One was sucking scented cashews and making curious hollow clicks with her teeth.

No one sat outside Grace's and Randal's door. For one unpleasant moment I thought that they were out; then I heard voices;

so I knocked loudly with the head of my stick. Grace's head appeared.

"You!" she called out in surprise. "I've come as a refugee," I faltered. She took the situation in in a moment. "Darling, you're drunk," she said. "Come in at once and be soothed and sobered."

It was wonderful to be with friends again. I felt safe—even safer than with the V.C. taxi-driver.

I did not notice at once that someone else was lying on the divan. "That's Michael," Grace explained. "He's taken refuge as well."

Michael looked at me with extreme suspicion, and I remembered that he was Grace's mad friend who had just been let out of a home.

"Loonies within and Nazis without," I said to myself and immediately hated the idiotic words.

I began to talk incoherently and joyfully. I still felt that I was going to be killed.

I cannot remember how it came about, but soon the conversation turned to schools. We may have been discussing something I was trying to write. Michael, who had been silent all this while, broke in now, in a deep, resonant, mocking voice, with these words: "Porta Vacat Culpa."

I swung round to him.

"How did you know that motto?" I asked almost sharply.

"Wasn't I there for four years?" he asked, with a long-suffering, patient smile, as if to show that the experience had indeed been an ordeal.

I saw Grace's face lighten with a smile. She felt relieved. She knew now that Michael would accept me. He was only nervous of complete strangers.

As we were still talking about this discovered link, the first bomb dropped. The swish, swish, suckling, eating, tearing noise made us jump to our feet, as if to fight some human enemy; then we ran into the little lobby away from the glass of the windows. The thud came and the huge steel-framed building gave the slightest, tenderest shudder in answer to it.

"Does it always do that?" I asked.

"When it's near," Grace answered flatly.

I was sober and chastened now, but with something else thrilling through me.

We shut ourselves up in the tiny box of the lobby, for bombs began to fall one after the other. At one moment, when the swooping scream was loudest, Grace uttered the clear, round words: "I am terrified." They had no color, which made them very real.

"Don't be silly," Randal said in his thin, Chinese philosopher's voice.

Michael was still discussing and remembering all sorts of school happenings: cheatings, beatings, secret meetings; runs, walks, games; masters, maids and romantic friendships.

I fed his flame and enjoyed the fire, too. The night wore on; my drunkenness wore off. The others spoke of it almost as a past thing.

"D. drunk is almost Byzantine," Grace said. And I saw the phrase as something in a copy-book, to be laboriously traced by endless generations of children.

"Let's go on to the roof," Randal suggested. Grace and Michael did not want to go, so he took me up alone.

We stood by the parapet, eight stories above the ground, looking down on to the spire of a church. The cone at the top of the spire had been sliced off in an earlier raid, leaving a tiny platform.

The wind blew over the black city where wounds of fire were spreading and tearing contagiously. In the lulls of silence one could hear the crackling, lustful flames eating, eating—never satisfied.

"When the palace was hit," Randal said, pointing to Kensington, "the air was filled with a delicious smell of old wood burning."

"That was only your imagination," I thought, but said nothing.

Far off I heard the bells of fire engines and ambulances. I saw pictures of bells, ringing at Mass, when every head but mine was bowed—of bells on the ragged points of a jester's cap, remembered from some children's party—of the silver-gilt bells on a coral rattle which had been bitten and sucked by many babies.

"Whizz, whizz through the streets. Get there, get there, get there!" I shouted, then felt very foolish.

I tried to imagine what it would be like down in those black, empty streets. I wanted to go down, to wander about, to see the sights, the stillness and the fear, the blackness of the corners.

"Don't be ridiculous," Randal said coldly; "you know you'd be terrified out of your wits."

We left the roof and went down to the flat again. Grace had asked Michael to blow up the "lie-low." We arrived while he was still puffing out his crimson cheeks. When it was inflated he took it into the bathroom and lay down with his head under the fat, swelling pan. The rest of us lay in heaps on the divan and in the armchair.

Fewer bombs fell. The barks from the guns began to be more isolated. The tired, frightened city seemed to be gradually contracting after its climax. I lay quite still, waiting to be swept away on a wave of sleep.

It was late when we woke. Out of kindness and squeamishness we did not look at one another carefully but smiled and were happy, stressing, exaggerating with words the awful night.

"Isn't it wonderful, the morning, the sun, the blue sky, breakfast, everything?" we sang.

I toasted the bread. Michael laid the tea-trolley with mad precision—each fork and knife and spoon harshly regimented.

We sat down and ate. How delightful it was to feel dirty and squalid and to be accepted like that. Nothing mattered but our liking for one another and our pleasure in life.

Grace went about with streaming hair, looking like Picasso's "La Soupe"; then she pinned it up into a careless bird's-nest, which would have made even the most slovenly rook ashamed.

We left the washing-up—all the sordid remains. We threw them down and streamed into the park and the sun.

At first we could not understand it; a sort of huge snow had fallen. Enormous flakes lay everywhere. Then we saw that it was paper, burnt and charred all round the edges. The giant confetti was caught in the trees, floating on the water, carpeting the ground.

I picked up a sheet which had been licked by the flames into the shape of a landscape-gardener's lake. Strangely enough, it bore the picture of a fire. In the black woodcut an antique fire engine raced gloriously, with plunging horses, while a gendarme pointed the way flamboyantly.

"Look, look at this strange fluke," I said to the others.

"Keep it forever and ever as a souvenir," Michael advised solemnly.

"No wonder those fires burned so brightly. They were paper-mills," mused Grace.

Here and there we saw new bomb-holes between the ancient trees. Green, torn leaves and branches lay on the ground, looking wounded and human.

"I like your silver-knobbed stick," Michael said crazily, turning to me. "I never dare do things like that."

I had never thought of my stick as particularly daring, but now I was self-conscious. We talked of all the vanities of life, of lovely clothes and food and precious stones. I was feeling hollow inside, with drumming head and sick taste in my mouth, but everything seemed new, saved, relished again after years of deprivation. The dancing boats on the water—the absurd and naughty toilets of the water-birds—our own unshaven squalor—the mad talk of philosophy—how delightful they all were.

Michael was planning the post-war world.

"Anarchism's the only thing!" he shrieked ecstatically. "Anarchism! Anarchism!" he shouted, as we all linked arms and started to run over the grass.

Evergreen Seaton-Leverett

I first saw her driving down the main street of the old inland watering-place which I was exploring. It was impossible to miss her, since she drove in a dark-green limousine belonging to King Edward the Seventh's reign. Beautiful brass carriage lamps glistened on either side of a chauffeur and footman, whose uniforms were also of dark green. She sat, perched up behind them in a glass box, a plump little woman, her brilliant terra-cotta hair topped with a sort of black satin cottage-loaf.

As the car drove by very slowly, she smiled and bowed to the people on the pavements with the greatest good nature and impartiality; she might almost have been parodying a royal personage. The round red face was crumpled and creased with so much smiling, but what was interesting was to see something in it to make me feel that a few of the smiles were for herself. She seemed to be enjoying her own preposterousness, laughing at it a little. It was as if she were saying something as simple as, "Oh, Lordy, Lord! The dear people in the street, and me sitting up here like an old aunt sally!" The little eyes were watering with amusement and pleasure; once she dabbed at them, then looked up to heaven, and again I could imagine her exclaiming, "Oh, Lord!" The mouth was a little open all the time. Before she was past me, I remember thinking: "She holds her head rather stiffly. Is she afraid that it might shake? If she wore jet bugles on that hat, would they still go on trembling after the car had stopped?"

My heart bounded at the spectacle she made in her progress down the street; for the world has become so mean that we no longer expect to be given the chance to stand and gape in admiration. When it comes, we are almost shocked, made to feel guilty. There is a return of that dreadful fear that seems to hang about all true fairy-stories. Fairy godmothers, in spite of their goodness and magnificence, are sinister; golden coaches that suddenly appear may as suddenly disappear, leaving deserving girls in rags by the kitchen fire.

I thought of all this as I turned down a narrow alley leading to the common. Who could the woman be? Was she some obstinate old dowager, refusing to be jostled out of the habits of her youth? She looked too sweet-natured to be anything so tight. Perhaps she was a singer, an actress from the past, who still loved to draw men's eyes. Hugging the thought of her to me, I looked up; and there she was again in reality, sailing up the road that lay between me and the gorse bushes.

At the corner of the alley I waited to watch her approach. There were few people here, so for a moment she had stopped smiling and bowing. Her eyes were down on her gloves; she seemed to be playing a sort of delicate pat-a-cake with herself, placing one chubby hand on another, stopping sometimes to pick and pluck at her sleeve. In front of her the chauffeur and the footman sat so stiffly that they reminded me of two green bottles waiting to be uncorked.

When the car had almost reached me, some peculiar spirit took possession and I found myself bowing and smiling—almost as extravagantly as she did these things herself. The moment she noticed me, her face lit up; she fluttered her hand, then turned to wave again through the oval bevelled glass at the back of the car.

What had I done? Had my excessive civility made her mistake me for a friend? Or was she interested quite simply in anyone who seemed to wish her well?

I stood staring after her until the car bowled round the corner and was lost in the trees.

I was not to find out any more about her until several months later when I was again in the town. While walking along the upper common, I suddenly came face to face with someone I had not seen since school days. I was sure of him because I remembered at once that he had lived in the town all his life. After our first exclamations and surprise, we sat down together near some great slabs of rock and started to smoke cigarettes. All round us children played amongst the rocks, climbing over them, squeezing between them, laughing, screaming, digging in the sand that had collected in nooks and crannies.

Soon I was asking all about the wonderful woman with tomato hair.

"Oh, but don't you know?" exclaimed my rediscovered friend. "That's Evergreen Fanny."

My mind at once rejected the silly name, but I waited in silence to hear more.

"She's years and years old, nobody knows quite how old; my mother says she was seventy, twenty years ago."

Extreme age was something I had not associated with the woman in the car.

"She's an amazing ninety, then," I said. "She looked more like sixty when I saw her."

"I know, that's the extraordinary thing; she never seems to change. Mother says she's looked exactly the same ever since she can remember. That's why everyone calls her Evergreen Fanny."

"Does your mother know her personally?" I asked.

"Yes, in fact she's about the only woman Evergreen enjoys seeing. But she loves men. If you like, I'll get Mother to ring her up and ask if we can go along this evening for drinks. Are you free?"

I nodded eagerly.

"I shall always remember first seeing her," Alec Gale continued. "I suppose I was about five. My mother had taken me shopping, and on the way home we ran into Evergreen. We met her on the pavement in front of the hotel, only a few yards from where we're sitting at this moment. The brilliant red hair and fantastic clothes made such an impression on me that I couldn't take my eyes off her. All the time she was talking to my mother I was staring openmouthed. At last Evergreen turned and wagged a finger at me archly. 'Isn't it sweet?' she said. 'I do believe the dear boy is admiring me.' My mother, whose guess was a good deal nearer the truth, bundled me off before I could say anything too frightful."

I was silent, remembering the effect of strangeness on myself as an infant. There had been a man who rode a blue bicycle and sang psalms at the top of his voice . . . But Alec was speaking again. "Of course, it isn't real," he said.

"What isn't?"

"Why, the hair. It's a wig. The nurse who came to look after Mother when she had pneumonia told us that Evergreen had three: best, second best, and everyday. At night she keeps all three on tall stands at the foot of her bed. But I'm not going to tell you any more about her; you must see her for yourself. As soon as I go home, I'll get Mother to telephone. Come to tea with us and I'll take you along afterwards. Her house is only just around the corner."

He gave me his address and we stood up.

"Till this afternoon, then!" he called, turning to wave to me before disappearing over a ridge. I thought I caught a glint in his eye, as though the idea of introducing me to Evergreen afforded him a wicked pleasure. Memories suddenly came back to me of the simple-minded Casanova's delight in being taken to see a real duchess, and of his extreme discomfort when his malicious friend disappeared, leaving him in the clutches of the ancient and lascivious woman.

"But why should you think of anything so absurd?" I asked myself. "Evergreen does not appear to be in the least lascivious; and even if she were, she would probably not have the slightest inclination to be lascivious with *you!*"

That evening, as Alec led me from his house to Mrs. Seaton-Leverett's, I was filled with doorstep fears and anxieties. I had never before been to see someone simply out of curiosity, and it seemed to me that I was bound to be found out and punished in some way for my impertinent inquisitiveness.

We turned the corner and began to walk down a street of late Victorian houses showing seventeenth century Dutch influence. Terra-cotta plaques, elaborate gables in steps, broken pediments and heavy cornices diversified each simple family box. We stopped in front of one where a tiny crimson windmill whirred beside a cement pool fringed with jagged, skull-like glints. Not far off, emerging from a privet bush, a little cement girl, also painted crimson, lifted her frilly skirt invitingly and rudely. Looking up, I saw that each window box to the house was a miniature crimson fence with five-barred gate in the middle. The scarlet of the geraniums behind fought interestingly with the crimson lattice-work. All these commonplace garden ornaments had been given a strange grim twist by this blood-red color.

Alec led the way up the path and rang the bell. The door was opened by the footman I had seen in the car, but how different he looked without his cap and uniform! He was young and weak, with thin damp hair, and bluish flesh about his nostrils. His suit was of dark greasy serge. He asked us rather breathlessly to wait in the dining-room while he announced our arrival to his mistress.

As we passed through the narrow hall, I just had time to look up and see that the lampshade was a Japanese paper parasol hung upside down. The bright flowers and birds looked old, dust-greasy and fly-blown. There was the faintest smell in the air of ivy, ancient meals, tomcats, upholstery and fungus. It filled me with a strange disturbance, perhaps because it brought so vividly to mind the phrase "A living tomb." What did it mean? A tomb for living? A tomb that was alive? This house was both.

All the curtains were drawn in the dining-room and three electric bulbs dressed in red crêpe-paper crinolines shone down on the table, making the yellow-grey oak look pale and dirty and naked. The rest of the room glowed darkly and rosily. I heard the whirr of an electric fan and turned to find one in the corner, colored ribbons streaming from its guard. It had the soiled gaiety of the Japanese sunshade and I was made to think of long-forgotten fancy-dress balls on battleships.

Seeing that the mirrored overmantel was stuck all over with cards, I went up to glance at some of them. They were invitations to garden parties, dinners, weddings, balls and christenings. All were yellowed, curling at the corners and thick with furry dust, so that they had an almost artificial air, as if they had been made to look old for a stage production. The few I read were all from peers. I remember best the garden-party invitations from the two marquesses whose places lay on either side of the town.

"She's kept every invitation she's ever had," whispered Alec, sliding up to me stealthily. "When she offers you sherry she'll tell you that it's one of the last bottles from the cellars of her grandfather's castles; she's been saying it for years. Actually she gets it round the corner where we do."

His jaunty interruption broke up my mood. I wished I had been left alone to contemplate the rosy butcher's shop glow, the dust, so thick that it had grown spiders' legs and arms, the grandees' cards, and the writhing water-lilies on the shoddy art-nouveau sideboard. How was it that Alec, after seeing this interior, could still think of Mrs. Seaton-Leverett as a comic figure?

But now the ill-looking young man had returned to take us to his mistress.

"This way, please, sirs," he said in his resigned, breathless voice. He led us up the stairs, glancing back many times as though he were afraid that we might not be following or that we had not yet learned to climb stairs properly and might be needing his help.

Whenever his eyes were off me for a moment I turned to study the wall opposite the banisters. It was decorated with pages from a wallpaper sample book pasted haphazard over the original dingy surface. A page of imitation brickwork followed a page of glossy marble. Purple grapes hung close to fantastic wood-graining and a square of meat-red damask. There was part of a frieze of pastel crocuses and a horny patch of Lincrusta panelling. My eyes began to rove and falter. The patterns and textures set before me were as bewildering as the profusion of dishes at a banquet.

And when we reached the drawing-room, or boudoir, if that is a fitter description, and the man withdrew, leaving us alone, my eyes skimmed with such rapidity from object to object that I felt dizzy. Everything was known, commonplace, but in such incongruous relation to the next object that it became startling. The bow window was draped in coarse grey lace; from the middle of each opening a large Easter egg, decorated with varnished scraps and tinfoil, hung down forlornly, reminding me of pictures I had seen of bombs in readiness to drop from airplanes. Photographs covered the walls, and between these, especially round the fireplace, were large saucepans and frying pans, tied back with tasselled curtain cord, sometimes stuck with a posy of artificial flowers, a bow, or a tiny flag. A larger Union Jack covered an occasional table on which stood flimsy glasses, a plate of candied cherries, a plate of strident pink coconut ice and a decanter with sticky dribbles from the lip. For me the room evoked extraordinarily the atmosphere of the Near Eastern brothel. Although I had never been in one, I had always imagined just such dirty lace, such chi-chi paper flowers, such sickly wine and sticky sweets. But there was one great difference. This room was sunless and a little damp. Perhaps the chill was all the more evident because one knew that this was no spider's parlor decked to lure in stupid flies, but a parlor decked for no other purpose than the owner's quirkish humor. She was alone with her scraps and tinsel, her Easter eggs robbed of their chocolates long ago.

A door opened and footsteps sounded in the passage. She stood on the threshold looking in at us. I had not expected anyone quite so short. Her black skirt was short. The sleeves of her white silk jersey were short, revealing puffy pink arms. She again wore a black silk hat; but this one was tall and straight-sided, with the narrow brim pulled down to her eyebrows, so that only little puffs of red hair showed above each ear lobe. One chubby hand poised on her breast made me feel that she might burst into song.

"Ah!" she said, moving towards Alec serenely and jerkily, rather like a toy duck on little wheels. "Naughty boy for neglecting me so long!" Still holding one of Alec's fingers, she turned to me. "Now tell me what his name is—I'm sure I shall like it."

Alec introduced me.

I found myself hoping that she would approve of my combination of sounds.

"Oh, that's *very* nice. I like that."

She said it over to herself, savoring it on her tongue as some tea-taster might sample his latest blend. A new picture jumped into my mind. I was not a person; I was just three syllables moving about and talking.

Mrs. Seaton-Leverett sat down in a basket-chair near the fireplace. One hand was still on her bosom, and since her fingers played a perpetual tattoo on her breastbone, my eye was often caught by the dusty twinkle of her rings. They gripped the chubby fingers as brass bands grip the cormorant's neck; or were they more like tiny sparkling boa constrictors forever tightening their death-hold?

I was able now to take in other details of her dress. The blue-and-white check, which hung down over the black skirt, was not a proper apron, but only an unhemmed piece of cloth pinned with two huge safety pins at the waist. Other smaller safety pins held strips of lace and ribbon in position aslant her bosom, so that she looked as if she had just returned from an investiture where some outlandish prince had decorated her with all his strangest orders. I pictured her going into shops, buying these snippets of lace and braid and ribbon, pinning them across her bosom at once to enjoy the effect.

She offered us the sticky sweets and sherry, and, sure enough, she told us that the sherry was one of the last bottles from her grandfather's cellar.

"It should be good, it should be good," she repeated airily; "my grandfather put it down years ago."

A slight pang passed through me; I could have wished that Alec's prophecy had not been so perfectly fulfilled. I was all for Evergreen. I wished her to be mysterious and unaccountable, baffling to those shallow people who came to smile or laugh.

My eye was caught by the glistening surface of a large photograph.

"Oh, that is a picture of your car, isn't it," I said, over enthusiastically; "I like its body very much."

Her face lit up. "You do like it? That is nice. But, my dears, it has been *such* a trial. It has had to have a whole new engine. It appears that they couldn't do anything more with the old one. It has been a great expense, but I'm hoping now that it will go smoothly for many years."

For a moment she seemed to forget us; her eyes wandered to the window; she drummed on her bosom and murmured in a far-away voice, "Yes, yes, yes, it has been a great expense, but it's a nice car. I do like a car to be a car."

I cast about in my mind for something else to say, afraid of allowing Evergreen to sink too deeply into her daydream. Could I say anything about the decorated frying pans on the wall, or the old Easter eggs? I wanted to know their history, the reason for their preservation; but perhaps Evergreen would resent my curiosity; perhaps she would open those round little eyes wide and I would be made to feel like a pet pug who has misbehaved on the drawing-room rug.

It was Evergreen herself who broke the tension. Still in her faraway singsong voice she began to tell us about her great-nephew who had inherited the grandfather's castle.

"He *is* a naughty boy," she mused, shaking her head; "he's got rid of the place to the National Trust—the whole village as well, if you please! And he never consulted any of us. He shouldn't have done it, it wasn't right."

"But aren't you glad that it will always be preserved now?" I asked, trying to say the soothing thing.

"Yes, but that isn't the point; he shouldn't have parted with it without letting us all know."

Evergreen was still shaking her head, but her expression had softened; she seemed to be willing to excuse her nephew's naughtiness, because, if the truth were to be told, she really admired his boldness, his decision, his high-handed behavior.

I nibbled a piece of coconut ice, sipped my sherry. The footman came to the half-open door, then slipped in furtively, a box entirely encrusted with tiny iridescent shells in his hand.

"Excuse me, madam, the cigarettes," he murmured, putting the box down on the Union-Jack tablecloth.

"Oh, how clever of you to remember, Henry!" said Mrs. Seaton-Leverett affectionately. "I'm afraid I never think of offering them, because I don't smoke myself."

As soon as Henry had left, she turned to us and said: "I'm not at all happy about him. You know he's not strong, and now, with this new Government Order, I'm so afraid they'll take him off and put him in some dreadful factory or other."

"But surely not!" protested Alec. "They can't do things like that yet. He's in a perfectly good job here with you."

"Oh, do you think so? I'm so relieved. I felt that they might say that he was much more necessary somewhere else; but he ought not to do anything strenuous, he mustn't have strain, he can't stand up to it." Evergreen's solicitude was charming.

But was this to be all? Were we only to have light gossip about her car, her nephew and her servants? Would none of the fantasy of the house get into the conversation? Every tinsel flower, every saucepan and miniature flag held a secret, some thought or feeling embalmed in it. The whole house seemed filled with tiny, unseen presences. They were all waiting for us to go; we were prying, curious people, the outside world. Evergreen fenced with us politely, kept us at bay. However long we stayed she would utter nothing but friendly platitudes.

I could see that Alec was growing restless; everything pointed to our going, yet it was very reluctantly that I rose to my feet. I wanted to stay with Evergreen alone. I wanted to hear her talking in that dreamy far-off voice, describing the ancient balls, the marriages and christenings.

"What, are you going, my dears?" she asked, suddenly taking notice of us standing before her, ready to hold out our hands. "Now, you must come again, both of you, soon. I liked your name so much; what is it?" she added, turning to me.

Delicate Henry showed us to the door; he seemed more resigned, more patient than ever. From the top steps of the porch he smiled at us, rather as a dying man might smile a brave farewell to his wife and children.

I did not look round until we had walked a few paces down the road; then some wish perhaps to see the crimson garden ornaments for the last time made me turn my head. My eyes travelled to the window boxes on the first floor; there was Evergreen, standing in the bow window with the dirty lace curtains pulled aside. She was staring down at us with a curious look of incomprehension on her face. It was as if she did not know who we were, or what we were. She would look thus, I felt, at the wood lice and other strange insects found under a stone. She was not hostile, but on her guard, a little repelled by what she saw. Hers was a ghost face at the window in a dream; and then the glass pane turned it into a drowned face staring up from the bed of a clear river. She had taken off her hat, so that the unbelievable hair rose up from her forehead like a sulky flame. The unyielding eyes beneath were still upon us; the mouth had not yet found any reason for being pleased.

Turning away abruptly, I tried to speak to Alec, to share some fragment of my thoughts with him. I wanted to say: "She is a prisoner in that extraordinary house; each object binds her with a spell." But how hollow it sounded! How artificial! He would only laugh. I could not express the half of my thoughts; they were as unformed, as numerous and impossible to catch as tadpoles in a pond.

Soon afterwards I heard of Evergreen's death. I heard, too, that she had divided her fortune between Henry and the chauffeur. It was difficult to imagine Henry enjoying thirty or forty thousand pounds; he had been so self-effacing, so breathless, so fragile. How would he bear the great weight of Evergreen's money? Had she dealt him a blow from another world, finally flattened him out under a pile of bank notes?

Alec told me that the house was empty now, that all the crimson ornaments were gone and the windows blank; but I knew that the spirits of the paper flowers, the invitation cards, the colored streamers, and the frying pans would always lurk there for me, together with the figure of Evergreen at the window, the amazing sullen lazy flame of her hair curling up into the shadows.

A Fragment of a Life Story

For some reason I have begun to think again of that late January afternoon at the beginning of the war when my curious fat friend Touchett took me to the parish hall to see a religious film. The film was thirty years old, and Touchett kept telling me this, wanting me to marvel at its age.

I had gone with him to strange meetings before. Once it had been to a lecture on Corporal Punishment at the Baptist Hall, where he heckled the poor schoolmaster until I became very embarrassed. And another time we had left the adult school hurriedly when some of the adult scholars, not caring for the political tone of the speaker, began to throw scalding coffee and the rather solid buns which had been provided for refreshment.

I had been very ill; so I told Touchett now, when he asked me to go to yet another meeting, that I did not feel strong enough for scenes. He assured me that the parishioners would behave perfectly.

But as we took our seat at half past three on that sullen afternoon, something seemed to click inside me. I couldn't bear the smell of the parishioners' furs, or the sight of the tatty bows on their hats. I couldn't bear the smell of the raw wood chairs, or the feel of their rush seats through my trousers. I couldn't bear the blistering, disintegrating flicker of the ancient film. The silver spots and smears tore across the camels, transfixed the asses, raced down the flat-roofed buildings, and made Jesus' face into a painful jigsaw puzzle.

There is no doubt about it, I was overcome with the horror of living. It was too disgusting for any words.

I jerked myself to my feet and pushed roughly by Touchett, who quavered after me in a babyish whisper, "What's wrong with you? Are you going to be sick?"

Still looking straight in front, I said: "I can't bear it anymore; it's awful!"

"Don't you like the film?" he asked. "It'll get even better soon; and, as you know, it's thirty years old, and has probably been preserved specially for us by Providence."

Anyone not knowing him would have thought that he was serious. There were subdued murmurs of "Hush." I made for the door blindly. I seemed to be almost fighting my way to it. I half fell as I caught hold of the handle.

The cold air blowing on me struck me as pleasant in some way, but I could not tell why. I did not seem able to explain anything to myself. I even wondered why the light was so weak on this winter afternoon.

I began to walk down the town. I crossed the bridge and still followed the High Street until I came to the great black station-yard where the trains were shunting and snorting. On the other side of the road, outside the public library, a youth stood, whistling mournfully and hunching his shoulders. He wore no overcoat, and several buttons of his shirt were undone, so that his meager chest could be seen. But his lips were the color of watered milk, and the smart nickel belt-buckle quivered against his flat stomach.

Fascinated by his bravado, I stared for some moments; then he noticed me, and glared back so balefully that I let the wind sweep me on at once.

I looked up at the spire of St. Stephen's Church. It appeared to me as a huge sharpened stake, put there by God for an instrument of torture. I imagined a gigantic body hurtling down from heaven and landing on this spike, pierced through the belly, the arms and legs spread-eagled and turning like windmills in their agony. I saw the long golden hair hanging down to the earth in heavy ropes and nets, enormous drops of blood caught and held between the strands. I saw the wonderful Ancient British chieftain's face—like Caradoc's in an old engraving—with flaxen moustaches round a crying Greek statue's mouth. The eyes I saw as a statue's eyes, too—blank and blind.

All this time, while I gazed so long at the tower, a policeman must have been watching me, for he now called out jocosely: "Can't you tell the time yet, mate? You counting it up?"

I wanted to spit on him, to swear, to shock him, to wake him up. How I hated all policemen!

I started to run up the hill, towards the doctor's house. He had been in my mind all this time. I pushed through the dripping bushes at the gate; one of them had an aromatic smell which I shall always remember, for, as I passed, I tore off a piece and crushed it between my fingers. I ran round to the drawing-room window, concentrating on the smell of the crushed leaves, knowing that I was storing it up in my memory.

Already the curtains were drawn, but I flattened the side of my face to the pane and saw, through a chink, the corner of a cream-painted bookcase, the edge of the standard-lamp, and a few strands of dog-basket. The walnut glow of the wireless, the treacly stain on the deal boards, and the dove-grey carpet, struck me as more than ordinarily smug and complacent.

"Quiet good taste," I murmured to myself; then, liking the silly words, I said them again quite loudly. They rang out in the stillness. I was in a terror, expecting the window to be thrown up at any moment. But nothing happened; only the little Aberdeen moved. For a moment it crossed my line of vision; and I thought that it looked exactly like an amazing little middle-aged, middle-class gentleman.

"O little Aberdeen," I prayed,
"Sitting upon the floor inside,
"I'd, free from any thought of sin,
"Become your melancholy bride."

The idiotic rhyme struck me as so full of meaning that I remembered again with hot shame the time when, as a child, I had asked: "Grandpa, what would happen if a man married a dog?" This, too, had been "free from any thought of sin." I had merely imagined a rococo scene with a fat spaniel, dressed in a veil and orange blossom, emerging from a Gothic Revival church on the arm of a well-groomed gentleman. But my grandfather had been too outraged and shocked to say more than: "Don't speak of it! Don't speak of it!" And so my question had gone unanswered.

Now, as I watched the final tremble and creak of the basket's edge, as the dog settled, I felt deserted by all the world. I knew that no one anywhere would ever have pity on me again. I saw all the hard granite faces set in a long range against me. I walked up hills and down valleys between avenues of granite faces.

And suddenly I felt that I must get into the house, that I could no longer stay outside. I guessed that the French window of the study would be unlocked. I turned the handle very softly and slipped into the dark room.

I could almost smell the medical books and the rack of neglected pipes. I huddled into the heavy curtain behind the door, and for a moment felt comforted, because I was no longer outside; but at the thought of the cold garden I was so overcome with sorrow for myself that I began to cry quite uncontrollably. I made noises like an animal or a musical instrument, squeezing out my breath or hissing it in through my teeth, muttering things that finished on a little scream, like steam escaping. I nursed my crying, wishing for it never to stop.

When at last the drawing-room door opened and steps came towards me, I crouched down lower to the ground in an ecstasy of hope and fear and shame. I wanted to become smaller and smaller—to become a kitten, a rat, a mouse, crouched at someone's feet in the dark.

The light was switched on, and there was a moment while he looked round the room before seeing me behind the door.

"What are you doing in here?" he asked, assuming that tone of shocked surprise which nurses use when children wet themselves. "You mustn't get into people's houses and hide behind doors, you know!"

He pulled me up to my feet and held me against him, to steady me, for I was trembling violently with lust and fear. For a moment I felt secure and serene. I no longer had to think for myself. I was even being held up and supported physically. Oh, it was lovely! I wanted to walk about, closely guarded like this forever. I dug my fingers into his arm fiercely, trying to get at the bone through the flesh.

Then, very gently, I felt him withdrawing. He still held me, but there was a tiny gap between our bodies, and his arms had gone rigid. I was so enraged that I flung away from him and made for the window, cursing and swearing at him with all the filthiest words I could remember. "You bucking feast, you ruggering bat!" I screamed.

He called my name urgently, and seemed about to follow me into the garden, but something made him change his mind; for, the moment I was outside the French window, he came forward and bolted it sharply. His face seemed almost wickedly triumphant, as he looked out at me through the greenish glass.

"Go home and go to bed," he said sternly, before he turned away. I rushed round the corner of the house and plastered my ear again to the drawing-room window. I heard him come in and say something to his wife and her friend. One of them answered him.

"What a pity!" she said. "He's so young. It must be terribly difficult to know what to do."

I stood there fascinated and delighted—they were talking about me! I strained to hear every word, and was rewarded with remarks about parents, money, curious taste in clothes, and undirected sex life. All the cruel words were varnished and stuck together with treacly pity. I screamed out against the appalling caricature. My screams set up a tiny, wiry vibration in the window glass. I could feel it on the tips of my fingers.

There was no answer, unless the silencing of the voices could be called an answer.

A sudden thrill and exaltation passed through me. I ran to the front door and rang the bell, hardly knowing what I did. The maid let me in just as he crossed the hall. He came towards me purposefully. I started to shout.

"What an amusing time you all must have discussing me! Do go on, I want to hear some more." Then I sighed and laughed very stupidly.

He caught hold of my arm, and was about to put me out of the door, when I shot out my other hand and clutched the banisters. They creaked and moved as he pulled at me roughly. I was amazed; he was using force! Why, he was even hurting me, and he was a doctor! I was exhilarated. Never again would I have to believe that he was entirely good and right. He was being brutal!

My protests grew as my strength gave out. I had to let go of the banisters, and he was jerking me nearer and nearer to the door. I kept on laughing and shouting and swearing to show that I did not care, that I was not almost mad with horror at this last treachery.

With the final desperate jerks I saw the strong hairs on his arms, as his cuffs rode up. "Very black hairs, very strong arms, and very gold cuff links enamelled with school crest," flashed across my brain. I knew now that he had lost his temper. It was wonderful. A sort of pure triumph of evil the moment seemed to me.

The door slammed, and I sat for a moment on the step where I had fallen. Quite suddenly I decided to go home and try to kill myself. I had the little black box of Prontisil tablets he had prescribed for me. I was sure that they were dangerous, for he always asked me anxiously how I felt after taking them.

I ran down the hill. Although my body was still weak, I was filled with a seething energy. The policeman stared at me again as I dashed past the church. This time I did spit, but not until I was several yards away from him.

I crossed the bridge and looked down for one second at the swirling water, half lost in the gathering darkness.

"If he were here to see, I'd jump straight in," I said aloud.

I ran up the road and let myself into the garden. As I put my key into the front door, I heard someone moving in the sitting room. I pushed open the door and saw Touchett by the fire.

"Hullo," he said, smiling sleepily. He looked exactly like a fat "doctored" cat; I could even imagine whiskers and a tail.

"I thought I'd come round and see what was wrong. Why did

you rush off like that?" he asked. "You *were* stupid, because you missed the crucifixion, which was marvellous. The agony! And the thunder and lightning effects!"

This careful innocence would have enraged me at other times, but now I felt radiantly alive and able to appreciate and embrace everybody and everything.

"Ask Lydia to bring in the supper," I said; "I'm just going into the other room to change my shoes."

I went into my room and sat on the bed, on the velvet-covered eiderdown which I liked so much. Automatically, I began to unlace my shoes, until I remembered that this was not at all what I had come to do.

I picked up the little black pillbox with its edging of brilliant magenta. My name, with Esquire after it spelled at full length, looked curiously pompous and important. I opened the box and pulled out the cotton wool; underneath lay the Prontisil tablets in their glowing nest. The magenta flushed their whiteness from all sides. I counted the tablets. There were sixteen.

"Surely," I thought, "sixteen tablets should have an appalling effect, if taken all at once."

I filled a glass with water and sat down again on the bed. Quite methodically I put the tablets one after another into my mouth, and washed each down with a gulp from the tooth glass.

"It's easy," I thought. "I wish I had some more."

Looking round the room for anything else to take, I had the notion of swallowing a little pair of curved nail-scissors, or of crushing the glass tumbler between my teeth; but I dismissed these as extravagant ideas.

I stood up and heard the last little gurgle inside me, as the final pill and gulp of water chased each other down. "I've really done something!" I thought. My gaiety mounted up into a huge exuberant wave.

I burst into the other room and saw the steaming soup on the two trays in front of the fire. Touchett was waiting for me politely. Greedy people always do wait politely.

"Have some soup, dear Touchett, some lovely steaming soothing soup." I shouted. I snatched the decanter from the bureau and slopped a lot of sherry into both soup bowls.

"Now you've probably made it cold," said Touchett petulantly. He bent over his bowl and took delicate little sips; then, finding it to his liking, he started to empty the spoonfuls down his throat with rude sucking noises.

"You are unbelievably disgusting," I said, feeling quite affectionate towards him. I slopped more sherry into two glasses, but forgot to stop pouring, so that a little golden waterfall splashed from the glass to the tray, and from the tray to the carpet. My first thought was for a damp cloth; but then I realized with a shock that, in a little time, messes on the floor, far worse than this, would no longer worry me.

"I could even throw butter at the walls," I thought, "and it wouldn't matter."

At the thought of butter, I spread my biscuits thickly and began to eat. I had become as hungry as a domestic pet.

"I must enjoy every moment of *my* Last Supper," I told myself. I poured out glass after glass of sherry for myself and Touchett, until the decanter was empty.

"Now that's finished and there isn't any more," I said. I felt unhappy.

Touchett gave me a suspicious look; he had placed two of his nicotined fingers on either side of his right eye, and seemed to be propping the lids open. It was a curious trick which I had noticed before.

"Why should you want any more sherry?" he asked. "You usually drink nothing at all, and I can hardly ever get you into a pub."

I felt a creeping tingling and swimming in my head. I became terrified and thrilled. Suddenly I burst out with what I had done. I wanted to shock and horrify.

"I've just swallowed sixteen Prontisil tablets," I shrieked, "and I'm beginning to feel very peculiar."

Touchett gave me an utterly blank stare, like a child looking over the palings of the infant school playground.

There was a moment of complete silence, then questions gushed out of his mouth.

"What are they? Are you all right? Why did you do it? Are they dangerous?"

He jumped to his feet and leaned forward, breathing heavily. I could smell the tobacco, the beer, the sherry, and the soup all mixed up.

I tried to calm him.

"Don't be stupid, don't be stupid. I only feel a little queer."

I seized a dish and ladled roast potatoes on to his plate. He loved Lydia's roast potatoes. But Touchett was frightened. He heaved his great body about in the chair and plucked a cigarette from his pocket, not looking at the potatoes. Then he started to wolf them without any of his usual signs of enjoyment. No smacking lips or eager eyes for the next mouthful.

"Why did you do it?" he asked again, thoroughly irritated with me for spoiling his evening.

"I'm still quite all right," I said, "and we must finish our meal in peace."

My head was reeling and my eyes seemed to be focusing curiously, so I shut them and saw myself as a small boy standing upon the dressing-table in red-and-white striped socks. I was standing on the dressing-table so that I could see my socks in the mirror. At that moment I loved the reflection of my red-and-white socks better than my mother, my father, than all my family put together.

I opened my eyes again and looked at Touchett. I could tell from his sharp furtive glances that he was about to jump up and leave me.

"Those nicotined fingers!" I thought. "Why, there's even a brown patch on the end of his nose! And those unspeakable teeth!"

"Touchett," I said sharply, "you ought to have your teeth seen to."

He looked at me.

"You seem to be very censorious all of a sudden," he said.

"But wouldn't you like to be dashingly handsome with a new 'guinea set'?" I asked.

He drew himself up and looked very haughty and dignified.

"I'm terrified of dentists," he said quietly. "Don't bother to bring out all the old claptrap about fear of dentists being linked with self-abuse. I know it all very much better than you do."

I stretched out my hands and said: "Don't go!" Whereupon he lurched to his feet like a frightened bullock.

"You go to bed," he urged, "or get the doctor."

The drumming was rising to a crescendo in my ears. As he pushed his way clumsily to the front door, I followed, snatching up a stick in the hall. We began to walk rapidly in the direction of his house.

My legs were becoming curiously heavy, but I laughed and sang and cracked stupid jokes, saying how disgusting it was to desert someone who was dying. When we got to the fork at the "Star and Garter" I shouted again.

"You can't go! You can't! What's going to happen to me? I can't be abandoned like this. It's shameful. You're a monster."

It was midnight. The lights were burning in the silence. Nothing moved.

"It's like a stage set," I thought; "and I'm the chief ranter."

"Shall I take you to the doctor's?" Touchett asked halfheartedly.

"Which one?"

He mentioned a name I did not know.

"Yes," I said—"if I can get there."

Then I saw the craven, lazy light come into his eyes again, and he veered away rapidly, saying: "Good night. I really must get home. Go back to bed quickly."

I screamed oaths and blasphemy after him, still half in fun; then, alone, beginning to be frightened, I wondered what to do.

Somehow I dragged myself home; past each appalling lamppost. The fire was still burning in the sitting room. I told myself that there were things to burn, while I was still alive.

I took all the notebooks with my poems in them, and some letters, and threw them on the flames.

The poems crackled gracefully and disappeared, but the imitation leather book backs sizzled, fried and flamed until the chimney caught fire. Up, in the heart of the wall, I could hear the roar of the burning soot.

"Quick, quick!" I called to Lydia. "Bring some water; the chimney's on fire."

She ran in with two blue enamel saucepans. I snatched one from her and threw the water into the grate with delight.

When water hit flame there was some sort of explosion. I jumped back. The room was filled with grey smoke. I saw Lydia like a ghost through the smoke. A little piece of scalding ash struck my cheek.

"It's all right," I said savagely, to stop all her exclamations.

Then I lay down on the sofa and thought that the time had really come. I was in some way losing all the salt and virtue of my senses. All was dumb, muffled, and thickened disgustingly. It was as if all my thoughts were reflected in some ghastly fun-fair mirror, the sort of distorting glass which is never funny, always frightening.

I held my breath for twenty seconds, and then gabbled out the name of Touchett's doctor to Lydia. I spoke so rapidly that she could not understand me. When I repeated myself, she gave me a long look, and then went to the telephone rather unwillingly.

I swayed into the bedroom and fell down on the bed. I lay there wriggling and lashing about, not being able to stay still for a moment, because of the soaring, swelling pain in my head, and because of my fear at the approach of the new doctor.

At last he came. He stood in the middle of the room, not saying anything; then he turned me roughly towards him.

"What's all this?" he asked sternly.

"He's just like a prefect who's discovered some peculiar goings-on in the disused cricket pavilion," I told myself. "He looks just like one, too—square head, pink mouth, wide shoulders. Skin smooth as the back of a child, as they say at the B.B.C."

I thought all this because I was very frightened of the doctor and wanted to give myself some courage and bravado; but it was no use, I had none. A terrible wave of self-consciousness made it impossssible for me to look at him, but I jerked out something about the tablets, and waited for his awful words.

Suddenly his prefect's manner dropped from him.

"First of all I think we'll try to make you sick," he said with businesslike gaiety. I laughed; the anticlimax was so funny, such a delicious relief.

He went in search of mustard, hot water, and a spoon.

I drank the yellow stuff in gulps, and waited, expecting to be violently sick. I imagined a horrible bright orange cascade of vomit from my mouth. I hated to be sick in front of the doctor. But nothing happened.

"No go?" he asked, looking at me enquiringly.

"I don't think so," I said. "Does it matter, if I'm not sick? Will it be serious?"

"You'll have the hell of a headache for the next day or so, but that's about all," he said with hearty malice.

I felt dashed. He was laughing at me. I was ridiculous and puerile. I did not know one drug from another. I was ignorant.

"Will you give me something for my head?" I asked, for by now it felt as if it were about to boil and crack open.

"Much better not," he said. "You've taken quite enough for one night!"

He laughed and joked, teasing me, making a fool of me; then he suddenly broke off and said, "The ridiculous is sometimes very near to the sublime."

I was startled; the remark was so sententious, so out of character. He's saying it specially for me, I thought; specially to make me feel good inside again. And I was very grateful, and tried to forget my resentment at his seeming unconcern about the Prontisil tablets.

At last he took up his hat and his case. He came forward ceremoniously, like a prefect again, only this time a nice prefect, congratulating someone on playing well in a match.

"Let's shake hands," he said.

I sat up in bed and held mine out. We shook hands. It was not silly, although it was very artificial.

Shaking hands is much more solemn and full of meaning than kissing, I thought. You kiss your aunt, you kiss your pet cat, but you never think of shaking hands with them like this.

I cannot tell whether I slept that night. I know that I first felt a certain happiness and comfort which was soon swallowed up by the terrible pain in my head. I know that this growing, bursting pain made me open and shut my eyes. Each time I opened them I saw the white mantelpiece palely glimmering in the darkness. The mantelpiece seemed to bend and cockle and become alive. Its flatness twisted into things that were nearly arms and legs. It seemed to swell towards me, then recede. And I seemed to spring out to it and back, like a tennis ball on a piece of elastic. I sang hymns to the mantelpiece and prayed to it. It brooded there, a squat flat deity, giving off waves of evil power.

When next I became conscious, it was bright daylight. Lydia had brought my tea; it lay beside me steaming in the little terra-cotta Chinese pot. I felt glad and happy—I felt horribly sick and soiled. Then both feelings, and many more, were all submerged, as wave after wave of realization broke over me. I saw that nothing was changed; either in the world or in me.

A Party

Fat Bertha Swan had bounced into the still-life room, given her invitation and bounced out again, shouting, "And see you damn well come in fancy-undress—you won't be let in otherwise."

Ian, painting alone in one corner, had smiled. He liked Bertha—even her exaggerated uncouthness and her absurd swearing amused him. He would certainly go to her party.

But now, as he sat on the bed in his room, he wondered what exactly fancy-undress meant. He supposed it meant fig leaves, loin-cloths, straw skirts, saucepan lids; but he wished he had asked some of the other students what they intended to wear. The knowledge would have given him more confidence.

Going over to the chest of drawers, he pulled out his faded mauve bathing "trunks" and looked at them doubtfully. He remembered buying them with an unexpected postal order sent to him on his fifteenth birthday two years ago. His aunt had not thought mauve a very suitable color for a boy, but he had liked them even more just because of her disapproval. Now moth holes stared up at him from important places; but these could be hidden. He had just been into the park to pick up some large plane leaves. He was going to sew a few on the shorts; the rest he would make into wreaths to wear round his neck and on his hair. Would they look like vine leaves? And would he look like Bacchus or was he much too skinny? Perhaps no one would guess that he was supposed to be a pagan god. He put his hand up and started to rub his scalp roughly. His hair at least was satisfactory, for it was short and curled tightly; although it was so strong and vigorous, the fear that it might one day all fall out sometimes came to Ian in his black moments. How terrible old age must be. How did one learn to bear the degradation?

He sat down again on the bed and started to sew the plane leaves on the shorts; next he made the wreaths, binding the stalks together with black cotton. He worked quickly and deftly, enjoying the task.

He stood in front of the mirror, wreathed and garlanded, his small feet bare. A little tingle of pleasure passed through him. The effect was better than he could have hoped. But how was he to travel to Catford in this state? He would have to put his leaves in a suitcase and dress—or rather undress—rearrange himself at Bertha's. There was not much time to spare; he pulled on his grey flannels and navy-blue sweater, buckled up a pair of old sandals and ran to catch the bus.

Outside the small suburban house three cats wearing collars were fastened to a young oak tree. Ian saw that the tabby wore a blue collar, the ginger a green one, and the black Tom bright scarlet with brass studs. Bertha had often spoken of her cats' dislikes of visitors; Ian supposed that she had put them here to sulk on their own. They certainly looked disgruntled.

Charming, heavy, swart Bertha, dressed all in Union Jacks, opened the door herself. A smooth round pillar of stomach divided her bunchy brassiere from her frilly skirt. She screamed, jumped up and down like a pneumatic road-drill, then hustled Ian into a bedroom on the ground floor. There he found the clothes of all the other guests strewn about him carelessly. He shivered a little as he pulled on his leaves, gowned himself and hung the garland round his neck. He tried not to feel naked and horribly defenseless. He longed for one of those awe-inspiring gorilla bodies. No one would dare to laugh then. If he clutched the garland close to his chest, hiding his nipples, he might feel a little more protected. But Bertha gave him no time for further anxious brooding. She burst into the room and cried:

"Oh, but, Ian, you look sweet. What are you? A sort of little woodland sprite, or what?"

Overcome with confusion, Ian could only mutter savagely: "I don't know. I'm nothing in particular, although I had thought of trying to come as Bacchus."

"But you can't look nearly loose enough for that," shrieked Bertha, taking his hand and pulling him into the living-room.

Mrs. Swan lay on the sofa in the bay window, her vast breasts and hips swelling up before her like miniature mountain ranges, one behind another. She wore black velvet trimmed with curtain lace, round her neck mauve pearls as large as sugared almonds glistened. Her face was unpainted but so heavily powdered that it looked as if it had grown a thick white fur.

"I'm always so pleased to see Bertha's friends," she said. "Dear young people all, I'm sure. I can't get about easily now, so it's a special treat to see new faces."

There was something strangely mortifying in her universal indulgence. One was dismissed as Bertha's friend, a dear young person, nothing more. Ian looked about him uncomfortably, his anxious smile becoming more and more fixed. What could he do with himself? Where could he go in this crowd? Nearly all the other guests were from the art school, but their nakedness had turned them into strangers. Stocky little Bobby Davies was holding Veronica Tooth's hand as usual, but he was only wearing a strip of imitation leopard skin and she looked like nothing so much as a large tablet of oatmeal soap tied with ribbons.

The lame youth, Treff Rowse, wore an elaborate *papier-mâché* codpiece which he must have modelled himself. Painted on it in bright colors was a terrifying face with staring eyes and wide-open mouth. One tape between his legs, one round his waist held it in position. His buttocks were quite bare. For the first time Ian saw his poor withered leg. It was like the thin white stalk of a dying plant. How could he treat it so cruelly? How could he expose it to them all? But Treff seemed perfectly indifferent to it and everything else. He was in a sort of trance, crooning to himself and moving his arms and shoulders, quite lost in one of his never-ending variations and perversions of "Dinah."

There were a few people whom Ian did not know. He guessed that one of them must be Baby, Bertha's younger sister. She had transgressed all the rules and come in a boy's jacket and trousers with a rather dirty scarf wound round her neck. Ian had been told that Baby had a passion for collecting books, which she hardly read, and that she pretended to enjoy smoking a foul little pipe made out of some pithy root with a surface like a lizard skin. Ian felt in sympathy with Baby because she, too, was younger than the others and clearly very shy. She was so shy that he was afraid even to catch her eye.

But who could that other heavily dressed person be? That nun with white bands swathed round her face? Her clothes must be authentic; she had everything—even the heavy crucifix dangling from her girdle. Perhaps she was a real nun; but could a real nun be persuaded to come to a party, and such an undressed party? At that moment the young nun thrust her hands down and straddled her legs. She seemed to be searching vainly for pockets. Her pleasant broad face puckered and she gave a deep laugh. Ian knew then for certain that "she" was a man.

People were gathering round the nun to examine her clothes and ask questions. They stroked the rich folds of her habit and one even picked up the crucifix shamefacedly and held it close to his face. Ian heard a girl say, "Nuns never look at their bodies; they bathe in cotton shifts that come right up to their ears. It must be so difficult chasing the soap under the wet folds."

"I've got the hang of it at last," replied the nun and everybody laughed.

Ian, finding himself near the door, felt that it was a good moment to slip out.

There was nothing in the hall but a great coarse needlework hanging done by Bertha. Fat golden lions with rosy tongues lolled under giant arum lilies. The hanging went strangely with the corrupt, genteel wallpaper frieze of autumn leaves. Ian stood admiring it for some moments; he had always felt that Bertha was one of the most talented people at the school. The thought of her talent made him depressed with himself. He passed on into the dining-room, not thinking of what he was doing. Here the food was already laid out on the long table. It was childish and appetizing. There were jellies and trifles, sardines and stuffed eggs and chocolate biscuits. On the sideboard stood carafes of lemonade, something which looked like raspberry syrup, and bottles of cider. All round the walls Baby's books reached from floor to ceiling. Starting in one corner with *The Treasures of Peru,* Ian glanced quickly along the lines until he came to *The Proceedings of the Sexual Reform Congress* by the door.

Bertha, leading the other guests in to eat and finding him there, immediately accused him of gluttony.

"What are you doing in here?" she demanded. "Have you been picking the decorations off the trifle? I can soon tell how many sandwiches or biscuits have gone."

"I haven't touched anything, Bertha," Ian protested, made to feel thoroughly guilty by her mock indignation. "I was just looking at Baby's books. Hasn't she got a lot?"

"Yes, haven't I?" said Baby, suddenly emboldened and coming forward to his rescue. "Do you like books?" She spoke as if they were avocado pears, or some other food for which a taste has to be acquired. There was no question here of weakness or excellence of different volumes. Books were books—things to be hoarded and treasured and touched.

Ignoring the food on the table altogether, Baby led Ian round the room again, sometimes crouching to pull out a large book, sometimes climbing to find a small one. Behind his polite exclamations Ian's thoughts kept turning to sardine toast and trifle and lemonade. All at once Baby awoke to her duties as hostess. She shovelled several things on to two plates and returned to their corner.

"I'm afraid you must be hungry," she said, offering him the things that he would not have chosen himself. They ate leaning back against the shelves. A greedy clatter of knives and forks arose from the table. Mrs. Swan had dragged herself up from the couch and was moving weightily round the room suggesting a cucumber sandwich here, a stuffed egg there, a glass of grenadine or a cheese straw. Ian noticed that parts of her mauve pearls, having lost their nacrous surface, had come to look like fungus puffballs or snakes' eggs. Spoons were already being dug into the bowls of decorated trifle. Some people were eating their little silver balls and some were not. Ian wondered for the thousandth time how they were made. He had wanted to know since his first infant party. Could it be that they were silvered with mercury? And mercury was poison—it made your teeth drop out.

The din was subsiding a little. Bare arms were thrown out contentedly along the backs of chairs. Smoke rings and spirals floated up. Pink tongues flickered round the last drops of sour-sweet cider in the glass-bottomed tankards. Out of the window the sluttish back gardens and sheds were fading into each other. The room was filling with shadows, so that the rows of books seemed to be closing in on the seated guests. Bertha struck a match and lit the scarlet candles in their curious makeshift holders, contrived out of raw potatoes sliced in half. From the open scullery door came the gentle dripping of a tap and the ghosts of yellow soap and cabbage water.

For a few moments the guests sat there comfortably enjoying the workings of the food inside them and the calm excitement of the gathering night. Mrs. Swan had sunk into the gnarled arm-chair at the head of the table and was drumming on a plate with her pudgy fingers. Satisfied little rumblings and gurglings arose from her enormous body and every now and then the lowest murmur of words escaped from her lips. She seemed to be praying or chanting to herself.

Suddenly Bertha jumped up and broke the peace.

"We must all play Sardines," she insisted, running to the window to blot out the last of the light.

"Oh, Berty-darling, let's have a little quiet," groaned Mrs. Swan. "It never does to jig about after food. If you do, it turns on you."

"You can't have quiet at a party, Mother," Bertha said, blowing out the candles and disappearing. She could be heard drawing all the curtains in the other rooms.

Soon the darkness was full of whispers and stealthily moving bodies. Ian made for the scullery door and stumbled down two unexpected steps, knocking over a metal tray or a dustpan. Some-one very near him laughed nervously at the clatter and he drew his feet back, afraid that the unknown person would trample on his toes. He could smell the sink now and the tang of shoe polish.

Ancient food smells came to him, but he could find no one hiding in the corners. He left the kitchen, felt his way up the two steps and passed into the hall. Opening a door, he found himself in the bathroom—a cold white glimmer came from the bottom of the bath. He touched a soggy sponge and shivered. But the bathroom, too, was empty.

As soon as he opened the next door he became aware of stifled giggles. He ran his hand along the wall until he grasped a bare leg. The giggle turned into a little shriek. Something touched his head, bounced away and touched it again. A handle on a chain. He was now in the lavatory and people were huddled round the pan, some even standing on the seat. A hand stretched down to help him up. He managed to wedge himself between the other bodies. They clung together there, surging and swaying and giggling. Ian's toes curled over the lip of the seat. He imagined himself as a primeval monkey standing on a branch in the chattering forest.

All at once he felt a hand exploring him. It ran tentatively down his arm, flickered over his stomach, one finger dipping for no more than an instant into the tiny cup of his navel before travelling on to his other arm. The hand had clutched his now, was kneading it excitedly in little rushes, rather as loving cats bite each other's necks. Distractedly Ian put out his free hand and touched a crucifix. The shock of the cold little metal body sent a shiver through him, starting a hot prick of sweat along his upper lip. On his ear farthest from the crucifix he could feel warm damp puffs of breath. He listened for a moment, caught a characteristic whistle and gurgle in the nose, and knew that he must have Bertha on his other side. Now he could feel her starched Union Jack skirt scratching his side.

The anxiety of not understanding exactly what was happening was rapidly undermining Ian's calm. Who could be fondling his hand so greedily? Could the nun have mistaken him for Bertha? They both had naked stomachs. Perhaps in his excitement the nun would not notice the great difference in their bulk. Had Bertha not mistaken him, but decided to tease him with these preposterous blandishments? Perhaps it was the nun who had decided to make a fool of him. This thought of maliciousness from a stranger was particularly hurting. The final confusion arose when he began to imagine that the hand belonged to someone quite unknown. There must be five or six other people standing on the seat, all within easy reach of him. Any one of them could be making a mistake in the dark. He was sure that there was some mistake or some intended cruelty. His own hand had gone stiff with discomfort and unhappiness. Yes, it was true; no one could ever love him.

He was just plucking up courage to snatch his hand away when the last person stumbled on their hiding place and the little crowd broke up, streaming out of the confined space to laugh and talk and stretch in the hall.

They played Sardines for a long time. Once Ian hunted with Baby. Under cover of darkness she had grown bold enough to smoke her little fiber pipe. When she lit the match, Ian saw her pinched face with the delicate nose and clear pink cheeks. Her pale hair, scraped behind her ears and tucked under the slouch cap, glistened for an instant. She looked remote, fanatical, consecrated in some way—but to what? To her book-collecting? He kept with her because he liked the glow which quickly grew and faded whenever she sucked at the pipe. There was a dumb fellow-feeling, too—not strong, but there. Ian, trying to explain it to himself, could only think of aspects of Baby that were not in themselves very winning. She had nothing to say; her mysterious preoccupation dulled her response to other people. She seemed to enjoy flouting her body. The scraped-back hair, the dirty scarf, the rough boy's clothes, gave her a secret pleasure. While she stood alone, her eyes far away, it was easy to believe that she had a contempt for "ordinary" people, for their cocksure silliness and unreality.

Ian grew so tired of stubbing his toes on unexpected pieces of furniture, of waiting breathlessly in the dark, that at last he crept up to the French window and let himself out into the garden. The night wind blowing on his hot skin made him shiver, but he welcomed it. He went over to the cats. They were all lying down, like the lions in Trafalgar Square. The tom had made one of those amazing smells, fascinating and horrible in their pungency, their power to evoke all scenes of human squalor and misery. Ian squatted on his haunches near the cats and made sucking, cheeping noises in a forlorn effort to please them. Strangely enough the tabby roused herself and ambled up to him. She began to rub herself against his thighs. The feel of her soft fur on his bare flesh was delicious, but somehow vaguely shaming. Like some solemnly planned voluptuousness, it was too soft, too yielding, with no tang in it. Bertha was wrong about this cat, at least—she certainly showed no dislike of strangers. The tabby, trying to climb up on his knees, clutched at his chest when she found herself slipping. Ian gave a little gasp as the claws dug into his flesh. He put up his hand and felt a little trickle of blood. He licked it from his fingers, savoring the saltiness on his tongue. Then he gathered up the cat in his arms and held it against his body. It was like nursing a huge silky cocoon, a baby wrapped in folds of slime, a purring seed about to burst from its velvet pod. He bent his head, cooing over the cat as if he would send her to sleep. She patted him once with her paw, ran her rough tongue over his skin, then nestled herself more snugly in his arms. The feathery brush of her fur, rising and falling, rising and falling, began to tickle just under his armpit. As a child he remembered his father tickling him there until he was unable to scream anymore, until he felt he must go mad or die if the torture did not stop. The sensations came flooding back, turning the gentle tickle into something intolerable. The cat, as though she read his thoughts, turned in his arms and tried to struggle out, but perversely he held her, flattening her against him. In her alarm she gave him a savage little bite so that he loosened his grip; then she leaped away till the leash jerked on her neck, bringing her down, dejectedly. She was like a minute slave, bitter at the thoughts of her bonds. Ian stared down at her for a moment, then he turned abruptly and walked back into the house. He held the bite of his left pectoral muscle, but there was no blood this time. He knew just how it would look; there would be tiny white tooth marks, the skin abraded round the edge, as if he had been paper too much worn by india-rubber.

In the house the game had changed to Murder, but Ian was not to know this. Every room was still in darkness. Mechanically he crept about in search of the group of hiders. He was becoming more and more weighted and oppressed, and yet, at the same time, somehow hollow, as if he were a cave through which the wind was blowing. "Morbid" was the word his aunt would have used for him. She always made the adjective sound particularly disgraceful, and Ian, against his will, gave it the same coloring.

There was a slight rustle in the darkness beside him, a little rush, then suddenly two hands were round his throat, pressing on his windpipe. He cried out in fear and his unknown attacker chuckled demonishly. He knew it was only some game, but he could not beat down his panic. If only he weren't lost in the stifling darkness! If only he could rid himself of the shock of those hands round his neck!

The lights were switched on. Bertha looked round and asked: "Who's been murdered?"

Ian, still collecting his wits, put up his hand like a schoolboy: "I think I have."

"Then lie down, you fool. You're supposed to be dead."

He lay down on the floor obediently. Bertha came up to him and saw the smear of dried blood from the scratch on his chest and shouted out gleefully, "It's murder all right, there's real blood!"

Bending lower, she described the tiny white punctures with their purplish centers. "Ian, what have you been doing?" she asked ominously. "Have you been teasing my cats?"

"Of course not. The tabby liked me very much. She wouldn't leave me alone."

"No, I see she wouldn't. She's bitten you. Why did you upset her? I've told you they hate strangers."

Bertha looked down at him balefully, as if she, too, hated him for trying to seduce her cats. They were *hers.* She would share them with no one.

The others were growing tired of this wrangle. If they were not to play Murder properly, they might as well forage in the dining-room for more food and drink before thinking of going home.

Gradually they disappeared from the room, leaving Ian still lying on the floor with Bertha standing over him. He was content to lie there; the strangeness of it rested him. If he stood up, he would have to face Bertha on her own level, contend with her ridiculously. How could she wish to possess her cats so entirely that she resented any attention paid to them? It was so absurd it saddened him. He would find it difficult still to think of Bertha as a great comic bouncing figure with something specially worthwhile and sensible deep inside. She seemed silly now, in her attempt to dramatize a trashy jealousy; she was like a girl on the pier determined to have a scene over some "boyfriend."

When Bertha saw that Ian would not get up, that he had insolently shut his eyes, feigning sleep, she, too, left the room, loudly complaining as she went: "Bloody fool to touch my cats. Next time they'll scratch your mucking eyes out."

Ian had to smile, Bertha's fatuous extravagance still tickled him. He sat up and saw the clock on the mantelpiece. He had missed his last bus by more than half an hour. The thought of the long journey home made his heart sink. He would be walking through miles of streets until early morning. He felt quite unequal to it, too tired to do anything else but lie down again on the floor. He wondered if Bertha would let him stay where he was for the night. He hated to ask after the trouble over the cats, but he was just about to go in search of her when he heard the swish of heavy skirts and turned his head to see the nun in the doorway. The white face bands were undone; it was clear that she was about to take off the whole head covering. In spite of knowing that she was really a man, it was a shock to Ian when she exposed cropped brown hair. The blunt, slightly freckled face underneath suddenly fell into place. Its heartiness ceased to be disquieting. One no longer felt that one was in the presence of the games mistress at some athletic convent.

"Are you sleeping there?" asked the nun, grinning to see Ian still on the floor.

"Well, I don't know yet; I'll have to ask Bertha. You see, I've lost my last bus."

"That's easy. I can put you up if you like—better than lying there. The floor gets damned hard after a bit."

It took a second for Ian to adjust himself to this idea, then he decided. "That is very good of you. Are you sure you don't mind?" Perhaps this was the friend he'd been waiting for, he must wait and see, he wanted so to talk to him alone.

At last the party was breaking up, coats and hats were being dragged off the huge pile on Mrs. Swan's bed, and Ian soon found himself walking along the cold pavement with the nun, habit off and trousers on.

They passed a row of little villas and the nun said: "That's where a strange fortune-teller lives; she's got red hair and she's sixty and she always wants me to go and see her."

They walked on until they came to a main road and saw the rows of silent shops. Up to one of these the nun led Ian. It was a barber's shop, and when the nun had found his key they went up the steep stairs into the darkness. It was so still, one felt all the people breathing quietly in the closed rooms. They made their way to the front. The nun switched on the light and Ian saw that there was butter in a molded glass dish and ham on a blue-ringed plate with other food laid out.

"This is my supper," said the nun. "Will you have some too?"

"I don't think I could," answered Ian, then added: "You know, I don't even know what your name is."

"My name is Don Billings."

"And mine is Ian Whyte."

The meal was dreary and a little sinister—so late at night—with all the sleeping people round.

"I lodge here with the hairdresser," said Don. "Her hair is red, too, but I think it's real, I think she's very fond of me; you see, I help her wash up sometimes. We must be quiet when we go upstairs else we'll wake her up. She's got a husband, too, but he's a traveller."

Slowly they groped their way up the stairs, Ian touching the shoulder of Don, until they came to the top floor—they passed the bubbling cistern, and Don gently opened the door of his room and shut it after Ian. They were in darkness. Ian saw the small grey square of the window, smelled the smell of bedclothes and waited until the light was switched on; then he saw the chest of drawers with white china knobs and the little picture standing on it. It was a reproduction of a landscape by Derain. A hot sandy road between dark trees with rich shadows and an eggshell sky. It was beautiful—and Derain was Ian's new discovery. He liked Don more than ever.

"My girl gave that to me," said Don, "because it's like somewhere we know."

"Is that all they like it for?" thought Ian.

Don was undressing, he pulled his shirt over his head. How brown his skin was with light golden hairs. He was firmly and neatly built. Ian admired him standing, so obviously solid and strong with his trousers resting on his hips. "He is like a miniature navvy with all the edges polished," he thought.

Don put on old flannel pajamas and turned back the bedclothes.

"You get in first and I'll switch off the light."

Ian did so and looked up at the ceiling. The night was so warm in this little attic and it was so strange to be in a different bed.

Don got in and they lay there close together, their warm bodies making the clothes seem a little damp. Don talked about his girl and many friends. Ian felt very lonely. It was nicer sleeping in bed with someone else; one wasn't so lonely.

"And yet I used to hate human contacts and always want to be on my own," he thought. "I wonder if I shall like it if he turns over and wakes me up?"

So gradually they dropped into sleep and the next thing Ian knew was that the sun was shining on him palely through a mist and that there was a scream of trams on the road. He looked at Don, who was still asleep. There he lay, pajama jacket open, his bare throat throbbing gently, with the golden hair at its base. There was a slight new stubble on his chin and upper lip and there were freckles round his closed eyelids.

"This is a nice friend to have," thought Ian. "And now I must leave him and get on one of those screaming trams to go home. I must borrow a book so that I can come back to return it another day." Looking round, he saw on the chest of drawers a book on Maya civilization.

Gently he pressed Don's arm and watched his eyes open, then slowly they both got up and took it in turn to wash in the cold water from the jug. Ian put on his trousers, rolled up the mauve bathing suit, then, turning to the chest, said: "Don, may I borrow this book?"

"Yes, do."

Don was sitting on a chair, still undressed, and Ian, not waiting to be asked to breakfast, held out his hand and said: "I must go now, as they must wonder what has happened to me at home."

Then he ran down the stairs and let himself out into the early morning air; clutching the book, he walked quietly towards the tram stop, saying over and over again to himself: "You can never tell, I might never see him again."

A Picture in the Snow

Yesterday, in the cold bright sunlight, we drove through the snow to our nearest town to do some household shopping and to find, if possible, a small spare part which was needed for the car.

We tried garage after garage, turning down side roads, going from one end of the town to the other, without success. We ended our search by cruising along a wide road on the outskirts, no longer with any idea of finding the spare part, but simply to enjoy the sight of the snow on the houses and gardens for a little longer before turning home.

All at once I was aware of a gap in the thick plantation of trees and shrubs on the right. I looked up the bank and saw that two new building sites had been cleared at the top, but as yet no building had been begun. There was a clear view of the great house behind.

The sudden unexpected sight of its twisted chimneys, its stone mullions, its stepped gables, the whole Edwardian solidity and comfort of it brought back vividly another afternoon nine years ago. I found myself concerned for its fate, angry that the trees and bushes screening it from the road had been torn up so ruthlessly. It was almost as if it had been some house of my childhood, cherished in many happy memories; yet I had only seen it once before.

On impulse I asked G. to turn into the drive, feeling fairly certain that the house must be empty. If it were not, our car should arouse little interest; we would probably be taken for builders, architects, or any of the other people who had to do with the two cleared sites in the garden.

Halfway up the drive we came upon three old women; they were talking together with much gesticulation. One leaned towards another as if she would breathe in her face until she convinced her or made her lose consciousness; the third gave us a quick, darting look, then hooded her eyes in an attempt to make us think that she had taken no notice, that we were not impressed on her memory for days and nights to come.

I was glad when we were past the old women. I said to G.: "Let's just go to the end of the drive, turn round and come back quickly."

As we wheeled round in front of the stone porch with its flat Tudor arch, carved coat of arms, and oriel window above, I was just able to read the word "home" on a new bronze plaque. The old women were explained to me then; they were patients probably suffering from slight mental disturbances.

"So it has come to this," I thought; "Mount Lodge is now a 'home,' and the garden is being torn up so that two little annexes can be built for nurses and doctors."

Once more my mind went back to the afternoon nine years ago when I first saw it and learned something of its history.

I had been walking in the town; I think I was coming away from the public library where I had been searching for something in a reference book. I was deep in my own thoughts, with my head down, but I became aware of footsteps behind me. They seemed to be hurrying, then a shadow loomed over me and I looked up to see a very tall, very plump man of about thirty-five passing close to me on the pavement. As soon as he was a few yards in front, he seemed to slacken his pace, almost as if he were waiting for me to catch up with him. He ambled so slowly that I did indeed draw level with him in a moment. Before I knew quite what was happening he had turned, bent down towards me with a tentative smile, and was saying in a surprisingly baby voice: "Oh—you look interesting; do tell me about yourself."

I was too taken aback at first to do anything but notice that the end of his pug nose was quite brown from tobacco smoke; it looked as if it had been toasted. But how was I to answer his extraordinary remark? The little rhinoceros eyes were still upon me. I must think of something to say.

"Does 'interesting' mean 'peculiar'?" I asked, as unconcernedly as possible. "Do I need a haircut? Or is it my clothes? Perhaps, when you passed me a moment ago, I had a faraway 'doped' expression on my face."

"Oh no!" the piping voice protested. "But I'm sure you write or paint or do something interesting. I've seen you several times."

I immediately felt spied upon, as if this fat man had been hiding in doorways and side alleys to catch me out in some discreditable practice.

"Well, what do *you* do?" I asked, retaliating.

"Nothing very much at the moment, I'm afraid; but I've always had a great interest in politics, psychology and literature."

"In that order?" I asked.

Again the flickering uncertain smile.

"Yes, perhaps now; but my childhood dream was to become a writer. I had almost finished quite a novel by the age of eleven. I still have it in my bedroom; some day I must run right through it and see what my maturer judgment makes of it."

A delicate little titter, like sparrows chattering in the eaves.

We were walking together now as if we had known each other for years. The fat man had insisted on falling into step with me; if ever the rhythm was broken by my disregard of it, or by some obstruction on the pavement, he would give an absurd little skip and come down again on his left foot in time with mine. I half expected him to begin intoning: "Left, right, left, right, left, right," in a sort of sleepwalking boy scout's voice.

As we marched in this military fashion, I was able to take in other aspects of my new acquaintance. His stained grey-flannel trousers flapped against his legs rather flimsily; instead of a belt, he wore an old silk tie threaded through the loops at the top. His vivid blue jacket sagged and bulged at the sides, making it clear that he was in the habit of stuffing his pockets with all manner of objects. His face was round and pale, but whenever he turned to me I noticed again that the little eyes twinkled from beds of much darker flesh. It was almost as if he had once been given two black eyes which had faded at last to these dusky circles. His lips were dark, too, and full; some of their darkness was again due to tobacco stain, and the first two fingers of his right hand might have been carved out of mahogany.

When we reached the top of the town where the road divides, I slowed my pace, meaning to say good-bye and take the right branch; but my fat friend refused to let me go. He stood in the middle of the road imploring me to go back to tea with him.

"Oh, do come back," he said; "there is no one at home. We can have such a pleasant chat. I do hate being left on my own."

His baby voice was so insistent, so appealing that I found myself resisting stoutly; then some sudden spark of curiosity burnt down all my defenses and I was thanking him meekly for his kind offer.

"My name is Whittome," he said: "but please call me Danny—all my friends do—isn't it frightful?"

I felt called upon to give my own name. There is something formal, something sobering about an exchange of names; one is made conscious of self and the lack of intimacy that exists between that self and the new companion. We walked on in silence until we came to the gates of a small late-Victorian red-brick villa called Elm Dene; the name, in fresh white letters, was painted on each solid gate pier.

"This is where we live now," said Danny.

Was there the slightest ring of apology in his voice? I wondered about the unnecessary "now"; it seemed significant.

He led me past the neat carpet-bedding, under the involved cast-iron porch, and into a rather dark dining-room with blue and white plates and vases on a shelf above the panelling. Tea for one was already laid on the large pale walnut table.

The maid must have heard us enter, for she came to the door already carrying the tea tray and an extra cup and plate. She put down the silver teapot and a rather unusual hot-water jug on a stand over a spirit lamp. Before she left I saw that she was old and that her grey-white hair was piled rather clumsily under her wide old-fashioned cap; it escaped at the back in sad little curls and wisps. She seemed to treat Danny with a weary indulgence, as if she had known him too long to be surprised at anything he did.

My eyes fixed on the delicate blue spirit flame; the hot water jug above seemed more fanciful, more luxurious than the other tea-table appointments. Did it belong to an earlier period in the Whittome fortunes? What sort of a house was this that I had entered? And was it going to be difficult to get away?

Danny had begun on the toast greedily, but only after a painful hesitation because both brown and white bread had been used.

"Which is nicest," he asked anxiously, "brown toast, or white toast?"

"Both are nice," I said prosaically, rather in the tones of a patient nanny; although he was so much older, his childish importunity, whether natural or assumed, had the effect of making me feel "in charge" of him.

His fat dimpled hand still hovered above the toast dish. The two brown fingers looked like little chipolata sausages dancing in the air. He finally plumped for white toast, stuffing a whole finger into his mouth and champing noisily. He seemed to revolve the toast round and round, and as he did so his body heaved from side to side, reminding me of pictures of Dr. Johnson; or was he more like an enormous praying mantis?

"My father won't be back for some time," he said, with his mouth full. "He still goes up to the city three days a week."

I said, "Oh, I see," not knowing what else to answer. Things were going very badly indeed. I wished that I had not given in to my foolish impulses and trapped myself in this dark room with its ponderous walnut furniture and coarse blue plates and jars. Danny perhaps could tell that I was eager to escape, for almost before I had finished the last morsel of my cake he was pressing a cigarette on me, as if trying to keep me with him for at least another quarter of an hour. It was clear that he preferred any company to none, that he had a hatred of being left alone.

"Come up to my bedroom and see my books," he said, catching at another method of keeping me a little longer.

I followed him upstairs and down a narrow passage. He

opened a door and I found myself in a little room where every piece of furniture, except the iron bed, was heaped with books. There were piles on the floor, even the tiny fireplace was blocked with them. Danny flopped down on the bed and began to open volumes on his knee. Sometimes he would thrust one towards me, pointing out a passage, a title page or an illustration. They were most fairly well-known novels of the twenties and books on psychiatry with lurid case histories printed in the appendix. There were political books, too, but these I found so dull that I can remember nothing at all about them.

My eyes strayed to a small photograph above the bed. I saw a little boy of four or five, dressed in white party clothes after the fashion of the first years of the century. He looked both plump and petulant. The rich glow of his silk socks and jersey made it easy to dismiss him as the traditional "pampered darling"; yet there was an attractive seriousness about the face, as if the child already had thoughts for his own future.

"Guess who that is," said Danny, puckering his face gleefully.

"Too easy," I answered. "It's you, of course, in your party suit."

"Did you really recognize me?" he asked, a wistful humble note creeping into his voice. "Yes, I was a promising, pretty child; and now I've got fat and almost given up hope of ever doing anything at all."

He was angry, not so much with himself as with Fate for playing this dirty trick on him. How dared she make him fat and take away his hope!

He bent down and pulled a suitcase from under his bed. Opening it, he began to rummage until he had gathered eight or nine faded green exercise books together.

"Shall I read you bits from my childish novel?" he suggested tremulously.

"Yes, do," I said, feeling quite eager to listen. Surely the novel of a child of eleven would have something interesting about it!

He opened the first book, smoothed the page, then shut his eyes and exclaimed: "No, no, I can't. I might be terribly disappointed in it; it might spoil it for me forever. Besides, you haven't seen the setting yet. I'd like to show you where we used to live; then, if I do decide to read you bits, you will have a clear picture of the background."

He stood up, all agog for me to follow him. We went down the back stairs and out into the garden. He was secretive, wishing to surprise me with something, so I asked no questions. We crossed the lawn behind the house and came to the vegetable garden. At the far end Danny unlatched a little gate and led me down a narrow path between thick hedges. Soon we were in the shadow of a solidly built stable and coach house. Danny pushed through a gap in the hedge. I followed and found myself looking down into a white cucumber frame where baby chickens cheeped and fluttered round their mother. Danny bent down, grasped one rather anxiously and began to cherish it in his hand, murmuring baby language to it. Was this what I had been brought to see? The chickens were very pretty, but I had no wish to pick one up, to feel the trembling little bunch of feathers struggling in my hand.

"Aren't they sweet? Aren't they sweet?" chanted Danny with half-closed eyes; then he seemed to remember what he came out for. He put down the chicken and led on through the bushes. We passed the cobbled stable-yard and came out on an overgrown drive banked on either side with rhododendron, laurel, holly, box and other ornamental shrubs. I noticed a forlorn lamppost with broken glass and empty bulb socket; leaves surged up to smother it. A few more years and it would be lost. The drive twisted artfully. Danny was hurrying now, as if he were impatient to confront me with what lay at the end. His excitement was rising. Under the great weight of his belly his twinkling feet seemed small and neat and extraordinarily agile. I thought of him as the Minotaur charging down the windings of the labyrinth.

We turned a corner and he stopped suddenly. "There it is," he almost squealed; "that's where we used to live."

I saw the mechanically picturesque outlines of Mount Lodge for the first time, the studied disorder of mullions, transomes, archways, spandrels, parapets, gables, dormers, crockets, finials, and diapered chimneys piling up and up, bewildering the eye so that it clung for relief to some minute detail—a carved leaf, a shield, a chip in the stone dressings, a damp patch on the brickwork.

"What a whopper!" I said, knowing that it would please Danny.

"Yes, isn't it," he agreed, between giggles of sheer pleasure. "My father built it in 1905. I can't think why, really, because it was always too big and mother much preferred picnicking in a little cottage she had. Still, he would insist on it; it's supposed to have cost about 17,000 pounds. Perhaps it gave him a feeling of achievement. In those days he was rather a flourishing stockbroker; but things aren't the same anymore; we finally had to leave the house six years ago. It has never been let; nobody wants such a large place. The gardener still lives over the stables and keeps plants in the greenhouse. Those were his dear little chickens we saw."

We began to walk towards the house, climbing some stone steps to a terrace before a great bay window. I peered through the dusty glass and saw elaborate parquetry and a plaster ceiling heavy with bosses.

"That's the drawing-room," Danny explained eagerly; "and there's a morning-room, a library, a billiards-room and a conservatory as well. Unfortunately I can't let you in because my father hides the keys ever since I allowed a rather wild friend, who'd lost his last bus home, to sleep in the conservatory. The irritating creature amused himself by breaking panes of glass. I'd never have let him in if I'd known he was so tight."

I was moving round the house, looking in at all the windows, while Danny pattered after me, describing the past in disjointed snatches. He had so much to tell; he could only spend a moment on each episode.

"Of course, once we went rather grand and had a page with buttons all down the front; the funny thing was that he and I belonged to the same boy scout patrol or pack or whatever it's called. We used to meet in the evening and pretend that we'd never set eyes on each other before. Then there was the time when my mother asked an Austrian count to stay. In a morose fit he locked himself in his bedroom for hours and hours, until we all felt that he must have committed suicide. He came out at last, calmly playing with the cat. Do you know what I used to say to people about this cat?"

"I can't think," I said absently.

"I used to say: 'Have you ever seen a cherry colored cat with rose colored paws?' When they shook their heads, I'd tell them that I had one and show them Tinribs with his *black* body and *white* paws. They never thought of black cherries or white roses." Danny giggled as if somebody was tickling the soles of his feet with feathers. He saw me looking at the rough tussocky grass which swept away in an ever widening fan until it reached a curving bank rather like some primitive earthwork.

"Of course, this was such a marvellous lawn, but it hasn't been mown for years. Once we had a garden party and I dressed up in all my mother's beads and rings and brooches and sat in a darkened tent, pretending to be the gypsy fortune-teller. Nobody recognized me and I prophesied terrible things—financial disasters, and deaths, and the most peculiar love affairs."

At the back of the house we came upon a desolate little patch fenced round with miniature palings. Danny opened the tiny gate and stood in the middle of the weeds.

"And this is *my* garden," he announced dramatically; "I've had it ever since I can remember."

"You don't seem to have done much work in it lately," I said. It was curious how Danny forced one into the position of nurse or schoolmaster. Why should *I* censure his laziness?

"Oh, I can't keep my mind on anything these days. If only I could, I'd have more important things to do than a child's garden; but I worry and worry and worry and nothing gets done—nothing!"

He was staring at me desperately; his bottom lip looked swollen, as if it had been stung by bees. It trembled a little. I turned away and remarked brightly on the first thing that met my eyes.

"Is there a pond behind all that dry bamboo grass?"

"Yes, it's terribly overgrown and weedy now, but we used to have a tiny boat on it. One of my mother's fantasies was that we should one day sail about on it, eating chocolate creams of every imaginable color—a white one, a pink one, a blue one, a green one, a mauve one, an orange one, a lemon one—can you think of any more colors?"

"What a quaint conceit!" I said laughingly, still trying to keep Danny from his black thoughts.

"Yes, she was like that . . ."

His voice trailed off. I imagined that his mother was dead, that he was dwelling on his memories of her.

"She used to paint quite a lot, you know," he added. "Would you like to see some of her pictures? A few are still stored in one of the stables, I think."

I followed him towards the cobbled yard. We entered a stall

and stood over a manger, turning back watercolors in narrow white frames. There was a still-life of anemones, jade beads and a little gilt Buddha; there were several garden scenes, bright with herbaceous borders; more ambitious landscapes of churches, rivers and autumn woods.

"Is your mother still alive?" I asked at last, shirking the difficult task of saying anything about her painting.

"Oh yes, but she's had to go away, if you understand what I mean. She has a little cottage near the sea. It's better if she only comes over occasionally to see us."

I didn't understand, but it was clear that I could ask no more. Mother perhaps was a little mad.

Danny replaced the pictures with neurotic exactitude, easing each corner into perfect alignment with the next.

"Let's go back by those winsome little chickens again," he said.

We started to push our way through the bushes. I heard a car in the drive and thought little of it, but Danny stopped at once.

"Who can be coming here?" he asked, exaggerating his perturbation. He turned back with a noisy crackling of dead twigs. A large black car swished by, then stopped. I could see the rounded top of a hackney-coach label. Someone was getting out, a rather beautiful, "overblown" woman in a sable coat thrown open carelessly. She wore no hat and the light glinted on her snugly waved, greying auburn hair.

"Darling!" she exclaimed, swaying gracefully towards Danny, "they told me that you were probably in here; I suddenly felt I had to come over and see you both. Aren't you pleased? Now take me back and give me a lovely strong cup of kitchen tea—that's what I want."

Danny was gazing at her open-mouthed. Mechanically he bent to kiss her. "But we never expected you. It's one of Daddy's London days; he isn't home yet."

"D'you ever know when to expect me?" the woman laughed. "It doesn't matter about Daddy; I can wait."

"Oh! But I have a friend in the bushes," said Danny, remembering me.

"My dear, what an odd place to have him, or her! Please introduce me at once."

The handsome woman came towards me, peering from side to

side. I emerged from my hiding-place and waited, smiling awkwardly.

"What must you think of Danny, leaving you to pine in there?" the woman said, holding out her hand.

Danny had followed her excitedly.

"This *is* my mother," he explained, his voice mounting higher and higher. His excitement expressed itself in little snorts and grunts. The delight he felt in being able to show her to me seemed to crown his day.

"Has my son been showing you our old house?" she asked. "I suppose in my heart of hearts I think of it as 'a dear old place,' although it was never really 'me'; Ronald was the one who would insist on it. Still, I have my memories, such odd ones some of them."

Danny's mother began to bite her pearls; she fiddled with them till she had the diamond clasp in her fingers. It flashed and winked at me like a knowing eye.

"What has this great son of mine been doing lately?" she asked, still addressing me, but never waiting for an answer. "Anything? Or nothing at all?"

She put her hand up to Danny's shoulder as if she would shake him playfully.

"How often have I said, Danny darling, 'men must work and women must weep'? But with no effect; he doesn't take the slightest notice. He's the laziest lump in all Christendom."

She tried to give him a little push, but his great bulk nearly overbalanced her. She reeled and her face came near to mine. I saw the heavy powder on the rather uneven skin, the slightly bloodshot corners of the handsome eyes. The delicately shaped and painted lips parted. There was a sudden breath of spirits. And then I understood.

Danny was watching me closely, giggling at the consternation on my face; he seemed to be waiting for something else—for the complete exposure of his mother? I turned and walked rapidly away, afraid to listen or look back.

That last scene was printed on my mind; it had lived with me for these nine years, so that I found myself extravagantly sorry at the change in Mount Lodge and the garden. It was almost as if it had been a house of my childhood, cherished in a hundred memories.

Ghosts

The first story I ever wrote was a ghost story. I wrote it at school for the last English lesson of the term. I remember the tremor of excitement that ran through me when I heard the master, so like a rather strong-smelling black retriever, giving out the announcement for preparation.

As I had been taken to see Knole in the holidays, my mind immediately turned to those wonderful rooms for material. I stole the ostrich plumes off James I's bed, the silver sconces off the walls, the brass locks presented by William III to the Cartoon Gallery, and the eighteenth-century proportions of the Venetian Ambassador's bedroom.

I panelled my imaginary room in pine and finished it with a

heavy cornice. From a cracked punch bowl came the faint scent of mildewed rose-leaves, and a hissing fire of green branches spat and danced on the scratched marble heath. The hangings of the fantastically high bed were of rose madder damask, faded in parts to tawny, dried-blood color, and they were so rotten that they had to be held together on a new foundation by countless lines of cross-sewing. It gave me a great pleasure to describe all these remembered details.

In this grand bed I put myself to sleep, after having blown out the eight candles in the four sconces. As I wrote, I became more and more involved in my own story.

Suddenly, in the middle of the night, I awoke and found myself staring up into the dome of the terrifying bed. I lay sweating, wondering what was going to happen.

I remembered a line, perhaps from Ecclesiastes or the Psalms, "the hair of my flesh stood up," and it seemed such a perfect description of my feeling that I put it down word for word.

Gradually, from the depths of the room beyond the bed, a lighted figure emerged. It was no ordinary ghost, rattling bones and chains, but a beautiful woman, tall and sweeping and not young—ageless, like the queens in fairy tales.

She glided up to the bed and stood there, twisting her rings and mouthing painfully. She wanted to tell me something and she was dumb!

I can't remember how I ended my story, but I suspect that I left it dangling in the air, as most true ghost stories are left.

I liked my story too well not to feel alarm when the time came for it to be read out by the black retriever. What if he should maul it and make it appear ridiculous!

I sat near the back of the class, and he took several other stories first. One he refused to read in its entirety because a great parade had been made of visiting nightclubs and "coming home with the milk."

I looked at the "unwholesome" boy who had so successfully added to his reputation for wickedness by writing in this way, and was amazed to see how calm he kept under the master's contemptuous glance.

With an exasperated crackling of pages the black retriever spat: "I can't read out any more of this appalling stuff!"

Such scorn would have withered me for days, but the boy who

specialized in vice just wore a bored expression; "blasé" I think he would have called it.

When at last my story was reached, I stopped breathing and waited for some dreadful pronouncements; therefore I was astonished when I heard the master say: "Now this at least has something good about it. The writer has tried to create a romantic atmosphere, and whatever he has described he has first seen very clearly in his mind."

This was intoxicating enough from the black retriever, who, I thought, disliked me. To be called "the writer"! But when he began to read my story soberly, as though it were "real literature," my heart was filled with gratitude. I listened to my own sentences with only a bearable amount of embarrassment, and knew in a moment that I wanted to be a writer.

All went well until "the hairs of my flesh" was read out. Instantly laughter broke out all over the room and voices called out: "Oh, I say, Welch, do they really stand up?" "Oh Welch!"

Unwisely rushing to my own defense as a writer by referring them to my august source, I protested: "But it's in the Bible! You can read it there."

This started a second storm of laughter, groans and mockeries. I thought: "Let them laugh. Everything is ridiculous if you like to make it so." I even began to laugh myself. . . .

Then I forgot all about this story, until sometime later when I had left school and was staying at a friend's house near the sea in Sussex. Besides myself there was one other guest, and as we sat on the sunlit lawn, shelling peas for supper, she started to tell me of this true experience.

She had gone up to stay at a large old house, I think in the Midlands. Her room was in the eighteenth-century part, with walls panelled to the ceiling, and heavy sash windows.

Immediately my mind flew back to my own story, and although she told me that her bed was modern, uncanopied and very comfortable, I still saw her in my ancient plumed bed with the crimson curtains moving in the draught like furtive animals.

She read a little as she lay in bed, then she switched off the lamp and went to sleep.

In the middle of the night she was woken, just as I had been in my story; although it was not a beautiful woman that she saw, but a huge filmy egg, made out of mucus membrane and lighted from within. It floated slowly through the darkness until it was above her in the bed. She saw with horror then that the egg-shaped glow encased the face and shoulders of a man. The shoulders were naked and just below them the body dissolved into stringy, phosphorescent mucus. Round his head was a squirming halo of the same. The flesh was of an extraordinary ruddiness, and exaggeratedly tight, as if the image had been blown up with a bicycle-pump.

The young man was grinning at her, showing his white, animal teeth. On his forehead were hot brown curls and the needle points of his eyes bored into her.

Fascinated, she watched the face until it disappeared on the other side of the bed, then she lay still, wondering what it could be, until, most surprisingly, she fell asleep again.

In the morning her host and hostess told her that the image appeared in various parts of the house, not only in that room. Sometimes it sailed down the passages. The face and shoulders were all that could ever be seen. They had no explanation to give for the appearance of the image, except a rather unconvincing tradition about a young man, a villain and an ancestor of theirs.

For a moment after the end of the story we went on shelling peas in silence. The pods, as they were ripped open, made a sucking noise, like mouths gasping for air. My mind was busy comparing the true experience with my invented one. I could think of nothing but ghosts; I was filled with the idea of them.

And jumping up restlessly, I left my companion, and the peas in the china basin, and the empty pods on the lawn; and I wandered a long way until I came to a black pool almost surrounded by tangled thickets. I knelt down and dipped my hand in the still water. My fingers were magnified into fat, curling grubs. Baring my arm, I stretched down till I felt rotting branches and twigs soft as horses' noses. I pulled, and a mossy, peeling antler rose dripping from the pond. Delving still deeper I came to a pie of excrement and leaves, layer on layer, and limp and black as chow dogs' tongues.

It was evening now, with the sun setting. I looked up at the turquoise sky, then down at the stirred-up water where black motes like pepper starred the pinkness of my tingling arm. From across the pool a dull blind window suddenly flashed back the dying fire of the sun, and a rush of birds streamed out above me. I saw the woodman's ruined shelter of branches tied together, and his pile of bark peelings turned now into a mass of dead mottled snakes.

Everything at that moment held a secret. Everything was haunted. But human eyes were not the right eyes, and my ears would never hear.

Anna Dillon

Anna Dillon looked in her bicycle basket to see that she had everything for her picnic: thermos of coffee, Ryvita bread, cheese, minute parcel of butter, a little honey in an old cold-cream pot, her precious ration of chocolate, an early, brilliantly red apple. They were all there; so was her childish paintbox, her block of paper and her book.

She waved her hand to Mrs. Eames, who kept house for her, and rode away from the cottage with a light heart. She was going to spend the whole afternoon by the river, in her favorite spot where the rich cornfield swept down to the magenta loosestrife and the varnished yellow daisies. There was a certain tree there, against which she knew she could lean and be at peace.

To look at Anna Dillon, one would have taken her for a girl in radiant health: the glinting, curling, toast-colored hair, the delicate brick-dust tint of her cheeks, the clearness of her hazel eyes that sometimes were quite green, all these seemed to point in that direction; but it was not so. Anna was tubercular. Many precious months of her life had been spent in sanatoria. Now she was better and was living very quietly all alone in the country, with only Mrs. Eames as companion, nurse and housekeeper. Her parents had died while she was still a child. Both had left her a little money, and now that she was twenty-one she had chosen to live away from the rest of her relations. They disapproved, but could do nothing. They also placed perfect trust in Mrs. Eames to let them know if Anna's condition in any way grew worse.

Bicycling along, Anna forgot all her troubles, including her deflated lung, until her too-impetuous pedalling in the hot sun made her gasp slightly.

"Go slow, you idiot," she told herself; "then you'll manage perfectly well."

When she got off the main road she even forgot the war; there was nothing to remind her of it except the jog-trot droning of the few aircraft circling overhead. They were ancient biplanes, used for instructing new pilots. Their shapes in the sky struck a curiously old-fashioned, nostalgic note.

Anna left the lane and rode down a bridle-path which led between a hop-garden and a cornfield. The hops with their creeping tendrils were already draped fantastically and beautifully from the wires to the poles. The path was rough, with here and there a piece of sharp tin or glass embedded in the cinders and baked mud. Anna avoided all these bits as carefully as possible, and at last reached the riverbank, feeling rather jolted. She crossed the old wooden bridge and wheeled her bicycle along the towpath until she came to her favorite place. Here the cool shade from the overhanging tree spread round her. She knew that she must not sit in the sun because of her condition.

Anna took the things from her basket, blew up her air cushion and lay back against the tree trunk. She seemed to have the whole river and the surrounding fields to herself. Nothing stirred, except fish in the river and birds in the trees. The fish sometimes leaped right out of the water showing their silver bellies. A gust of wind came to ruffle the surface of the water and to make the rich cornstalks grate against each other dryly. Anna spread her Ryvita with butter and cheese and began to eat hungrily.

As she ate, she read her book. It was an old novel by Mrs. Henry Wood. It really was very amusing. Whether the humor was intentional or not, did not matter in the least.

By the time Anna had reached the chocolate and apple stage, she felt utterly content. Her milky coffee comforted her, in spite of the heat. She let her hands trail through the silky blades of grass, then she felt in her bag and took out her cigarette case. It was of engine-turned gold with a diamond clasp. She had given it to herself as a present when she thought she had some money to waste.

"You oughtn't to take a thing like that just loose in your bag when you go out in the fields or by the river," Mrs. Eames said. "You're bound to lose it one day."

"How should I take it then? Padlocked round my neck?" Anna had asked.

"You oughtn't to take it at all."

"But I love pretty things—I enjoy my cigarettes much more out of this case than out of a paper packet."

"You won't talk like that when you've lost it in the river or the long grass," Mrs. Eames warned her.

Nevertheless Anna still took her cigarette case with her, and now she opened it and fitted one of the white tubes between her lips. She lit it and puffed contentedly for some minutes, wondering what subject she would choose today for her little watercolor sketch. She was modest and lighthearted about these, admitting that she only did them for her own amusement. One day she hoped to become more serious.

She got up and, taking her block and paint-box, walked a little farther along the bank to get another view. She thought that she might do two willow trees, some boat-houses, a gate, and their reflections in the water.

As she looked across at this group, she became conscious of someone lying close to her in the grass. A slight bank and the length of the thick tussocks of grass had completely hidden the outstretched form until she was almost upon it. Now she looked down into the sleeping face of an airman. He had taken off his jacket and shirt, and he lay there in the full glare of the sun in his startlingly white singlet. His arms and legs were thrown out carelessly, as if he had fallen down exhausted. Sweat glistened between the bleached hairs of his very neat moustache. His brown face shone.

Anna was startled by the beauty of his calm eyelids and his mouth washed clean of all expression. Without thinking of the heat on her back or her standing position, she bent over her board and tried to get down the significant lines of his face. She worked feverishly, afraid every moment that he would wake and see her standing over him. But she soon became so engrossed that she forgot his humanity and studied him as she would a rock or a stone.

Anna smudged with her finger impatiently, trying to get the deep shadows round the eye sockets. It was while she was riveting her gaze on this part of his face that his eyes slowly opened. He looked straight into her blankly for a moment, then a grin spread from his mouth, up his cheeks, curling and broadening his nostrils and crinkling the skin round his eyes.

"You know I charge a slight fee for this," he said sleepily, yet at the same time just managing to cock an eyebrow.

"I *am* sorry, I really must apologize," said Anna in great confusion. "The fact is that I was walking along, looking for a landscape subject, when I suddenly came upon you. I could not resist trying to get something down while you slept. I do hope you are not offended."

"Fully realizing the powers of attraction my extraordinary beauty must wield over any nice girl, I am graciously able this once to forgive and forget." The man's face showed not the flicker of a smile. Anna arranged hers to match. "That is extremely good of you. May the humble artist be allowed to present her modest drawing as some slight recompense for her effrontery?"

Anna held the sheet of paper out to the man bowing her head in a ceremonious gesture. He took it, at the same time raising himself and reclining on one shoulder in a lordly way.

"But my dear, it's perfectly frightful!" he said with simulated surprise. "I had no idea I looked like that when I was asleep. I shall be careful never to do it in public again."

"I expect that what offends you is my ineptitude. In many ways I prefer the sleeping to the waking expression." Anna smiled sweetly.

"Oh naughty! Don't let's go on sparring anymore. Will you

believe me when I say that I think your bracelet's very pretty and that I may have seen worse faces in my time."

Anna looked down self-consciously at her big amethyst and silver bracelet, and then began calmly to sketch the man in his new position.

"Still making use of me!" he cried in mock surprise, but taking care not to move.

"That's right, keep still," Anna said approvingly, then she lapsed into silence for some time. Only the scribble of her pencil could be heard and the delicate lapping of tiny wavelets against the overhanging banks. The man held his position well, and although he wore a wry smile, he was very patient. At last he said, "If smoking is permitted, will the artist put a cigarette between her model's lips? She'll find a case in the breast pocket of the tunic."

Anna put down her pencil abstractedly and went across to the tunic. When she turned it over and saw the wings on the pocket a tremor ran through her. She liked to touch the cloth; it gave her great pleasure. She found the case and opened it. It was empty except for two cigarette cards and an address on a torn piece of paper.

"You've smoked them all," she said. "Just wait a moment and I'll go back to my bicycle and get you one of mine."

She returned with her case. It glinted in the sunlight.

"Aha—I see I have to do with an heiress," said the airman in a stage villain's voice. He had not moved at all. The pose was held perfectly.

"It's nothing but vulgar ostentation, I'm afraid," said Anna. "There's nothing behind it at all." She fitted a cigarette neatly into his mouth and lit it for him. They puffed together silently.

"What's the time?" The airman asked after some minutes.

Anna looked at her watch.

"It's nearly four."

There was another pause.

"It's a pity we haven't got a little kettle and a fire here, so that we could make tea," the man said.

Anna thought for a moment and then said abruptly, "Why not come back and have tea with me? Mrs. Eames would be overjoyed to get it for a real live airman." She spoke as lightly as possible, and mentioned Mrs. Eames to reassure him.

He looked at her penetratingly and then said shamefacedly,

"You know, I wasn't cadging when I said that about a little kettle and a fire."

"Of course you weren't! I only wondered if you'd like to come back and have tea with me; I live quite near."

"I would," he said seriously.

Anna stood up. "I'll just get my bicycle and put the things from my picnic lunch back in the basket," she said, walking away so that he should have time to put on his shirt and tunic.

She waited by her bicycle, until she saw him coming round the corner, looking very trim and smart, now that he was properly dressed. She saw that he was a squadron leader.

Anna rode very slowly beside him. They talked quietly. There was no more bantering, although they sometimes laughed. Anna opened the gate and called out to Mrs. Eames, "I've brought a real pilot home to show you, Mrs. Eames! Can you give us tea?" Mrs. Eames looked at Anna's companion and just said, "Oh, sir!" Although the airman did not know it, this was a tremendous tribute. Mrs. Eames had long ago given up calling anyone "sir," considering it undemocratic.

After her first moment of admiration, she looked at Anna enquiringly.

"This gentleman very kindly sat for me while I was trying to sketch on the riverbank," Anna explained. "We both felt thirsty, so I suggested coming back and asking you to make us some nice tea."

Mrs. Eames flew into the kitchen to get things ready. Anna knew just what to say to please her. She also knew that Mrs. Eames would be thrilled to get tea for the unknown airman.

Anna took him into the tiny living-room and showed him her things.

He looked along the bookshelves quietly, then said, "How pretty and peaceful it is here."

Anna's eyes shone, "Do you like it?" She was delighted with his simple praise.

"Yes, the pretty striped curtains, the bright old china figures and the cups on the rack, the roses in the silver bowl and the nice polish and lavender smell."

"Sit down and be comfortable," Anna pressed him. He sank into a corner of the sofa and seemed quite content to gaze about him and be at peace.

Anna saw the great need he had of peace. She guessed that he had gone to the river to get away from everybody and everything. There was an almost terrifying look of strain about his eyes when he thought he was not being watched. But underneath she could see the real broad, straightforward nature, that was only waiting to come back and take possession—that now expanded in the quiet cottage rooms.

Mrs. Eames came in importantly, bearing the silver tray, the Georgian silver teapot, sugar basket and cream jug. She had unpacked them all from their box and tissue paper and polished them in a flash for the unexpected visitor. Anna beamed her approval. She was not quite so certain when she realized that Mrs. Eames had used some of the Earl Grey tea. Men so often preferred Indian to anything else, that she was afraid he might not like the flavor. But she was reassured when he said, "I haven't tasted tea like that since the war began."

She pressed him to eat some of the toast—a tomato sandwich—one of Mrs. Eames's crisp shortbread biscuits.

They they both sat back and smoked in silence. Anna realized that they knew nothing about each other, and she was content to leave it so. She wanted always to think of him just as the airman she found sleeping by the river. She hoped he would ask no questions and tell her nothing.

He didn't, he simply sat quietly on the sofa puffing his cigarette until it was finished. Quietly Anna walked across to give him another. She held a match for him too and their hands touched. She felt the slight tremble of his hand through all its strength. She saw the golden hairs glinting on it. She did not want to take her own hand away; she wanted to go on having contact with this quite often vivid almost ruthless life, so different from her own tenuous stream.

He looked up straight into her eyes through the smoke; then his hand closed on hers and he pulled her down very gently beside him on the sofa. She sank down willingly enough, content not to think at all, only to savor this wonderful new peace and security. She lay against his side in the crook of his arm. Through the uniform, rough to her cheek, she could feel his steady heart beating. Big Ben—Rock of Ages—she thought of all things set and steadfast. Her head rose and sank as he breathed. His large hand played through her hair. He delicately stroked the glinting strands.

"Where shall I be this time next year?" he mused in a whisper close to her ear.

Impulsively she put her hand up to touch his eyelids, to smooth and stroke the hairs on his upper lip.

"Don't let's think of anything but now," she said. I am fatally ill; you go through untold dangers almost every night, but let's think of nothing but our peace and safety now.

He bent his head down to kiss her. She raised her lips and put her arm with a childlike gesture tightly round his neck, so that the crisp stubble at the back of his head pricked her bare arm.

"Oh, darling," they both sighed together and then laughed at their unanimity. They lay there, holding each other tightly, savoring each second, knowing that too soon they would be torn apart.

Mrs. Eames, with the greatest good sense and feeling, did not come in to collect the tray. The tea grew cold in the pot, but Anna got up at last and went across to pour another cup for her unknown friend. They drank the cold tea together from the cup. She parted his lips, pushed a biscuit between his ivory teeth, then nibbled the other end herself. Their noses touched. They laughed and rubbed them together lovingly, like Eskimos.

Suddenly he held her to him so tightly, that she felt she could not breathe.

"Oh, darling," he gasped out, "I shall always remember this marvellous day. You can't think what you've done for me, giving me this wonderful peaceful time. I shall have to go soon and we may never meet again, but this moment will always be, crystal clear, perfect, nothing can ever change it."

His words so pierced Anna that she felt the tears on her cheeks wet and hot. She did not bother to restrain them but cried quite simply and freely against his shoulder.

"Oh, life is so awful," was all she could say.

"No it isn't, darling; it's just life—no use to kick and strain—got to take it as it comes." He paused a moment and still seeing that Anna wept bitterly, added, "Let's have some music to cheer us up! Where's the wireless? I'll turn it on and see what's going."

Very gently he undid her arms round his neck and went to switch on the wireless. He tuned into a program of gramophone records of the twenties. The silence of the cottage was broken by the plaintive lyric "—Diamond bracelets—Woolworth's doesn't sell Baby—Till that lucky day you know darn well baby—I can't give you anything but love."

"Come on, dance a little, darling," he said, holding out his hands.

"We can't in this tiny room," Anna replied, but nevertheless she wiped her eyes and stood up. He grasped her, supporting her against him, so that she felt no weight in her body, then they swayed and moved gracefully to the old music. He guided her between the pieces of furniture but often they stood still in one place like Eastern dancers, only moving their bodies and their arms.

"It's heaven, you really do dance all my cares away," said Anna fervently. "I seem to forget about the war, forget about the fact that I may be dead next year."

"That goes for me too," he answered, pressing his strong lips to her thin crimson ones. She clung to him, seeming to need all his support.

"Now darling," he said very gently, "I've got to go, else I shall be late." He held her at arm's length and looked deep into her eyes.

"Don't go," she cried clutching at his arm.

"I must; but I think we'll meet again. I think one day we'll see each other on the riverbank again and we'll come back and have tea just like this." He said no more and turned to jerk down his tunic and pick up his cap.

She ran to him to help, patted a hair from his shoulder, determined not to make this parting too difficult for him. She folded his ear with her hand, kissed the side of his cheek and whispered softly, "Good-bye darling. I'll pray for you every night. And one day we'll meet by the river again."

For some reason they both of them left it vague in this way, superstitiously afraid of fixing a day.

Anna watched her airman walking down the path alone. She saw him turn into the road. He walked jauntily with a determination. It was clear that he was steeling himself, keying himself into the right mood for the grim night's work. "God, keep him safe—God, keep him safe," Anna found herself saying over and over, in a low voice. The agony of parting pierced into her and twisted like a knife, but she did not cry. "We've had our lovely time. We can only ask for the smallest crumbs, never dare to ask for more. If he should be killed tonight; if I should die tomorrow, we still have that. These are the tiny things we live on, they only must suffice."

She looked out of the window. The lane was blank now, only the waving flowers in the garden and the feathery trees. Quietly Mrs. Eames came in and took away the tea things. She soon reappeared and looked at Anna solicitously. "Shall I read that nice book to you, Dearie," she said comfortingly, "while you go on with your pretty cross-stitch work?"

Anna nodded and smiled and pulled her work towards her.

Mrs. Eames sat down and took the book in her lap. "What a nice young gentleman that was! Did you see his decoration ribbon, I couldn't tell now what it was but I saw it." She went on, "He'll be dropping in again, I wouldn't wonder, now he knows where we are. He enjoyed his tea all right." She chortled, thinking of the empty plates.

"Yes, he'll come back, won't he?" said Anna fervently, and in her heart she tried to cover the cold stone which chilled her there.

In the Vast House

When I was small I lived with my grandmother—all alone except for the servants—in a big house. All around was the spreading park which shut out the world. Everything was very still in the house, there were only the voices of the servants which could sometimes be heard through the closed doors and the singing of my grandmother's canary. It was a green bird in a wonderful Chinese cage of silver-gilt set with coral and lapis lazuli.

My grandmother was very old and queer; she always wore the old-fashioned cravat and tailcoat of a man. Below the waist I do not think she ever wore any outdoor clothes, as she always sat in a wheelchair with a rug tucked round her legs. Her hair was yellow grey, brushed forward into romantic wisps about her ears to which were fastened two black pearls. She would sit all day by the French window in the library looking out across the park. Sometimes she would grunt and swear to herself.

She did not really like me very much and I was either left alone to do as I wished or else put in charge of Will, the footman.

He was tall and broad and I loved him dearly. If I were playing on the floor, while he was serving my grandmother at her table at the window, I would creep up and kiss his strong legs. He would shift his feet slightly to show that I tickled, whereupon I should do it again until my grandmother, hearing my heavy breathing and my giggles would shout, "Geoffrey, come out from under the table and stop teasing Will." Then she would turn to Will and say, "Take him away, Will, and give him a good flogging if you think he needs it." She always spoke of any form of corporal punishment, however mild, as flogging.

Will, with a shamefaced repressed grin, would then bend down and say, "You come along with me, Master Geoffrey." I would feel his big hands groping for me under the table and the scratch of their hard palms as they brushed my face and legs. Then I would be borne up by those arms, which always seemed to me like an iron crane, and held against his warm hard chest. I would feel the regular hammer of his heart against me and like this, we would leave the room, myself an anxious but willing prisoner. When the library door was shut and we were in the wide, portrait-hung corridor, Will's nature would expand and he would lift me onto his shoulders and walk with a swaggering step, sometimes running and lunging. I was delighted and terrified and would tighten the grip of my legs around his neck, so that the short hair at the back of his head would prick my flesh and he would shout out that I was choking him and would bring his chin down onto my knees and expand his neck muscles. I would relax my grip and he would hold my hands up and would pretend to be a dancing bear with a monkey on his back.

If it were after lunch and the time when I should rest, he would often take me to his room which was in the dome at the top of the house; he would climb with me, still on his shoulders, up the narrow servants' stairs and at last would throw me down on his narrow, white counterpaned bed. His face would often be shining with sweat after so much horseplay and the veins would stand out on his large hands which were covered with the red-gold hairs which I liked so much. I used to think that his hands looked as if they were dusted with powdered gold, when the sun shone and made the fine hairs glint.

When he had made me settle myself to rest on the bed, he would take off his coat and sitting down by the window, he would begin to stuff his pipe and find the sporting news in the paper.

I would watch him through the slits of my half-closed eyes, my eyelashes knitting together and making a veil through which he appeared.

I would see the slight furrow, as his eyebrows were brought in and down by his concentration on the scores. The white sleeves of his shirt would be rolled up and the blur of gold hair would lie like a bloom over the flesh of his arms. They were as thick as my thighs and I exulted in their hugeness and strength.

My eyes would pass from him to the dressing table where the swing glass would be hanging drunkenly, and where the photographs of Will's sweetheart and his sailor brother would stare back at me. Will's sweetheart had soft hair, like a mouse's nest, and calves' eyes that focused on a future of which she seemed terrified.

His brother was in a gym vest and sailor's trousers, sitting on a cardboard rock with arms akimbo. His eyes seemed to say, "What next, what next? I've done all that's expected of me so far."

I would watch a fly sitting on one of Will's studs and then hear it buzz as it threw itself against the mirror, trying to fly through it.

Perhaps at last I would doze off and when I awoke with a slight feeling of sickness, I would see that Will's chair was empty and that his pipe, with the ashes still in it, was on the window sill.

I would steal across to the window in my stockinged feet and pick up his pipe. I would wipe the mouthpiece and then put it in my mouth, pretending to be Will.

The taste of the burnt tobacco would sting my tongue and fill me with nausea and strange pleasure.

If he had left any clothes lying about, I would slip them on furtively and feel my warmth releasing the pleasant smell of Will's body, so that I seemed to be lapped and enveloped in him.

If I heard him approaching, I would hurriedly wriggle out of his garments and pretend to be putting on my shoes. When he came in he would help me and then bend my face up to him and draw his strong fingers through my hair as a comb. He would take me down to the Varnished Room, where tea was laid every afternoon, and leave me there alone until he had fetched my grandmother in her wheelchair. I would sit by the hissing fire and look round at the room which never ceased to amaze me. It had been decorated for an ancestress in the eighteenth century and everything was painted or lacquered in it. The ceiling and walls were panelled in wood and painted with strange, erotic scenes from the classics, the doorway and wainscot, window frames and chimney piece were green and red marbleized wood and there were columns and architectural ornaments with wreaths of flowers. The varnish with which all this painting was covered had mellowed to deep amber and the whole room, ceiling and walls, was polished once a month with beeswax so that it glinted and glistened from sunlight and firelight. The furniture was mostly Venetian, gilded and painted and decorated with old engravings, mixed with Chinese cabinets covered with thick lacquer on which were incised faded peonies and flying birds. There were Chinese jars filled with dried rose leaves, so that when Will took the lids off before my grandmother appeared, the breath of a hundred summers rose faintly from them. Every year another handful of petals was put in and the jars were so large, it would seem that they would never be filled.

On the mantelpiece and on top of the tallest cabinet were octagonal silver vases, swelling in the middle, which held faded ostrich plumes dyed yellow, crimson, green, and blue, darkened with dust and age. From the center of the room hung the great chandelier of Venetian glass decorated with colored flowers and leaves and bristling with wax candles.

While I was staring at all these things, the door would open slowly and my grandmother would be pushed in by Will. The corners of her mouth would be pulled down so that it looked like the sagging slit in a pillar-box. Her eyes would go straight to the tray by the fire, where the silver kettle and the spirit lamp with the honey jar shaped like a Grecian urn and all the other tea things were laid out. Then, when her chair had been wheeled up to the fire, Will would leave us and we would settle down silently to eat the soft floury scones, the toast, the sandwiches and the cakes. I was only allowed one piece of cake and would nearly always choose the rich, black plum cake which was made with molasses.

My grandmother would eat greedily, with great concentration, and when she had finished she would lie back in the wheelchair and restlessly turn the rings on her fingers and pluck at her cravat pin, running her hand endlessly up and down the lapels and seams of her coat. Sometimes she would take a book from her lap and read to me, but she would never finish the story and always left me in a terrible state of suspense. Once, while she was reading one of the Ingolsby Legends, I noticed that her voice was thickening and faltering. I grew red and squirmed on my chair. I did not know what was going to happen. At last she stopped reading, letting the book fall into her lap and flattening her hands out on it with a smack as it fell. She threw her head back against the chair, looking up at the ceiling and cried out in a voice heavy with grief: "Emma used to love this one, the ghost always frightened her so." She was crying bitterly by now and I sat, as still as a mouse thinking of what I knew of Aunt Emma, as I called her.

When my grandmother had married she had told my grandfather that Emma must come to live with them too. He was ready to agree to anything at that time and so Emma had come, and thenceforward my grandmother and Emma had lived a vital life almost totally excluding my grandfather. While they were fishing, or riding, or boating on the lake, he would be left to wander morosely in the park or to read alone and unwanted in the library.

At last, worn out with boredom and disappointment he had died. His loss was hardly noticed except that Emma and my grandmother now hardly even bothered to disguise their passion. They shared the same room and were inseparable in everything. When Emma suddenly died my grandmother completely withdrew from everyone, living alone in the vast house until when my parents died I joined her.

Constance, Lady Willet

Constance, Lady Willet, looked at herself in the glass and put a little more powder on her already rather thickly coated nose. She consciously over-powdered in this way so that the effect should last for several hours. She thought of herself as a handsome woman, and she was. Thick neck, broad cheekbones, widely set apart brown eyes which were only ever so slightly discolored, and pretty reddened sullen mouth all made up a pleasing whole. She thought once more that she was really wonderfully preserved for sixty-three.

She put the puff back into the box with the Reynolds' Angel Faces on the oxidized silver lid, and then pulled her gloves on. As she looked down at her half-hoop of diamonds and her wedding ring she thought of her husband. He had only been dead a few months. Poor Harold; he hadn't had a very happy life. She'd been a disappointment and their son Mark had been a disappointment and then business had done badly and he'd lost a lot of money, and on top of everything else to die so painfully!

Constance left her bedroom and went down the break-neck cottage stairs which opened straight into the long low sitting room. Mark was sitting by the fire reading *Fourteen, The Diary of a Schoolboy.* He had found it on one of the shelves of the rented cottage. He looked up at his mother and then turned his face away rather furtively. He had only lately come out of prison where he had been sent for refusing to do his noncombatant duty.

He was afraid of his mother because her attitude changed almost hourly from loving understanding to the most jingo patriotism and then back again. Having no money, his allowance having stopped at his father's death, he was forced to live with his mother. He knew that she wished to be rid of him, that she did not like his large, rather dirty presence continually about the place. She was always telling him to go to the Labor Exchange and get a job on the land; to make an appointment with the dentist; to eat less greedily; not to scatter ash on the carpet. He was nearly forty and very unhappy and worried. His wife had left him long ago.

"Are you going into Tunbridge Wells?" he asked with an attempt at brightness.

"Yes," said Constance, "I've got some very necessary shopping to do. Now remember darling," she added firmly, "you're to be out of the house for the whole day, as I've told Mrs. Cousins to clean it from attic to cellar. I shall be extremely annoyed if you hinder her in any way. You're not to come back till I return this evening."

Mark nodded his head, and then asked rather hurriedly for a little money so that he could buy some cigarettes and have his lunch at the Green Man across the common. His mother felt in her purse, then drew out two half-crowns and handed them to him importantly. "Darling, do try to spend less," she said; "you realize, I suppose, that we're as poor as church mice now. Or perhaps you don't. As you've never done a stroke of work all your life, I suppose you still have no idea of the value of money. You've certainly romped through your own as if it were water."

Constance stopped talking, wondering if this last metaphor were quite all it should be. Mark muttered something meek and conciliating, whereupon his mother broke out again, "I think you're much too submissive. I wish you wouldn't always agree with me, it's so dull!"

Mark was about to frame a reply, but his mother swept out of the room with a perceptible swish, calling out, "Now remember!"

Constance patted her soft wool dress and straightened the charming little bunch of different-colored wallflowers which she had pinned to her bosom. The diamond chips glinted in the brooch which had belonged to her mother. It was made in the form of her father's regimental badge. She began to walk down the village street to the bus stop. Sunlight pierced through the heavy trees and dappled the warm-colored roofs. Constance felt happy with her shiny American cloth shopping bag on her arm.

The bus was rather crowded but she found a place and sat contentedly looking out of the window.

Poor darling Mark, she thought, no money, no sense, no stamina. Only a silly Edwardian baronetcy and the weakest of literary urges. Those teeth, his growing stomach and his disappearing hair—what *was* to be done? She simply couldn't have him about the place forever, and yet if she gave him a tiny allowance and told him to go away, he would get so very much worse, and she would feel horribly pinched. For the hundredth time she added up her various sources of income and saw that the total came to no more than 325 pounds a year. In spite of her own and Mark's extravagance, she blamed poor Harold for not managing better in some way before he died.

But Constance was clever at putting unpleasant things out of her mind, so when she alighted in Tunbridge Wells she was able to give her whole attention to the people in the streets and the objects in the shop windows. Living in the rented cottage in the tiny village had given her an excitement for the town, like that of a young girl in an eighteenth-century novel. She was content to gaze in shop windows, however meagerly stocked; and to watch the passersby. She wondered where they came from, where they were going to. She made up stories about their journeys and destinations.

Across the road was an arts and crafts shop. Constance made straight for it and looked at all the little painted gnomes, brass door-knockers, embroidered kettle-holders and fancy window wedges. At the back of the shop she saw the dearest tea-cosy all made of brightly colored felt in the shape of a brooding hen. Constance longed to waste her money on it, so she went in and asked the price.

"Ten and six, Madam," the very young girl said.

Constance thought for a moment; she had very little more than three pounds to live on till the end of the month, but she quickly brushed this thought aside and decided to have the cosy. "Then when Mark is in late his tea will always be hot," she assured herself comfortably.

Constance went out of the shop and wandered further up the High Street. She knew that the Pantiles were a snare and a delusion, that the soul of the town was no longer there. She thought it a shame that there were not delightful little luxury shops under the colannades.

When she reached the station she decided to leave her serious shopping until after she'd had a cup of coffee and a cake at Wynn's. "I'll feel so much fresher after that," she thought.

She sat down at a little table and watched the chattering women all round her. She felt a little lonely. She wished she too had an amusing woman friend to laugh and gossip with.

"But then I quarrelled with all mine long ago," she told herself stoically. She enjoyed catching snatches of conversation, some of them rather improper.

She lingered over her coffee, smoking three cigarettes, and when at last she got up to go she found that is was nearly one o'clock. All the shops would be closing for lunch. She hurried to the greengrocer and was just in time to buy a lettuce and a cooked beetroot before the door was locked.

Constance wondered what to do. She did not want to go back to the cottage without doing her shopping, yet if she stayed she would have to wait a whole hour.

"Of course in the old days I could have gone to one of the hotels and had lunch, but now I couldn't possibly afford it, especially after having bought this darling tea-cosy." She hugged the parcel to her protectively.

She saw that the pub across the round on the corner had opened and that men were going in.

It might be rather fun to ask for bread and cheese in a place like that, she thought. She crossed over and walked slowly past the door. She caught a glimpse of the bright handles glistening and someone behind the bar, but she did not go in. She decided to walk further down the town and find a more attractive pub. She was going to enjoy her adventure. I haven't been in a pub for so long, she thought. Something bobbed about on her hat; a part of the heavy ribbon bounced up and down. This for some reason gave her a gay irresponsible rakish feeling.

Constance passed the parish church and climbed a little way up the hill out of the town. There she found a pub on the right-hand side of the road which satisfied her. She went in and exercising all her charm asked if they would give her some bread and cheese. The daughter of the house was very polite and was about to show her into a private room, when Constance suddenly said, "No, I'll have it in the corner of the bar, if I may, it's more companionable." She gave the girl her brightest smile.

While the girl was getting the bread and the cheese and the cucumber she had suggested herself, Constance looked round the bar. It was dark and low, but everything was clean with that humble sort of spit and polish cleanness, which has no trimmings.

One *can't* enter a pub without drinking *just* a little something, Constance told herself. She thought that she would order a glass of sherry, if they still had that wine. The thought of sherry reminded her of an episode with poor Harold. She admitted that she had been naughty and difficult, but after she had pulled herself together and they had made it all up, she remembered asking Harold very sweetly if she might have some sherry before dinner.

"Of course, my dear, if you will promise me to take no more than a lady-like amount," he had replied.

Somehow the prim words had angered her, had made her go hard inside. She had laughed metallically and said, "Darling, what an absurd measure! What *is* a lady-like amount?" Then she had drunk eight glasses straight off and had not appeared at dinner.

But all that was past now; she had forgotten all that unfortunate part of her life, Constance told herself. She knew now how to manage her temperament. She was peaceful.

The girl brought her bread and cheese and Constance asked for the sherry. A glass of dark treacly liquid was placed before her. Constance put it to her lips. She smelled again the clinging alcoholic smell; she loved it and it frightened her.

This is absurd, she said, and drank the sherry down so that the image of it should not frighten her. She began to eat the bread and cheese and to cut up the cucumber. The cheese was very soapy.

Perhaps another glass of sherry will give me more appetite, she thought. She waved her empty glass gaily, and the girl came to fill it from the bottle. Constance drank it down as she had the first, because she did not like to see it standing before her.

The bar was filling up now. Workmen, shop-assistants, a few travellers and soldiers stood about and talked in quiet undertones. Constance felt depressed by their lack of vivacity. They really are half dead, she thought. She wondered if a little whiskey and soda would lighten her heavy feeling. She remembered how, in the early days of their marriage, she had liked to sip Harold's drink while they sat close together in a huge armchair in his study.

She beckoned the girl towards her and gave her new order. After that she ordered two more whiskeys. They gave them to her in such tiny glasses and she could add so little soda water that they were gone in a moment.

Constance had eaten as much bread and cheese as she wanted. She decided that to make her meal complete, she must finish with a liqueur. I wonder if they have any cherry brandy? she asked herself. She went up to the bar, to look at the bottles on the racks behind. The men politely made room for her and she wedged herself in between them, feeling warm and friendly. She made some amusing remarks and the ones nearest to her turned and laughed. She opened her gold cigarette case and offered it round. The girl behind the bar told her that they had some cherry brandy—the only liqueur they did have, as it happened.

"How lucky!" said Constance gratefully. "It's my favorite." She offered the soldier on her right a glass as well. He blushed and said, "Thank you, M'am, I've never tasted that." "I'm glad then to be able to widen your experience. I always want to do everything I can for any gentleman in khaki," replied Constance banteringly. The soldier blushed again and held his tiny little glass of red liquid up to hers. They both drank their thimblefuls down in one gulp and Constance immediately ordered two more. She went on ordering cherry brandies until the girl said that she must keep some in the precious bottle for other customers.

'"Quite, quite," said Constance, now sublimely sweet-natured. "I only hope we haven't had more than our fair share already." She began to talk to the soldier about the house Harold had built for her in the first days of their marriage when rubber was doing extremely well. She told him with childish delight about the morning-room, the billiard-room, the flower-room, the grape-houses. She described the gardens vividly, the croquet lawns, the rose garden and the Japanese water garden with stepping-stones and irises.

The soldier loved to listen; it was like a fairy-story to him. Constance had quite forgotten the masculinity of her audience and was now describing minutiae of her tea-gowns, the velvet-lined sleeves and amber girdles; the silver spirit kettles, Earl Grey Blend, *foie gras* sandwiches and anchovy toast. Then she described her pets, her Abyssinian cat Gut, and her darling white Pekinese Po, who would bite everyone.

"Time, gentlemen, please," and the girl's officous collecting of all the glasses broke through her stories. She lingered a moment more and then the soldier suggested that they ought to be going, the doors were about to be locked. Constance settled up her final bill and then started to walk very carefully to the door. She wished the soldier and the girl behind the bar would not watch her; of course she lurched if they made her self-conscious!

Outside the door the soldier looked at her rather anxiously, then saluted stiffly, thanked her and walked away rather too rapidly.

Constance felt horribly alone. She began to wander down the hill with black misery in her heart. She had nowhere to go and nothing to do. The girl came running after her and handed her the broody-hen tea-cosy which she had forgotten. Constance thanked her and looked after her yearningly as she disappeared once more into the pub.

The wind was blowing, the sun was shining, people passed her, Army lorries hooted and dashed past dangerously. Constance's misery became so acute that she leaned against some railings and began to gasp.

"You all right, mother?" someone asked insolently. She saw two other faces smile.

Constance haughtily drew herself up and continued down the hill. Walking was becoming more difficult. Unaccountable things seemed to happen, her movements were not linked together harmoniously.

Constance began to sing very gravely and softly "Lead kindly light." The difficulty of fitting all the words into the tune always fascinated her and she also felt in her sadness very close to God.

But it was no good, the terrible black melancholy was growing on her. Outside the church, close to the traffic lights so gaily red and green and yellow, a buzzing and splintering of sparks rose to a crescendo in her head. A curtain as of some thick grey and black material fell across her eyes. Blindly she put her hand up, then leaned against the old soft brick-work of King Charles the Martyr's Church and was violently sick. The stream of orange vomit gushed onto the pavement. For a moment Constance stood utterly still and rigid, her eyes turned up to heaven, then she fell, still rigid as a stick. Her body smacked smartly on the hard paving stones, she rolled a little and lay in the gutter, close to the neat curb.

Constance was not unconscious for long, but when she came to a young policeman was bending over her. She hated at once his self-important expression, his stupid eyes, his brutal mouth. "What's your name?" he said harshly. "Constance," she answered weakly.

The young policeman and a few loiterers tittered. "Surname and address," the policeman insisted implacably.

Constance tried to clear her mind.

Oh Harold, Harold darling, thank goodness you're not here, she thought. Then she spoke in an untrembling voice.

"Willet is the name. Lady Willet, Garden Cottage, Langfield."

There was a slight stir of excitement in the small crowd. The policeman was still unbelieving.

"What did you say—*Lady* Willet?"

He seemed unwilling to write down anything so palpably untrue in his little book.

Constance nodded her head curtly and tried to sit up, she still felt horribly sick and faint but she was not going to show it to this reptile and these loiterers. She made as if to get up. The policeman said, " 'Ere, be careful!" but supported her in his arms.

"Send all these idlers away, Constable," Constance said grandly; then she nearly fell down again.

The policeman began to feel rather harassed. "Move along there, haven't you got anything to do?" he asked the crowd. They fell back a little. Then very slowly he maneuvered Constance across the road and onto the common. He walked her up and down there for some time. Gradually she became clearer and steadier.

Full Circle

I remember it well, that still night before the war, when I walked up to the entrance of the majestic house. The last glimmer from the dead sun was still hanging in the air. It lighted up the curious twisted chimney shafts and baroque gables, dramatizing them, so that it was difficult to tell whether the houses were Elizabethan or Victorian.

I pulled the long shaft of the hand-bell and heard it echoing down what I imagined to be a stone passage. Soon there were footsteps and the door was opened to me by a footman with striped waistcoat.

For a moment I was surprised and rather taken aback by this uniform, never having seen it in real life before. I had imagined in a cloudy way that if people still had footmen, they dressed them like hotel waiters. Now this nineteenth-century relic delighted me. I looked at his smooth, good-looking, commonplace face and said,

"Can you tell me where I can get a bed for the night near here? I'm walking along the Downs to Winchester and have lost my way."

He looked at my rucksack with a darting, rather furtive look, as if to read my intentions from it; then said in a soft voice,

"There's nowhere, unless you choose to go back to Steyning."

"How far is that?" I asked.

"About three or four miles."

I saw that I would get nothing more from him. He was waiting, not too politely, to shut the door. He wanted to get back to the wireless in the servants' hall or to his book by the fire. I felt, for some reason, that the family was away and that the servants had the house to themselves.

It was on the tip of my tongue to ask if he could not put me up somewhere in the house, but I had not the courage to listen to the weak excuse he would probably make for refusing. So I let him shut the door gently in my face.

Now I was surrounded by the night again, with nowhere to sleep "unless I chose to go back to Steyning." His wording seemed ironical. As if anyone would "choose" to walk back three or four miles after having walked twenty!

I crossed the cobbled court and stood by one of the stone urns which punctuated the balustrade. The coarse park grass on the other side lapped right up to this low wall. I heard the noise of animals chewing in the dark and to the right I thought I caught the glimmer from some crack between the curtains of a window. I wondered if the dark mass could be a cottage. I decided to climb over the balustrade and walk across the park to see. As I passed, sheep coughed, rose jerkily to their feet and ran away to lean against the trees in fright. Sometimes I would see them with their rumps in the air, their front legs still bent under them in an involuntary attitude of prayer. They seemed unable to move; then suddenly their legs would flick straight.

As I drew nearer I saw that the light was moving. A man was carrying a lantern out to his beasts. I felt glad that I would not have to knock again at a strange door.

"May I shelter in one of your outhouses?" I asked, hoping that my voice would not startle him.

He turned round abruptly, then came towards me with the lantern held high.

"Where do you come from?" he asked, shining the lantern on my face.

"I am on a walking tour. I have been up to the big house, but the footman said that I'd have to go back to Steyning if I wanted a bed."

"They wouldn't help you there!" he said contemptuously. It was contempt as much for my ignorance as for the inhabitants of the house.

He stood silently for a moment, looking at me. I thought he was going to ask me into the cottage, but when he spoke, it was to say,

"Come along with me, I'll show you where there's some hay."

He took me across the tiny farm-yard and led me to a shed which joined the barn. The smell of the hay met me as I stood in the doorway. The man had gone in and was stirring it up in one of the corners.

"You ought to be all right there," he said.

I eased my rucksack off my shoulders as I thanked him. Leaning against the wall I realized how tired I was. I hoped that he would leave me so that I could sink into the hay.

I did not have to wait, for after one further swift glance at my face he said good-night. I watched the lantern swinging across the farm-yard and waited until it had disappeared into the cottage and the door had clicked behind him. Then I undid my belt, kicked off my shoes, and after wrapping myself in my raincoat, lay down to sleep.

I was so tired that the events of the day kept passing before my closed eyes, running and mixing together in that fantastic, restless way. Cows in their stalls nearby shook their chains or knocked against the wooden walls.

Just as I began to wonder if I should ever fall asleep, I felt the delicious sinking and fading of consciousness. I lay like this until something jerked my eyes open. I was not yet fully awake but I knew that the dim light had changed in the shed. It was darker still. Someone was standing in the doorway.

"Who's that?" I cried out in alarm before I realized that it must only be someone from the cottage.

"It's all right, mate," the man said in a soft voice. He came towards me and sat on the edge of the pile of hay. I saw then that he was only a youth, two or three years younger than myself. I thought that he was probably the son of the farmer. He had a pleasant face but his lips and eyes were sullen. He seemed almost on the point of tears.

"What's wrong?" I found myself saying against my will. I did not want him to think me curious.

There was no answer for a moment, and I thought that he had resented my question, until he suddenly burst out,

"Would you let your father still beat you if you were eighteen?"

"Not if I could help it," I said with a laugh, trying to make the atmosphere lighter.

"No more would I, and I haven't!" His voice reached almost to a shout on the last words. "Just look at that," he went on, turning his back to me for my inspection. In the dimness I could just see dark stains on the white shirt. They might have been oil, mud, or blood. I said nothing, and in his impatience he pulled his shirt over his head. Then I knew what they were. On the white flesh were raw wounds and long bruises.

"He made my brother help him tie my hands to a tree, then he did that with his belt," he said. "But he won't do it again in a hurry; I've treated him the same way!"

"What have you done?" I asked fearfully.

"Kicked him in the belly till he was sick on the floor!" The youth laughed and leaned back till the hay pricked his wounds and he flinched.

If the man with the lantern was his father, I wondered why I had heard nothing. He had certainly not been "kicked in the belly till he was sick on the floor" when he led me to the shed, and if the incident had happened after he left me I surely would have heard some of the inevitable noise through my half-sleep.

However, I determined to ask no more questions. I accepted the fact that a father had beaten a son who was too old to be beaten and that the son had replied by kicking the father in the stomach.

My companion showed no desire to go back into the house; he said that he would stay with me, out in the shed till the morning.

He lay on his stomach, trying to ease his back into the most comfortable position. I had ointment for blisters and scratches in my pack. I got it out and rubbed some gently on the less important wounds (I could do nothing about the others). His flesh seemed burning, and I could feel how his whole frame trembled if I hurt him.

When I had finished he groped in the dark, then found my hand and held it firmly, as if to thank me.

Almost immediately after this he fell asleep still touching me. Moving as little as possible I put away the ointment and lay down beside him. His smooth breathing and the warmth from his body lulled me. Soon I too must have fallen asleep, for I remember waking later at the climax of some violent dream in which my companion or someone like him only rather older, was standing in a doorway watching a woman take a tray of cakes from the oven. She seemed quite unaware of his presence till he sprang at her, pushing her onto the kitchen-range and snatching the cakes with his other hand. I awoke at the terrible scream she gave as her hands and face touched the hotplates of the stove.

I opened my eyes. My companion still lay close to me in the hay with his hand on mine; but his breathing seemed to have grown thicker and I thought that I smelled an unpleasant odor from his body, an unkempt, unwashed smell which had not been there before. I supposed that the warmth had drawn it out from his old clothes. I tried not to think of it and composed myself for sleep again, hoping that I would not dream.

But I did. Scene after scene of squalor and brutality passed before me. The youth was always the chief actor. In each scene he seemed to be heavier and coarser than in the last. I was always the helpless spectator, hidden in some cupboard or spying through some skylight, from the roof.

In my last dream I saw him following a little girl across a Common. She was pretty, she danced gaily as she went along, throwing stones into the air and skipping. I saw him steal up behind her and grasp her round the waist. She screamed but he put his hand over her mouth and dragged her underneath the bushes. I saw him pin her hands down and kneel on her legs, spread-eagling her. Then he tore at her clothes, and I awoke with such horror that I found myself sweating; while my throat was sore with dryness. For a moment I lay there collecting myself, inexpressibly thankful that it had only been a dream. I thought I would tell my companion when he woke of the horrors I had dreamed about him. It would amuse him. I could still feel his body near me and his hand on mine. He was very still, so I did not disturb him.

Although I kept my eyes shut, I knew that it was day, because of the red glow of the light shining through the flesh of my eyelids.

As I became more conscious of my surroundings I noticed the unpleasant smell again, but there was no doubting it now. It was the smell of human dirt, despair and squalor. His hand on mine seemed strangely rough and horny and there was a coldness pervading his whole body. I thought that he must have been chilled in only his thin shirt and trousers.

I sat up, opened my eyes and looked down on my companion. Then in a moment I had jumped to my feet and lay back against the wall, my legs and arms trembling from shock.

A strange man lay there, and his face was grey and seamed and filthy. A line of dried dirt ran round his open, grey-lipped mouth, and a dribble of saliva was caught in the stubble on his chin. The strong hair on his chest frothed out of the rents in his sweat-blackened shirt. He was utterly still. I could not understand how my convulsive jump had not wakened him.

Then I knew.

I ran to the cottage door just as I was, without my shoes. The thick mud pushed through my woollen socks and lay in little cushions between my toes. I fumbled with the buckle of my belt as I rapped on the door.

The man I had seen the night before slowly opened it. He held a towel in his hands and his arms were dripping.

"What is it?" he asked grudgingly, thinking, I suppose, that I had come to borrow something.

"Quick, there is a man in the shed. He is ill."

I knew that my voice was much too loud, but I could not control it.

The man pushed past me, still carrying his towel. When I caught up with him he was kneeling by the man in the shed. He had torn away what remained of the other's collar and was holding his head between his hands. Then he let it fall back on the hay and stared at it.

"It's our Tom," he said half to himself, half to me. "I haven't seen him for twenty years." And in quite another voice he added, "Go and tell my sister Annie to come quick."

I started to run back to the house, but a woman in a white apron met me. The strings of it were flying in the wind.

"What is it?" she asked in agitation. "What's wrong?"

"Your brother's in the shed, he wants you," was all I could say.

I did not go back. I left them together and waited with my stockinged feet sinking into the mud.

I heard the woman begin to weep and through the dark opening I saw her throw her apron over her face. It seemed a curious, almost stagy gesture. "He has come home to die, he has come home to die," she kept on repeating.

Then I heard the man calling me. "Young man, will you help me?" he asked.

I could not bear to touch it, but I went in and picked up the boots behind my back so that I would be able to walk without looking at it.

We laid the body on the parlor sofa. The man looked at me and said, "He was our brother. He ran away twenty years ago because my father beat him for going out with girls. But before he left he got my father in the cow-stall and kicked him so that when we found him he was half dead. He only lived for six months after that. But Tom didn't know what he'd done!" he added passionately.

I wondered why the man had told me this terrible story, but then I realized that he had again been half talking to himself for his voice changed, as before, when he said,

"Now I suppose I'll have to go for the police."

It was then that I had the unreasoning fear that I might be charged with the murder of their brother.

I thought, while I waited to be questioned, of the youth who had come in the night before, and of how he slept touching me, while I saw in my dreams all the terrible acts which had made him into the tramp who lay beside me when I woke in the morning.

Weekend

Grace lay on the bed face downwards, her hair in greying wisps, against the pillow; her hand still clutching the little fabric suitcase. From outside came the voices of the farmer's wife and daughter.

After a time she got up, went to the small mirror over the chest of drawers and straightened her hair, then she went slowly down the dark stairs to the parlor where tea was laid on the big rosewood table. Mrs. Bulmer, hearing her come down, brought in the teapot and set it down without saying anything.

Grace went to the bookcase and looked at the titles of the books. They were old novels and bound volumes of *Chamber's* magazine. She chose Delia Blanchflower and taking it to the table, she propped it against the teapot and sat down.

She ate slowly, her eyes on the book until it got too dark to read. Then she pushed back her chair and stared into the fire, thinking of herself.

Her thoughts were flickering and uncertain like the fire. She could hardly look at some parts of her life without wincing, but here in the stillness some of her fears seemed to evaporate and she kept repeating to herself, "I can stay here until Sunday night."

Grace got up and went to the window which looked onto the farm-yard; everything was fading and merging together, soon there would be no light left; the heap of dung steamed slightly and the cows kicked the sides of the barn and rattled their chains. A young man passed, his work finished, a satchel slung over his shoulder. The smoke from his cigarette blew in at the window and Grace caught the white gleam of his open shirt.

She shut the window and drew the curtains and sat in the firelight until Mrs. Bulmer brought the lamp. It glowed and made a soft pool with Grace at the edge. She tried to read her book but could not rest, so she went to the door and slipping across the dark hall she let herself out as silently as possible. The cool air met her and all the night smells coming from the animals and grass and flowers. She made her way down the hill towards the village. Its lights were twinkling faintly through the trees.

She wandered into the empty street and the voices coming from the inn; she climbed the steps to the black church and saw the pale glimmer of the diamond-paned windows; she smelled the yews and the long wet grass brushing on her stockinged legs. The voices were louder now, the inn door had been opened, someone had crossed the street. Grace got up to go home, she came to the lane, grown high with cow-parsley and nettles, and made her way along it over the stile and through the meadow past the dim bulks of cows, like stranded ships, still grazing.

It was not until then that she saw the other figure. It was walking slowly and she soon was close behind. It swayed a little, then fell down. Grace ran up and bending over recognized the man who had passed her window at the farm.

His eyes were shut and his mouth was open. She smelled the smell of beer and knew that he was drunk.

"Shall I help you to get up?" she asked stiffly. He opened his eyes and stared at her. "All right, if you like," he answered. She knelt down and got his arm round her neck and tried to pull him upwards. He was too heavy and fell back.

She tried again; he slowly staggered to his feet and she held him swaying. Her legs were like two buttresses and her arms were linked around his waist. Slowly she felt him sinking again. Each button on his shirt scraped on her arm as he sagged until she lost her balance and fell with him into the deep wet grass. Her arm was pinioned beneath him and he was lying heavily on her side. His breath was on her face and suddenly his warm hard mouth, the rigid bone beneath, was pressed hard against hers and she felt his tongue trying to find the opening of her lips.

She pushed against his throat with her hand and felt the Adam's apple rising and falling as he gulped. She grabbed at his flesh and felt the coarse strong hair on his chest. At last he lifted his head and lay back and she swiftly jerked her arm from underneath him and scrambled to her feet. He lay there still and in a minute began to snore. "I can't leave him here," she thought. "He'll lie here all night and probably be dead in the morning."

She pushed him sharply with her foot and said loudly and clearly, "Get up and go and put your head in the stream to sober you down."

He mumbled, "I'm not drunk, not bloody likely," and rolled over on his face. Then his attitude changed, and his face seemed to lighten as he said, "But I wouldn't mind a swim neither."

He knelt up unsteadily and bending down his head he put his hands over his shoulders and began pulling his shirt slowly over his head. He was like a ghost in a pillow-slip, headless and lumbering, then off it came and he seemed to be a white pillar of marble growing out of the tree trunk of his trousers. He sat down and pulled off his shoes and socks and his toes like tight bracken fronds seemed to uncurl.

He stood up and let his trousers fall to the ground. Even the activity seemed to have sobered him. He walked towards the stream and felt it with his toe, then slowly the two shafts of his legs sank into it and he was swallowed up to the waist. His nipples were rigid with cold and his nails were blanched. Grace saw him dive like a porpoise and then his long arms thrashing the surface. He was shouting now and warbling as he lay on his back, arms outstretched, his wet hair glistening in the dark.

He ran up the bank and out into the grass which the moon was just beginning to silver. He was combing his hair with his fingers and rubbing himself with his shirt. Grace sat by a tree trunk and watched. He came up and pulled her to him and kissed her again. She did not resist this time. His flesh was like cool, clean rubber.

He finished his dressing, putting his jacket on without his shirt. They walked towards the farm, leaning on each other, she still supporting him a little. When they got to the wicket gate into the garden he said, "This is where I'll leave you," and slipped round to the back out of sight.

Grace walked up the brick path, wondering if she would find the door still open. It was locked. She rang gently and the old bell went clanging through the house. There were footsteps and a grating as the door opened inwards. Mrs. Bulmer looked out, her eyes like duck's eyes, evil and suspicious. "Oh it's you," she said. "I thought you'd gone upstairs, so I locked up." The hall was black and Grace made her way slowly across it and up the stairs, slippery with oil cloth. The air in her room was warm, with the smell of the birds that nested in the eaves and of the wallflowers in the jam jar heavy on it. Grace looked at herself in the glass by the light from her candle and saw her greying hair. "Thirty-four's not very old," she kept saying to herself as she took off her clothes and wearily rubbed cold cream into her face. "Tomorrow I shall be going back to Miss Moulton's registry office for maids and mistresses and I shall be listening to the likes and dislikes of maids and mistresses and writing letters to maids and mistresses." She said it like a parrot while she brushed her hair.

The bed was cold and the cotton sheets dragged at her flesh. She looked at the grey square of the window and felt the breeze blowing in on her face.

She woke to see Mrs. Bulmer bending over her and to smell the strong tea in the cup with the gilt trefoil on it.

She heard the birds and someone whistling in the yard. She drank her tea then got up to see if it was him. He saw her as she came to the window and looked away. She was cut and mortified. She dressed and went to her lonely breakfast by the fire; the sun streamed onto the table. She sat and read while Mrs. Bulmer prepared her a lunch to take out, then went upstairs to put on her outdoor shoes.

As she came out into the yard he passed in front of her, the water from the buckets he was carrying slopping out as he walked. She followed on behind the barn, but he never turned his head and she saw the gold stubble at the back of his head glisten as the muscles of his neck moved.

He went into the barn and she heard him talking to the calves.

She had her picnic amongst the buttercups, throwing her bread crusts onto a stone for the birds to find, then she buried the litter from her meal in a rabbit hole and walked slowly back through the fields to the farm to pack. Mrs. Bulmer was surprised when she said she was going. She said, "I thought you was going to stay as long as you could, I thought you was going on the 9:16." But Grace shook her head and left for the station.

Touchett's Party

On an evening in the first autumn of the war three young men met in the Edwardian drawing-room of a house on the outskirts of a small provincial town. They had been asked to dinner by an older man, who wished to give a party because he had won 15 pounds on a horse race.

Touchett came into the room and greeted his guests ceremoniously, in order of seniority. The first he took notice of was Wilmot, a very well-made, smallish man of about twenty-six, with film star teeth and tiny black moustache, and the remains of a charming north-country accent. He had been the leader and organizer of the local Fascist party, until the whole thing had disintegrated in a curious scandal.

The rumor in the town was that one night a lady member of the party had been divested of her clothes, then tied in a crucified position on the blackboard easel and painted with silver paint, until she resembled the little statuette which used to be seen on the bonnets of Rolls-Royces. There had been a peeping Tom or some busybody of a policeman—in any case, the party had ceased to exist the year before the war began. Wilmot was now in the army with three stripes and only the mildest questions asked about his past. In this the authorities were perfectly right; Wilmot only wanted to belong to some harsh cast-iron organization, and the army admirably fulfilled these wants; therefore blackshirts no longer had any attraction at all. He said that he wore his with his huge brass-buckled belt to dig the potatoes in.

Markham, the second guest, was younger; nineteen, or twenty at most. He had been the sub-editor of a small local paper and was now violently pacifist, admitting quite openly that the thought of bombs and guns was too terrifying for words. He had soft, floppy, damp-looking hair, a rather pretty face with a prominent chin and good jaw line. He sometimes fluttered his hands with a too convenient and conscious grace.

The third was myself. I had been lying naked on the roof of a nursing home at Broadstairs for four months, so I was very brown and felt extremely well and lively. I had been asked chiefly, I think, because I had a baby Austin. We were to drive in this to the country inn where Touchett had ordered dinner.

Touchett was hugely fat and babyish and, with extremely bad teeth and rather winning ways, he would often recite rhymes about "pusillanimous pandas" or "two halfpenny stamps look less than a penny one, Never refer to the honorable anyone." Then would come long lines of Swinburne or A.E. Housman.

Touchett had never done anything all his life and though nearing forty, still lived a sort of schoolboy's life in his father's house, with consequent fears about being late for meals, not making too much noise, and anxieties over pocket money. True, the pocket money now was spent on beer and cigarettes, not on sweets, although Touchett retained a passionate love for them when other people paid for them.

Touchett's extreme tallness took away slightly from his huge stomach, but I always marvelled slightly when I saw him squeeze into the front seat of my minute car. He would always slam the door with extreme ferocity, which exasperated me.

We stood for a few moments laughing and joking before setting out. Markham made a coarse remark and Wilmot and I guffawed rather extravagantly, already getting ourselves into the mood of the evening.

Touchett put his dimpled finger to his nicotine-stained lips and said, "Shush, shush, my father's just coming down to dinner in the next room."

I looked at his pursed mouth and saw that even the tip of his nose was stained brown. The stain on his lips seemed to have solidified into hard little cakes.

"Let's go quickly," I said, "then we can feel free."

We left the house, shutting the door in a pantomime of furtive quietness. Immediately we'd wedged ourselves into the small red car and I had swung out of the gates, a gay babble broke out. Touchett passed his cigarettes about (this marked it as a special occasion, usually they were never offered to anyone).

Wilmot put two in his own mouth, lighted them both, then passed one over my shoulder and fitted it neatly in the corner of my mouth.

"Thank you," I said in surprise. I remember as I smoked and drove, the curiously melancholy effect of the bronze chrysanthemums seen in the light which was about to fade.

As we drove along the quiet roads, the intensely green landscapes seemed dead and flattened out. The waning light, in a last fling, somehow strengthened and vivified the color at the expense of obliterating the contour. It was at that moment just before all is lost in a scale of greys, silvers, blacks and duns.

I parked in the yard of the country inn and we bundled out. The inn was called by the name of the family who lived in the historic house nearby. The arms were everywhere displayed in freshly painted blue and red and silver.

"Azure, gules, and argent," I thought to myself, enjoying the pomposity.

We entered a hall where warming pans and two grandfather clocks vied with engravings and garden plans of the nearby house, which had been torn from old topographical books. There was also a nostalgic picture, rather good, of a lady in flowing drapery leaning on a windowsill fluttering her hands despairingly on an empty bird cage. Outside was the callous idyllic landscape of a dream village.

We passed through this room, after leaving coats and sticks or hats on the stand. The next room held a bar like a catafalque of gaily painted wood. Saucy cocks with huge tail feathers strutted on the glasses, the shakers, the trays, the shelves, on every place where there was room for this emblem.

The colored bottles against mirror glass looked fascinating and medicinal, like something in the druggist's shop.

"What shall we have," said Touchett excitedly, thrilled at having fifteen pounds to squander on his friends.

"I want lemon gin," I said decisively. Wilmot and Touchett had whiskey and Markham a dry martini.

Being a Saturday night, the place was already full. A collection of curiously clothed people passed continually through the room to get to the dining-room. There were people in evening dress, people in rough tweed, people in rather greasy pin stripes, elegant ladies with wool beads round their necks and others with string shopping-bag snoods over doubtful blond hair.

We settled ourselves in a corner by the fireplace. Markham dragged a large armchair across the room, as there were not enough seats round the table.

Almost immediately, the owner of the inn, an extremely stalwart-looking lady, came in and after deliberately wheeling back the armchair, substituted a hard and imitation Windsor in its place.

"This won't take up so much room and people will be able to get into the dining-room, the other one blocks the way," she said firmly and brightly and rather insolently.

We all looked at her and became rather intimidated; she had such a complete air of mastery. She wore a tweed coat and skirt of nondescript color; her hair matched almost exactly. There was something fleshy and horsy about her, and the Eton crop and the masculine leather elbow pads on her jacket gave a twist of depravity to her appearance.

We found ourselves making the appropriate jokes when she had taken herself off with her rather rolling yet officious stride.

The waiter who brought our drinks was extremely fat and white, fatter than Touchett and almost as tall. He seemed terribly harried and every remark was somehow a supplication and a whine.

As we sipped our various drinks, Touchett told us a horrific tale of the boiler bursting in the kitchen and deluging this fat waiter with scalding water and steam.

"Wasn't it frightful," Touchett said with childish relish, "when the doctor came to undress him, his skin peeled off with his clothes! They were stuck together!"

I knew that Touchett was exaggerating and embellishing this story, fantastically, for although the fat waiter looked white, he did not look as if his skin had been peeled off from head to foot.

We each had one more drink, then sailed into the supper-room. We were late and so it was completely full except for our reserved table. This was in the middle of the main room. To one side a glassed-in balcony thronged with tables and people hung over the courtyard.

"We must have champagne," Touchett said, taking the wine list and pondering. He ordered what he wanted and waited for the excitement of white napkins, pails of ice, tin foil, wine-corks, and fanciful Victorian shallow glasses.

Unfortunately for Touchett, these last, the very symbol of champagne drinking, did not materialize. Apparently we were to drink our wine out of the deep bulbous standard glasses which were on every table.

"But these aren't champagne glasses!" Touchett protested with a whimper, but not so loud that the waiter might hear.

"Won't they do?" I asked anxiously, not wanting arguments or trouble.

"Nobody will know that we're drinking champagne," he complained, laughing at himself.

"Oh yes they will, Touchett. Their eyes are all glued to the fat bottle glistening with dew."

We tried to content him by talking in this way.

When the asparagus was brought, Wilmot, rather exaggerating his rough-diamond role, said flatly, "How do you eat it?"

"Pick it up with what God gave you, and insert it in the right hole," said Touchett naughtily.

"Suck them like dummy-tits," said Markham, who by now was just the slightest bit rowdy.

This unfortunate remark was said so loudly that it rang through the crowded room. One could almost hear it echoing against the walls.

Markham's face went red, his eyes glistened. We gave each other kicks and thumps and taps under the table to restore order. The fat waiter hovered round us smiling indulgently but still somehow being pathetic and cloying.

We were almost the last to leave the dining-room. We had eaten one roast chicken greedily and Wilmot had insisted on using the wooden toothpicks in the most ostentatious manner. The longing to *"épater"* was abroad. Our remarks became more and more doubtful.

Touchett licked up his pink and white ice cream lovingly and swallowed my wafer in one mouthful when I offered it to him.

The champagne had made me feel full of sadness and foreboding. I thought of the war which hadn't really begun yet. I idly stared at another much younger waiter whose skin where he shaved looked raw and tender and maltreated. This somehow too was very sad.

We were all moving out of the dining-room now into a room which seemed to be full of divans and screens. I could tell that the waiters were pleased to get rid of us. I felt that in some way we were not quite behaving properly.

Are we talking too loud? I asked myself. Are our jokes too indecent? Are we showing off? Do we look dishevelled? Can the other diners hear the personal remarks we make about them? Are any buttons undone or ties crooked?

We settled ourselves two on a divan and two in chairs.

"We must have lots of liqueurs," Touchett insisted.

He ordered Grand Marnier, Benedictine and Green Chartreuse, and, because the hotel would soon not be allowed to serve any more drinks to nonresidents, we each sat with two or three different-colored little glasses before us.

The fiery extraordinary taste of the liqueurs mixed with the coffee, the asparagus, the chicken, the ice, the champagne. This moment I'll always remember, I thought, because the taste of the liqueur has printed it forever on my mind. I'll see Markham sitting opposite me looking over-excited with his hair flopping over his face, very gay with monkey eyes sparkling. Such a boy, as old ladies would say. I'll see Wilmot looking nice and thug-like with flashing teeth, but tolerant and loosened-up also. Such a man. I'll see Touchett rather like a naughty self-indulgent yet solicitous mother who both wants her children to enjoy themselves, yet not to be as debauched as she is herself. I'll see this forever; yet even now it's passing and will never come back. Next year some of us will probably be dead.

The waiters were now asking us politely to leave. Other guests, no doubt residents, looked at us with curiosity and a certain amount of superciliousness. I hoped there was not going to be trouble.

"Let's go," I said. "They want to close up here. We can all go back and sit at my place."

We all stood up and then made our way through the bar to the hall. The proprietress gave us a firm look and a good night and we were outside.

As soon as we had fitted into the car, Touchett began to sing a song called "Balls to Mr. Bangelstein." The chorus to this song was so infectious that we were soon all shouting it. We yelled it as we shot past the grey medieval palace with its huge central hall. The front façade and one wing were completely refaced in early nineteenth-century stone, but this could not be seen at night, only the great carcass brooded alone in the fields dwarfing the tiny village built beside it.

We climbed the hill and passed the gates of the private lunatic asylum. I wondered if we should wake any of the lunatics with our singing. I imagined one loose in the gardens, under the great spreading evergreens. Perhaps I should see a grey face pop over the wall as the car whizzed along. My mind played with many fancies, but I could not rid it of the thought of death which brooded over everything. I hugged this thought which made the night so precious.

At the gate of my flat, which was on the ground floor of an early-Victorian house, the others all bounced out and waited for me to unlock the door. In spite of their rowdiness and singing, there was an indefinable politeness and delicacy, a sort of gentlemanliness which is especial to drunk people. It is I suppose the feeling of give and take, and tolerance, the milk of human kindness.

They threw themselves down on the sofa and the chairs in my room. I went to get glasses and cider and whiskey, for I had no beer in the house.

When I came back, Wilmot was making remarks about two large wooden angels I had just bought.

"But they're frightful," he said. "They make me think I'm in a Roman Catholic cemetery."

"And what about that awful tapestry cartoon on the wall. Look at that horrible dirty little cupid sticking a dart right into that poor girl's bosom. It's unfortunate that there should be a damp stain just at that place too, while Venus looks on and smiles smugly with a disgusting, knowing expression. 'Sacred and profane love.' Your room really is too disgusting, Denton. It's like a Surrealist chapel, nothing quite what is expected or where it's expected."

It pleased me to hear the boorish remarks. I knew that they did it to please me.

Touchett sat back in the one armchair and Markham lay on the hearthrug and leaned back against his fat cushiony legs in their dirty grey flannel tubes.

"Stop tickling," screamed Touchett girlishly. "I can feel your hair tickling through my trousers. Oh, my skin is so sensitive. I shall go mad if you move your head and tickle me any more."

Markham rubbed his head up and down on Touchett's legs as an animal rubs itself against a tree trunk.

Wilmot and I sat on the sofa; we by now felt extremely friendly towards each other. I poured out whiskey for him but refused to give him any water. He threaded his arm through mine and we clinked glasses ceremoniously in what I had always been told was the German fashion. "Surely they can't always do this before drinking," I said hazily. "Think of the time it would take!"

Touchett by now had become so hysterical from the tickling that I was afraid his screams would wake the dead, to say nothing of the neighbors. "Try to be quieter, Touchett," I implored shakily.

Touchett got up and ran across the room trembling delicately like a blancmange.

"Stop it, stop it, Markham you wicked boy," he yelled in ecstasy.

Markham leaped up to chase Touchett, but Wilmot dived from the sofa and did a low tackle, grasping Markham's legs and bringing him down. There was a struggle on the floor. My little marble-topped table went down with a crash. I saw the marble fall out of its socket and lie on the floor like a curved wet slab of fish.

"Order, order," I screamed, "you'll spoil my bibelots." But no one took any notice. Markham with straining and grunting struggled to his feet, although Wilmot still trapped his ankles fiercely.

The more he struggled to free himself, the more Wilmot tugged at his trousers, until at last something ripped and the trousers slipped over Markham's hips like a flag slipping silently down the pole at evening. They gathered in concertina folds round his ankles, half enveloping Wilmot's face.

We all let out a yell and hoot to see Markham there in his dangling shirttails. Touchett, who had flattened himself against the wall as the struggle took place, now let out a piercing laugh and groan and disappeared into the hall. I heard him fumbling with the latch. Wilmot in devilry let Markham go and the last we saw of them was Markham hobbling with the trousers still round his ankles pursuing Touchett across the dark little strip of lawn outside the windows. Markham had a glass of whiskey in his hand which he had snatched up as he left the room. I wondered if I should ever see the glass, intact, again.

I let the curtain fall back into place and turned to Wilmot.

He looked very smoothly and creamily pale, beautiful, I thought. He said nothing.

"I'll drive you home," I said. He followed me out to the car still without saying anything. Then as he stood with his hand on the door, he leaned forward and was violently sick onto the road. He made no excuses, but quietly held himself in control until the paroxysm was over. He repressed any slightest sign of weakness, pain or despair which nearly always accompanies vomiting. When he felt better he quietly began to curse and swear at me, asking me how dared I try to get him to go home by offering to drive him, and saying that he had been taught as a Fascist to fix bastards like me and that nobody succeeded in managing him.

I felt chilled by this outpouring of hate but I pretended to take no notice. "Don't let's go home if you don't want to," I said.

"No, sorry, I was only being bloody-minded," he said getting into the car, all smiles and ameliorations, patting my arm.

I started to drive and Wilmot talked more and more accommodatingly and more and more soberly. By the time that we had reached his mother's bungalow he was treating me as he would a distinguished stranger. I was sorry that politeness had taken the place of everything else. We went into the little match-boarded sitting room with its brown velour curtains and brass-studded leatherette chairs. Two eighteenth-century pastel portraits of Wilmot's mother's Swiss ancestors looked down on us. It flashed through my mind that I had never thought of Swiss people having ancestors.

"My real name is Edouard, but people call me Eddy—that is the people who are not entirely in sympathy," Wilmot added with a smile.

"You must have something to drink," he said. "I know you will—there's some good sherry."

He creaked across the passage to the dining-room. I listened to either Wilmot's mother or his sister turning over in bed. Every minute sound came through the beaverboard wall.

Wilmot and I drank the very dark sherry from thin little machine-chased glasses; then I said that I must be going.

"God knows if I'll get home, I've just remembered how low the petrol is."

"Oh I'll fix it, I'll suck some out of my sister's car," said Wilmot in a very workmanlike way.

"She'll be livid," I said.

"Oh she probably won't notice."

We went into the outbuilding where the sister's dilapidated little car stood amongst the coops and other disused instruments of the chicken farm.

Wilmot found the short narrow tube, then kneeled down on the dusty ground and began sucking up the petrol. He looked very strong and square and preoccupied. Suddenly the petrol came up and Wilmot wiped his hand across his mouth, saying, "Christ, I nearly got a mouthful!" He let the petrol dribble into a bottle. "That's enough, really," I said, "you'll empty her tank."

Wilmot held up the bottle.

"Do you think that will be enough? It's only about half a gallon."

I said "yes" hastily. We poured it in. Wilmot and I shook hands warmly. "Good-bye," he said, "and thank you for the fine party."

"It wasn't my party," I said, "it was Touchett's. Don't you remember, he wanted to spend his winnings."

"Good God, I'd forgotten. We none of us said anything to him because he pushed off like that with Markham after him. We'll have to thank him another day."

I started the car and waved to Wilmot in the dim hut.

"Good-bye, good-bye," I said.

He waved back. I could just see the little black moustache and the smudge of white teeth.

Those teeth will probably be scattered all over the place next year, I thought, and the glossy moustache will have melted quite away. I looked at the dim fields, and the sheep crouching or munching the grass. The autumn mist was hovering a few feet from the ground.

At home the fire had at last burnt out. I saw the little table, forlorn on its side, an empty frame with the marble slab some few feet off. I saw the empty glasses and the tousled chairs, the cigarette ash everywhere. The wooden angels looked down, the cupid and Venus in the tapestry cartoon shook and eddied a little from a draught.

I left the dismal room and went to the garden gate again. I leaned against the iron bars and played about with the toe of one of my shoes in the grass. My shoe touched something hard that tinked. I bent down and after feeling about for a little, picked up the glass which Markham had run off with. It had been carefully put down and was still full of whiskey. I held it up to my lips, but the smell made me feel sick, so I poured the liquid onto a flower bed where it made a gentle hissing noise.

I wondered how far down the road Markham had been able to run with his trousers round his ankles. The amusing picture could not make me smile.

Forlornly I went back into the flat, fell down on my bed and tried to sleep.

"Everything comes to this," I kept repeating to myself mechanically.

Alex Fairburn

Alex Fairburn bent her fair head nearer to her work and counted the stitches of her petit-point. The fire stretched and yawned at her feet and through the thick curtains she heard the bell-like trickle of the water in the drain pipes. It was seven o'clock on an autumn evening and she was alone.

She had spent most of her time alone since she had left Jack. The thought of him twisted something inside her. It was not hate or fear that she felt but just shame—to have made such a mess of their marriage from the very start. She could not bear to think of it. They were both so stubborn, nobody but a fool would have imagined that they could live together. But at twenty-one she had been a fool and now two years later she realized just how large a one. She thought of Jack with his thin pointed eyes and mouse-soft polished hair, the smallness of his bones and the egoism of his face in repose (the sort of face Little Lord Fauntleroy might be expected to have in the days when his goodness had begun to wear thin), the queer smell of his feet when he took off his socks and the sparkle of his nonsense at a party. Then she thought of her resistance to his will, her foolishness, the beauty of her face and the wealth which made her independent of him. Everyone told me not to marry him, she thought. Daddy said he hadn't enough money and Mother just said don't, but I did and then made everything much worse by behaving so stupidly when I found out my mistake. As if drinking too much could ever make you forget that you had married someone so like yourself that he was unbearable.

When Alex had left her husband she had gone to a psychologist and been analyzed. There had been the endless journeys to the little upstairs room in Wimpole Street and the tense sound of her own voice answering questions and saying whatever came into her head. It had all been so formless and floundering and yet the psychologist seemed to have a pigeonhole for everything. She left halfway through the course and then she found religion.

She went to stay with a friend in a country town where the Oxford Group had sent a mission and one night at a friend's house she met some of the young men and women from Oxford and suddenly became very enthusiastic. She read her Bible daily, applied only the minimum of make-up to her face, and settled in a cottage in the country, near the sea.

The petit-point work was all part of the scheme and of course there was no drink in the house.

Her family thought it peculiar but they were so encased in their wealth and the selfishness which it bred that nothing really got through to them from the outside world. They came once or twice to the country cottage and thought it "very jolly," but wanted to know if she was not very lonely there. Alex replied that she was not, with brittle overemphasis.

She could indeed scream with boredom at times. She had asked all the friends she could think of to come down and spend a few days with her, but had so overpowered them with her conviction of the meaning of life and had bullied them so with the confidence that this conviction had given her, that they all in turn had left before their time was up and now she was left alone. Even the Belgian maid had gone that very day.

Now that it was autumn, things seemed even drearier and she didn't know what she would do next.

The needle darted in and out of the canvas, never had anyone been so savage about doing petit-point before. Alex thought of the pattern which she had bought ready painted in the shop opposite Harrod's. "It may not be creative," she said to herself, "but at least it's work. What would I do without it?"

The click of the garden gate broke through her concentration and she looked up, hands on the work in her lap, waiting for the bell to ring. It did not, but she heard the thud of feet walking along the wet path to the back door, then there was a knock and she went to open it. The beads of rain were dropping from the low eaves and through their strings she saw a dripping figure, young and grey in the evening light.

"Excuse me, miss, but could I put up in your barn tonight? I'm on the road and it's that wet."

Alex looked at the speaker again quickly. He had tow-colored hair and a thick-square mouth. His ragged jacket and grey flannels were heavy with rain and Alex caught the gleam of newspaper through the cracks in his squelching shoes.

"Come in," she said hurriedly, acting on impulse. She stepped back into the kitchen and held the door open for him. He followed her sheepishly, hanging his head and fingering the straps of the greasy knapsack on his back. "Won't you take off your wet coat and dry it by the fire? Of course you can stay here tonight." Alex went over to the boiler and stoked it. It was still on, luckily. She opened the door and arranged the clothes horse in front of it.

The young man, still tongue-tied, was easing the knapsack off his back, his eyes glazed and unmeaning.

When Alex turned from the fire she saw him standing there by the kitchen table. He had taken off his coat and it was hanging from his lowered arms and dripping steadily onto the tiled floor.

She realized with a shock that he wore no shirt, only a dirty sweat-stained singlet such as stokers wear and she saw the pale hair on his chest over the low semicircle of its neck.

His whole attitude was so shamefaced and dejected that she hardly dared to look at him. She took the coat gently from his hands and arranged it across the horse. A thin steam rose from it carrying the smells of the man and his tobacco with it.

"Would you like a hot bath?" she said suddenly; then feeling she had been tactless she added, "You've got so wet, I should think you need warming up." A wan smile lit his face, making it look quite weak, and he replied, "All right, if yer like."

"Come on then, I'll show you the way." Alex was bustling now. She led the way up to the landing and fumbled in the dark linen cupboard for a clean towel. Her hands fastened on its rough comfort and she drew it out. She smiled self-consciously when she saw its color by the bathroom light. It was pale lilac and monogrammed with her initials—a part of one of her wedding presents. She turned on the taps and poured the Russian pine essence into the bath from the great green bottle that stood on the mirrored shelf.

The little room was filled with its scent and the clammy steam which frosted the taps and shining tiles.

Now that she had no excuse for staying longer she went to the door and turning, said, "Don't put your wet things on again after your bath, I'll find you something else." He gave a half-grudging obedient nod and she shut the door.

Outside in the dry warm and darkness of the landing, Alex's mind raced. This new Samaritan feeling had entirely seized her and she did not stop to analyze it. She felt her way to her bedroom and went in. The lamp by the bed glowed under its peach shade and by its dim light she searched in the bottom of the chest of drawers for the sailor's trousers she had bought in Gravesend and worn once or twice on the beach in the garden.

She found them and held them up. She had had to buy them large as otherwise her feminine hips, slight as they were, would not get in the tight top part of the trousers. She hoped he would be able to wear them. She looked amongst her jerseys and found the largest. It was thick with a high polo collar and she had worn it for riding.

When Alex had done all that she went quickly to the dressing table, adjusted her hair and touched up her light make-up with lipstick and powder; then she went to the bathroom door and said, loudly so that he could hear through his splashing, "I've got some clothes here for you. Will you give me your own to dry?"

She heard him get out of the bath and walk towards the door, then the door opened slightly, and his hand and forearm with the golden hairs glistening on the pink flesh were thrust forward, holding the sopping clothes and shoes. She took them with an involuntary fastidiousness and walked down the stairs. In the kitchen she put them with the coat in front of the boiler and went to the larder. The smell of cold and fat was disagreeable, but there was a dish of spaghetti which the maid had prepared that morning and also several tins of soup and fruit.

The milkman had left the regular quantity of cream she had every day and Alex felt that she had almost enough to make a meal.

She turned on the electric stove and put the spaghetti in the oven and the soup in a saucepan on the hotplate. Then she hastily laid the table in the kitchen and poured the tinned loganberries and the cream over a sponge sandwich which she had found uncut in a tin.

She looked at the table and felt that she had done all she could. The sight of the tumblers made her realize that there was nothing in the house to drink but water. Her scruples were quite gone by now and she wished she had something to offer him. Then she remembered the bottle of whiskey she had bought last month when her white Alsatian was dying and the vet had told her to feed it on whiskey and white of egg. She had been so distracted at the time that she had rushed to the nearest pub and bought a whole bottle. Her dog had only lived two days after this and so there it was still almost full.

She had put it out in the garage to get it out of the house and now she ran out to get it. It was still there in the corner, covered with a few cobwebs.

She brought it in and wiped its neck and stood it on the table. There was no soda water, so she stood the water jug next to it. She could hear him fumbling on the landing upstairs so she called out, "There's no light up there, can you find your way down?" She could not quite hear his low answer but in a few moments she saw him standing in the doorway, still red from his bath, wearing the sailor trousers and her jersey. He had combed his hair with his fingers and it coiled in rough order on his head. The gold stubble was still on his cheeks and chin but the dirt had gone and as he moved forward she caught the glint of his bleached eyelashes as they shone in the light.

The steam from the wet clothes was filling the room and as they sat down to eat, drifts of the warm human air blew between them. He ate gingerly at first, then gaining confidence he applied himself with concentration and Alex ate methodically too to keep him company. She saw that his hands which moved so steadily were still mooned with black at the tip of each fingernail.

"Would you like some whiskey?" she asked when the soup had been finished. "Thank you," he said looking at his plate with the embarrassed grin playing round his mouth and his eyelids.

He did not wait to watch what instrument she used for the spaghetti but said, simply, "I'm afraid I don't know which tool to use."

Hurriedly Alex replied, "I should use any one you like." Then, feeling this unhelpful if polite, she added, "I'm going to use a knife and fork." She quickly picked up the knife she had not intended to use and began eating.

Every now and then he took drinks from the glass of whiskey and when it was empty she filled it again without asking him.

She noticed that the food and drink were heating him. A light dew of sweat made his face shine. The atmosphere in the room was warm and steaming, like a laundry.

When they had finished the loganberries she said, "You go into the other room and make up the fire, while I heat the coffee." She showed him the door across the landing and then went back to the electric stove. She could hear him banking up the fire and then the stillness when he had finished. The coffee and milk which she had mixed in the saucepan frothed up to the brim and she snatched it away before it should bubble over.

She placed it as it was with the cups and sugar on a tray and went with it across the landing. When she opened the sitting room door she saw him standing in front of the fireplace just staring at the picture above it. It was a Dutch flower piece—not stimulating—and his whole body seemed so hopeless that she guessed he was not looking at the picture but quite through it.

He turned when he heard her, but did not offer to help her. He just hung his head.

Alex drew the little table in front of the sofa, the only really comfortable piece of furniture in the room, and then fetched the cigarettes and chocolates from the desk.

"You must be so tired; won't you sit down?" she asked, indicating the sofa.

He leaned back stiffly in one corner as she poured out the

coffee. She passed it to him with the sugar. The cup slipped in the saucer and she saw his face give a start and lurch.

When they had both taken cigarettes he quite surprisingly leaned forward and struck a match for her. The light from it gave his impassive face a false animated glow—as the rose lights in butchers' shops enhance the color of the meat.

He breathed rather deeply after his meal and she saw that he was getting hotter than ever in the heavy sweater. Feeling that conversation was impossible she got up and went to the wireless and turned it on softly.

As she sat down again, she noticed that his eyes had a more unfocused, less staring look. The muscles of his face were less tense and his long legs in the wide sailor's trousers seemed more relaxed.

The music was formless and unmoving, it was difficult to know who would appreciate it, but looking at him again, she realized, with sudden alarm, that his lips and nostrils were twitching and that his chin was thrust forward stubbornly. "Oh Lord, don't let him break down," Alex prayed swiftly to herself. "What shall I do?" Then she sprang up and went into the kitchen to fetch the whiskey. She brought it back with the tumbler of water and two glasses on a tray. She let her hand fall on his shoulder as she set the tray down. She could feel the heat and the trembling of his body through the wool. "Cheer up, let's have a drink." She spoke harshly and brightly and she could see him stirring and contracting as if he were gathering himself together. He gave her a low sound of acknowledgment and nodded his head.

She moved nearer to him on the sofa so that she could pour out the whiskey from the little table in front of him. She put a lot into his glass and only a little into hers. She did not like the taste. She hoped it would cheer him up. As he put the glass to his lips she heard it ring against his teeth. He was trembling. He drank it in large gulps so that he would not have to go on holding the glass. Then he began to choke. This was too much for him. He gasped, choked, and wept all at once. Alex prosaically knelt on the sofa and thumped his back. He was breathing with great sighing gulps now, his body lying open, arms thrown out and legs straddled, exhausted by the paroxysm.

Something caught at Alex as she saw him lying stretched in the corner of the sofa. She leaned across him, her long neck arched, and bent her lips down to his cheek. He made a movement with his face away from her. She lay against him and heard his heavy heartbeats, then slowly she stretched her hand out over his head and switched off the reading lamp. The light from the fire played on the ceiling and walls and shook light from every polished object that it caught. There was no noise but the rain, the hissing of the damp wood and his deep breathing.

She put her arms carefully round his neck and lay on his chest. The weight of their two bodies together made the sofa sag. They slipped to the ground, narrowly missing the table with the whiskey tray, and lay together there on the bearskin rug in front of the fire. He put his big arms round her drowsily and she felt the heat from his body eating into hers. His face was glistening with sweat. Alex knelt up by his side and pulled the thick sweater up from his waist. At last she got it over his head and only his arms lay imprisoned in it, stretched out above him. She looked down at his face and he smiled, his eyes half closed. He drew his hands out of the sweater and holding them up, drew her down so that her cheek was against his chest. It felt to her skin like fine grass scattered on satin. She closed her eyes and whenever she opened them she saw the light of the flames gilding the white top of his body.

They did not go to bed that night but lay in front of the fire on the bearskin, dozing and waking. Alex got cushions and rugs and banked up the fire.

Towards dawn she went soundly to sleep and woke two hours later to see him standing over her and looking down. He had changed into his own clothes and the straps of the knapsack were across his shoulders.

"I must be going," he said and shifted his feet nervously. Alex jumped up, the whole of the memory of last night returning to her. "Don't go, don't go yet. You must have some breakfast." She sped into the kitchen and found two kippers and began making toast and coffee.

He stood in the doorway, watching her and not saying a word. Sometimes he looked at the kitchen clock. They ate their meal in silence, then he got up and went to the door. "Good-bye," he said. Alex couldn't stop him or say anything, she could only stare. She watched him go out and heard him walking down the path and opening the gate into the road; then she came to life and ran after him. When she got to the gate he was already a little way down the road; he turned and gave her a rather clumsy, distant wave. It stopped her from going further. She slowly turned back into the house and sat down again at the breakfast table, leaning her head down on it with her arms curved round. She shut her eyes and felt the smell of kippers and butter and coffee piercing through her thoughts. She lay some time like this, then resolutely she sat up and brushed her hair back. She looked at the congealing fat on the plates and the mahogany skin of the eaten kippers, the dregs in the coffee cups and the smears of butter and marmalade on the small plates.

She cleaned it all into the sink and began washing up. When she had finished she stoked the boiler, then went into the other room. The rugs and cushions lay on the floor in front of the fire which was out and there were her jersey and sailor's trousers which he had worn. She looked at them and did not move, then swiftly she bent forward and gathering them up, she held them close to her face and smelled them. The smell of his body clung to them still. She folded them and put them down on the sofa, then she cleaned away the rugs and the whiskey and the coffee cups. When the room was tidy, she switched on the electric fire as she had not remade the open one and, fetching her Bible, she sat down to read. When she had finished her chapter she sighed, and taking up her petit-point made the needle dart in and out of the canvas. She worked faster and faster, trying not to think at all, but she kept on saying to herself in endless repetition as the stitches grew: "I didn't even give him sixpence, I didn't even give him sixpence."

The Diamond Badge

When I'd come to the last word on the last page, I felt I had to write to him at once. There seemed an urgency about the business which I did not stop to question. I sat down at my little desk in the window and there, surrounded with leaves and the sound of the birds in the garden, began my foolish letter. I say foolish, because even as I wrote, I knew I was extravagant, strained, curiously false in the words I chose to express my gratitude and enthusiasm.

What would an author think at receiving such a letter from an unknown woman? It was quite clear to me that he would probably be contemptuously amused, a little exasperated; but there would be some pleasure in receiving such tribute, and who was I to guard my dignity and deny him the only repayment I could make? I licked the envelope, pressed it down and went out to the letter-box before I could change my mind.

As I walked back down the lane, through the evening air, I felt released, as though I had got rid of something, drink or waste food, that was burdening my body. It seemed the most wonderful thing in the world to give out all the time, things that were wanted, expressions that no one would bother and understand, smiles they could not see, and songs they'd never hear. I went into my little kitchen and started to heat some coffee and boil an egg for my supper.

The answer came in five days' time. If he were to write at all, I had been prepared to wait, since the publisher would have first to forward my own letter. Then there might be other delays. He might be travelling or living abroad. This promptness therefore both delighted and nonplussed me. I had to steel myself for a meeting earlier than I had imagined it to myself; but I had asked for it; and now he invited me to tea on the Friday, only three days away. I began rather agitatedly to plan what I should wear. Going up to my room, I opened the cupboard doors and looked at all my clothes, hanging patiently, like so many squashed flat criminals. They were nice clothes, but I had grown a little too used to them. In the end I decided on a trim coat and skirt, a little severe for me, but becoming. With this I should wear a stiff, frilly white shirt with my one and only valuable brooch, my father's regimental badge in tiny diamonds. I was aware of the rather painful gentility of such a choice. I did not really wish to present myself as nothing but a dreary English gentlewoman, but the memory of my letter returned to disquiet me. I was determined to underline the sobriety in my character in an attempt to neutralize some of the letter's excessiveness.

He wrote from a village some thirty miles away in the next county, but the journey did not sound difficult. He gave me the name of the station, the time of the train and said that his friend, Tom Parkinson, would be there to meet me in the car. Somehow all this care and solicitude struck a slight chill into me. I felt that he must often have arranged for strangers to visit him. It was as if he made a business of never denying himself to anyone, because he so despised the pomposity of ambitious little people who tried to add to their importance by a lack of all response. Then the thought came to comfort me that he might still be genuinely pleased to see people who had enjoyed his book; for, although it had been out for a year or more, it was his first book and he could not yet be so very celebrated. I had never heard his name mentioned, only read it in one or two reviews.

Tom Parkinson was there to meet me. I knew him by his searching, rather anxious eyes. They were not the eyes of a man about to welcome wife, sweetheart or friend; they were too guarded, too ready to save the stranger from embarrassment. I liked at once his beaky nose, his tallness which was yet not overwhelming, the bank of dingy fairish hair flopping over his forehead. The sleeves of his open-neck shirt were rolled up and his beltless trousers seemed to hang on his hips rather precariously; they were slack round his ankles as if they dragged on the ground behind. I knew just what the hems would be like at his heels—caked with mud and beginning to fray.

When we shook hands, I saw that he had tiny red veins under the tight brown skin on the sides of his arched nose; they were not in the least unpleasing, and the nondescript color of his eyes soothed me. I guessed that we were almost exactly of an age, but I hoped, rather pointlessly, that he was the elder by a year or so.

He took me out to the dilapidated Morris and we started to climb the hill into the town. It was a squalid little country place, only called into being, I should imagine, by the building of the station in the middle of the last century. The one or two older buildings looked as if they had once been solitary farm-houses.

Soon we were out of the one main street and climbing another hill through frothy orchards and bare hop-gardens. The contrast between excess of blossom, thick and heavy as curdled milk, and the naked poles linked to each other by lines of tingling wire, sent some sharp feeling through me. It was as if a Rubens woman, rich in the glow of her fatness and beauty, were stripped the next moment of all her flesh, so that one had nothing but the gaunt skeleton, almost heard the little bones of hand and foot tinkling.

We came at last to a narrow lane down which Tom Parkinson turned the car. It was hardly more than a track and we bounced in our seats as the wheels mounted the ruts or sank into them again. I tried to prepare my face, to wash self-consciousness and stain right out of it. I longed to look in my mirror, but somehow, with Tom Parkinson so close beside me, the gesture seemed too calculating, too businesslike. Might not his straightforward nature jump to the conclusion that my titivating was due entirely to an imbecile wish to fascinate his friend in the first moment of our meeting? I contented myself by opening my bag and fiddling about until I had the mirror out of its pocket and could just see my nose and lips shining up from the dark interior. I bent my head a little and saw my eyes. They did not reassure me. They looked steady and hard and fierce, as frightened eyes are apt to do. I simpered at myself, then smiled genuinely to remember my mother doing this when I was a child. I had thought her so utterly ridiculous.

We were slowing down. I looked up to see a converted stone farm building over the hedge on the right. The part which had once housed carts and rakes was now glazed in. The three great windows with their thick white bars gave the place an attractive air of comfort, even of luxury. There were no ugly creosoted beams, no leaded casements or quaint "lanthorns" on either side of the door, just the white paint and the rough silvery stone walls. At one end the building rose to two stories. I guessed this must once have been the stable and loft. The long loft door, with a little projecting roof over it and the wheel for a pulley, was now also glazed.

Tom took me in and I saw how bare the large ground-floor room was. It was not as I would have had it at all, but I felt soothed. On the tiled floor was thick satiny rush matting in a pattern of squares bound together. The walls seemed to be the natural oatmeal color of undistempered plaster. Over the mantelpiece was a rich still-life of glowing fruit, peonies, dahlias, sunflowers and enormous shells; indeed everything was larger than in life. The heavy impasto was a little distasteful to me, and I found myself repeating the old phrase: "Excrement on canvas."

The puritan room was really rather a bore, but I found myself dwelling on it and almost appreciating it because it was so unalarming; and to be calmed at that moment was all that I craved for. Tom let me look about, not hurrying me in the least; then he called up the stairs: "Andrew, we've arrived."

I heard an answering call, deep, rather musical, a little too social, as if the whole situation were "tremendous fun." In spite of this slight false note, I was attracted to the voice; I knew that it was trying to make me feel at ease.

We climbed the polished oak stairs. Once I looked down on the long sober room. From this unusual viewpoint the large chairs with their red and white striped cushions and their loose covers of rough linen looked extraordinarily inviting. I had the childish longing to jump over the banisters and land in the middle of the broad sofa.

Tom opened the door on the narrow landing and said: "Here we are."

I followed him in and felt myself holding out my hand dazedly to the little person on the bed. He was terribly deformed, his hands all twisted and his body seemingly telescoped into itself, so that he was broad but perhaps only three feet tall. He had a smooth oval face with rather delicate features. His hair was red and a little silky fringe ran right round to his jaw line, framing his face and making him look like a particularly well-groomed ill-disposed monkey. He wore no moustache, so I could watch his pink lips clearly. He licked them as his eyes lit up and he said: "I'm not *in* bed, only *on* it; I like best to loll here in my room. Don't you like to be a little up in the air? How right they were when they made all town houses with their drawing-rooms on the first floor!"

I said: "Yes, it's nicer to be off the ground, to be able to look out a little farther."

Tom had brought a chair up for me and I sat down, placing my bag beside me, refusing to clutch it as I wished to do.

All this time Andrew—already I named him this in my mind—was watching me with his small bright eyes. They seemed to be brimming with expectation. I think he was waiting for me to betray some sign of horror, or pity for his condition; then, I felt the eyes would have bubbled over and he would have gloated. I wanted him to get no satisfaction from me. I wanted this to be the most prosaic tea-party that had ever taken place. Already I angrily regretted giving in to impulse and writing that letter. I resented not being warned before I broke my way into this different world where nobody wanted me in particular. Why had I not been told of Andrew's condition? I found myself childishly blaming some mysterious, unknown being who should have told me everything beforehand.

Tom reappeared with the tea tray and I felt easier. There were some very good rock cakes which he had made himself. As I ate and drank and talked, I was able to look about me in little snatches. Andrew's room was more gargoyly and frilly than the downstairs room. There was more to offend, surprise and interest. A great pile of exercise books and typescripts balanced, seemingly in absolute confusion, on a table near his bed. There was thick dust on some of them; it was clear that he would not have them touched.

Andrew did most of the talking, shooting out questions, telling gay little anecdotes, laughing, and swivelling those bubbling eyes of his. Tom sometimes murmured a word or smiled his lazy, rather private smile, which had something very slightly irritating about it. I suppose it kept one out. He seemed determined to enjoy his joke alone.

Andrew never mentioned books, and when I felt I ought to say something about this one which had so impressed me, he scowled, turned away and said: "Let's not talk about anything so embarrassing."

The evening wore on, and still I made no move to go. I seemed to be fascinated, held in a house where there was no place for me. It was almost as if I were waiting for something to happen. A smell of cooking rose up the stairs, and instead of getting to my feet to say good-bye, I asked Andrew if I might go down to the kitchen to help Tom. He said: "Oh, do. He'd love that."

Then almost before I was out of the room, I caught a glimpse of him turning the pages of a book of old engravings of the Seats of the Nobility and Gentry! My eyes had caught the title as I sat drinking my tea, and I too had wanted to look inside.

I knocked tentatively on the kitchen door. Tom came to it frowning a little, holding a frying pan which was still sizzling from the electric hotplate.

"Can I help?" I asked, looking up at him anxiously. I wanted to be doing something to prove my usefulness, to clear away the impression that I was one of those people who stayed too long. I still don't know why I didn't leave politely at just the right moment after tea.

"Well, the kitchen is awfully small for two," Tom was saying rather pointedly. It was clear that he wanted me out of the way. "But if you like to lay the tray for three in that corner near the larder door, I think we won't be too much in each other's way."

"I say, is it all right my staying to supper?" I asked in a rush.

"Oh, of course; we were expecting you to."

Tom turned back to his frying and I set about laying the tray without more ado. I knew how irritating it was to be asked continually where things were kept, so I did my best without talking to Tom, searching in cupboards, pulling out plates and forks and knives until I had what we should need. I saw that we were to have fried fish and potatoes and some early lettuces. There didn't seem to be any fish knives and forks, so I put ordinary ones; then started to make a French dressing.

"I won't put it over the lettuce in case either of you don't like it," I said.

"Oh, but we both do," replied Tom rather absently, his mind still on the perfect browning of the potatoes.

I shredded the lettuce with my hands, tearing each leaf into small bits, then I poured on the dressing and tossed the fragments about till they were all covered and glistening slightly from the oil.

"I don't bother to do it nearly as well as that," said Tom looking down at the bowl approvingly. I felt glad and hoped that he would stop classing me as just another nuisance to be borne good-naturedly.

"If you don't have to be back tonight, why not sleep here?" he said suddenly. "It would save me having to take the car out in the dark; the lights are rotten."

"But I haven't got pajamas or a toothbrush or anything," I said, quite taken aback; "besides, what about Mr. Clifton?"

"Andrew? Oh, he wouldn't mind; it's no trouble to him. All we've got to do is to make up the bed."

Matters were left like this, till we climbed up to Andrew's room, Tom carrying the heavy tray of fish, potatoes and salad, I following with the coffee which was still dripping through the percolator.

When we had both sat down near Andrew's bed, with the trays on stools before us, Tom suddenly said: "Oh, Susan Innes is staying the night; it's much easier than getting the car out with those hopeless lights, and she hasn't got to be back for anything. I'm letting her have my new toothbrush; it's still all done up in cellophane."

Andrew turned to me with a metallic smile and said: "That's fine; we won't have to hurry at all then over the meal."

"But is it all right?" I asked miserably. "What must you think of me coming to tea and then staying the night?"

"It will be nice," Andrew said in his smooth bland way. "We so seldom have anyone to use our spare room."

All through supper I felt strained. Andrew's gaiety was

brittle. His amusing maliciousness made me uneasy. What would he do with me when I had gone? He would tear me into little pieces, as I had torn the lettuce. I began to wish I had left hours ago. It is terrible to be with people who are intelligent and can understand, yet who cut themselves off with a high wall of indifference. It is far better to be with crude people who do not realize half the time what they are saying or doing. One is not so lonely or so lost.

The lack of contact between me and Andrew, even between me and Tom, made me long all the time to be doing something for them, so that at least they would look back on me as a help in a practical way, a sort of temporary housekeeper who knew her business, even if she were good for nothing more.

"What can I do?" I asked as soon as supper was over. "Can't I so some mending? I should like that; it soothes me."

"Do you need soothing?" Andrew asked with his bright unwarm smile.

"Don't we all?" I shot out, rather too fiercely. "But seriously, I saw an enormous hole in the heel of Tom's sock—I may call you Tom, I hope? If you have any more like that, they ought to be done at once."

Would they mistake my longing to be doing something for a cloying motherliness? Would they think it coy to use Tom's name, then to ask for permission? Perhaps the worst transgression in their eyes would be that I had had the impertinence to mention the hole in Tom's sock. I didn't care, I was past caring. I felt that I had floundered from the beginning and might just as well go on floundering. I was on the brink of that strange desperate wish to throw all defenses down and appear utterly ridiculous in the eyes of the enemy.

"That's very good of you," Tom was saying gravely. "I have some socks that need doing, but there's not much wool. Will you mind using all the wrong colors?"

"Of course not," I said; "if you don't mind wearing the peculiar darns."

He brought me some newly washed socks and some skeins of what looked like embroidery wool. There was a brilliant magenta color and some salmon pink. I started to work at once. The huge egg-shaped holes gaped at me, but I soon had some of them neatly crisscrossed with the bright wool. The darns looked strangely theatrical; they reminded me of the artistic patches on the Pied Piper's cloak, or on the breeches of a stage peddler.

We spoke little as I worked. Andrew looked at his book of engravings and Tom puffed and sucked at his pipe. I hated the juicy bubbling it sometimes made. Gradually the light faded in the room until at last I had to put down my needle. Andrew's book lay on his chest. He seemed to be staring up at the ceiling, or were his eyes shut? I wondered how it was that I could seem so domestic and settled with them and yet be so completely cut off.

"Would you like the light?" Tom asked thoughtfully, seeing me put down the sock and lean back.

"No, I'm sure you're tired of those old socks," broke in Andrew; "don't do any more. Let's just sit in the gloaming, or dusk, or whatever other cozy name you wish to give it."

We sat in silence. I could just discern the little dumpy figure of Andrew on the bed. Somehow his richly striped dressing-gown, turned now to black and pale grey, made me think of a squat cold-cream jar, or a fat tube of toothpaste with the used part neatly rolled up. I pondered on his terrible deformity, guessing that he must have been born in that condition. I remembered the girl at school, so quick at lessons, so respected by all the other children, who had been born with just such a deformity—the normal-looking head, the twisted hands, the rigid little legs and thick body. Without realizing it at once, I began to endow Andrew with the qualities we all had given her. He was the brilliant person—"brilliant" has a special, almost magical meaning for children and simple-minded people. He was wonderfully brave, fighting all the time, refusing to be beaten by his handicap. He had a loving nature and never complained. I even remembered to tell myself that his body did not matter; it was not the *real* person. The real person one day would be freed from his shackles.

It was some moments before I realized that all these blindly held beliefs about my schoolfellow hardly fitted Andrew at all. They were all lies or deceitful half-truths. He was not "brilliant," his book was mercifully free from that quality, and his conversation, though animated and amusing, was on a level with the conversation of a hundred other people I had known. It was almost as if he refused to give the best of himself; he needed that for a more serious purpose. Perhaps he was brave in the way that we all are forced to be brave when faced with something inevitable. But I could not believe that he had a loving nature, or that he never complained. If his attitude to me as a stranger was any guide, he was certainly not very attached to his fellow beings. His affability was only on the surface; and I was sure that Tom often had to listen to long diatribes against people and circumstances.

The last and greatest lie was that his body did not matter. Of course it mattered, terribly, horribly. It was the thing that mattered most when one first met him, and, although I knew it would matter less as one came to know him more, indeed was already not quite so important to me, it would always be there to jolt one at unexpected moments, to keep him as a person apart, a special case.

I saw his head turned towards me now in the darkness. He seemed to be thinking about me for the first time since we'd met. I moved a little uneasily in my chair, making the wooden joints creak.

"I'm afraid you must find it dreadfully dull here," he said at last.

I answered in the same vein of conventional politeness.

"It's not dull at all, it's very good of you to have me. I feel rather guilty about staying the night when I really only came to tea."

Tom quietly got up from his chair and went out of the room, carrying one of the trays. I felt that I had been left to talk to Andrew alone. I was not grateful to Tom for his tact.

"It is rather wicked to play such a trick on you, to let you come here without any warning. Things must be so utterly different from what you expected." Andrew spoke suddenly with a curious mixture of taunting and solicitude in his voice. I was completely nonplussed and could only repeat myself.

"It was very good of you to have me." Then on a lower note I murmured, "I see no trick. I asked myself."

"Yes, but what did you expect to find?"

"What do you mean?" I asked repressively, because I knew only too well. I have seldom been so grateful for darkness. He could see no expression. The red mounting to my cheeks was hidden from him. Only my voice could betray me. My determination to control it made every muscle tighten.

"Oh, I see; you won't play the truth game," he said amusingly. "Perhaps it's just as well. It's stimulating, but it's also rather painful. The trouble is one remembers for too long afterwards."

"I can't play any game, for I'm utterly at sea. I don't know why I wrote to you, or why I came, or why I'm staying the night when I was only asked to tea."

Andrew seemed to consider my outburst for a moment or two; then in a very gentle, almost a tender voice, he said: "Isn't it strange, I can't think why either."

For an instant the rebuff hung in the air. It was an outrageous little sentence that had nothing to do with me; but when it flashed down to pierce me, I was so startled that I jumped to my feet.

"I'd better go, I can't stay here," I said. Rushes of mortification seemed to sweep over my words even as I spoke.

"Oh, please don't misunderstand me," Andrew implored. "I simply meant that it is often impossible to understand the reason for one's own actions. How much more impossible to interpret the reasons of others."

Is that what he had meant? Or was it a skillful side-stepping? Had my whole attitude during the visit been one of wrongheaded suspicion? Had I read far too much into harmless words and looks? I was too confused to think anything out. I only wanted to be alone. Without saying anything more I moved towards the landing. Andrew was careful to say good night, in case I should be coming back. The slippery stairs and the cool, polished rail were soothing to me. I felt the uninhibited quality of the living-room rising up to bathe me round with its peace. There was a light from the kitchen. Tom was there filling a hot-water bottle.

"I've just thrown your bed together. This is to put in it, although I think it's pretty well aired already."

He held the bottle out to me and I took it gratefully. It seemed a symbol of his thoughtfulness.

"Thank you *so* much," I said with too much feeling; but he did not look uncomfortable. He led me across the living-room and opened another door. I was in a little room of sprigged chintz and scrubbed oak furniture: very much the spare room, or the bedroom in some tasteful country hotel. The naked wood seemed to be declaiming, "I'm honest—no tricks about me. I haven't even any wax on me."

"Do you think you've got everything you want?" Tom asked. "The bathroom's just next door. I've put the new toothbrush out."

I thanked him again for doing so much for me and he said, "Oh, that's nothing," then added something silly like "Don't let the fleas bite."

After coming back from the bathroom, I half undressed, then snuggled into the warm bed. The moon was up in the sky, surprising me with its face, for I had noticed nothing as I sat in the dark with Andrew. Its discouraging light seeped into the floor in a hard unfeeling square. Even as I gazed at it, fascinated by its unearthly, dusty chill, I heard the nightingales quite near the house. Their song, so overlaid, so caked with human imaginings, struck me tonight quite differently. I could not read unending heartache or sad sweet unreasoning joy into it. They appeared to me as watchmen, paid to guard the house, who sang and warbled mechanically to show that they kept awake. This curious conception of them grew into a conviction. It was then that I must have fallen asleep.

I awoke to find Tom bending over me. My heart was beating very fast and through mists of half-consciousness I tried to remember what had terrified me. I was still frightened. Little cries which I did not utter kept rising in my throat, then sinking back, as if to lie in wait until my control should weaken. Tom's beaky nose was near, half a threat and half a reassurance. He loomed over me like a small thundercloud, or a grizzly bear, all furry at the edges.

"Are you all right now? Are you awake?" he asked gently. "You were calling out. I expect you had a nightmare."

"Was I making an awful noise?" I asked excitedly. "I can't think what I was dreaming of. I hardly ever call out in my sleep."

A sudden wave of shame swept over me. This final scene was all that was needed to damn me in their eyes forever. I saw Andrew in the future turning to Tom and saying: "Don't you remember that ridiculous woman who began screaming in the middle of the night?"

But Tom was still looking at me anxiously.

"I came in," he explained, "because I thought something might have got through the window and frightened you. The trouble about sleeping on the ground floor is that cats do sometimes jump in, and hedgehogs and dogs make strange noises just outside."

In my alarm I had sat bolt upright in bed. Now I was shivering. I clutched my bare arms and shoulders, both for warmth and to hide my half-dressed state from Tom. Without seeming to notice anything, Tom pulled up the eiderdown and settled it round my shoulders. He did not immediately remove his arms, so that they hung round me as if he had forgotten about them. Heavy and comforting, they were the arms of a sleeping friend. I was incongruously reminded of the "Babes in the Wood." It seemed probable that the nightingales might soon all hop into the room, carrying leaves in their beaks to make a blanket over us. In our hanging together there was a drowsy cessation of strain, a loosening of bands. I could feel the relief of tears dammed up behind my eyes. I waited for them unconcernedly.

It was then that I heard the slight noise outside the door. There was a delicate knock, then Andrew's voice, much lighter and more fairylike, almost whispered: "May I come in?"

Without waiting for an answer he turned the door handle and stood in the square of moonlight. Seen in that aluminum deadness, with the dark strips of his dressing-gown turned into velvety sooty eels, he made one think at once of a dwarf at the Court of Spain painted by Velásquez. He had that everlasting, unmoving, expressionless quality. He watched and listened. The skirts of his dressing-gown stirred very, very slightly. This made him appear more monumental than ever.

I was pleased that Tom did not immediately remove his arms from me. It would have been such a mean and paltry gesture. In his sleepiness he gradually let them slip, then turned his head and exclaimed: "Oh, hullo, Andrew. Susan's been having nightmares."

"I heard her cry out and wondered if anything was wrong," Andrew said, still standing quite still.

Tom began slapping his flanks and feeling in his pajama jacket pocket. It was a sort of dumb show to express his need of a cigarette. I told him to look in my bag on the table. I guessed the cigarette would be slightly scented from my powder and I knew he would not like this; but I took a sort of perverse pleasure in thinking that with each puff he would be not very favorably reminded of me.

"And *I've* got some sweets in *my* pocket," Andrew said suddenly. He was like a child vying with his schoolfellows. He came towards my bed holding out the paper bag. I took a sort of butterscotch toffee and started to crunch it appreciatively. Meanwhile Andrew was making efforts to scramble on to the end of my bed. I knew he would hate to be helped, so I let him pull himself up laboriously. He lay back against the wall to rest.

"You don't mind us like this all round you, do you?" he asked, turning to me abruptly. He still spoke in his new light voice. He seemed to be afraid of breaking up the stillness of the night. I felt how right he was.

"Of course not," I said, "it would be nice to talk a little in the moonlight."

My new ease startled me. Andrew no longer held any terrors. I was almost about to fall into the trap of treating him as a pet, a kitten or a marmoset. My only anxiety was that he would have heartburnings over finding Tom's sleepy arms around me; for I had already quite convinced myself that, if he loved anyone in the world, it was Tom, and that his love would not be of the sharing kind. I tried to study each feature in the moonlight. I thought he looked a little wistful, a little far away, like a child who knows his fate is in the hands of others; but perhaps this was imagination. In my present outflowing mood I was too prepared for emotion and pathos in everyone. Tom sprawling near me, half on the low bedside table, half on the edge of the mattress, was extraordinarily comforting. He said nothing, but pulled at his cigarette and blew out the smoke with a noisy unself-consciousness that I loved to hear. The shadow from his head and shoulders fell across my face, shrouding me protectively. I delighted to look out from my cave at the long arched shape of my body under the bed-clothes. In the moonlight it was like one of those medieval coffins of silvery stone, or like a great cocoon wrapped round in its web of a thousand thousand strands. I was balanced between thoughts of death and birth in a wonderful "now" of living. The nightingales were still singing. Once more they were transformed, this time into a bird orchestra performing chamber music while we took our light refreshments of butterscotch and cigarettes. I saw them in my mind, comic as crows, or the monkey musicians in Dresden china. They cocked their heads, swivelled their beady eyes and muttered like parrots.

Andrew held his sweets out to me again and I took two in a sort of sheer exuberance, a throwback to childish slyness and greed. We munched and crunched, making a noise of footsteps on a shingly beach. I wondered what Andrew was thinking. He had suddenly become in my eyes so much less important. I took it at first that this was entirely due to the change in my own attitude; but now the slightest of misgivings stirred for a moment. Had he become innocuous and almost childlike because, for the time being, he had retreated into himself to think and plan? Had he pulled in his head and left his grotesque little tortoise body, hard and strong, to be patted and patronized by soft pink fingers? The thought faded almost as soon as it had awoken. Andrew sitting there on the end of my bed, his little drumstick legs stuck out straight before him, was almost as comic and endearing as the nightingale orchestra I had imagined.

Again I caught myself out in a sentimental dodging of what I really felt. He was like my fancied bird orchestra, not because he was comic or lovable, but because he, like birds performing human actions, was sinister and a little frightening.

Giving my hand an angry little pat, I sat up more in bed, wriggled my shoulders under the eiderdown and determined not to spoil the present moment by barren wonderings. It was enough that we were watching the moon through the night, happy in our sleeplessness, thinking our thoughts, as though we had to be serious about the business of living forever.

They left me just before dawn. Andrew and I had eaten all the sweets, Tom had smoked all my cigarettes. We had talked in lazy snatches, enjoying our own and each other's truisms. They had been solemn and deep and soothing in the stillness of the night.

As I lay on my pillow, alone once more, I thought of Tom. There had been no need for anything when he had left. A word or sigh would have jarred me through and through. Even a look would have seemed horribly crude and furtive. He kept his face averted and called good night airily, laughing at the hour. I leaned from the bed giving all my attention to Andrew.

"I hope you'll sleep," I said, "I'm afraid my nightmare has ruined your night."

"Oh, I like a vigil," he answered quaintly; "I mean a communal one. That's why I liked the air raids in the war. One sat about and drank tea and felt cozy because of the danger."

He left me with this last word which is always spelled in red capitals in my mind, I suppose because I once must have seen it as a child written thus on some mysterious electrical contrivance barred round with iron spikes.

I could not go to sleep again, but I lay there resting, smoothing out all talk from my brain until I became aware of the first cold weariness of the dawn. It seemed amazing that this watering misery, as sordid as a slum, could conquer the monotonous magic of the moon, but it grew and grew in strength, filling out the trivial anxieties of the day in front of me, until I knew that I must get up and dress. I shuddered at the anticlimax of breakfast, the embarrassment of good-byes and thank-yous, the business of starting the car and arriving at the station in time for the train. The thought suddenly came to me that I could escape everything by leaving now, on foot, before anyone was astir.

II

I went over the the little writing table, so smugly waiting for the guest to write his letters on a rainy afternoon. Yes, there was paper in the drawer—all nicely engraved, with envelopes to match. I sat down and wrote a hurried note to Andrew thanking him for having me and explaining that I was leaving early so as not to dislocate his morning's work—he had told me that he worked from breakfast to lunch—and because I wanted to be back at my cottage before the grocer called with my weekly provisions. Poor excuses, but they would have to do.

I was careful not to leave Tom's name out altogether but to mention my appreciation of his good cooking and his thoughtfulness in preparing my room. I hoped that they would both come one day soon to stay with me for a night or two. I ended on this rather matey, tit-for-tat note. We might have been dull old friends arranging our yearly visits to each other; but I could not be bothered with refinements of thought or word. I wanted to be off. Besides, after last night I felt a sort of comradeship that permitted most things.

Never again would I look on Andrew as a devilish little dynamo about to vibrate with terrifying inhuman power. I had the secret of him; and Tom . . . I cut short the smile which was curving my lips. I would not indulge my thoughts until I was in the train.

As I finished dressing and collecting my few possessions together, the alien notion of pretending to forget something and leaving it behind came into my head. Tom would find it when he came to strip my bed. He could take it as he liked, as a symbol of my thoughts for him, or just as carelessness. In either case it would give him the excuse for writing to me. It seemed necessary to arrange such little matters. The novel excitement of even such a simple scheme possessed me. I looked about for something suitable to leave. . . . My handkerchief? My gloves? My powder-puff or lipstick? I should be uncomfortable without any of these; besides, wasn't there something a little too frail and human about them all? They were too animal and intimate. I had never in my life found anyone else's handkerchief without a slight distaste. Even lost gloves had a pathetic look that was almost squalid.

My eyes lighted on my brooch, genuinely forgotten until now on the little shelf above the bed. What could be better for my purpose? It was beautiful in itself and yet personal. The fact that it was valuable added to its usefulness; it would be returned to me for certain.

The little diamonds winked at me and I had a momentary pang. What if Tom should overlook it, or consider it of little value, not connect it with me, and give it to the girl who came in to clean twice a week? What if it should get lost in the post? My sudden surge of feeling for my brooch made me imagine the most unlikely catastrophes. But I left it there, letting myself out of the French window with the feeling that I was deserting an old friend.

The grass was soaking. I walked as quickly and silently as I could towards the lane. The chickens, locked in their house, heard me and clucked. I muttered to them and passed on. My shoes were not suitable for much walking. I spoiled them on that morning; but I enjoyed the cool squelch of dew between my toes. I was only sorry that the heels were not lower, for they made the walk to the station more tiring than it need have been.

I sat in the narrow ladies' waiting room, hours too soon for the train that went in my direction. Milk cans were banged about as if they had been sacred drums in a Buddhist temple. I was told that the first passenger train would be for London, so I decided to go up, do a little shopping perhaps, then return to my cottage from Victoria. It would be better to do this than to wait for five or six hours.

I did not arrive home until early afternoon. How tired I was, with the dusty heavy tiredness of sleeping in one's underclothes, of meeting new people and being jerked into new feeling. The trip to London had put the finishing touches to my exhaustion.

As I turned the key in the lock the uncontaminated stillness of my house rushed out to welcome me. I loved it all again for the thousandth time. Treasured pieces of furniture and china stood about the room like utterly reliable custodians, deaf-mutes pledged to me for life. I went upstairs and turned the taps on in the bathroom. I was pleased that I had made the color so raucous in this usually chaste white room. The bath, hand-basin, and pan were strawberry pink, the walls the shiny yellow of a buttercup. Curtains of vivid cerulean-blue plastic material let through a preposterous light, reminding one of glaciers and mammoths and Ice Queens. The harshness of the black and white rubber floor jumped up to the eyes in a dazzle.

I put into the hot water handfuls of bath-salts almost as gaudy in scent as the fittings were in color. Lilies of the valley, enormously, swooningly large, suddenly crowded into the steamy room, sucking up every particle of air.

I wallowed in the water, lying like a dead sheep, half on my side, only moving sometimes to steam my face with a hot flannel. And afterwards in my bedroom, lying on my bed, I opened my secret store cupboard where I kept food for just such an occasion as this. I had had no breakfast or lunch, only a cup of coffee in London, so I fell on the biscuits, the dried figs and chocolate. I made watery cocoa on my spirit stove, then dropped in an enormous spoonful of marshmallow mixture, sent to me from America.

It melted like whipped cream, covering my cup with a thick froth. When the tepid bubbles broke against my lips, I was reminded in some confused way of "Old Man's Beard." I saw the hedges wreathed again with the grey skeleton flowers.

I dropped a lump of chocolate into my drink to make it even richer. The chocolate melted slowly, sticking to the spoon and the sides of the cup. I enjoyed smoothing it out and letting the smears dissolve. I was a child again, playing with mud pies.

It was dangerous to wonder why such a glow of happiness had settled on me. It might dissipate if analyzed. There was the soaking in hot scented water after tiredness and dirt, the food after hunger, my own chosen refuge after the banalities of Andrew's spare room; but at the back of everything, pumping radiance into every material comfort, was the thought of Tom. Just that, no questions about him, no probings; I hardly even knew what I wanted of him, certainly not his presence at the moment. I had left so early that morning partly so that I should be able to think of him and not see him again.

Looking down I caught sight of Andrew's book on the bottom shelf of the table, the book that had started the whole *adventure,* if that was quite the right word. Now that I knew Andrew, how differently the sentences would read. I would not look at it again; I had no wish to force the readjustment of opinions. I would not jar myself in any way. I wanted to sail on forever in my smooth contentment. I could feel sleep coming, closing round me, until I was in a tingling, buzzing, tomb chamber of mole velvet.

In the days that followed I waited for a little registered parcel with the address in an unfamiliar hand. I tried to guess how Tom would write. I thought of smallish, untidy yet businesslike letters. There would be no scrawling, no flourishing "o's" and "d's" and "s's." Of course, it was possible that Andrew would write instead of Tom. It would not matter. I waited calmly to hear from either of the friends in the little stone house with the large white windows. That my brooch was still with them made a connection that pleased me. I almost hoped that it would be kept a little longer.

But as the days passed into weeks and I still received no parcel, I began to wonder what had happened. Had Tom overlooked it on the shelf above the bed? He would not, in all probability, be very particular about dusting. Had the girl who came in to clean found it or taken it without a word, to wear with her new evening dress at the dance at the village hall? I wondered whether I should write to Andrew. It would be easy to pretend that I had been looking everywhere for it, and had at last come to the conclusion that I must have left it in his spare room. But I was held back by the hope that one day I should go to the door and find the postman with the little parcel in his hands. Wrapped round my brooch would be a long letter from Tom. How much better to wait for this than to agitate and receive a correct little note from Andrew. I began to insist to myself that I should soon hear from Tom, that the understanding, so suddenly and mysteriously born that night, could not die away to nothing. It was growing in this fallow time, and I must not hurry it. I told myself this, but despondency was gathering. Gradually I gave up waiting for the postman's knock. A sort of dullness settled over me. I was too inert even to write for my brooch. I thought of it, as I thought of Tom, as something rather unreal that had existed for me long ago.

In my strange new sluggish state it was easy for Prudence Dawe, an old school friend, to persuade me to go and stay with her for a week. I put up almost no resistance. I could see the surprise on her face when she came to fetch me in her car. Always before I had made innumerable excuses, showing quite clearly that I preferred my solitude and my own bed.

When we arrived at her commonplace, comfortable house, I was made to wait in the drawing-room like a true guest, while she bustled about in the kitchen preparing the tea. She was singing gaily, happy, I suppose, to have me to gossip with for the next seven days. I felt almost warm towards her and because I could not look at her room with any pleasure I went up to the gate-legged table covered with magazines. Prudence read many as a sort of duty. She liked to be thought intelligent and up-to-date. I picked up the latest number of a literary monthly and took it to the fire. It was autumn now and cold. Vaguely I wondered what had happened to the whole of the summer. It had drained away unused and unenjoyed. My last bright memory was of the blossom and the nightingales in spring.

I opened the magazine and saw two reproductions of pictures that seemed bad in the extreme. Their dreary affectation was horribly exposed by the camera. They were as obviously cheats as the spirits photographed at a séance. I turned over the pages, ignoring a learned article on the heart cries people scribble on the walls of public conveniences, and two long poems by a well-known French poetess.

I came on it at the end of the magazine, just before the reviews and the advertisements. It was clearly the tid-bit, the delightful new short story with which to finish the feast. It was headed "The Diamond Badge" by Andrew Clifton.

I had no need to read it; indeed, I don't think I could have brought myself to look at even the first page. I suddenly knew a lot of things—what had happened to my brooch, why Tom had never written, why Andrew had seemed so harmless and childlike all at once. He *had* retreated into himself to think and to plan; this story was the result. The tortoise head *had* been pulled in, leaving me to pat the stony shell with my silly, soft, patronizing fingers.

I thought of him prowling round my room after I had left,

seeing the glitter of my brooch and climbing up on the bed to seize it. He would bear it away as a prize, cherishing it while his story developed. I never expected to see it again now—or him, or Tom. I was cut off forever. Andrew would keep my brooch; it would be a scalp, a sort of legal confiscation.

But I was wrong. When I returned from Prudence's, I heard a little plop as I opened the door. Something had fallen from the broad ledge beneath the letter slot. A tiny parcel lay on the mat and I recognized Andrew's spiky writing on the label. I gazed at it for a moment without moving, but Prudence was behind me, waiting to come in. My mind was in a maze, all my feelings dulled and fuzzy. My only clear thought seemed to be, "And he hasn't even registered it." With a sort of mock indignation I said it over and over again to myself. I picked up the parcel and put it on the side table, not having even enough interest to open it.

Brave and Cruel

On a lovely late summer evening, soon after the end of the war, I went to return some books to a near neighbor of mine in the country. As I walked down the lane to her house, everything was very still; the fields, the trees, the hedgerows seemed to be held in a dream. Because of this wonderful calm, I was all the more surprised to find Mrs. Bellingly in a state of high excitement. I had expected her to be lying on her garden-bed under the gnarled damson trees, perhaps lazily shredding French beans for her supper, or painting her nails with thick, dull coral varnish; but she was inside the house. She came hurrying to her front door and began at once to say: "You must, you simply *must* come to coffee tomorrow to meet really *the* most ravishing young man. I've only just met him myself. He doesn't know anyone else here, and I've said I'll do all I can to get him some friends of his own age. It is all quite extraordinary; I came home last night to find one of those sports bicycles thrust into my hedge, apparently abandoned. I didn't do anything about it at once, thinking that someone would probably turn up to claim it; but by this afternoon I had almost made up my mind to telephone the police, when who should appear but this delightful creature! My dear, a complete madman! He saw my easel in the garden and came straight up to me saying: 'Oh, you're an artist, and I've been looking everywhere for someone to do my portrait!' Then he began to explain about the bicycle. He said he'd thrown it down the night before, because he was too impatient to ride it any longer. He'd thumbed a car and got home in less than half the time."

"How unusual it all sounds!" I said.

"Oh! there's masses more to come. I asked him in to tea and he told me all about himself. His name is Beaumont, and he has been a fighter pilot. He told me the most thrilling stories. He won the D.F.C.; then he was wounded, poor boy, and had to spend months in hospital. He was bitterly disappointed when they told him he couldn't fly any more. I don't quite know what he's been doing since he left the air force; but he's only just come to live in this neighborhood, and that's why he's so keen to get to know other young people. He asked me particularly if I knew any nice girls, so I've told Katherine Warde to come in too tomorrow. I shouldn't be surprised if she falls for him at once. He's a very dark boy, almost swarthy—I suppose it must be southern French blood—then he has this glistening hair brushed back, and the most laughing, dancing expression I have ever seen. He can't keep still a moment. While he's talking, he prowls up and down and uses his whole body to accentuate his meaning. Poor boy! He must have had frightful experiences as a pilot. I expect they've helped to make him so excitable; but he's not in the least depressed, no one could be more bursting with spirits."

As she lay back on the sofa in her long room and told me all about this new friend, Julia Bellingly herself seemed bursting with spirits. Although she was a grandmother, she often displayed all the bounce and gusto of a hearty schoolgirl. She had retained that leathery quality. She would tell preposterous jokes, poke fun or wolf her food. But she also possessed a mature handsomeness that was remarkable. She had been, as she playfully—seriously sometimes—explained "an Edwardian beauty." She had sat to one of the fashionable painters of that period. Each new visitor would be taken to her bureau and shown the large brown photographs of her portrait. The original was in some public gallery.

She stretched out her hand now to the little old mahogany paint-box that held her cigarettes, and I had to try to strike a match on the worn side of a long case, decorated with brocade and a bedraggled gold tassel. When the cigarette was lighted, she went on with her story.

"If you'd come just a tiny bit earlier you would have seen him. He borrowed my torch before he left; he thought he might be out late tonight and he has no front light. I do hope he brings it back safely tomorrow—I told him to come to coffee, partly to meet Katherine and you, and partly to settle about his portrait. He is really anxious for me to do it. 'I would have liked it for my fiancée,' he said. But when I asked him, jokingly, if he'd want me to paint her too, he said: 'Oh, good lord no! She was ugly as sin. She was a nice girl, but ugly as sin. Besides, she's dead now.' Isn't he an extraordinary person! The most extraordinary young man I've ever known. He didn't seem callous, just matter-of-fact. I suppose one can't go through all the terrible experiences of modern warfare without being changed in some way."

"No, perhaps you can't," I said, not knowing quite what to think of Julia Bellingly's young man. I got up to go back to my supper.

"Now do please come tomorrow at eleven," Julia urged. "Just for once you can break your rule and come out in the morning. You can fit your writing in *any* time. I *do* want you to meet this amazing Beaumont."

"All right, I'll come," I said, showing rather more reluctance than I felt, since I was always being told to "fit my writing in," as if it had been some jigsaw puzzle.

Before leaving, I slipped into the cloak-room to replace the borrowed books on their shelves. Mrs. Bellingly had consigned all her books to this little closet. "Never clutter up your house with books," was a piece of advice she often repeated.

* * *

The next morning was fine and clear, so I took a picnic lunch with me in an old schoolboy's satchel and went down to Mrs. Bellingly's on my bicycle, intending to ride on and have my meal in the fields or by the river after I had met M. Beaumont.

Mrs. Bellingly's front door, as usual, was open. I knocked and called out; then walked into the hall. I heard voices in the drawing-room.

"Come in!" Mrs. Bellingly shouted in her rather military voice. I could tell that she was gay. Perhaps she had begun already to tell some of her jokes.

Flat blue-grey pancakes and wisps of cigarette smoke floated across the broad bars of sunlight from the windows. Someone came towards me at once, saying: "Oh, he's got leather pads on the elbows of his jacket! I do like that, don't you?"

As he turned to Mrs. Bellingly, I was able to glance quickly from top to toe of the "ravishing young man." To me this was certainly not quite the right description. His face, because of swarthy skin and harsh but well-formed features, seemed saturnine in spite of animation. There was a thickness and heaviness about him altogether. Thick hair swept back from his forehead; he had rather small compact square teeth. He wore an Italian shirt of white towelling and his bare arms were crisscrossed with dark hairs. Dark hairs sprouted too through the maroon cord lacing the shirt at his throat. His trousers were of dirty blue corduroy, mended across one knee with coarse stitches. He was tall, but his waist was not quite thin enough, so that his deep chest, the basket of his ribs and the waist merged together, reminding me too much of a tree trunk. He spoke with extreme exuberance and simplicity, and some of his words had a disarming cockney charm. It was impossible for me not to respond at once to his friendliness.

"So you've written a book," he said; "fancy being able to do that! It's marvellous."

He picked up Mrs. Bellingly's copy, which lay on a stool near him, and began to turn the pages hurriedly, sometimes stopping to glance for a moment at one of the decorations, then hurrying on, as if in search of some particular passage.

"Mr. Beaumont writes too," said Mrs. Bellingly in the decisive tone she used when more than ordinarily vague.

"No, no, you've got it wrong!" Beaumont exclaimed boisterously; "I said I'd *like* to write."

There was a pause in which he seemed to be thinking. Suddenly his face lit up and he turned to me.

"I say, old boy, what about us collaborating? Isn't that an idea! I've got the material, and you can knock it into shape."

I smiled, because I was surprised at being called "old boy" so suddenly; even the words themselves seemed strange to me. They had the pickled preserved flavor of a past fashion. I asked him what he wanted to write about. Did he want to describe his experiences as a fighter pilot?

"Yes, that too," he said quickly; "but I'd been thinking of life on the road—driving lorries up to Scotland. You see, that's what I've been doing since I came out of the R.A.F." He glanced towards Mrs. Bellingly, then added: "Of course I only did it for the experience, but I know all about it—all the swear words, all the slang, how the chaps pick up girls on the road."

Here he wrinkled up his nose, grinned, and winked.

His hair had fallen over his forehead, so he jerked it back and ran his fingers through it roughly; then he pulled a little black comb out of his pocket.

I wondered what Mrs. Bellingly was thinking. Did she want to hear more about the lorry drivers and the girls on the road? Perhaps she did not care so much for the vigorous combing; or did that too give her a sense of warmth and coziness? It was difficult to tell from her face since, except for gaiety or gloom, it was usually inexpressive. The cloudy blue eyes were too much like children's "agate" marbles and her complexion was too hidden under peach-pink foundation cream. I felt though, that she was as charmed as ever by Beaumont, and only hoped that others would not carp or find fault.

I heard the garden gate groan, and looked out of the window to see Katherine Warde pushing her bicycle up the path.

Her head was bent forward a little, so that I could see the crown of her rather artfully arranged hair. The curls and ridges gleamed golden in the sun, but the rest of her hair was brown. In that glimpse she looked as silent and brooding as I had often known her to be. I wondered if Beaumont would enliven her or make her more silent than ever.

When she came into the room, I thought again how pretty the short thick nose and the clear coloring were. They made her face charming, in spite of the slight look of mulishness. Only the mass of hair with its discreetly bleached waves and ends did not entirely please me. There was so much of it, and it seemed to make her small figure almost top-heavy.

Mrs. Bellingly introduced her to Beaumont; she gave him a quick dutiful smile, then composed her features again and looked about the room in the indifferent way of a confused person. I brought her a cup of coffee as a protection and we began to talk in rather low voices about life at her art school in London. She was taking the drawing and painting examinations, but hoped secretly to be able to give up teaching for theatre design; she longed for some job with a ballet company.

Beaumont was talking to Mrs. Bellingly in much louder tones. He seemed to be explaining how he thought conquered nations ought to be treated; I heard the words "honorable capitulation" several times, and each time he pronounced the "h" of "honorable" with great harshness and vigor, as if in this way to drive the adjective deeper into Mrs. Bellingly's consciousness.

Just as I was listening with one ear to their conversation, so, I noticed, was he casting us a glance every few moments. At last he stopped talking to Mrs. Bellingly, dropped his hands to his sides and looked straight at us. A broad smile spread over his face, he turned his eyes up to the ceiling and said, as if to the air, "I think Katherine is very shy of me; I wish she wouldn't be."

Then, when Katherine looked away hurriedly, he added, this time directly to her, "Katherine, don't be shy."

Katherine seemed overcome. I felt that she wanted to run behind the large sofa and crouch there in hiding. Her eyes darted from object to object in Mrs. Bellingly's very crowded room. Like a dealer at a sale she skimmed over the Staffordshire figures, the ruby and white Bohemian glass, the glittering Empire lusters. But it was a relief to see that Beaumont did not share her embarrassment. He had come towards us impulsively and was now describing his behavior in air battles.

"Of course, I was very cruel," he said; "I *am* very cruel, you know. I can't help it; I had to give the devils all I'd got. I couldn't stop myself. I used to love to 'sew' a train—just like your machine, Katherine, sewing a piece of cloth!" Here he prodded the air with his finger, then laughed gleefully.

Soon we were all asking him questions. Even Katherine had nearly recovered from being told not to be shy. Beaumont told his stories with a great many arm and leg movements. We might almost have been in the airplane with him. He showed us delicate white scars on his arms and one above his right eye. He explained that they were shrapnel wounds. Sometimes the one above his eye made him feel dizzy and filled the eye with blood.

"When I get angry, it goes quite crimson," he said.

He was now so warmed to his subject that he looked at none of us. He stared through the wall of the drawing-room, as if he saw something in the sky, far above. His hands were slightly raised, his eyes shone, and his lips seemed wet. All at once he dropped his eyes to me.

"We've *got* to write a book together," he said; "think of all this grand stuff going to waste! What a book we could do! It would make you famous."

I raised my eyebrows and gave the little laugh that might have been expected. He was piqued by my lightness and frowned.

"Don't laugh, I'm serious," he said; "it would be good." Then, as if the strain of being serious were too much for him, he allowed a wicked grin to spread over his face.

I looked at the ormolu and gunmetal clock and saw that it was after twelve o'clock. I knew that Mrs. Bellingly would soon want to be left to prepare and enjoy her lunch alone. I too wanted to ride on and have my picnic by the river.

When I stood up, Beaumont rose too.

"Which way do you go, old boy?" he asked.

"Oh, David's always going down to the river to picnic alone; isn't it strange?" said Mrs. Bellingly in a tone of mild suspicion and resentment. She disapproved of pleasures that she could not share.

"Mind if I tag along some of the way?" Beaumont asked: "I've got an appointment with someone out in that direction."

I was quite pleased to have Beaumont as a bicycling companion, but I wondered where he could be going, since the lane I took down to the river ended in a cornfield and there was no house near, except the lock-keeper's.

All three of us said "good-bye" to Mrs. Bellingly together. Beaumont shook her hand up and down while he thanked her for lending him the torch and promising to paint his portrait. The first sitting was arranged for the next morning, and it was settled that Katherine should be there too, to avail herself of this fine model. Mrs. Bellingly, as she made the arrangement for Katherine, seemed to intimate that Katherine should do more work in the holidays, that she, Mrs. Bellingly, when a student at the Slade in the first years of the century, had covered many canvases during the long summer months.

Beaumont and I wheeled our bicycles beside Katherine till we came to her house on the corner of the main road. Here she glanced quickly at both of us, smiled, wiped the expression off her face almost at once, and said "good-bye" solemnly. As she turned away, she gave a little duck; she might have been trying to escape the chopper in the game Oranges and Lemons. She walked towards the house with a sort of morose unconcern. It was as though she were unknown to us, and we were making her self-conscious by shameless staring.

Beaumont and I mounted our bicycles and rode round the corner. As soon as we were out of sight, he leaned towards me and said in a low, amazed voice: "I say, Dave, isn't Katherine shy! I wonder why she is. I didn't frighten her, did I, with all that cruel talk? I can't help it you know, I *am* cruel."

"No, I don't think it was that," I said; "it is meeting people for the first time that she finds difficult. Mrs. Bellingly rather overpowers her, tries to manage her too much, don't you think? But of course, she *is* a very easily embarrassed person."

For a moment or two we rode on in silence; then Beaumont turned to me again; very suddenly: "I'm wondering if you can keep a secret." He was mysterious, full of his secret, smiling because he had the important thing to tell.

"I suppose I do look very indiscreet," I said.

"If I tell you, you won't think it's silly, you won't tell anyone else?"

He raised his eyebrows, making wrinkles on his forehead. He was still smiling, with his mouth a little open; he longed to tell me but wanted too to keep me in suspense. It seemed to be a sort of game.

"Well," he said at last, "I've been thinking about marriage lately, and now I've met Katherine, I think I'd like to marry her. Don't laugh, I'm dead serious."

"But you've only seen her once," I said, quite amazed by the unreal sound of his words.

"I know, but she's my type. What a good egg that Mrs. Bellingly is to bring us together! You see, Dave, I want to settle down. I never used to; it's only come over me just lately. But now I want to marry and have a baby girl."

"A baby girl!" I exclaimed. It was impossible to tell what this extraordinary person would say next.

"Yes, don't you like them too? I don't know what it is about them; they're sort of soft and—" he seemed to be searching for a word—"cuddly—I don't know. Anyhow I'd like to have a little baby girl of my own."

"Katherine is very young, you know. I don't think she is nineteen yet," I said, for the sake of saying something. I found that I could not treat Beaumont's marriage plans seriously.

"That's all the better; a wife should be a few years younger than the husband, don't you think? And you could take a girl like Katherine *anywhere,* couldn't you? Isn't she pretty! And I bet she'll learn to dress before she's twenty-one; to look really smart, I mean. She looks very nice now, but it's sort of in a young-girl-student way, isn't it?"

When he spoke again, it was with the same secret air that he had used before, the same smile, hesitation, drawing in of cheeks.

"You know Dave, I haven't kept off it, I've been as bad as the next man, I've had lots of women—too many; but I've always been careful to keep myself clean. That's what matters; keep yourself clean."

Was I about to be lectured on hygiene? Or was he talking of souls? Nothing seemed unlikely.

We had now almost reached the corner where I should have turned to the left, to go down to the river; but when I told Beaumont this, he seemed so disappointed, and he persuaded me so energetically to stay with him on the main road, that I gave up my plan. I found that he had never meant to take the turning to the river. His appointment was with someone in the nearest market town. I agreed to ride on with him until I came to the top of a hill, lined with old beechwoods. I would picnic there instead.

As soon as I had decided to do this, he said impulsively: "I like you, Dave. You wouldn't mind going up in the air, would you? You'd be all right. You'd make a grand pilot."

All I could do was to exaggerate the surprise in my voice as I said: "I! make a good pilot! What do you mean?" Was Beaumont trying to make a fool of me?

But flattery so preposterous and blundering still works some charm. Perhaps the untruth itself enriches, frees the flattered person, for a moment, from his own idea of himself.

"You know I'd be absolutely hopeless," I said coldly. I had not used his name so far, although he had already shortened mine to Dave, and perhaps he noticed this now and wanted me to call him by some name, for he said:

"Don't call me Beaumont, it's such a mouthful, call me Micki—all my friends do; only you must remember it's spelled with an 'i' not a 'y.' You see it's short for Michel. I really belong to an old French family."

"How interesting," I said, waiting for more details.

"Yes, but you see I haven't ever lived in France, because my father went to New Orleans as a young man. My father's dead now, and so my mother has settled herself in rather a nice little flat in Chelsea." There was a slight pause, then Micki added, "I just know a few facts about the family. They were quite important people, you know—not exactly noble, but highest provincial gentry. The name should really be *de* Beaumont, but I don't bother with the de."

By this time we had begun to climb the long hill leading to the beech woods, and Micki was looking very hot. On leaving Mrs. Bellingly's house he had put on the jacket which hung over his handlebars, to prevent it, I suppose, from slipping off as he rode; but now he was getting so hot that I suggested he should stuff it into my bicycle-basket on top of the brown satchel, holding my picnic.

"Fine, but will it get in, old boy?" he asked.

We stopped and he pulled it off with relief. He looked at it in his hands, then said: "It's only a bought thing, isn't it awful! Perhaps it would look better if it had leather on the elbows, like yours. The wife of my great friend, squadron-leader Minton, is always giving me tips on dress and *she* likes leather elbows."

"My jacket only has leather pads because the tweed was wearing through," I explained, not quite understanding the importance he seemed to attach to them.

Micki held out his bare arms and gazed on them. They looked very dark against the towel shirt. The short sleeves stuck out above the swarthy biceps like minute fairy wings.

"You're sunburned," I said.

"No, I'm not; it's the filthy Latin in me." He clucked his tongue and shook his head musingly.

We climbed on until we reached the first bend, before the steepest part of the hill. As we turned, an orange lorry appeared round the bend higher up the hill, then rushed and rattled past us. The driver called out. I took no notice, thinking that it was only some ribaldry, but Micki dropped his bicycle at the side of the road and ran back, shouting to me over his shoulder: "Wait a sec, will you? I know this fellow."

I sat down on the bank and watched Micki chasing the lorry. It pulled in to the side and stopped; Micki raised his head and talked to the man in his high driver's seat. Standing there in the road, laughing, waving his arms and shaking back his hair, he seemed different to me—more lithe and slender, with a greater ease about him.

But when in a few moments he ran back, he seemed just as he had been at first.

"I used to know that chap well," he said between deep breaths; "he's very aristocratic—French origin too, you know. He used to wear a reddish beard."

We began to push our bicycles again, but we had only climbed a few paces when another lorry passed us, this time going up the hill. It was heavily laden with logs, and the engine chugged painfully. When it came to the steepest part of the hill, it stopped, swayed a little, then rolled back to where we were.

"Look out!" Micki cried, although I had already jumped up on the bank in case the lorry should slide any nearer.

"You've always got to be careful of those things," he added in the same excited voice.

I wondered what made him warn me in such an alarming, grim way. Had he seen a lorry roll back and crush someone? Or did he like to make little incidents seem more important?

The lorry had now swung into the middle of the road and stopped again. Steam belched from the radiator and rose up in a white curling, waving tree. Micki ran out to the driver and said: "You'd better let her cool off."

The driver just smiled at him wearily, indifferently. He asked Micki to put bricks behind the wheels and Micki ran to the bank where there was a whole pile, next to the black and white St. John ambulance post.

He wedged two behind each huge front wheel, then the driver climbed down and stood in the road, still saying nothing, only smiling wanly at Micki's agitation and excitement. He looked very young, and he seemed too tired to be either particularly grateful for Micki's help, or irritated by it. He seemed to be asking with his heavy eyes and faint grin, "What's all the fuss?" And Micki, when he felt this indifference, became restless, almost shamefaced, as if he had been emptied and cast aside. He pulled up his bicycle and hurried on, until the sweat trickled through his thick eyebrows and rolled into his eyes. He paused to wipe his face, then said with all his old animation: "Let's find a good place and rest at the top of the hill!"

At last we were there. We sat down on a green bank close to a granite drinking trough, and Micki took out his comb again. He ran it through his damp glistening hair several times, then he turned to me and said: "Dave, do you think I speak very badly? Mrs. Minton, that's the friend's wife you know, is always telling me I'm much too careless. She says I say 'knaow' instead of 'know.' You'd tell me too if I pronounced things wrong, wouldn't you?"

I was touched and surprised and confused. In an effort to be easy, I asked laughingly, "Is Mrs. Minton herself such a 'beautiful pronouncer'?"

"Well, old boy, she *thinks* she is, but I'm sometimes not so sure. I'd like you to meet her though, she's very nice; and *he* was my best pal in the R.A.F. They've got a daughter—only fifteen, but lovely shaped breasts and very quiet and sweet. There is a son too, but he's a little bugger. He's got one of those mean natures. I thought I liked him all right at first, but when I asked to borrow something last week—he's got a special sort of engineering tool you can't buy now—he hid it and then said he couldn't find it. Funny having a mean streak with such a grand guy for a father."

"Are you sure that he hid it?" I asked. "It might really have been lost."

"It wasn't lost," said Micki scornfully; "I was looking round the house and I found it stuffed behind a lot of his clothes in a cupboard; that was a queer place for it, wasn't it? Besides, I know he doesn't like me much. He sort of looks at me suspiciously sometimes. There isn't any reason for it; it's just his meanness."

"Do they live near here?" I asked, feeling that Micki wanted to tell me more about his friends.

"No, not very near—just outside Brighton. They've got a lovely place there, you'd like it, Dave—sort of terraced gardens, and at the bottom a hard court, a squash court and a little bathing-pool. I can go there whenever I like; my room's always ready; but of course I don't like to make use of their offer too much. They're a grand family though, and Mrs. Minton seems to take a real interest in me. She's always telling me what to wear and what to say. She agrees that it would be a good idea for me to get married, and she says she'll try and fix me up herself, if I can't find anyone I like; so, if Katherine isn't having any—!"

He gave a loud laugh and threw himself back on the bank, tucking his hands behind his head. Again I wondered if he wanted his love at first sight of Katherine to be treated seriously or as a great joke.

He stretched out his arms and started to examine them just as he had done on taking off his jacket.

"God! I wash and wash and yet my skin is just as filthy-looking," he exclaimed.

I realized now that this was one of his habitual remarks but this time he spoke with such simplicity, *really* as if talking to himself, that I was reminded at once of the story of the blackamoor who searched everywhere for some magic potion to turn him white.

After a few more minutes' rest, Micki sat up and said: "I haven't got much to do in the town—only see a chap who owns a big garage. You sit here and have your picnic and wait till I come back; then we can ride some of the way home together."

"Oh, I shall go into the woods and find a good place before I eat my picnic," I said; "and then I might stay there reading for some time; so don't expect me to be on the road for certain when you come back, will you? I may find another way home through the woods, but if I don't, I'll try to meet you here. How long do you think you'll be?"

I wanted a rest from Micki; it had come upon me suddenly that he was an exhausting companion. Perhaps I made my feeling too clear; for he said with aggrieved conviction: "You're not going to wait, you devil." Then, apropos of nothing, he added: "Of course, after Uppingham I went on to Christ's at Cambridge, you know."

I wondered cloudily if there *were* a Christ's at Cambridge. Micki contrived somehow to make even simple facts sound improbable.

Before we parted, Micki looked down at the water in the horse-trough and said: "Let's have a wash, Dave!"

He buried his face deep in the water, splashed it all over his arms, then pressed the button of the drinking-fountain so that a jet gushed out and hit him in the eye. He laughed up at me and the hard white teeth made his skin look almost khaki. There was the redness of his tongue too, as he flicked it round his lips to drink up the drops trickling down his face. Drops threaded themselves into necklaces along stray hairs, or dangled from the wet rat's tails above his eyes.

"You press the button, Dave, while I have a drink," he suggested.

The button was very stiff. I pushed with both thumbs and Micki stretched his mouth wide open to receive the frothing gush. It struck against the back of his throat, choking him with its bubbles. He spluttered and swore and laughed again.

I left him, still coughing and swearing, and climbed up towards the woods. Before I disappeared, he waved to me, and my last glimpse was of him trying to dry his face and arms on a large dingy red navvy's handkerchief; then he swung his leg over his bicycle and was gone.

I went deep into the woods and, after some time, found a glade where the sun filtered through the beech leaves and fell on rich green cushions of moss and the black water of a little pool. I settled there, with my back against a tree trunk, and started to unpack my satchel. I had cheese and crisp bread and a little butter, then chocolate to be eaten with a fresh sour apple, and a thermos of milky coffee.

As I ate and drank, I glanced sometimes at my book, but chiefly I gazed at prospects through the wood and thought of the strangeness of Micki Beaumont.

He seemed to fit into none of the holes he dug for himself so industriously. He was not the French near-noble, the English public schoolboy and undergraduate, the R.A.F. pilot, or even the amateur lorry driver. Yet I wondered too if he was not a little bit of all these things mixed together in the most unexpected way, to make a strange new pudding.

I stayed in the woods till after five o'clock, partly because it was so delightful there, and partly to make quite sure of missing Micki on my way home. I hoped to see and know more of him; but on another day.

II

We met again the next week. Mrs. Bellingly asked me to tea, telling me that she had invited one or two other people to celebrate Micki's engagement to Katherine. The notice had been in that morning's paper.

I was so used to Mrs. Bellingly's mistakes, extravagances, and wild twistings of the truth, that I only opened my mouth and eyes in a kind of goggle of mock astonishment.

"But it's true!" she insisted, picking up the paper and passing it to me. The notice was already underlined in bright crayon. I began to read: "The engagement is announced between F.O. Michel de Beaumont, D.F.C., only son of Mrs. R. J. de Beaumont of Inverness. . . ." Here I stopped and turned to Mrs. Bellingly: "But Micki told me that his mother had a flat in Chelsea; he never mentioned Scotland. He talked of New Orleans; I can't remember anything else."

"Yes, I didn't quite understand the Inverness part," agreed Mrs. Bellingly; "because he only told me about the Chelsea flat; but I daresay she has a place in Scotland as well. Poor boy! he doesn't seem to get on with her very well. In spite of his fine war record, she appears to take very little interest in him. Sometimes she doesn't write for months, and she's nearly always out when he calls at the flat. I suppose she's one of those women who live just for their bridge, or their clothes, or whatever it may be."

"She wasn't described to me," I said; "he only told me that she'd lived in Chelsea since his father's death."

"Oh, he's told me *so* much. The poor boy's nerves are in a frightful state. He seems to long to make a confidante of one, and sometimes he comes out with the most astonishing things. In his confusion he contradicts himself too. Of course, the ordeal he's been through is bound to have left its mark."

As I listened to Mrs. Bellingly, I was again puzzled by the strange effect she produced when she used soft words. They came out in all the usual places, but the tone was so brassy that they were made to sound almost mockingly sentimental. And yet I knew that there was no hint of mockery in her words—either for herself or for her subject.

When the afternoon came and I had put on a suit and was tying up my shoelaces, I heard Micki calling up to my window from the lane. He had come to hurry me and take me back to the tea party. I felt the weight of his footsteps sinking into the ground under the window. As he bounded upstairs, the little house trembled. Although he moved so quickly, there was a deadness about the weight of his body.

He began at once to admire my Donegal tweed and some brightly checked socks. He rubbed his hand over my sleeve, then looked closely at the flecks of color in the tweed and marvelled at their variety. He himself had on a Prussian-blue shirt of a curious silky linen. His tie and hairy fawn jacket were much lighter in tone. On his feet were heavy brogues. Eyes and hair glistened, and he laughed and talked so much that there was almost always the gleam of teeth as well. I felt sure that Mrs. Bellingly would consider him more ravishing than ever.

After looking carefully at some other clothes that lay about, Micki went across to the open door of my hanging cupboard and examined each suit. I wondered at this close attention; he might have been the owner of secondhand clothes shop.

Suddenly he said: "We had a pilot at the 'drome. He was just like you. He wouldn't stand a spot of dirt on his machine. Christ, he was fussy! We used to call him Louise, but that's only a nickname. He wore marvellous pearl-grey satin pajamas. Hardly anybody dared to tease him, but you could, Dave; he'd let you, because you're so like him. I'll ring the 'drome and see if he's still there. 'Go on, bastards! Get it clean!' he's shout at the guys working on his machine, then he'd walk up and down flipping his

hands. 'Polish it, you swine!' he'd call out; but they didn't mind they thought he was grand."

Here Micki broke off to give me an imitation of his friend walking up and down beside his machine. He rolled his eyes swayed his hips, and lisped most preciously.

Although the act was so old and commonplace, there was such a spirit of fun and devilry in Micki that I had to laugh.

"Louise was very brave, you know," he said, "*and* cruel You're very brave and cruel, Dave, aren't you?"

He seemed to want me to confirm him in his fantasy, so my impulse was to say "No" loudly and perhaps a little rudely. wanted to stop all further comparisons and other personal remarks

We went out into the lane and started to walk toward Mrs Bellingly's house. When we were at the gate, I looked through the rose arch and saw people already sitting in the garden. The little group on the lawn looked very brilliant; Mrs. Bellingly's garden furniture was painted canary yellow and powder blue. The canvas of the chairs was in broad stripes of white and yellow, and the tablecloths were candy pink. Raucous green-ringed cups stood on these cloths, quite overpowering some older, more beautiful gold-sprigged china; but the silver teapot held its own, flashing back gleams from polished sides. It was like a little lighthouse, surrounded by dark, forbidding rocks; for all the guests looked dark against the brilliant furnishings.

Apart from Katherine, there were four others: a Mrs. Talbot, perhaps seventy years old, slight and spare, dressed all in black, even down to the fine stockings on her sparrow's legs—her grand-niece Pamela, who had a haughty expression and some unfortunate spots—Pamela's baby girl with palest floss-silk hair—and, last of all, a Mrs. Charles in a steel-grey coat and skirt, fitted tightly over squat hips, so that she looked like a neatly packed grey paper parcel. Only the face under the gunmetal straw hat was different in color. It had a tawny glow and a fullness that are not supposed to be English. On first seeing her I had been reminded of Red Indian squaws and gypsy clothes-peg makers, until the more likely explanation of Jewish blood had come to me.

All these people had been introduced to Micki before he came to fetch me, but none of them showed pleasure at his return. They fixed their attention on me as the new arrival, or talked brightly to

Mrs. Bellingly, offering unnecessary help with the teacups or little tables.

I wondered why Mrs. Bellingly had asked such people to meet Micki; they were not even well known to Katherine, who sat amongst them silent, rather too composed, with gold daisies in her ears, and her hair swept up in a new, more becoming fashion.

Micki knelt down on the tartan rug and held out his arms to the baby girl, but she, after looking up at her mother's discouraging face, turned away from him with some complaining sound. Micki took no notice, but began to twirl his large hands over her head and make gug-gug, goo-goo noises. His long hair fell over his eyes; he shook it back and called over his shoulder, "She's shy, Dave, but isn't she grand! Can't you see now why I want a baby girl?"

I saw the look of distaste on the mother's face. Her absurd stiffness so annoyed me that I dropped down at once on the rug to give Micki all the support I could. I guessed that this might encourage him to further extravagances, but that would have to be risked. At least I should be near, and he would not have to shout his embarrassing remarks.

He began to tumble the baby girl on the rug and, in spite of wild protests, to give her grizzly-bear hugs. The floss-silk hair was tousled, the stiff little skirt pulled up, to show pink panties and a line of less pink stomach. Tears soon followed, and then at last the mother, Pamela, turned to Micki and said exasperatedly: "Oh, *please* don't upset her too much."

"I didn't want to upset her, poor little thing!" Micki protested; but Pamela had already turned back to the others, who were discussing their gardening problems and pleasures. I could see, beyond Pamela's head, the rigid lack of interest on Mrs. Bellingly's face. The blue eyes were two smoky pebbles, washed up by the cold sea, and the mouth had set into a dark crimson line, finishing in sharp little down-curving fishhooks. She hated gardening and left her own to become a wilderness, except for the small patch of lawn on which we were sitting. She did not want to hear about Mrs. Talbot's gardener's operation, the bomb damage to the grape-house in the war, and how the best muscatel vine had died at last, the absurdities of the dog and the hedgehog in the potting-shed. She wanted to make her women guests take notice of Micki and

appreciate him, and, since delicate methods had failed, I guessed that less delicate ones were about to be employed. In order to hear more, I got up off the rug and carried a plate of chocolate biscuits back to the tea table.

The first break in the tedious garden topic was seized on by Mrs. Bellingly; she turned to Mrs. Charles and began at once to talk of Micki, his bravery, his interesting French descent, his vitality and fire, the special quality in his looks which made them so acceptable to a painter. She never spoke softly, and now her voice rose with her enthusiasm. I wondered if Micki could hear his praises—he would certainly have enjoyed them; but perhaps he was too busy trying to comfort the baby girl with more hugs, although hugs had caused all the tears in the first place.

Katherine, I think, heard every word. She showed no sign, unless she kept even stiller than before; but she seemed to be drinking in the remarks and storing them away. I wondered if she wished that Micki would abandon the baby girl and talk to her, or whether she preferred to be left to herself, before these disapproving women. Micki did sometimes call out to her, asking her to admire the baby girl, or telling her with much gusto that he would be wanting one of his own just like her by and by; but Mrs. Bellingly was the only person who paid her marked attention as the engaged girl. She had begun to call Katherine "dear" in her peculiar sweet-hard tone; she smiled on her much more and tried to control the impulse to give orders. The effort was not made for nothing; the smiles and discipline seemed to be making the rich peach-bloom quiver a little. The face underneath had always lived a life of its own, but sometimes signs broke through the marshmallow armor-plating.

By the end of Mrs. Bellingly's praises of Micki, Mrs. Charles's expression had hardened into a leathery simper that would have been most affronting to anyone just a little more aware than Mrs. Bellingly; for tea-table politeness veiled disbelief so thinly that the features seemed to be saying, "Oh, but how droll! How too amusing of you to take up this attitude! Of course, anyone can see that the man is dreadfully common and almost certainly some sort of trifling impostor, but you choose this romantic view—so original."

Mrs. Charles's smiling rejection of every word at last became clear even to Mrs. Bellingly. A pause stretched itself into a silence. Mrs. Bellingly turned away impatiently and asked me to fetch the cigarettes from the drawing-room.

Soon afterwards Mrs. Talbot struggled up from her low deck chair to say good-bye. Standing on those fragile black-silk legs she looked very tottery and ancient; but there was a great lump of pride and malevolence behind her pale little eyes, and I thought that it was this lump which was her driving force. Insolent pride and ill-will carried her through the day, kept her from dying, from melting into nothing. I thought that each year to come would make the little beady eyes clearer and paler, until they were nothing but two sucked acid drops. All color would drain out of her, leaving only the pure venom.

Pamela took the child up like a bundle of sticks and followed her great-aunt. She smiled a general good-bye, then the mouth drooped too suddenly, disparagingly, as if she had dismissed from her mind everything but the child's evening meal and bath, her husband in the army across the sea, and the problems of her own face and body. Mrs. Charles lingered a little, sitting forward in her chair, so that her smooth gray rump poked out assertively, giving me the fancy that perhaps, after all, this was the most important part of her and she should be turned upside down at once.

She left, still smiling her tight smile and acting her extremely correct English lady's part, giving nothing away and yet making her dreary meaning only too clear.

When Julia Bellingly had seen the last of her stiff-necked guests to the garden gate, her breast seemed to fill, to rise up like a proud figurehead's. She returned to us impatient for the pleasure and amusement that the others had spoiled.

"Katherine, let's go on with Micki's portrait," she said; "and you David can stay and do a drawing. I'll give you some nice prewar Ingres paper and red chalk."

We followed her into the long drawing-room, where two easels had been set up near the fireplace. Micki at once took up his position and said: "Am I right? Do I look right? Is my head at the right angle? Is that good? Does it look good?"

He held the arms of the shabby *bergère* and tilted his chin, anxious for our spoken approval, afraid that we might withhold it through inattention or lack of generosity.

"That is fine, Micki," Julia Bellingly said: "just a tiny bit more to the left—nearly—nearly. Now hold it, and we can begin at once!"

I had been placed on the sofa with drawing-board, paper, chalk and art cleanser—a very large and temptingly soft india rubber, which I pinched and kneaded and thought of dreamily as "a miniature pound of baby's flesh." I began with no very strong desire to draw Micki, but soon grew interested and found myself accentuating the bridge of his nose, the length and the slant and the slight bulge of his eyes, the peculiar heaviness of his jaw, and the good rich shape of the lips above. I noticed for the first time that his ears were less well-formed than the rest of his features, they had a punched, ill-treated appearance and they stuck out a little; but the dark wings of hair, sweeping back, sometimes flopping over them, helped to disguise this.

Micki at first sat very still, so still that the eyes fixed in a stare; he might have been falling into a trance; but after about a quarter of an hour he grew restless, twitched his nostrils, glanced out of the corners of his eyes, and said, "Can I see now? I want to know what they're like. Do you think any of you have got me yet? I want to move now."

"Oh, but just a little longer!" Mrs. Bellingly protested. "You haven't sat any time yet, Micki."

Micki took no notice and jumped up to look. I felt that he would not like mine so I leaned over it and busied myself with the art cleanser. But he was not to be put off; he already knew the other two pictures and only stopped to note what progress had been made. He praised Mrs. Bellingly's and told Katherine that she had not quite caught his expression yet; then he came over to me saying, "Let's have a look, old boy; what have you been making of me?"

For a moment he looked at my drawing in silence. It was clear that he felt a little shocked by it. I began at once to explain that portraits were often very unlike the sitters, and ought never to be taken to heart. They were sometimes just exercises, where lack of skill, love of distortion, a hundred other things, overlaid the likeness.

He said: "Oh, no Dave, I like it all right; it's fine. I just thought at first you'd sort of made me look kind of peculiar."

He gazed at it for a little longer, then went back to his chair, and I thought I heard him murmur something to himself.

After this, the sittings grew shorter and shorter, and the rests turned into entertainments. Micki performed and the rest of us watched. When first we came in from the garden, I had noticed Katherine's cherry-red gramophone and thought how strange it looked, sitting on the slender early piano, which Mrs. Bellingly persisted in calling a harpsichord. Now Micki went over to it and put on a record of the R.A.F. March Past. He had bought it only that morning and kept telling us that it was a fine thing, and that Sir Walford Davies was the composer. As soon as he heard the music, Micki began to strut up and down the crowded room, swinging his arms stiffly. All at once he jerked his head to our side and kept it there, his eyes fixed rigidly on us, while he marked time, lifting up his knees preposterously and shooting his arms straight out until they looked as long as monkey's arms.

This moment of taking the salute was the most uncomfortable of all, far worse than Micki's tricks with the child on the rug. I glanced away, smiled, tried to look at him again, still smiling, but there was no escape for me. One thing I knew, I must not look at Katherine or Mrs. Bellingly. I must not even think of their expressions.

Micki stopped drumming on the floor, the hands dropped to his sides, and the fierce solemn look melted. He smiled and said: "Ah yes, that's how we used to do it. It was grand!"

Picking up a book off the low stool in front of the hearth, he sat down, opened the book on his knees, and began to tell us about it. It was all to do with the air force and he had bought it that morning, when he bought the record of the march. It was *absolutely* true to life and was by Hector Bolithiero—at least, Micki's very personal pronunciation of this name sounded a little like that. There were added syllables, making the name roll and lilt, reminding me of Lillibullero.

After the book, we were asked to admire a spotted scarf, of a pattern much favored by pilots, Micki explained. This too had been bought in the morning. It was as though Micki had gone out to collect three symbols of his past career; and now that he was showing them to us, his excitement rose. He knotted the scarf round his neck, jumped to his feet again and waved the book.

"But you ought to put my wings in!" he exclaimed. "Couldn't you do it in silver paint? I could show you just how they go."

He moved towards Mrs. Bellingly's canvas, as if about to

scratch out wings in the wet paint with the end of one of her brushes.

"No, Micki, no! Don't touch it!" she cried; "I'm not doing you in uniform, and it wouldn't look right at all to have your wings on an ordinary shirt or jacket—whichever I finally decide to have you in."

"But how will anyone know I've got wings then?" he asked indignantly, "*or* the D.F.C.? The ribbon ought to be underneath the wings. I'll draw them out on a piece of paper and tell you the colors. You could get silver paint, couldn't you, for the wings? They ought to be silver, you know. I'd like them to flash!"

"Now I think that's enough about *your* portrait for today," said Julia Bellingly; "you won't sit still any more, so we can't really get on. What I want to know is, would you like me to do a portrait of Katherine for your wedding present?"

"Just Katherine, or both of us together?" asked Micki, his voice brightening towards the end of the question.

"Katherine alone, of course; I'm already painting you."

"Yes, but wouldn't it be grand to have one of both of us!—me sort of looking into the distance, and Katherine sort of looking at me."

Mrs. Bellingly said nothing. She may have been suppressing some tart remark on vanity, which she thought unsuitable for the engaged ears of Katherine, or she may only have been changing over to another subject in her abrupt capricious way; for when next she spoke it was to say: "Oh, Micki, do run up and see if you can do anything to the clock in my bedroom; you promised to mend it."

Her guests were usually asked to work.

As soon as Micki had gone upstairs, it was suggested that we should tidy the room.

"That boy turns it into such a bear-garden with all his marching and striding about—to say nothing of the mess of our own paints and easels."

Katherine and I began to plump out the cushions on the sofa and straighten the rugs. Mrs. Bellingly went over to Micki's chair and turned over the fat squab in the seat. She was patting and prodding the ragged brocade, when suddenly she screeched: "Oh, that wretch has loosened the arm of my *bergère* again! And I glued it so thoroughly only the other day. Just look what he's done with all his lurching and wriggling. Why can't he sit still like anyone else?"

She almost ran out of the room and we heard the misleading patter of her small high-heeled shoes on the hall tiles. It was as if a delicate young doe had tripped into the house. We heard her take a rush at the steep little box-stairs, then there was the muffled rumble of voices in the room above.

They came down hand in hand, Julia Bellingly, the nurse, dragging Micki, the great naughty boy.

"Now look, you're going to be shown exactly what you've done," she said, leading him up to the chair. She might have been the severe owner of a new puppy, about to rub the little creature's nose in its "business."

"You are a very bad lad; you've broken the arm of a valuable old chair, which has already been mended once very carefully by me."

Julia Bellingly banged each word into him as if it had been a nail. Micki stood by her, eyes down in mock repentance, an embarrassed smile on his half-open lips. Very gently he began to swing the arm still held by her. Then they were holding hands, swinging them, up and down, up and down, looking into each other's eyes, smiling, laughing. Micki's hair had fallen over his face. The tassels dangled, the square teeth glistened. Julia Bellingly wrinkled up her nose, then tried to make a stand for severity.

"It's no use turning it into a joke and trying to get round me; I'm really cross."

But her face belied her words—and they went on swinging hands.

"You know, we needed people like you to come round with the mobile canteens," Micki said to her solemnly. "Some of the women were terrible—all stuck up and a bit sexy. What chaps like is the *older* woman full of good sense and fun."

The mistimed, misdirected flattery fell to the ground between them, killing the smile on Julia Bellingly's face. She seemed not to care for the part of older woman full of good sense and fun. There was a hint of outrage, as if Micki in his calculating, scheming simplicity had at last insulted her intelligence.

"We'd better stop now," she said stonily; "we'll get nothing more done today."

She began to gather up her brushes and to wipe them on an old linen rag.

"I'll just look at the grandfather clock too," said Micki, eager to do anything to regain favor. "I'd like to get every clock in apple-pie order for you."

He went over to the old clock and opened the case. Julia Bellingly did not forbid him. He kept moving the pendulum and the position of the stand on the floor, waiting there until good humor should be restored.

Katherine finished wiping her brushes, shut her paint-box, then stood up to go home. I looked at her. Here was the girl who was going to be married, but it didn't seem real at all. Could many people be married in this way? Were they just caught up in a halfhearted game of ball? Was she excited or happy? Did anything show on her face? Perhaps the tiniest spark of perplexity glinted sometimes under the heavy layers of calm.

Mrs. Bellingly took her into the hall and I was left alone with Micki. Shutting the clock, he tiptoed across the room to me. He put his arm round my shoulders and muttered close to my ear: "Everything's going fine, old boy. I like her and she likes me."

I felt his breath on my cheek, the rather tingling grip of his fingers round my shoulder. He was secret and triumphant, wanting me only to share, to question nothing. Still cupping my shoulder with his hand, he stood away from me, as if to show me his radiant expression, or perhaps to see my answering pleasure.

"And you must be best man," were his last eager words, before he left me abruptly to go to Mrs. Bellingly, who was calling.

I myself said my good-byes and thank-yous, then left by the side door. I wanted to be alone to think over the afternoon.

It was like some Punch and Judy show or pantomime; it had that slight touch of insanity and squalor—emphatic characters playing extraordinary parts—strangely threatening because they seemed so meaningless and unrelated.

There was the silent Katherine, Mr. Punch's baby, the victim whose head would be dashed against the scenery sooner or later, then Mrs. Bellingly, was the strident willful Judy with perhaps a touch of the Widow Twankey. Mrs. Talbot, Mrs. Charles, Pamela and the baby girl had been a chorus of wicked ugly sisters, curiously alike in spite of all differences of age and appearance.

Micki had been Punch, of course, both sad and a little sinister, with the hangman's rope somewhere very near. But what had I been? I tried to think as I pushed through the overgrown garden, then climbed over the fence into the lane.

Once more the days passed and I did not see Micki myself, but I heard from Mrs. Bellingly that he was now living in the house with Katherine and her mother. The vicar had applied to the bishop for a license, and all the other arrangements for the marriage were being made. An old friend of the family was to give Katherine away—"And you are to be best man!" said Mrs. Bellingly, turning to me gaily to watch my surprise.

"But it's absurd!" I exclaimed. "I never took him seriously. He ought to ask one of his air force friends, someone who really knows him."

"No, he doesn't want one of them; he's determined to have you," she answered comfortably.

There was a pause, then I said slowly: "I don't think anything would persuade me to go to church as best man."

I left almost at once to go to Micki.

I found him in the living-room of the Wardes' house with mother and daughter. The room with its grim black beams and great sooty open fireplace oppressed me. Some romantic music, perhaps by Tchaikovsky, was coming from the wireless and Micki was jigging and swaying to it, while Katherine watched him from a cushion on the floor with the head of her old decrepit dog in her lap. Mrs. Warde, who had come to the door to let me in, now stayed by my side, and I found myself sitting with her on the low sill of a curious window, which jutted out like a large arrowhead into the derelict vegetable patch, where once the lawn had been. In her rust-red shirt and velveteen trousers Mrs. Warde looked rather plump and young and anxious. She had the embarrassed movements of Katherine with less of the imposed calm. She advanced impulsively, then grew suspicious in spite of herself, so that conversation with her was a sort of shunting in and out of a dark tunnel.

I found it difficult even to mention the marriage. All I could bring myself to say was, "I expect you are awfully busy."

"Yes, we are," the words came in a rush; "and Katherine's not much good, you know. Most of the time she's out, or upstairs with her dog and her paints, so it's left to me to arrange everything."

"Doesn't Micki help?" I asked.

"Yes, he does try; but he's so full of ideas, he wants to do everything at once, and of course that's just the way to get nothing done at all."

As she spoke, Mrs. Warde glanced across at Micki, and I caught just a flash of that strange dazed interest, that capacity for watching and marvelling which some young parents show.

"This music's a bit like the 'Warsaw Concerto'," Micki suddenly called out, perhaps because he felt that we were lost to him, in our pointed window.

"That's a grand thing, isn't it?" he added. "We had a sergeant who played it the whole time. He threw himself all over the place." Here Micki shook his hair over his eyes and clawed the air like a mad gorilla on a chain. "God! the sweat *poured* off him! He thumped so hard I thought he'd break a string. The next minute he'd be off in his plane. Nothing but playing the piano and dropping bombs!"

Micki played the piano on the air for a little longer, clucking his tongue and rolling his eyes at the same time; then he came out of his frenzy and turned to me.

"You're going to be best man, Dave, aren't you? It's all fixed."

"Oh, no, you must ask one of your *real* friends," I said in my agitation, then tried to cover the unfortunate adjective with, "someone you've known for a long time."

I stopped, afraid of offending Katherine and Mrs. Warde with more signs of my eagerness to escape. Micki's feelings seemed less important, because less capable of being hurt. I wondered why this was so, and it came to me that, from the very first, he had appeared to expect only a light, amused response, never a deeper one. Perhaps the greatest moment of truth had been at the top of the hill, when I wanted to go into the woods to eat and read, and he wanted me to wait for his return from the town. He had known then that I would not wait, and his annoyance had given me a glimpse of something underneath all the jigging and vivacity. There had been too the moment when, breathing on my ear, holding my shoulder tight, he tried to will me to suppress my uneasiness, to accept his success without question.

But Micki was talking to me again. "Don't get stage fright, Dave! All *you've* got to do is not to lose the ring. Just think what *we* have to go through!"

He put his hands on Katherine's shoulders and rocked her backwards and forwards; and because she sat stiffly with her legs tucked under her, she looked like one of those little weighted dolls that cannot fall over.

I appealed to Mrs. Warde.

"Micki ought to choose one of his air force friends, oughtn't he?"

She fluttered her eyes and was not quick, so Micki answered for her.

"No, I don't want any of them, they'd come drunk or something; I want you, you're just the ticket."

I rebelled against being used in this way. I was not a doll to be taken out of its box on special occasions.

"I shall never be anyone's best man," I said, jumping off the windowsill; "they seem so—so peculiar."

What had I done now! The faces of Mrs. Warde and Katherine were quite blank, making it all the easier for me to read reproach into them. I wanted to say good-bye at once and get out of doors again.

I murmured some more correct excuses then went quickly to the door, but Micki's voice followed me still.

"Nonsense, Dave, you'll do fine as best man—you'll see! When the day comes you'll be all agog."

He came with me into the hall; I was afraid he would offer to accompany me home, but I contrived somehow to get out of the front door and then out of the garden gate without him. I walked down the road, enjoying the freedom and the air, determined not to hear if he should call after me. Once round the corner I felt safer.

But another complication was waiting for me at home. A note had been left and the writing was unknown to me. I read it hurriedly. "So sorry not to have found you in. There is a matter I feel I ought to discuss with you as soon as possible. Could you call at my place sometime today? I shall be at home all afternoon and evening.—Mildred Charles." That was all.

The urgency, the mystery, the shortness all reminded me of the cryptic notes I had sent and received as a child—notes tucked under stones, stuffed into tree trunks, buried in the ground, or sealed in little tins to float down the river, out to sea, to the other side of the world.

But what had possessed Mrs. Charles that she should be playing this game at her age, and with me, almost a stranger, and so clearly out of tune with her?

In spite of my lack of love for Mrs. Charles, my interest was pricked and I looked forward to visiting her. It was almost certain that she would talk of Micki, but just because it was not absolutely certain, room was left for the most extraordinary imaginings. Would she warn me of some secret danger to myself, some hidden threat I could not even conceive of? Would she lay before me all the difficulties of her private life, then ask for my advice? Or did she want me to read through the sixteen school exercise books of her novel in manuscript before sending it to my publisher with a glowing note? Perhaps she wanted me to paint a conversation piece of her white Pekinese playing with an embroidered ball near her goldfish pool. Perhaps in a mad whim she had left me all her money, and, wishing to carry the eccentricity even further, had decided to tell me herself of my good fortune.

Because I had let my fancy roam, and because her note had reawakened in me the excitement and faint alarm of the secret messages of childhood, I felt a little dashed when I found Mrs. Charles bending over one of her knife-edged flower beds. She wore a pair of thick stained leather gloves, but otherwise her clothes were as dark and neat and unexceptionable as ever. Her strictness was somehow mortifying. One had to marvel at the inhuman gloss, even while feeling frustrated by it. She stopped digging round the plants with her trowel and led me towards the house. The path was straight and sharp like the flower beds, the grass on either side shaved so flat that now, in the summer heat, it had begun to turn a golden brown in patches.

Once under the protection of the dark little brick porch she began.

"It's about that poor girl that I felt I ought to see you. I knew it would be hopeless to tackle Mrs. Bellingly; she's so—under the influence."

"Under the influence!" I exclaimed.

"Well, under *his* influence then—there! I've had to say it, one can't beat about the bush in these affairs it seems."

"You mean Mrs. Bellingly is under the influence of Micki Beaumont?"

"Yes, but that, of course, is her affair. She, no doubt, is well able to take care of herself; but it's that poor girl I'm so worried about. Something must be done to prevent this iniquitous marriage. The vicar's daughter told me this morning that everything is arranged for Monday. You realize today is Thursday!"

"Yes, the marriage is extraordinary to me too, quite unreal. I've never been able to take it seriously; but if they really mean to get married, I don't see how anyone can stop them. Mrs. Warde seems to like Micki very much, and the vicar by this time has probably had the license from the bishop."

"But does no one realize that the man's an impostor, an out-and-out rogue?"

Mrs. Charles grew duskier than ever, as if darkness and not blood had flushed up behind her skin. By now I had been led into a very white little parlor. There was the glistening paint of the broad cottage windowsills, the frozen lines of glazed chintz pouring down to the fawn carpet. The chintz had a feather design, a gold feather and a brown floating forever down white cascades. An armchair and a very small sofa, covered in the same material, stood on each side of the fireplace. Between them was an early Victorian rosewood table with embroidery under a glass top—a pretty wreath of flowers worked in silks and wools. Three miniatures in thick black frames spotted the far wall. That was almost all that the room held.

I wanted to look about me for a moment, not to answer Mrs. Charles's question so I found myself saying rather lukewarmly, "You feel sure then that he's an impostor?"

"Sure! Aren't you, then? Wouldn't anyone be sure who had eyes in his head—ears—I was almost about to add a nose."

Mrs. Charles laughed delicately at her own lapse into coarseness and class hatred. I was a little fascinated by it, wondering just how far she would allow herself to go.

"I think I've explained so much away by telling myself to remember that he landed on his head," I answered.

"I don't believe he's ever even been up in an airplane."

"But I've seen a photograph of him in his uniform with the wings plainly visible."

"What does that prove?" Mrs. Charles rapped out. Her manner was becoming more and more short and sharp, as if, being unable to confront Micki, she would accuse me in his stead.

"Now you must face it," she said, fixing me with her licorice eyes; "do you, or do you not feel that there is something very peculiar indeed about that young man?"

"I've always thought him strange," I replied unhelpfully; "he tells a lot of lies, but so do many other people. There was a boy at school who told me that he went to a fancy-dress party as a sea-horse in a tank of water. He had another story about his grandmother. When she died, she was taken up to Scotland and left on the top of an ancient tower, so that the birds of the air could pick her bones."

Mrs. Charles was becoming impatient.

"But we are not dealing with a schoolboy's fancies! I don't think you grasp the seriousness of the situation."

"I do think it's very serious for Katherine, and I hope that something will stop her from marrying Micki, because he seems to me to be very irresponsible, even a little mad."

"If you think in that way, you will certainly help me to prevent the marriage." Mrs. Charles looked at me quickly to see if my expression was contradicting her words.

"But what *do* you intend to do, and how do you think I can help?" I asked.

Here tea was brought in by a large weary old woman in black to the ground. I felt that her weariness, which showed so plainly in her grey cottage-loaf cheeks, was caused by years of uneasy obedience to Mrs. Charles. She arranged the things on the rose-wood table with painful care. Mrs. Charles pulled her lips together and waited stiffly.

When we were alone again, she leaned towards me and said: "What I intend to do is to ring up my brother-in-law."

Mrs. Charles implied that her brother-in-law was powerful indeed.

"Oh, will he be able to help?"

I hoped my voice sounded irritatingly simple.

"Certainly he will—and this is where you come in; if you can give him all the details of this Beaumont's supposed career in the air force, he will then be able to find out if there is a word of truth in the story or not."

Over the teacups Mrs. Charles was warming to her detective work. She began to tell me all about the importance of her brother-in-law in the air force; and every fact was blown away as soon as she had dragged it up. For the rest of tea, I only remember vividly the obstinate shutting of my mind to every new pretension of genteel boast.

"But why don't you ring up your brother-in-law now if you want him to inquire about Micki?" I suggested, clutching at the first idea that came to me for breaking up the conversation.

"I had hoped that you would first go back and quietly find out from him all you could, so that we had something really solid to work on."

"I think we have quite a lot to work on already. You've heard what I know, and Mrs. Bellingly must have told you other things."

"What things?" Mrs. Charles asked suspiciously.

"Oh, I only meant other facts about him."

What had Mrs. Charles thought that I meant?

She sat for a moment in silence, her hands in her lap, one foot crossing the other and pointing outwards as if poised for a playful kick.

"Perhaps I *should* ring up Ralph straight away," she said, "so that he can begin at once with the preliminary inquiries. I can always ring him up again later, if more facts come to light."

She stood up, still musing, then walked quickly to the telephone in the little box entrance hall. I heard her asking for the number.

But things did not go well between her and Ralph. Because I had not listened properly to her story, I did not know where he was; he was probably at home, but I imagined him in a little hut on a vast airfield, listening to her questions, thinking them absurd, and cursing her under his breath.

Mrs. Charles had begun the conversation in her usual high, singing, rather gentle tones; but as each question, each description was received with less and less sympathy or interest, her voice seemed to sink, to check itself in the middle of an utterance, so that, towards the end, I heard fragments like these—"nothing to be done then?"—"find out more if I can"—"I hope I haven't—."

I hurried into the hall, to be by the front door when the conversation came to an end. She put down the receiver and smiled faintly and sadly at me.

"He says he can't do much at the moment—so busy; and he wants more details. I knew we ought to have had more facts."

"But Micki hardly ever tells the same story twice. There are so many variations," I said, trying to make her feel less solemn about him.

"How can *anyone* be taken in by him then?" she exclaimed in amazement; "how can the girl's mother allow him anywhere near her daughter?"

"Oh, she seems very fond of him herself. He has been living in the house for the last week or ten days. Don't you think romancing, lies, play-acting often come to be excused just as a sort of amusing eccentricity?"

"Well, I for one do not think them amusing. How a mother can gamble with her daughter's happiness in this way! How Mrs. Bellingly could have introduced the man, or even entertained him herself!"

Mrs. Charles looked up at me as I backed out of the door. I held out my hand and said hurriedly: "I'll certainly ask Mrs. Bellingly if she has told Katherine's mother exactly what she knows or doesn't know about Micki."

Mrs. Charles, still with the sorrowful expression on her face, let my hand go, then said suddenly: "Aren't women fools!—such absolute fools!"

"Why women only?" I murmured mechanically, beginning to wheel my bicycle down the path. When I turned to latch the gate, Mrs. Charles was still staring after me. She did not wave, she just stared as if she found the exposure of wickedness a thankless, exhausting task.

That evening Micki came to see me. I had been at the Gothic-shaped upper window of the cottage when he was approaching. As he loped down the narrow lane, his feet slapped heavily and carelessly on the ground, his arms flung out and back, and he shook back his unruly hair constantly.

I wanted to escape out of the back door, but knew that I must wait for him.

I heard him climbing the stairs; then he was in the room,

which I kept asking him to sit. At last he sank into it, with legs sprawled out recklessly, but hands together, finger touching finger, in the precise, ancient ecclesiastical convention. Slouched down in the chair as he was, his nose almost touched the hands; so he stuffed the first two fingers up his nostrils and began picking and probing.

He was gathering courage to say something to me; I waited, hating the passing moments, hating to have to listen.

Now he was fiddling with the thick dull metal bracelet of his watch. He had undone it and was holding out the watch, not exactly to me, but as if he would contemplate it himself. The bracelet hung and rippled like a dead snake trodden flat.

"That's a fine job of work!" Micki said admiringly, but still as if communing with himself. "I suppose it's worth twenty pounds, at the very least, any day of the week."

I moved about uncomfortably on the bed, then made myself look out of the window and assume an absent smile, to show, without using any words, how uninterested I was in watches.

"You wouldn't like it, Dave?" he persisted; "it's yours for—for twelve pounds."

"But I already have a watch," I said.

"Oh—then I wonder if you want a typewriter. I've got a grand little one that I'd let *you* have, perhaps. It's all white in a white case. It cost a bit though, I couldn't part with it under thirty. Would you like me to bring it along to show you?" He leaned towards me eagerly.

"I don't use one. I write everything with my fountain pen."

I felt very cold.

Micki gave me one swift, alarmed glance.

"All right, all right, Dave," he said, "it doesn't matter at all. I just thought you might want a watch, or a typewriter, and I wouldn't mind selling mine now, because this marriage is going to run me in for a bit of expense, and the allowance my father left me in his will is not coming through properly. Don't you worry though, old boy, I'll get by."

And I who had only been worrying about my own discomfort, had a twinge of that compunction which bites all the deeper because it carries with it a determination to do nothing at all to help. I wondered how one could be left an allowance in a will. Did Micki mean that all the money had been left to his mother on condition that she made him an allowance? But of course Micki was as ignorant of his real meaning as I was; he had only intended to deceive. That is what he would always be trying to do. There was no will, no allowance, no money—and there never would be. Poor Micki was doomed to lying and contriving for the rest of his life. He would contradict his own lies a hundred times a day; and in the end all his schemes would fail. He would be given only kicks, and every word he spoke would make more trouble for him.

I saw all this, yet I only wanted to get rid of Micki. I found that I could hardly look at him or speak to him. I knew that I ought to try to talk to him about the marriage; I ought to confront him with some of his lies and contradictions and ask him why he behaved so strangely, but I just sat, sullenly waiting for him to go.

"I was in Brighton yesterday," he said gaily.

I grunted an unwilling "Oh."

"There was a murder there."

I could do no more than wrinkle up my forehead.

Micki must have seen the lack of interest and belief, but still he longed to break through them, to make me laugh and feel warm towards him. He tried once more, then accepted defeat. It was as if he had said to himself, "It is hopeless to mention money; hardly anyone will stand for it. He's turned against me now and he'll never be the same again."

Or was it that a new idea had come to him? Whatever the cause, he gave up trying to appease me, slapped his hands down on his knees and said: "I'd better push off—masses to do before this wedding, and I expect you writer guys never get enough time to yourselves."

Now that he had decided to stop trying to get money from me, he seemed lighter and less anxious, but his eyes had a questing, faraway glint, and I felt certain that he would go down to Mrs. Bellingly, if he had not already been to her.

He left with the remark: "Now don't you forget, Dave, about being best man on Monday." But he spoke so lightly, with such lack of conviction that I did not even think it necessary to contradict him again.

At times did he too hardly believe in his marriage, I won-

"What's going to happen now?" I asked, with the sort of suppressed enjoyment that goes with that remark.

"Goodness only knows!" wailed Mrs. Bellingly. "I've told

dered. When he was out of the house the thought of him was more disquieting than his presence had been. I imagined him lurching along the lane, and I felt for the first time that he was dangerous in some way, that he held a threat. His anxiety might at this moment be turning into desperation. I saw him going into Julia Bellingly's house and frightening or cajoling her into giving him money. I thought of him struggling with her, knocking her down, then searching through all the stuffed drawers of her cabinets and chests, emptying out china, glass, silver, clothes and curtains that she herself had not disturbed for years.

I pictured these simple things, because underneath there was a deeper fear of Micki. He was like a madman, a drunkard, a ghost—some being that could never be reached.

I waited until I thought he would have entered Mrs. Bellingly's house, if he were going there, then I followed. I was soon outside the kitchen window, which was very close to the hedge on one side of the lane. I peered through a gap in the leaves and saw that the thick curtains had been drawn early. I listened and heard voices, a low peaceable murmur. Mrs. Bellingly seemed to be moving about, touching plates and saucepans while Micki talked to her and sometimes laughed. I tried to hear what they were saying, but the window had been screwed up, because of Mrs. Bellingly's fear of burglars, and only a faint sound reached me through the glass.

I stood about in the lane for some minutes, then the light went off in the kitchen. I imagined that they were carrying food or hot drinks through to the drawing-room. I could hear Mrs. Bellingly giving some directions in her military voice. There seemed little need for me to wait any longer.

But as soon as I was home, I wanted to be at the other end of the lane again. I felt that I might be missing something, and I wanted to talk to Mrs. Bellingly myself.

I drank some tea and read a book. When I felt that Micki must have left, I walked down once more. This time I found a crack of light at the side of one of Mrs. Bellingly's bedroom windows. I called up softly. In a moment there was a stealthy movement of curtains, then I heard her whisper: "Go round, I'll let you in." The whisper was like the harsh loud noise a soldier makes as he breathes on the buttons he is polishing.

As I waited by the front door, voices came to me from the

road. A man was chuckling and laughing and a woman made much lower, more murmuring replies. I ran round the corner of the house and stood by the coal shed, until the voices passed on down the road. When I came back to the front door, Mrs. Bellingly was peering out, shining a torch into the garden.

"There you are!" she said. "Why are you playing tricks?"

"I thought I heard Micki and Katherine in the road. I was afraid he was bringing her back here."

"For heaven's sake come in quickly then and let me lock the door."

"It's all right, the voices have gone down the road. I expect they were just out for a little walk with the dogs before bed."

Julia Bellingly shut the door behind me, then, still only by the light of the torch, led me upstairs to her bedroom. She was dressed in her man's bathrobe of yellow towelling, and she had taken off her make-up. Her hair was netted; the tight little grey curls looked like baby mice cowering in terror against her scalp. After clearing a chair for me by tipping corsets, stockings, and petticoat on to the floor, she lay back in the elaborate French bed and slid her feet under the coverlet. Pink light glowed down on her head from the little dome round which the striped bed curtains were gathered. Everywhere the warm light seemed to fall on cast-off clothes. They were heaped on chairs, tables, and some were even hanging out of the drawers of the fine, dilapidated walnut tallboy. A long gilt gesso table was covered with bottles, jars, pencils for lip or eye, tweezers, brushes, sprays, scissors, powder-puffs and pieces of cotton-wool stained peach-pink or deeper red. I thought that Mrs. Bellingly must have kept every cream and lotion she had ever tried; for some of the labels on the bottles and jars looked as if they belonged to the Russian Ballet and the Cubist period.

In this warm, quiet, dishevelled setting, we began to discuss Micki. At first Mrs. Bellingly could only move her head from side to side and repeat, "I don't know," between exasperated sighs; then she put on her tragic voice and said: "He's been here tonight, trying to sell me his watch."

"I thought so," I answered; "he tried me first. I followed him down to see what he would do here. How did you get rid of him?"

"Oh, just gave him something to eat, then wore him down with boredom—didn't speak much, just read my book."

breathing heavily and striding about, ignoring the armchair in

Mrs. Warde that I knew nothing of him before he threw his bicycle into my hedge. I've told her about all his lies and contradictions; but the silly woman won't listen; she's quite determined to go through with the wedding. Micki has won her over completely. Apparently there are times when he grows terribly anxious and excitable. His eye goes bloodshot, his face twitches. Mrs. Warde does what she can to reassure him; sometimes she sits with him because he can't sleep. On one of these occasions she tried to question him a little, but he put his head in her lap and burst out weeping. 'You want to do something for the boys who saved you in the Battle of Britain, don't you? Then let me marry Katherine,' he pleaded."

Mrs. Bellingly paused to raise her eyebrows and shrug her thick shoulders. "Of course, that sort of behavior has overcome all resistance and now Mrs. Warde won't hear a word against him. She just says: 'Wouldn't you do and say some rather strange things, if you had had to jump, wounded, from your blazing plane?' "

"Oh, but I haven't heard the details of that story, have you?" I broke in.

"No, but what does it matter? Micki tells so many stories. Poor boy! He has too much imagination to be satisfied with the truth. But let me go on with *my* story. When I found that I could make no impression on the Warde woman, I decided to go to the vicar. He told me that nothing could be done to prevent the marriage, if the bride's parents allowed it, and if the bride and bridegroom were not disqualified in any way from marrying. So now I don't know what to do; I feel at my wits' end."

To express her helplessness, Mrs. Bellingly dropped her hands on her stomach.

"But what has changed your attitude to the marriage?" I asked suddenly. "You seemed so keen about it before."

Would she answer or be frozen by my baldness?

"Oh, I don't know; I've had misgivings about his stories all along, of course, but I didn't pay much attention to them. I just thought as we all have done, that oddity was quite excusable in someone who had gone through so much; but when I heard that the license had been granted and the wedding fixed for Monday, I suddenly felt that it was all much too hurried, that they should really get to know each other before taking such a step. I realized too that Mrs. Warde still knew almost nothing about Micki's background—his family and so on. He had told us that his mother lived in Chelsea and he'd told us that she lived in Inverness, but she was not to be asked to the wedding, nor were any of his air force friends—why? I did think it strange; and now that he's been trying to sell things, because his allowance is not 'coming through' properly, I know there's something wrong."

"Did he tell you that he was in Brighton yesterday and that there had been a murder there?" I asked.

"No, he told me that he hadn't been to Brighton after all!"

"What can you make of it? Does he forget what he's said as soon as the words are out of his mouth?"

"I don't know what to think about his romancing, but I imagine now that he has been a boy in a garage or a workshop; he knows a lot about mechanical contrivances and is always longing to tinker at them, if they are out of order. My guess is that, because of this knowledge, he was drafted into the air force as a mechanic, and then his head was turned by the amazing deeds that were being performed all round him. He could not be content with the plain truth of a humdrum existence any longer, and so began telling the wild contradictory stories we all have heard. Whether he actually flew himself or was awarded the D.F.C., I can't say. I can't even tell whether he really was discharged on health grounds, he seems so fit. Perhaps they felt that his stories almost amounted to delusions and that the poor boy was too unstable for so arduous a life."

Julia Bellingly stopped talking; for a moment the room was quite silent. The piles of clothes, the bottles and jars, the old furniture and cherry striped curtains all seemed to have been listening too; and now one was aware of their sullen indifference, their everlasting brooding and waiting. The silly patterns on the bottles, the rubber suspender clips, held a strange aloofness and dignity.

I got up to go, then wondered if I should first stoop down to replace the underclothes on the little gilt chair. I decided not to and moved towards the door.

"Have a biscuit," said Julia, opening her painted bedside tin and tossing me a *petit beurre* tomboyishly. She laughed, then lay back against her pillows as if she were ill or had been through some terrible experience. She moved her head again from side to side and sighed, just to make sure that I should not miss her unhappiness and perturbation.

It was sad really, I thought, as I clambered down the stairs in the dark and let myself out, Mrs. Bellingly could never be the same with Micki again, she had found him out. There would be no more jokes about spiders and passionate kisses, skeletons and toilet rolls; no more descriptions of her first dinner party in Carlton House Terrace when, in her agitation, she tried to hack a piece off the plaster decoration, instead of helping herself to the entrée in the dish. Now she could not tell him again about the little girl who for her birthday was given a bottle of scent and a small trumpet, but was told not to worry the vicar with them when he came to tea. She was an obedient child, so she met him at the door with these cryptic words: "If you smell a little smell and hear a little noise, you'll know it's me."

Julia Bellingly loved this story and I was very fond of it too, although I must have heard her tell it at least six times. There were many other stories; Micki had listened to them all and laughed. Now he wouldn't hear them any more.

Before I fell asleep that night, I kept thinking of Micki in the house with Katherine and her mother. Would he be prowling from room to room, looking for money, and objects of value he could sell, or would even Micki see the madness of stealing from his future wife in order to help with the wedding expenses? Perhaps the disappointments of the day had been too much for him and he was weeping now with his head in Mrs. Warde's dressing-gowned lap. Perhaps he was telling her that his allowance was not "coming through" and that she must not even expect him to buy the wedding ring.

Since his last visit to me, I saw him always as a lost dog, forlorn, harassed, with an unenticing hint of danger that made one wish at once to get away from him. What warned one against him before he had opened his mouth? Was it the eyes staring, then circling? The badly related hand and leg movements? The scheming that was so obvious that one had a fancy of steaming, churning thoughts bubbling up against the walls of a glass skull?

IV

I did not dream of Micki, but he was in my thoughts again almost as soon as I had woken up and begun to drink my tea. There were now only two whole days before the wedding. That which had seemed so frivolous was coming nearer and nearer, insisting every minute on being taken more seriously. But still I had the feeling of sitting in the theatre and not believing in the play. How did the situation manage to be so artificial even at this moment? Was it that Katherine's face, always so composed and guarded, had never shown more than a tinge of satisfaction or perplexity over her lover's behavior? She and Mrs. Warde were sleepwalkers; their skin was like rubber; one might prick them with pins, but they would not cry out or wake up. And Mrs. Bellingly was like leather; she would cuff anyone who dared to approach *her* with a pin.

After doing a little work, I got up and dressed, then went out with my picnic to a lake in a park beyond Mrs. Charles's house. I planned to call on her after lunch in case she had found out from her brother-in-law anything about Micki's life in the air force.

I sat down on the bank near the reeds; the big carp jumped all round the great elm, which had fallen, and lay now like a small spiky pier, reaching almost to the center of the lake. Across the ripples, I could see the old house on the far bank, all its windows shining in the sun, brown and white cows grazing close to its grey walls. I hoped the old man who lived in it would not die for a long time; "for if he died," I thought, "people would not be allowed to roam at will, fish in the lake, sit on the bank, munching and reading as I am doing. The new owner would change all such slovenly ways."

I stayed there for more than two hours, then rode back to Mrs. Charles's cottage on the edge of the estate. As soon as I had entered her garden gate and could not retreat, I regretted coming. I did not want to listen to her, pick over her tid-bits, or even watch the ugly expressions chasing each other across her face; so it was with relief that I heard the old cowed housekeeper say: "I'm afraid Mrs. Charles is not at home."

It was delightful to be freed from the visit which no one had asked me to pay; I rode on lightheartedly towards home and met Mrs. Bellingly at the foot of the lane. She was just about to hurry into her house.

"Oh, it is terrible, terrible," she said in a despairing murmur; "come in, I must talk to you. I've had to keep my door locked all day, a thing I never do."

The head shook, the mouth twisted tragically, even the blue pebble eyes rolled up once with a baroque saint's beseeching air. I must be made to feel the horror of the situation, must not be robbed of excitement by lack of expression on her part.

We went into the kitchen and Mrs. Bellingly immediately put on the kettle and opened her painted tins to take out cake and biscuits. We were to have tea with our disturbances and horrors.

"I've tried again," she said, "I've done all I can, but the vicar's daughter says that everything is arranged for Monday. Katherine and Mrs. Warde have gone to London today to get the wedding clothes—have you ever heard of anything so rushed, how can they possibly buy a wedding dress in such a way? The license has been paid for—by Mrs. Warde of course. It seems that nothing more can be done in an *ordinary* way; but something *must* be done, and you and I are the only people to do it, even if we have to do something *extraordinary.*"

"What do you mean?" I asked, rather struck by Mrs. Bellingly's determined lips. She seemed to consider for a moment before answering in her tense stage-whisper voice. The teapot hung down in her hands, over the steam from the kettle.

"I've thought it all out," she began; "you and I must get Katherine into a car and take her to my daughter's, so that she won't be there to marry Micki on Monday."

"You mean kidnap her?"

"Yes, I suppose I do really. I thought we'd stop at the house tomorrow or Sunday afternoon and ask her to come with us to Nan's just for the drive. Once we had her in the car we could try our very best to persuade her not to marry Micki; if she wouldn't listen we could keep her at Nan's until after Monday."

"You couldn't keep her against her will," I said.

"I think we ought to do anything, even that, to stop the marriage."

"Do you think we should go to the police?" I asked, halfheartedly.

"Oh, no," Mrs. Bellingly said. As she spoke we both saw someone go past the window that looked on to the lane.

I went out at once to see if it was anyone for me, but while I was peering through the hedge, the man in some way returned to Julia Bellingly's front gate. When I turned back to the garden, there he was in the drive, holding some papers against his dark suit and fixing me with black rolling eyes. He looked alarming, menacing, and the comedian's thick eyebrows did not lessen the effect. In my agitation I confused him with a publisher who had refused my book and then been annoyed that someone else had taken it and he could no longer do business with me. Next I tried to tell myself that the man was an unknown tradesman. But he looked exactly what he was. He came up to me quietly and swiftly and said: "I'm a detective inspector, but there is no cause for alarm. Do you happen to know of anyone who goes by the name of Beaumont?"

Julia, who had joined us, nodded and tried to nudge me as if to say "It has come at last."

"Oh, yes," she said out loud to the inspector; "so you have come about him! We were only just wondering what to do."

Her voice seemed full of a sort of relief and childish awe.

"Come into the drawin'-room," she said, "we can discuss it there."

The detective sat down by the window, still secretive, important, baleful. He began to feel in his pockets, then brought out a card and held it out to us.

"Do you recognize this man?" he asked.

Three hideous likenesses of Micki, taken from different angles, stared out at us. He looked much thinner; he had a sort of hanged or broken-neck appearance—the eyes, the mouth and the head all slanting to one side. An indescribable air of degradation hung about him in each picture. To look at the horrible card made me feel ashamed. No one should ever be seen in that state, I thought. It seemed brutal and mean for the inspector to be showing us the card.

"Yes, we know him," said Julia with a little gasp; then she had the idea of proving it by showing her own portrait of Micki.

"Here he is," she said, dragging the easel forward, anxiously looking at her work, then at the inspector.

"Oh, yes, I see," he said solemnly, afraid of being thought unintelligent or inartistic. He wished to get away from the picture back to his questions, and Julia wanted praise and admiration for her work. The portrait was an absurd embarrassment blocking the way.

"Is he mad?" I asked, to break the spell.

At this, Julia's questions began to pour out. I was pleased that she was there to do all the talking and the answering; I could draw back and listen.

When her questions became too importunate, the detective put his hands on his knees, smiled like a cat, rolled his black eyes and said: "I'm afraid I'm here to ask questions, not to answer them."

"But *is* he mad?" she asked irrepressibly.

The detective said carefully, importantly, "This man is not certified, but I think he should be."

He paused to give his words their full effect.

"Of course, you'll appreciate the fact that we don't have photographs of people for nothing." He turned to us both with his fat cat's smile. "We haven't a portrait of Mrs. Bellingly, or of you, sir, at the station."

Julia and I smiled back uneasily.

"We've had trouble with this man before, but it was only by chance that we got to know of his activities here. He went to Brighton the other day and a police officer there had occasion to ask for his identity card. He did not carry it, so was told to report back to us. That started one or two inquiries and we discovered about his coming marriage, and the story of his supposed air force career."

"Is that quite untrue?" Julia asked.

"Quite, I think. He has been in the air force, but was discharged after a few months as being quite unfit for service."

Again there was a pause in which the detective gathered himself together for an important announcement.

"You must understand," he said, "that my hands are tied; I can't do anything for the moment, because a crime has not yet been committed; but I'm here to prevent *bigamy*."

"Bigamy!" Julia mouthed and savored the squalid word, turning it into an abomination of wickedness.

"Yes, it is believed that he already has a wife whom he visits at Brighton."

"Oh, poor Katherine, poor Katherine," Julia said without a trace of feeling.

The detective inspector then asked a great many questions about Micki's air force career. He wanted particularly to know what rank he had given himself and what decorations. At last, after more fat smiles and secret airs, he left, telling Mrs. Bellingly that he would be calling again later for more information.

As soon as he had gone, Julia and I sighed, lay back in our chairs and began to smoke cigarettes. We could not stop talking about him and Micki, and repeated the same questions and exclamations many times. We marvelled at his appearance just when I had said: "Ought we to go to the police?" We kept asking, "But bigamy! Do you really think Micki is married already?"

I left, quite exhausted by the topic, longing to get my mind on to something else, but feeling that I could not rest until I knew what was to happen to Micki.

Later that night I went down to Julia's again and we walked to the Warde's house together. There was a car outside; we recognized it as the village policeman's. We left, but came back later. The car was still there. There seemed no sense in waiting about; we could do nothing; so we returned to our houses to go to bed. I wondered if Micki had run away. I hoped he had. And I wondered what Katherine and Mrs. Warde were feeling.

How much had they been told, and how much had their feeling changed towards Micki? Everyone would be against him now, I thought; he would have nowhere to hide.

In the morning Julia Bellingly ran up my stairs and burst into the room. She began to flood me in a rush of words.

"Oh, it is awful," she said, "awful!"

She clasped her hands in her lap. She seemed to be clinging on to "awfulness," squeezing the very lifeblood from it. These are the facts that I pieced together from her story.

After stopping at the vicar's to pay for the license, the Wardes had gone to London and bought the wedding dress. They came back in the evening and found Micki at the house. He had managed to buy a wedding ring and showed it to them in its little velvet box.

"Won't it be lovely, darling," he said to Katherine, "when we are married!"

At this moment, just when all three of them were feeling so untroubled and affectionate, there was a knock at the door.

Katherine said: "Oh, I'll go, Mummy, don't you bother, you're tired."

Micki, who had run up the stairs to look down from a window, said urgently: "Don't go, Katherine, don't go!"

But Katherine answered: "Of course I must go, Micki, if someone is knocking."

She opened the door and two plainclothesmen advanced on Micki. He threw himself on Mrs. Warde imploring her to save him; then, when the policemen took hold of him, he began to hit out and scream so violently that they could do nothing with him. One of them had to run to get help from the soldiers' camp near the house.

Mrs. Warde had described to Julia the horrifying change in Micki's face when he knew he was caught. He had screamed and wept and clung to her; then at last he had fallen down on the floor stark and rigid, like a person in a fit.

After they had taken him away to the station, the policeman came back and interviewed Mrs. Warde. They told her that Micki's real name was Potts and that he was the son of a farm-laborer who had lived in a village eight or nine miles away. His father was now dead. His mother had quite despaired of him, but she had one other very honest son in the navy. Micki had been playing different parts and imposing on people ever since he was sixteen. For the last few years he had used the name of Beaumont. It was thought that he was already married and that he had two children, but this had not been proved. The police seemed to know more than they revealed. It appeared that he had often been in their hands. When they took him to the station, Micki broke down altogether and begged them not to put him in prison again. The scene, the policeman said, was terrible to watch.

All these jerky statements, together with many others, poured out of Julia Bellingly, chasing each other as they do on the page.

"Poor Micki," she said; "it's too bad. I think he is a case for the doctors."

Then she said: "Poor Katherine, it must have been terrible for her, when they took him away." Finally she began to protect herself.

"But I can't be blamed for bringing them together," she stormed; "I told Mrs. Warde I knew nothing of him before he threw his bicycle into my hedge. I told them all, but they were too foolish to listen. How can people be so unwise? Extraordinary to rush into things, to make no inquiries!"

It was interesting to watch the facts being twisted so rapidly. Julia was emerging as the wise, utterly levelheaded woman, who had watched the folly of others without being able to save them from themselves. *She* had never been unaware of Micki's real character. She had known him for what he was from the first.

Everything which did not fit in with this new picture was glossed over, or ruthlessly suppressed.

"He is remanded till September the fourteenth," she said suddenly; "I suppose we shall all have to appear in court. Won't it be frightful! But I shall just have to stick to what I have been saying all along."

Was this to be the end of Micki, this quick, violent scene, so unexpected because so like a set, arranged ending? The police breaking in just as the ring was being shown—the fighting and the screams.

I had only Julia's word for these last scenes, and she again had heard the story from Mrs. Warde; so I wondered how much had been made to fit into a traditional framework of drama.

In the days that followed Julia Bellingly would slur the clear-cut ending with new snippets of information which she had managed to pick up.

"Of course it's not true about the wife and children at Brighton," she would say; "it's only one of those stupid mistakes the police make. Just because he knows a woman down there with two children they jump to the conclusion that he's married to her. I doubt if they were even lovers."

Then at another time she came out with the remark: "You remember the scars on Micki's arms, and how his eye would sometimes go bloodshot?"

"Yes," I said, "he told us the scars were shrapnel wounds."

"Well, they were nothing of the sort. He once fell off his bicycle, scraped all his arms and the side of his face. A stone must have caught the corner of his eye, and that's what causes if to be bloodshot sometimes. Aren't his stories extraordinary! Everything has been turned to account."

Julia seemed perfectly detached about Micki now; she could mention his downfall, his lyings and contrivings without even a tremor of discomfort or pain. Only sometimes did she say "poor Micki" as if regretting something that had gone forever; and even then one felt that she might only be regretting his grotesque lumps of flattery. She seemed to have no conception of the unpleasantness of his present condition. The idea of him in prison appeared to fill her with a sort of grim resigned humor, as if the whole affair had been a game, and this was the accepted forfeit.

"When he was at school, you know," she said, "he used to tell the other boys such preposterous stories that they would set on him and call him a liar; then he would run to the village policeman and tell him that he had been attacked. Extraordinary for a boy to go to the police, don't you think? It's something he certainly wouldn't do now!" Here she laughed heartily.

September the fourteenth came, and Julia and the Wardes were called to give evidence. How thankful I was to have escaped the ordeal of standing up in court and talking about Micki!

Again I only have Julia Bellingly's description of the scene. It is fragmentary, and colored by her indignation at the words of the detective inspector, who spoke of her as giving Micki "some entertainment" at their first meeting.

"Why on earth did he use such ambiguous words?" she asked; "they might imply *anything*. I was furious. I wanted to call out that I'd only given the wretched boy some tea, but of course I didn't dare."

She told me little about her own evidence, beyond stressing her nervousness—I guessed that this nervousness had made her appear tougher than ever—Katherine and Mrs. Warde she hardly mentioned; but when she came to Micki, she began to act the scene for me, thumping with her fists and shaking back her hair as he did.

"He was quite extraordinary," she said; "he began by saying that he could not help making stories up and acting them; it was in his blood. Then he said the stories ran away with him, so that he couldn't control his behavior. He was sometimes amazed at his own inventions; but he was in their power. All this time he was gesticulating, talking very fast, just as he does when he gets excited. He went on and on, until at last he had to be stopped. The most embarrassing part was when he dragged in Katherine and asked if it wasn't natural for a man to want to marry the only girl he'd ever loved."

"What happened though?" I asked impatiently.

"Well, the things they caught him on were the photograph of him in R.A.F. uniform with wings and a D.F.C. ribbon, and the engagement announcement in the paper. He was given two or three months—I'm not quite sure which—for masquerading in the King's uniform."

"It is all over then and settled?"

"Yes, he's in prison now, I suppose. It seems a silly little thing to catch him on, when his real crime was trying to bamboozle that poor girl into marrying him, so that he could live on the family for the rest of his life."

Julia let her shoulders sag suddenly and gave a deep sigh. She had not enjoyed appearing in court, and now she was thoroughly tired. She began to murmur again about the detective.

"That absurd man, saying that I gave the prisoner 'some entertainment'! How frightful it sounds! What on earth will people think, if it's reported? They won't even know that I'm old enough to be his mother."

V

Micki went to prison and I thought that I would hear no more about him.

The latest disturbance was caused by an anonymous letter which Julia Bellingly received one morning. It was very spiteful, very petty, very incoherent; she had no idea who could have sent it. First she thought it was a woman, then she thought it was a man. So far as it made sense at all, it seemed to be accusing her of inordinate pride and snobbery. The author appeared to triumph over her, because of her indiscreet friendship with such a character as Micki. In involved sentences she was told that, after the degrading newspaper publicity, she would no longer be able to give herself grand and conceited airs.

"Whoever heard such rubbish!" Julia cried; "I who talk and

mix with anybody, just as the spirit moves me, to be told that I have a grand and conceited air!"

It did seem a strange document—written by someone in the habit of using a pen, the letters not large and florid, or too small and neat. I pictured a rather tight-faced businessman, who resented Julia's bright clothes and bags, resented her handsome face, so protectively painted and bold, resented her fat legs which moved so fast. Perhaps he had heard her voice bawling out a welcome or a good-bye—not a tremor in it, not a doubt. He had hated the parade-ground ring, and had put her down at once as an arrogant, pretentious woman in need of humbling.

Julia Bellingly made much more of an ado about the letter than I thought she would. She showed it to the cat-faced, rolling-eyed detective, who promised to do what he could about it. She wrote to the two papers that had reported the case and told them they had no right to mention her name, thus involving her in the unpleasantness of receiving anonymous letters. By the time she had finished, it was known throughout the neighborhood that she had had an abusive letter.

But the writer was not discovered and gradually the agitation died away. Julia spoke of the letter less and less and stopped remarking on the rudeness of the newspapers in not answering. Sometimes she would burst out again against the unknown person's absurd ideas about her, but she gave up trying to find out who he or she was, contenting herself with such expressions as, "ridiculous creature," "pathetic individual," "petty fool."

With the passing of interest in the anonymous letter, even the mention of Micki's name ceased for the moment. When I went out, I never came across the Wardes, so heard nothing from them; and Julia was silent because she was feeling more than ever that she was being blamed for introducing the impostor to Katherine and then encouraging the intimacy so wholeheartedly.

One person I did meet on one of my bicycle rides was Mrs. Charles.

"Oh, how lucky," she said, "that that dreadful affair was stopped in time!"

"Yes," I said, "lucky for Katherine."

"You see Mrs. Bellingly?" she asked.

"Almost every day—we live so close."

"I am not seeing her, just for the moment." She spoke with

tight competent lip movements, as if well able to manage all difficult situations. "She will be feeling so awkward about the whole distressing business. I shall give her a rest."

"I don't think she is very uncomfortable; I think she has shut it out of her mind," I said.

"Nevertheless I shall give her a rest," she answered firmly.

And I rode away, wondering if Mrs. Charles were withholding herself as a punishment, or out of a true spirit of tact.

Perhaps it was a month after Micki's conviction when Julia again came to me with news of him.

"Katherine has heard from Micki in prison," she said excitedly, "and what do you think the extraordinary boy says?"

"I can't think," I answered; "tell me."

"He says that he'll never love anybody else and that as soon as he's out of prison he wants to marry her. He says that if she's still in London, he'll join her there, get work, and then they can be married."

"But what does Katherine say? Will she answer?"

"I don't quite know; I've only heard from Mrs. Warde. Perhaps her mother will write for her. I must say Mrs. Warde still seems very sympathetic towards Micki; she even talked of going to see him in prison. After what has happened you would hardly believe it, but there it is. Life is so amazingly mixed and confused, isn't it?"

"Yes, people won't stay in their appointed places, they flow about like anything," I agreed.

"Mrs. Warde is furious that Micki was treated so roughly when he was arrested. She seems to be swinging over entirely to his side," Julia said.

"I suppose she got to know him so well when he was living in the house, that she understands the problems he has to deal with," I suggested.

"But no one can get away from the fact that he practiced the grossest deception on her and her poor daughter. When he was unmasked, the shock must have been terrible for a young girl like Katherine."

How curiously stilted our conversation was growing! Was is that we were talking about something that, for us, was dead and done with? Micki with his protestations, his insistence on continued love—could anything be sillier, less worthy of consideration? How could he go on pretending, even in prison? And although I did not know how Katherine had been behaving lately, I reproached her too for her infuriating immobility, her acceptance of all that came to pass. No other girl I knew could have been used as she had been used by Micki.

When Julia stopped talking, I took away with me only a sort of woolly exasperation at the foolishness of the whole affair.

Some weeks later Mrs. Warde did go to see Micki in prison. She described to Julia the strangeness of talking to him through an iron grille; then she went on to say how contrite Micki appeared to be. He blamed himself for everything, asked her pardon for involving her in so much trouble, and swore that he could never love anyone but Katherine. He said that he was going straight from now on, that prison taught you a lot of things, and that he needed it to sober him up.

Julia recounted this conversation quite uncritically, yet the hardness in her voice made it sound quaintly mawkish and humbugging. She increased this impression when she told me that Katherine had had another letter from Micki, even more passionate than the first. I could picture him writing it, bending low over the paper, hunching his heavy shoulders; then throwing his head back, shaking his hair, as his eyes lit up and the right worn-out phrase came to him. Those eyes would shift too from side to side, anxiously, as if he half-expected someone to spring up and prevent him from finishing his love letter. But at last he would be licking the envelope, showing a great deal of broad red tongue; and he would have that sleek far-seeing almost happy look of the scheming man. . . .

Then suddenly Micki was out of prison—early because of good behavior. I met Julia in the road, and she ran up to my bicycle, waving her painted canvas shopping bag and panting:

"I've just seen Micki! He was driving a huge yellow lorry full of milk cans."

"Did he see you?" I asked quickly.

"I don't think so; as soon as I recognized him I turned my back and crouched against the hedge. He was going very fast."

"So he has got work," I said.

"It would appear so, but his mother told the police he never kept anything longer than a few weeks."

"What happens?" I asked.

"He either does something silly and gets sacked, or just becomes restless and leaves himself."

"Perhaps he is turning over a new leaf; he told Mrs. Warde he would," I said, then added: "Do you think he has been to see her and Katherine yet?"

"I don't know, I must find out. I think I shall go along this afternoon."

Julia did go along that afternoon and discovered that Micki called quite often on the Wardes, in fact so often that Mrs. Warde was growing just a little anxious. He was so overwhelming, she explained, and he would not take "no" for an answer, although Katherine had retreated quite into herself and hardly showed signs of being aware of him at all.

"But we are both so sorry for him in a way," she told Julia. "He can't really help his difficult nature, and he's never had a chance; everyone has turned against him."

But it was not long before Mrs. Warde herself had to turn against him. He went so often to the house, stayed so long, worried Katherine so much with his attentions, that at last Mrs. Warde asked a male friend to make it quite clear to him that he must worry them no longer.

"He won't take any notice of her," Julia said; "he just puts his arm round her and tells her not to be an old sourpuss. What an expression! Is it American?"

"Do you mean to say he won't leave them alone?" I asked.

"Well, he will now, because this man has told him that if he goes there again, he, the man, will come round to kick him out of the house and inform the police."

"So Mrs. Warde is no longer sympathetic," I said.

"Poor woman, she's been so plagued to death that she only wants to be rid of him."

Ever since this day, when Julia had seen Micki in the yellow lorry, I was afraid that I too would meet him on the road. I pictured him hailing me exuberantly, stopping the huge lorry with a jerk, so that a great clatter of milk cans was set up. He would lean out of his high window, or perhaps jump down and begin pumping my hand and slapping me on the back. Then would come the flow of questions and suggestions. He might want me to write a book on prison life from the inside. He might want me to tell Katherine what an excellent husband he would make. Or perhaps he would only suggest coming round to the cottage in the evenings for talk and relaxation after work.

But I was soon to be relieved of this fear of meeting Micki. A few days after he had been forbidden the house by Mrs. Warde's male friend, Julia learned from a neighboring farmer that he had lost his job.

"He came later and later every morning, and was so careless that the farmer had to get rid of him," she said.

"Everyone is getting rid," I said.

"Well, what *can* you do with someone like Micki! He is hopeless—quite, quite hopeless."

Julia was the next one to be attacked. I was with her one evening, looking at some more Staffordshire figures she had just bought, when the telephone bell rang. She went into the hall, leaving the door open. I heard the delicate clip-clopping of her heels on the tiles, then the rather weary, supercilious, brazen "Hullo," which she always used on the telephone. It was as if she wanted to cloak her eagerness with this hard, bored sound; for she always was eager when the telephone bell rang. She would say: "Oh, that's only the coal man wanting to know when I'll be in." Or, "I expect it's for you; people are always asking me to take messages for you." And as she ran into the hall to pick up the receiver, one knew that she was telling herself these uninteresting things to keep her hopes from running away with her. What was it that she hoped to hear over the telephone? The voice of a wonderful new friend? News of a fortune left to her? I would never know, nor, I supposed, would she.

But on this occasion her voice, after the "Hullo," did not droop in disappointment; she said with quite a warm surprise, "Oh, Micki, it's you, is it?" Then there was a long pause in which Micki must have been saying something earnestly, for when Julia spoke again it was in a changed, much less gay voice: "No, Micki, I'm sorry, I can't have you here. You've already put me in one very unpleasant position; I can't risk having any more troubles and difficulties."

Again silence, while Julia listened to Micki. "You say you're different now," she suddenly burst out, "and yet I hear that you've been worrying the life out of poor Mrs. Warde and Katherine. I don't call that keeping to your resolutions."

Micki's next speech was longer than any of the others. I wondered what he could be saying to make Julia scrape her shoes on the tiles so restlessly. Then at last she was drawling in her old disdainful lazy voice: "I'm afraid I can't listen to such stuff any longer. I don't know what you're talking about; it sounds like utter nonsense to me."

She put down the receiver quietly and came back into the room.

"It was Micki, of course," she said: "I had to cut him off; otherwise he would have gone on ranting all night."

"What was he ranting about?" I asked.

"I don't know, some dreadful stuff about friends; he only liked *real* friends, people who stood by him in a tight corner. And why hadn't I stood by him, instead of giving all those facts away in court? And why had I turned against him now? Did I like kicking a fellow when he was down? Was I afraid to have him in the house, because he'd been in prison? There was more character inside a prison than out. And he only liked real friends, people who stood by him through thick and thin. He went on and on, repeating himself like a cracked gramophone record. At last I couldn't stand it any longer."

When Julia stopped talking, her set, moonstone eyes were staring into the distance; the faint wry smile of the invalid had come back to flicker round her mouth, just as it had done in the rosy, lighted bedroom before she had thrown the biscuit at me.

With a shake of her tight grey curls she rid herself of the contemplative mood; the filmy blue marbles came back to me and the room, the sufferer's smile grew much broader, until her teeth showed.

"Well, that's that!" she said, smoothing her hands over her bosom and down her apron. She so often wore aprons that I had come to look on them as an important part of her in the house. They were nearly always of brightly bound coarse linen or flowered curtain chintz. They were small, gathered bunchily at the waist, and always extremely dirty. It was strange, but I had never seen her in a clean one. Round the stomach the gathers and pleats, rich as an Elizabethan's ruff, gave an outline faintly and frivolously like an expectant mother's; and the greasy dirt on the arch flowers and colored bindings made me think of some gay teashop wrecked and defiled by hungry rioters, or the licentious soldiery.

"I hope he doesn't bother me any more," she said, sitting down; "I shan't know what to do if he turns up at the door. I shall just have to shut it in his face, I suppose."

There was a moment in which she mused.

"This is how I see it," she began again slowly; "one is interested in all kinds of people, one likes to see them, however strange their behavior; but when it comes to interviews and scenes with the police, one has to draw the line. One simply cannot be caught up in all that unpleasantness. One sympathizes, but one cannot be part of it."

I nodded, agreeing with every word, in spite of all the "ones" she had used. At that moment the dullest most hidebound people seemed far more desirable than those who brought after them all the squalor of detectives on the doorstep and policemen hiding in the hedge.

"I only hope he doesn't ring up any more," Julia said again.

But he did. There were two more telephone calls, and twice Julia put the receiver down in the middle of bitter recriminations. The burden of Micki's song seemed to be: "You are no true friend; you are a traitress who abandons her friends in their misfortunes," and Julia would reply: "You are a deceiver, a trickster without any backbone."

I imagined that there might be many more of those violently cut-short conversations, but after the third call there was silence.

Sometimes the thought of Micki would come into my mind and I would wonder what he was doing and where he was. Had he some new job in another part of the country? Or had he gone back to live on the mother who had despaired of him? I remembered all Micki's stories about this mother, how neglectful and uninterested she had been, how mean about money, in spite of the house in Inverness and the flat in Chelsea. Then I thought of the real mother, the Mrs. Potts, who had had to bring up her two sons on the meager wages of a farmhand. What must she think of Micki with his fancy new name and ancestors, his startling clothes, astonishing lies and prison sentences? Small wonder that she had given him up; what else could she do, since he had flown quite beyond her reach? How she must cleave to the sailor son! The one Julia had described simply as "very honest." He would be sober and sensible and pleasantly ordinary. He would give no trouble by catching himself in his own web of lies and deceits. Thinking of this brother reminded me of one of Micki's stories, one I had hardly listened to at the time; it was the story of an airplane that had been bought by Micki and his brother for—was it 2,000 pounds? They had begun to work on it in some mysterious way, improving it so much that it had flown faster than any other plane of its class. It is strange how little impression this story made on me when Micki told it. Was I used to his extravaganzas by then? Or was it that I was so uninterested in airplanes, and so ignorant of them, that I could be made to believe anything?

To muse in this way on another's life is to go round and round in a white mouse's exercising wheel. The beginning is the end, and the end the beginning; one longs more and more to travel just a little distance, to catch only a glimpse of something new, however small. It was because of this wish to know something more of Micki that I asked Katherine a very plain question the first time I saw her after his arrest.

It was almost Christmas-time before we met again. I had a friend staying with me, and, since he was fond of beer, I had taken him one evening to the Blue Anchor, the mournful little village inn. We were just about to go in when someone else appeared out of the darkness and shone a torch on the door and on us. A woman's voice said, "Hullo"; then I leaned forward and recognized Mrs. Warde. I was a little surprised to see her there, never having associated her with the Blue Anchor. Her arms seemed to be full of bottles, knocking and clinking together musically.

"A party of old friends has suddenly descended," she explained with an anxious little laugh, "and we've absolutely nothing to give them, so I thought the only thing to do was to collect all the bottles we could and try to get them filled with beer and cider."

My friend Ted had opened the door by now and the three of us went into the saloon bar—bottle and jug room. It was only when I was about to shut the door after us that I discovered Katherine trying to slip through the crack before it became too narrow.

"Katherine!" I exclaimed, "we never knew you were here too."

"I came with mummy to help her with the bottles," she said

hurriedly; "I've been padlocking my bicycle to the fence; thieves rush for the ones outside pubs, I'm told, and what would I do if I lost mine? I've already had my pump removed—while I was having my hair done last week. I was an idiot not to take it in with me."

I took Katherine up to Ted and introduced him to her, but Mrs. Warde was already talking to the landlord through the narrow hatch and did not notice us. Although Ted opened the door for her, she could not have realized that he was a friend of mine, for when he went up to her at the hatch and asked what she would like to drink, she turned and said stiffly, "Nothing, thank you."

"Oh, come on," coaxed Ted, not to be refused. "You must keep us company."

"But I don't even know you," said Mrs. Warde even more stiffly.

This little misunderstanding was not amusing at the time. Mrs. Warde's flushed face and hard mistrustful eyes seemed so cruel and powerful; she looked ready to eat up Ted, good-nature, bewilderment and all. The thought flashed into my mind that she was angry and suspicious because of Micki and the trouble he had brought her. I went forward at once to explain Ted to her. There was laughter, an apology, embarrassment; then Mrs. Warde said that she must be getting back to her guests with the drinks, but she felt sure that Katherine would like to stay with us a little longer, since the friends at home were only old people like herself.

Here Mrs. Warde laughed again, and she looked very young with her face still slightly pink from her anger. Below the short fur jacket I saw that she had on the velveteen trousers she was wearing when I went to tell Micki that I could not be best man.

Before Katherine had even protested or offered to help her with the bottles, Mrs. Warde said: "I'll see you later then, darling; I can easily manage alone, once I get them into the bicycle basket."

Ted went out with her to carry the bottles to the bicycle, and I was left with Katherine. Our drinks were waiting for us on the hatch board, so I brought them over to the silvered cast-iron table with the marble top, and we sat down together on the long bench against the wall. Above us hung a mid-Victorian overmantel, its broad expanse of mirror speckled and smoky, the gilt blackened on its frame of trailing madonna lilies, ivy, convolvulus and periwinkle.

Katherine's eyes were on the tawny cider in her glass; she seemed to be watching the bubbles rising to the surface like tiny divers. Her lips were together firmly, she looked more restrained, more self-possessed than ever. I saw that she still wore her hair swept up as she had rearranged it on her engagement to Micki; but nothing else of that time was to be remembered, it seemed; for when I said impulsively and too suddenly, "Have you heard anything more of Micki?" there was a discouraging silence. Of course it had been a mistake to ask in that simple, crude way, but I had felt the sudden longing for direct speech without any wary refinements or delicacy.

"But perhaps this isn't quite the place to talk about him," I added hurriedly, anxious now to clothe my bare question.

"No, I don't think this is quite the place to talk about him," Katherine agreed. She smiled at me with finality. I knew that I could never talk to her of Micki again.

Just as Julia had been the first to see Micki, so now the last glimpse of him was be hers also.

She came to me one evening in spring and told me that she had just returned from a shopping expedition. She showed me the blue and fawn striped jersey, the coral-red string riding-gloves, and the chipped little eighteenth-century enamel comfit box that she had bought; then, after I had admired each new possession, she said suddenly: "And who do you think was on the bus with me?"

It was as if this, the greatest plum, had been kept till last. I tried to think, but only one unusual person came into my mind.

"Was it your mad friend?" I asked; "the one who once sent you a parcel you were frightened to open because you thought it was a bomb, but it was really a lovely jar of ginger?"

"No, no," said Julia impatiently, "whatever makes you think that I should run into Thelma on a bus? She's probably miles and miles away."

"Then who was it?" I asked, tired of the guessing game.

"Micki, of course!" she exclaimed.

I wondered why my thoughts were still supposed to be fixed on Micki after all these months.

"Yes," she continued, "when I got on the bus, it was already very crowded, so I had to take a seat downstairs, although, as you know, I usually like riding on top. I was looking down at my shopping list to begin with, and I didn't take much notice of any of the other passengers, until we came to the top of the hill where the bus stops. I looked up then and noticed at the front of the bus a head of hair and shoulders that I felt sure I knew. Just then the man stood up and turned; it was Micki. He was very well dressed, in clothes I don't remember seeing before. I nearly made a sign to him with my glove, but he was looking the other way. As he passed he glanced down and suddenly recognized me. I was just about to smile and say something, when he jerked his head up and walked on, ignoring me completely.

"I turned to watch him get off the bus. He hesitated for a moment on the grass at the side of the road; he had half-turned his back, but I could see how new his clothes were and how well they fitted him. I could see too that he was glancing at me over his shoulder, out of the corners of his eyes. In that twisted position he looked so sly, so resentful. He seemed to be wishing me ill, like some—some wizard."

Julia sighed, then finished her story.

"My last glimpse was of him turning to walk up the little side road. Poor boy, he looked so lonely and so charming in his new clothes, with that dark rich hair brushed back and clipped crisply round his ears and down his neck. He never turned, never gave me another glance, just walked on alone, until he was under the trees."

"Did his jacket have slits at the back and leather elbow pads?" I asked, rudely breaking in, I am afraid, on Julia's mood.

"Yes, I think it did," she said a little petulantly; "but how did you know? And why should it matter?"

"Well, at least he has that, if he has nothing else," I murmured.

"What did you say?" Julia asked sharply.

"Oh, nothing. I just remembered that he wanted a coat like that."

"The tweed was a sort of mixture of mustard, earth and moss colors," she mused; "it suited him *so* well."

I thought of Micki pausing at the side of the road, so that Julia should see each detail of his new clothes—the clothes which gave him such a proud, armored feeling. She should be made to see that other people had not cast him off, that he had no need of her any more. She should admire him, just as she had at first; but now she should regret as well.

Then when he turned to go into the wood, he would be torturing her, murdering her with every thought for deserting him. But perhaps later the evil mood would pass and he would remember her stories and jokes and her great liveliness. Perhaps he would remember them long after everything else was dim. He might burst out laughing, when he was in prison again, or just when he was about to make businesslike love to another girl.

Here I looked up. There was some change in the room. Julia was about to cry; I could already imagine the great crystal crocodile drops trickling down her peach-bloom cheeks. And each crocodile drop would have something so painful at its core.

In desperation my thoughts raced back wildly to one of her most outrageous riddles, the one which began, "What is it that has twenty-two tits and a ball?"

I had not guessed, nor had Micki—nobody could ever guess; and so Julia was always able to cry out exultantly: "Why, a girls' hockey team, of course!"

Did Micki remember this one? Surely he could never forget it! The young bosoms bouncing so energetically as they chased the little ball over the grass. It was preposterous, irresistible.

And here, in spite of Julia's brimming eyes, in spite of all my efforts to be grave, a strangled sound, rather like a hog's snort, broke from me. I gave up then and let the smothered giggles out.